MYRA BRECKINRIDGE/MYRON

Gore Vidal was born in 1925 at the United States Military Academy, West Point, where his father was the first aviation instructor. Vidal's maternal roots are thoroughly political. As a boy, he lived with his grandfather, the legendary blind Senator T. P. Gore, to whom Vidal read. His father, Eugene Vidal, served as director of the Bureau of Air Commerce under Franklin D. Roosevelt. After graduating from Phillips Exeter Academy, Vidal enlisted at seventeen in the United States Army. At nineteen he became a warrant officer (j.g.) and first mate of the army ship *F.S. 35*, which carried supplies and passengers from Chernowski Bay to Dutch Harbor in the Aleutian Islands. While on night watch in port, he wrote his first novel, *Williwaw*, published in 1946, the year he was mustered out.

Vidal's early works include *The City and the Pillar* (1948), *Messiah* (1954), the short story collection *A Thirsty Evil* (1956), and two successful Broadway plays, *Visit to a Small Planet* (1957) and the prize-winning *The Best Man* (1960). Vidal also wrote a number of plays for television's "golden age" (*The Death of Billy the Kid*) as well as Hollywood screenplays (*Suddenly, Last Summer*). In the sixties, three widely acclaimed novels established Vidal's international reputation as a best-selling author: *Julian* (1964), a re-creation of the world of the apostate Roman emperor who attempted to restore paganism; *Washington, D.C.* (1967), the first in what was to become a multi-volume fictional "chronicle" of American history; and the classic *Myra Breckinridge* (1968), a comedy of sex change in a highly mythical Hollywood.

Myron (1974), a sequel to *Myra Breckinridge*, continued to mine the vein of fanciful, sometimes apocalyptic humor that informs *Kalki* (1978), *Duluth* (1983), and *Live from Golgotha* (1992), works described by Italo Calvino as "the hyper-novel or the novel elevated to the square or to the cube." Vidal also continued to explore the ancient world in the wide-ranging *Creation* (1981). *The Boston Globe* noted, "He is our greatest living man of letters."

Gabriel García Márquez praised "Gore Vidal's magnificent series of historical novels or novelized histories" that deal with American life as viewed by one family from the Revolution to the present: *Burr*

(1973), *Lincoln* (1984), *1876* (1976), *Empire* (1987), *Hollywood* (1990), and *Washington, D.C.* Vidal's interest in politics has not been limited to commentary; he ran for Congress in New York in 1960, and in 1982 came in second in the California Democratic senatorial primary.

Vidal's essays, both political and literary, have been collected in such volumes as *Homage to Daniel Shays* (1972), *Matters of Fact and Fiction* (1977), *The Second American Revolution* (1982), and *At Home* (1988). In 1993 his *United States: Essays 1952–1992* won the National Book Award. *Palimpsest,* Vidal's memoir of his first thirty-nine years, was published in 1995.

Vidal divides his time between Los Angeles, California, and Ravello, Italy.

ALSO BY GORE VIDAL

NOVELS
Williwaw
In a Yellow Wood
The City and the Pillar
The Season of Comfort
A Search for the King
The Judgement of Paris
Messiah
Julian
Washington, D.C.
Myra Breckinridge
Two Sisters
Burr
Myron
1876
Kalki
Creation
Duluth
Lincoln
Empire
Hollywood
Live from Golgotha

SHORT STORIES
A Thirsty Evil

PLAYS
An Evening with Richard Nixon
Weekend
Romulus
The Best Man
Visit to a Small Planet

ESSAYS
Rocking the Boat
Reflections Upon a Sinking Ship
Homage to Daniel Shays
Matters of Fact and Fiction
The Second American Revolution
Armageddon?
A View from the Diner's Club
Screening History
United States: Essays 1952–1992

MEMOIR
Palimpsest

MYRA BRECKINRIDGE

MYRON

GORE VIDAL

PENGUIN BOOKS

PENGUIN BOOKS
Published by the Penguin Group
Penguin Putnam Inc., 375 Hudson Street,
New York, New York 10014, U.S.A.
Penguin Books Ltd, 27 Wrights Lane, London W8 5TZ, England
Penguin Books Australia Ltd, Ringwood, Victoria, Australia
Penguin Books Canada Ltd, 10 Alcorn Avenue,
Toronto, Ontario, Canada M4V 3B2
Penguin Books (N.Z.) Ltd, 182–190 Wairau Road,
Auckland 10, New Zealand

Penguin Books Ltd, Registered Offices:
Harmondsworth, Middlesex, England

Myra Breckinridge and *Myron* first published in one volume in
the United States of America by Random House, Inc., 1986
Published in Penguin Books 1997

3   5   7   9   10   8   6   4   2

Myra Breckinridge first published in the United States of America
by Little, Brown & Co., Inc. 1968
Copyright © Gore Vidal, 1968
All rights reserved

Myron first published in the United States of America
by Random House, Inc. 1974
Copyright © Gore Vidal, 1974, 1986
All rights reserved

LIBRARY OF CONGRESS CATALOGING IN PUBLICATION DATA
Vidal, Gore, 1925–
Myra Breckinridge; Myron.
ISBN 0 14 11.8028 5 (pbk.)
I. Vidal, Gore, 1925– .   Myron. 1987.
II. Title.   III. Title: Myra Breckinridge.   IV. Title: Myron.
PS3543.I26M9   1987   813´.54   87–40002

Printed in the United States of America
Set in New Baskerville

MYRA BRECKINRIDGE

I

I am Myra Breckinridge whom no man will ever possess. Clad only in garter belt and one dress shield, I held off the entire elite of the Trobriand Islanders, a race who possess no words for "why" or "because." Wielding a stone axe, I broke the arms, the limbs, the balls of their finest warriors, my beauty blinding them, as it does all men, unmanning them in the way that King Kong was reduced to a mere simian whimper by beauteous Fay Wray whom I resemble left three-quarter profile if the key light is no more than five feet high during the close shot.

2

The novel being dead, there is no point to writing made-up stories. Look at the French who will not and the Americans who cannot. Look at me who ought not, if only because I exist entirely outside the usual human experience . . . outside and yet wholly relevant for I am the New Woman whose astonishing history is a poignant amalgam of vulgar dreams and knife-sharp realities (shall I ever be free of the dull lingering pain that is my peculiar glory, the price so joyously paid for being Myra Breckinridge, whom no man may possess except on her . . . *my* terms!). Yet not even I can create a fictional character as one-dimensional as the average reader. Nevertheless, I intend to create a literary masterpiece in much the same way that I created myself, and for much the same reason: because it is not there. And I shall accomplish this by presenting you, the reader (as well as Dr. Randolph Spenser Montag, my analyst friend and dentist, who has proposed that I write in this notebook as therapy), with an exact, literal sense of what it is like, from moment to moment, to be me, what it is like to possess superbly shaped breasts reminiscent of those sported by Jean Harlow in

4

Hell's Angels and seen at their best four minutes after the start of the second reel. What it is like to possess perfect thighs with hips resembling that archetypal mandolin from which the male principle draws forth music with prick of flesh so akin—in this simile—to pick of celluloid, *blessed* celluloid upon which have been imprinted in our century all the dreams and shadows that have haunted the human race since man's harsh and turbulent origins (quote Lévi-Strauss). Myra Breckinridge is a dish, and never forget it, you motherfuckers, as the children say nowadays.

3

I shall not begin at the beginning since there is no beginning, only a middle into which you, fortunate reader, have just strayed, still uncertain as to what will be done to you in the course of our common voyage to my interior. No, to *our* interior. For we are, at least in the act of this creation, as one, each trapped in time: you later, I now, carefully, thoughtfully forming letters to make words to make sentences.

I shall begin by putting my cards on the table. At this moment (writing the word "moment"), I am not the same Myra Breckinridge who was the scourge of the Trobriand Islanders. She is a creature of fantasy, a daydream revealing the feminine principle's need to regain once more that primacy she lost at the time of the Bronze Age when the cock-worshipping Dorians enslaved the West, impiously replacing *the* Goddess with a god. Happily his days are nearly over; the phallus cracks; the uterus opens; and I am at last ready to begin my mission which is to re-create the sexes and thus save the human race from certain extinction. Meanwhile, I live no longer in the usual world. I have forsaken the familiar. And soon, by an extreme gesture,

I shall cease altogether to be human and become legend like Jesus, Buddha, Cybele.

But my immediate task is to impress upon you how disturbingly beautiful I am with large breasts hanging free, for I am wearing nothing but black mesh panties in this overheated room, whose windows I have shut because it is the rush hour (6:07 P.M., Thursday, January 10) and beneath my window the Strip (Sunset Boulevard in Hollywood, California) is filled with noisy cars, barely moving through air so dark with carbon monoxide that one can almost hear in the drivers' lungs the cancer cells as they gaily proliferate like spermatozoa in a healthy boy's testicles.

4

From where I sit, without turning my head, I can see a window covered by venetian blinds. The fourth slat from the bottom is missing and so provides me with a glimpse of the midsection of the huge painted plaster chorus girl who holds a sombrero in one hand as she revolves slowly in front of the Château Marmont Hotel, where Greta Garbo stays on her rare visits to Hollywood. The window is set in a white wall on which a damp splotch resembles an upside-down two-leaf clover—or heart— or male scrotum as viewed from behind. But no similes. Nothing is *like* anything else. Things are themselves entirely and do not need interpretation, only a minimal respect for their precise integrity. The mark on the wall is two feet three inches wide and four feet eight and a fraction inches high. Already I have failed to be completely accurate. I must write "fraction" because I can't read the little numbers on the ruler without my glasses which I never wear.

5

I am certain that I can eventually capture the reality of Myra Breckinridge, despite the treachery and inadequacy of words. I must show you as I am, at this instant, seated at a small card table with two cigarette burns at the edge; one is about the size of a quarter, the other the size of a dime. The second is perhaps the result of a burning ash, while the first . . . But there is to be no speculation, only simple facts, simply stated. I sit now, perspiring freely, the odor of my lovely body is like that of new bread (just one simile, then I shall be stylistically pure), mingled with a subtle ammoniac smell that I find nearly as irresistible as all men do. In addition to my extraordinary physical presence, I studied the classics (in translation) at the New School, the contemporary French novel on my own, and I learned German last year in order to understand the films of the Thirties when UFA was a force to be reckoned with.

Now, at this arbitrary instant in time, my hand moves across the page of an oblong black notebook containing three hundred blue-lined pages. I have covered eighteen pages already; that leaves two hundred eighty-two yet to be filled, if one counts the present page of which I have used twelve of thirty-two lines—thirteen with these last words, now fourteen. The hand is small, with delicate tapering fingers and a slight golden down at the back near the wrist. The nails are exquisitely cared for (lacquered silver) except for the right index fingernail, which is cracked diagonally from the left side of the tip to the part where the flesh begins, the result of trying to pry loose an ice cube from one of those new plastic ice trays which so freeze that unless you half melt them under the hot-water tap you can never get the ice out.

There are limits, however, to describing exactly what I see as I write and you read. More to the point, one must accept the fact that there are no words to describe for you *exactly* what my body is like as I sit, perspiring freely, in this furnished room high above the Strip for which I am paying $87.50 a month, much too much, but I must not complain for a life dream has come true. I am in Hollywood, California, the source of all this century's legends, and tomorrow it has been arranged for me to visit Metro-Goldwyn-Mayer! No pilgrim to Lourdes can experience what I know I shall experience once I have stepped into that magic world which has occupied all my waking thoughts for twenty years. Yes, twenty years. Believe it or not, I am twenty-seven years old and saw my first movie at the age of seven: *Marriage Is a Private Affair,* starring Lana Turner, James Craig and the late John Hodiak; produced by Pandro S. Berman and directed by Robert Leonard.

As a small girl I used to yearn for Lana Turner to crush me against her heavy breasts, murmuring, "I love you, Myra, you perfect darling!" Fortunately this Lesbian phase passed and my desires were soon centered upon James Craig. I saw every film he ever made. I even have recordings of his voice. In Parker Tyler's masterpiece *Magic and Myth of the Movies,* he refers to James Craig's voice as "some kind of Middle Southwest drawl, a genuine lulu." I can certify that James Craig was in every way a lulu and for years I practiced self-abuse thinking of that voice, those shoulders, those powerful thighs thrust between my own and, if I may be candid, no matter what condition James Craig is in today, married or not, decrepit or not, Myra Breckinridge is ready to give him a good time for old times' sake.

6

Buck Loner is not the man he was when he was the Singin' Shootin' Cowboy of radio fame—movies too: he made eighteen low-budget westerns and for a time was right up there with Roy Rogers and Gene Autry. In those old movies he appeared to be lean and tough with slender hips and practically no ass at all which I don't find entirely attractive. I like a curve to the masculine buttock, on the order, say, of Tim Holt's in *The Magnificent Ambersons*. Mr. Holt, incidentally, decrepit or not, has a good time coming his way if Myra Breckinridge should happen to cross his path as she is bound to do now that Hollywood is finally, literally, at her feet (lovely feet with a high instep and naturally rosy heels, fit for any fetishist).

Today Buck Loner (born Ted Percey in Portland, Maine) is fat—no, *gross!*—with breasts even larger than mine. He is huge and disgusting and old, and obviously dying to get me into bed even though I am the recent widow of his only nephew Myron Breckinridge, the film critic, who drowned last year while crossing over to Staten Island on the ferry. Did Myron take his own life, you will ask? Yes and no is my answer. Beyond that my lips are sealed.... In any case, let us abandon *that* daydream in order to record the hard facts of this morning's encounter with my husband's uncle, Buck Loner.

"Never knew that boy of Gertrude's had such an eye for feminine pulchritude." This sentence drawled in the once famous Buck Loner manner was, I fear, the first thing he said to me as he helped me into a chair beside his redwood desk, one coarse redwood hand lingering for just a moment too long on my left shoulder, in order to ascertain whether or not I was wearing a bra. I was.

"Mr. Loner," I began in a careful low-pitched voice, modeled on that of the late Ann Sheridan (fifth reel of *Doughgirls*.) "I will come straight to the point. I need your help."

That was the wrong thing to say. To ask for anything is always the wrong way to begin a conversation but I am not one to beat about a bush, even a bush as unappetizing as Buck Loner. He sat back in his steel and black leather chair, a very expensive item selling for about four hundred dollars at the best office supply stores. I know. I worked one entire year at Abercrombie and Fitch, and so got an idea of just how expensive nice things can be. That was the year poor Myron was trying to complete his book on Parker Tyler and the films of the Forties—a book I intend to finish one day, with or without Mr. Tyler's assistance. Why? Because Tyler's vision (films are the unconscious expressions of age-old human myths) is perhaps the only important critical insight this century has produced. Also, Tyler's close scrutiny of the films of the Forties makes him our age's central thinker, if only because *in the decade between 1935 and 1945, no irrelevant film was made in the United States*. During those years, the entire range of human (which is to say, American) legend was put on film, and any profound study of those extraordinary works is bound to make crystal-clear the human condition. For instance, to take an example at random, Johnny Weissmuller, the zahftic Tarzan, still provides the last word on the subject of soft man's relationship to hard environment . . . that glistening overweight body set against a limestone cliff at noon says the whole thing. Auden once wrote an entire poem praising limestone, unaware that any one of a thousand frames from *Tarzan and the Amazons* (1945) had not only anticipated him but made irrelevant his jingles. This was one of Myron's insights that most excited me. How I miss him.

"How I miss him, Mr. Loner. Particularly now. You see, he didn't leave a penny . . ."

"No insurance, savings account, stocks, bonds, safety deposit box maybe? Gertrude must've left the boy *something*."

Buck fell into my trap. "No," I said, in a throaty voice with a small croak to it not unlike (but again not *really* like) that of the late Margaret Sullavan. "Gertrude, as you call her, Myron's angel mother, did not leave him one penny. All that she owned on the day she died, Christmas Eve 1966, was a set of bedroom furniture. Everything else was gone, due to a series of expensive illnesses in the family, hers, Myron's, my own. I won't bore you with the details but for the last five years we supported a dozen doctors. Now Gertrude, your sister, is gone with no one to mourn her at Frank E. Campbell's Funeral Church except Myron and me. Then he died and now I'm absolutely alone, and penniless."

During this recital Buck Loner directed toward me that same narrow-eyed gaze one detects in those scenes of Brian Donlevy whenever he is being asked a question about Akim Tamiroff. But confident in the efficacy of my ultimate weapon, I merely offered him a sad smile in return, and blinked a tear or two loose from my Max Factor Supreme eyelashes. I then looked up at the life-size photograph in color of Elvis Presley which hangs behind Buck's desk, flanked by two American flags, and began my pitch. "Mr. Loner, Gertrude, Myron's mother . . ."

"A marvelous woman . . ." he began huskily but no man alive can outdo *me* in the huskiness department.

"Gertrude," I positively *rasped* through a Niagara of tears

unshed, "with her dying breath, or one of her dying breaths—
we missed a lot of what she said toward the end because of the
oxygen tent and the fact she could not wear her teeth—Gertrude
said, 'Myron—and you too, angel girl—if anything happens to
me and you ever need help, go to your Uncle Ted, go to Buck
Loner and remind that son-of-a-bitch'—I am now quoting
verbatim—'that the property in Westwood just outside of Hollywood where he has his Academy of Drama and Modeling was
left to us jointly by our father whose orange grove it was in the
Twenties, and you tell that bastard'—I'm sorry but you know
how Gertrude talked, those years as a practical nurse left their
toll—'that I have a copy of the will and I want my share to go
to you, Myron, because that property must be worth a good
million bucks by now!' " I stopped, as though too moved by my
own recital to continue.

Buck Loner idly stroked the bronze bust of Pat Boone which
serves as the base for his desk lamp. A long moment passed. I
studied the office, admired its rich appointments, realizing that
half of the ground it stood on—some fifty acres of Westwood's
finest residential property—was mine. The proof was in my
purse: a photostat of Buck Loner's father's will.

"Gertrude was always a high-spirited gal, ever since she was
yea-high." He indicated what looked to be a Shetland pony; on
one finger a huge diamond glittered. "Poor Gertrude died most
horribly, Myron wrote me. Great suffering at the end." He
smacked his lips, the unmitigated shit, but cool it, Myra baby,
I said to myself, and half of all this will be yours. Sudden daydream: Buck Loner hanging upside down like a fat sack of
potatoes while yours truly works him over with a tennis racket
strung with copper wires.

"I never knew Myron," he added, as though this might somehow make spurious the relationship.

"Myron never knew you." I was deliberately redundant. "I
mean he used to follow your career with interest, collected all
sorts of stories about you from the old *Radio Times*. And of
course you were to have figured at some length in one of the

chapters of his book *Parker Tyler and the Films of the Forties; or, the Transcendental Pantheon*."

"How about that?" Buck Loner looked pleased, as well he ought to be. "I suppose my nephew left a will?"

I was ready for that one. I told him that I possessed three wills. His father's leaving the orange grove jointly to Gertrude and himself, Gertrude's leaving her share of the Westwood property to Myron, and Myron's leaving his entire estate to me.

Buck Loner sighed. "You know," he said, "the school ain't doin' too well." Phonetically that is not exactly what he said, but it is close. I am fortunate in having no gift at all for characterizing in prose the actual speech of others and so, for literary purposes, I prefer to make everyone sound like me. Therefore I shall make no further effort to reproduce Buck Loner's speech, except when something particularly vivid stays with me. Nothing vivid was said for some minutes while he lied to me about the financial status of the Academy of Drama and Modeling. But of course everyone in show business knows that the Academy is a huge success with an enrollment of one thousand three hundred young men and women, all studying to be actors, singers, models. Some live on campus but most live elsewhere and drive to school in their jalopies (a marvelous Forties word that I heard for the first time in *Best Foot Forward*—oh, to have been an adult in those years!). The Academy mints money.

When Buck had finished his tale of woe, I crossed my legs slowly and deliberately (my skirt was practically mini, my legs divine), and was rewarded by a noticeable increase in Buck's salivation. He swallowed hard, eyes on that triangulated darkness beneath the skirt, forever inviting the question: is it you-know-what or panties? Let him wonder! No man will ever possess Myra Breckinridge, though she will possess men, in her own good time and in ways convenient to her tyrannous lust. In any case, Buck Loner is a three-time married man whose current wife, Bobbie Dean, once sang with Claude Thornhill's band in the Forties, and is now a passionate Jehovah's Witness, forever saving sinners in back streets. Gertrude thought her common.

"Naturally, this is all quite sudden, Myra, I may call you Myra? Even though we never met but then you are my niece-in-law, and so practically kissin' kin."

There is a crash outside my window—was a crash (in the time I took to write "there is a crash" the tense changed). Two cars have collided on the Strip. I heard breaking glass. Now I hear nothing. If the accident was serious there will soon be the sound of a siren. More than ever am I convinced that the only useful form left to literature in the post-Gutenberg age is the memoir: the absolute truth, copied precisely from life, preferably at the moment it is happening . . .

Buck Loner made me an offer. While his lawyer and my lawyer work out a settlement, he would be happy to give me a job starting now and extending until the school year ends in June and all the talent scouts from TV, movie and recording companies converge upon the Academy to observe the students do their stuff. I accepted his offer. Why not? I need a place to live (as well as an entrée into the world of the movies), and so what could be better than a teaching job at the Academy? I will also enjoy meeting young men (though whether or not they will enjoy meeting me remains to be seen!), and the Academy is crawling with them, arrogant, cocky youths; several whistled at me in the corridor as I made my way to Buck Loner's office. Well, they will suffer for their bad manners! No man may jeer at Myra Breckinridge with impunity!

"Now we have an opening for you in our Acting Department—that's for movie and TV acting, we don't go in for stage-type acting, no real demand . . ."

"The theatre is finished . . ." I began.

"You can say that again." It was plain that he was not interested in my theories which reflect more or less Myron's thesis that this century's only *living* art form is the movies. I say more or less because though I agree with Myron that the films of the 1940's are superior to all the works of the so-called Renaissance,

17

including Shakespeare and Michelangelo, I have been drawn lately to the television commercial which, though in its rude infancy, shows signs of replacing all the other visual arts. But my ideas are not yet sufficiently formulated to record them here, suffice it to say that the placing of the man in the driver's seat (courtesy of Hertz) reveals in a most cogent way man's eternal need for mastery over both space and distance, a never-ending progress that began in the caves at Lascaux and continues, even as I write, in the Apollo capsule with its mixed oxygen environment.

"Your work load will of course be light. After all, you're a member of the family and of course I'm taking into account your terrible recent loss, though it has been my experience that work distracts our attention from grief in a most extraordinary way." While he was filibustering, he was studying a chart. He then scribbled a note and gave it to me. On Monday, Thursday and Saturday mornings I am to give an hour course in Empathy. Tuesday and Friday afternoons I teach Posture.

"You seem particularly well equipped to give the course in Posture. I couldn't help but notice how you looked when you entered the room, you carry yourself like a veritable queen. As for Empathy, it is the Sign Kwa Known [*sine qua non*] of the art of film acting."

We sparred with one another, each lying to beat the band. He so pleased to have me "on the team" and me so happy to be able to work in Hollywood, California, a life's dream come true and—as they used to say in the early Sixties—all that jazz. Oh, we are a pair of jolly rogues! He means to cheat me out of my inheritance while I intend to take him for every cent he's got, as well as make him fall madly in love just so, at the crucial moment, I can kick his fat ass in, fulfilling the new pattern to which I am now irrevocably committed. Or as Diotima said to Hyperion, in Hölderlin's novel, "It was no man that you wanted, believe me; you wanted a world." I too want a world and mean to have it. This man—any man—is simply a means of getting it (which is Man).

There goes the siren. The accident was serious. I stretch my legs. The left foot's asleep. In a moment I shall put down the yellow ballpoint pen, get to my feet, experience briefly pins and needles; then go to the window and lift the blind and see if there are dead bodies in the street. Will there be blood? I dread it. Truly.

BUCK LONER REPORTS—
Recording Disc No. 708—
10 January

                Other matters to be taken up by board in reference to purchases for new closed circuit TV period par agraph I sort of remember that Gertrudes boy was married some years ago and I recall being surprised as he was a fag or so I always thought with that sister of mine for a mother how could he not be only thing is I never knew the little bastard except one meeting in St Louis oh maybe twenty years ago when she was there with her third husband the certified public accoun tant and I remember vaguely this sissy kid who wanted to go to the movies all the time who I gave an autographed picture of me on Sporko that palomino horse that was and is the trademark of Buck Loner even though the original palomino in question has been for a long time up there in the happy hunting ground and my ass is now too big to inflict on any other nag except maybe Myra Breckinridge period paragraph what is the true Myra Breckinridge story that is the big question you could have knocked me over with a feather when she came sashaying into the office with her skirt hiked up damn near to her chin at least when she sits down she is a good looking broad but hoteyed definitely hoteyed and possibly mentally unbalanced I must keep an eye on her in that department but the tits are keen and probably hers and I expect she is just hungering for the old Buck Loner Special parenthesis start taking pee-pills again to lose weight zipper keeps slipping down which makes a damned sloppy impression end parenthesis period paragraph but what I dont like one bit is the matter of the will and I guess I better put Flagler and Flagler onto it first thing tomorrow it is true that the property was left me and Gertrude jointly but she always said Ted she said she never called me Buck she was the most envious broad that ever lived especially when I was right up there biggest star of them all after Roy bigger than Gene certainly but wish I had Genes eye for real estate that man is loaded of course I dont do so bad with the Academy but Gene Autry today is capital r capital i capital c capital h rich well I was better box office Ted Gertrude said you can keep my share of that lousy orange grove that our father threw away his life savings to buy just as the bottom dropped out of citrus fruit I never want to see or hear of it again is what she said more or less but naturally when word come to Saint Louis and later to the Island of Man hattan where she was living with that crazy picture painter that Hollywood was spilling over into nearby Brentwood and West wood and all the other woods were filling up with lovers of the sun and fun from all parts of the USA Gertrude did ask once or twice about our mutual holding but when I told her I needed money to start the Academy and needed the orange grove to teach in and maybe put a building on she was very reasonable merely saying that when the time came I was to help Myron to become a movie star as he was even better looking than I was at his age and besides could act the little fag she sent me all sorts of pictures of him and he was pretty as a picture in a drippy sort of way and wrote these far out pieces about the movies that I could never get through in magazines I never heard of in

England and even in French some of them were written I will say he sent them all to me including a long article type piece that I did read about so help me god the rear ends of all the major cowboy stars from austere aspiring Gothic flat ass Hoot Gibson to impertinent baroque ass James Garner shit exclamation mark paragraph Flagler and Flagler will be notified first thing tomorrow morning and told to examine with a fine tooth comb the deeds to this property and also to make a careful investigation of one Myra Breckinridge widow and claimant and try to find some loophole as I have no intention at all of letting her horn in on a property that I myself increased in value from a five thousand dollar orange grove to what is now at a conservative estimate worth in the neighborhood counting buildings of course of two million dollars maybe I should lay Myra that might keep her happy for a while while we discuss the ins and outs of our business meanwhile I better see if that fag nephew of mine left a proper will this will have to be gone into in careful detail by Flagler and Flagler and their private detective meanwhile she will be working here where I can keep an eye on her period paragraph check new TV makeup equipment write President Johnson giving him my views on subsidy for the arts in line with talk I gave to Fresno Rotary before Xmas those two kids are definitely balling and I don't like that sort of thing to be too visible on the campus particularly since she lives here in the dormitory and the matron tells me she is off with that stud every chance she can get and is always coming in after midnight a beautiful little piece she is and it may well be that the Buck Loner Special could straighten her out but I must proceed cautiously like they say as she is a minor of eighteen and naturally drawn to a male minor of nineteen six feet two and built like a stone wall who wants to be a movie star with sideburns a nice kid if he stays out of jail and I hope one day he makes it but meanwhile its his making her that I mind I mean what would her mother say her worst fears about Hollywood fulfilled I better tell the matron to give her a tough talking to or back she goes to Winnipeg as an enemy alien and deflowered virgin through no fault of yours truly remember to tell masseuse to come at five instead of six am getting horny as hell talking about the dear little thing from Winnipeg whats her name Sally Sue Baby Dee Mary Ann thats it Mary Ann Pringle and shes making it with Rusty Godowski from Detroit where else a nice dumb polack who maybe has that extra something that makes for stardom that masseuse better be good today

7

I write this sitting at my desk in the office to which I have been assigned in the west wing of the main building of what must be an incredibly valuable piece of real estate. I've spent the last few days prowling about the Academy and it's a most expensive creation, worth millions I should say, and half of it's mine, or at least half the ground it stands on. I have already contacted a good lawyer and presently he will surprise Buck Loner with my claims. Our case, I am assured, is airtight.

I find Buck Loner something of an enigma. No man can be as cheerful as he seems to be, as desirous of creating love as he says he is. Yet it is true that oceans of warmth flow from him to all the students, quite indiscriminately, and they seem to adore him, even those who are known as "hippies" and mock everyone (the argot is curiously rich out here, and slightly repellent: teenagers—already a ghastly word—are known as "teeny-boppers"!). Reluctantly, I find myself admiring the man, monster though he is. But then I shall soon break him to my will. Is there a man alive who is a match for Myra Breckinridge?

8

I sit now in a bus on my way to Culver City—and Metro-Goldwyn-Mayer! My heart is beating so quickly that I can hardly bear to look out the window for fear that suddenly against that leaden horizon marked by oil derricks, I shall behold—like some fantastic palace of dreams—the Irving Thalberg Memorial Building and its attendant sound stages whose blank (but oh so evocative!) façades I have studied in photographs for twenty years.

Not wanting to spoil my first impression, I keep my eye on this notebook which I balance on one knee as I put down at random whatever comes into my mind, simply anything in order to save for myself the supreme moment of ecstasy when the Studio of Studios, the sublime motor to this century's myths, appears before me as it has so many times in dreams, its great doors swinging wide to welcome Myra Breckinridge to her rightful kingdom.

I was born to be a star, and look like one today: a false hairpiece gives body to my hair while the light Max Factor base favored by Merle Oberon among other screen lovelies makes luminous my face even in the harsh light of a sound stage where I shall soon be standing watching a take. Then when the director says, "O.K., print it," and the grips prepare for another setup, the director will notice me and ask my name and then take me into the commissary and there, over a Green Goddess salad (a favorite of the stars), talk to me at length about my face, wondering whether or not it is photogenic until I stop him with a smile and say: "There is only one way to find out. A screen test." To be a film star is my dearest daydream. After all, I have had some practical experience in New York. Myron and I both appeared in a number of underground movies. Of course they were experimental films and like most experiments, in the laboratory and out, they failed but even had they succeeded they could never have been truly Hollywood, truly mythic. Nevertheless, they gave me a sense of what it must be like to be a star.

This trip is endless. I hate buses. I must rent or buy a car. The distances are unbelievable out here and to hire a taxi costs a fortune. This particular section of town is definitely ratty-looking with dingy bungalows and smog-filled air; my eyes burn and water. Fortunately elaborate neon signs and an occasional eccentrically shaped building make magic of the usual. We are now passing a diner in the shape of an enormous brown doughnut. I feel better already. Fantasy has that effect on me.

What to make of the students? I have now taught four classes in Posture (how to walk gracefully and sit down without knocking over furniture) and two in Empathy (I invite them to pretend they are oranges, drinks of water, clouds . . . the results are unusual, to say the least).

Though I have nothing to do with the Speech Department, I could not help but notice what difficulty most of the students have in talking. The boys tend to bark while the girls whine through their noses. Traditional human speech seems to have passed them by, but then one must never forget that they are the first creations of that television culture which began in the early Fifties. Their formative years were spent watching pale gray figures (no blacks, no whites—significant detail) move upon a twenty-one-inch screen. As a result, they are bland and in-attentive, responsive only to the bold rhythms of commercials. Few can read anything more complex than a tabloid newspaper. As for writing, it is enough that they can write their name, or "autograph" as they are encouraged to call it, anticipating star-dom. Nevertheless, a few have a touch of literary genius (that never dies out entirely), witness the obscene graffiti on the men's bathroom wall into which I strayed by accident the first day and saw, in large letters over one of the urinals, "Buck Sucks." Can this be true? I would put nothing past a man who traffics so promiscuously in love, not knowing that it is hate alone which inspires us to action and makes for civilization. Look at Juvenal, Pope, Billy Wilder.

In the Posture class I was particularly struck by one of the students, a boy with a Polish name. He is tall with a great deal of sand-colored curly hair and sideburns; he has pale blue eyes with long black lashes and a curving mouth on the order of the late Richard Cromwell, so satisfyingly tortured in *Lives of a Bengal Lancer*. From a certain unevenly rounded thickness at the crotch of his blue jeans, it is safe to assume that he is mar-velously hung. Unfortunately he is hot for an extremely pretty girl with long straight blonde hair (dyed), beautiful legs and breasts, reminiscent of Lupe Velez. She is mentally retarded. When I asked her to rise she did not recognize the word "rise" and so I had to ask her "to get up" which she did understand. He is probably just as stupid but fortunately has the good sense not to talk too much. When he does, however, he puts on a hillbilly accent that is so authentic that I almost melt in my drawers.

"I thank we gawn git on mahty fahn, Miz Myra" were his first words to me after class as he looked down into my upturned face, confident of his masculine primacy. He was, in fact, so close to me that I could smell the most appetizing odor of deodorant mingled with tobacco and warm boy. But before I could make a suitable answer *she* pulled him away. Poor child! She doesn't know that I shall have him in the end while

27

9

I can hardly bear it another moment! I am reborn or in the process of rebirth like Robert Montgomery in *Here Comes Mr. Jordan.*

I am seated in front of a French café in a Montmartre street on the back lot at Metro. Last year's fire destroyed many of the studio's permanent outdoor sets—those streets and castles I knew so much better than ever I knew the Chelsea area of Manhattan where Myron and I used to exist. I deeply regret the fire, mourn all that was lost, particularly the famous New York City street of brownstones and the charming village in Normandy. But, thank Heaven, this café still stands. Over a metal framework, cheap wood has been so arranged and painted as to suggest with astonishing accuracy a Paris bistro, complete with signs for BYRRH, while a striped awning shades metal tables and chairs set out on the "sidewalk." Any minute now, I expect to see Parisians. I would certainly like to see a waiter and order a Pernod.

I can hardly believe that I am sitting at the same table where Leslie Caron once awaited Gene Kelly so many years ago, and

I can almost re-create for myself the lights, the camera, the sound boom, the technicians, all converged upon this one table where, in a blaze of artificial sunlight, Leslie—much too round but a lovely face with eyes like mine—sits and waits for her screen lover while a man from makeup delicately dusts those famous features with powder.

From the angle where I sit I can see part of the street in Carverville where Andy Hardy lived. The street is beautifully kept up as the shrine it is, a last memorial to all that was touching and—yes—good in the American past, an era whose end was marked by two mushroom shapes set like terminal punctuation marks against the Asian sky.

A few minutes ago I saw Judge Hardy's house with its neatly tended green lawn and windows covered with muslin behind which there is nothing at all. It is quite eerie the way in which the houses look entirely real from every angle on the slightly curving street with its tall green trees and flowering bushes. Yet when one walks around to the back of the houses, one sees the rusted metal framework, the unpainted wood that has begun to rot, the dirty glass of the windows and the muslin curtains soiled and torn. Time withers all things human; although yesterday evening when I saw Ann Rutherford, stopped in her car at a red light, I recognized immediately the great black eyes and the mobile face. She at least endures gallantly, and I could not have been more thrilled! Must find where Lewis Stone is buried.

This is the happiest moment of my life, sitting here alone on the back lot with no one in sight, for I was able to escape the studio guide by telling him that I wanted to lie down in an empty office of the Thalberg Building; then of course I flew straight here to the back lot which is separated from the main studio by a public road.

If only Myron could have seen this! Of course he would have been saddened by the signs of decay. The spirit of what used to be has fled. Most dreadful of all, NO FILM is currently being made on the lot; and that means that the twenty-seven huge sound stages which saw the creation of so many miracles: Gable, Garbo, Hepburn (Katharine), Powell, Loy, Garland, Tracy and James Craig are now empty except for a few crews making television commercials.

Yet I must write the absolute·truth for I am not Myron Breckinridge but myself and despite the intensely symbiotic relationship my husband and I enjoyed during his brief life and despite the fact that I do entirely support his thesis that the films of 1935 to 1945 inclusive were the high point of Western culture, completing what began that day in the theatre of Dionysos when Aeschylus first spoke to the Athenians, I must confess that I part company with Myron on the subject of TV. Even before Marshall McLuhan, I was drawn to the gray shadows of the cathode tube. In fact, I was sufficiently *avant-garde* in 1959 to recognize the fact that it was no longer the movies but the television commercial that engaged the passionate attention of the world's best artists and technicians. And now the result of their extraordinary artistry is this new world, like it or not, we are living in: post-Gutenberg and pre-Apocalypse. For almost twenty years the minds of our children have been filled with dreams that will stay with them forever, the way those maddening jingles do (as I write, I have begun softly to whistle "Rinso White," a theme far more meaningful culturally than all of Stravinsky or even John Cage). I submitted a piece on this subject to *Partisan Review* in the summer of 1960. I believe, without false modesty, that I proved conclusively that the relationship between consumer and advertiser is the last demonstration of *necessary* love in the West, and its principal form of expression is the television commercial. I never heard from *PR* but I kept a carbon of the piece and will incorporate it into the book on Parker Tyler, perhaps as an appendix.

For almost an hour I watched a television commercial being made on the same stage where Bette Davis acted in *The Catered Affair*—that predictably unhappy result of the movies attempting to take over the television *drama* when what they should have taken over was the *spirit* of the commercials. Then I was given lunch in the commissary which is much changed since the great days when people in extraordinary costumes wandered about, creating the impression that one was inside a time machine gone berserk. Now television executives and technicians occupy all the tables and order what used to be Louis B. Mayer Chicken Soup only the name of Mayer has been, my guide told me, stricken from the menu. So much for greatness! Even more poignant as reminders of human transiency are the empty offices on the second floor of the Thalberg Building. I was particularly upset to see that the adjoining suites of Pandro S. Berman and the late Sam Zimbalist were both vacant. Zimbalist (immortal because of *Boom Town*) died in Rome while producing *Ben Hur* which saved the studio's bacon, and Pandro S. Berman (*Dragon Seed, The Picture of Dorian Gray, The Seventh Cross*) has gone into what the local trade papers refer to as "indie production." How tragic! MGM without Pandro S. Berman is like the American flag without its stars.

No doubt about it, an era has indeed ended and I am its chronicler. Farewell the classic films, hail the television commercial! Yet nothing human that is great can entirely end. It is merely transmuted—in the way that the wharf where Jeanette MacDonald arrived in New Orleans (*Naughty Marietta*, 1935) has been used over and over again for a hundred other films even though it will always remain, to those who have a sense of history, Jeanette's wharf. Speaking of history, there was something curiously godlike about Nelson Eddy's recent death before a nightclub audience at Miami. In the middle of a song, he suddenly forgot the words. And so, in that plangent baritone which long ago earned him a permanent place in the pantheon of superstars, he turned to his accompanist and said, "Play 'Dardanella,' and maybe I'll remember the words." Then he collapsed and died.

Play "Dardanella"! Play on! In any case, one must be thankful for those strips of celluloid which still endure to remind us that once there were gods and goddesses in our midst and Metro-Goldwyn-Mayer (where I now sit) preserved their shadows for

all time! Could the actual Christ have possessed a fraction of
the radiance and the mystery of H. B. Warner in the first *King
of Kings* or revealed, even on the cross, so much as a shadow
of the moonstruck Nemi-agony of Jeffrey Hunter in the second
King of Kings, that astonishing creation of Nicholas Ray? No.

10

Seated at a table in the Academy cafeteria. It is three weeks to the day since I arrived. People want to sit with me, but I graciously indicate that I would rather make these notes. They respect my writing at odd times in public places. There is a rumor that I am with the CIA.

While waiting just now to be served today's lunch specialty, a chili con carne that looks suspiciously like Gravy Train, a concentrated dog food which California's poverty-stricken Mexicans mix with their beans, I noticed, as always with a certain pleasure, the way the students go about playing at stardom.

A fantastically beautiful girl called Gloria Gordon holds court at one table, wearing a silver lamé evening gown, cut to the navel, while rock-and-roll singers do an impromptu number in the center of the room, to the delight of the western stars in their boots and chaps; a pleasure not shared by the motorcyclists in their black leather, bedecked with swastikas and chains, radiating hostility, so unlike the Easterners who are solemnly catatonic in their Brooks Brothers suits and button-down collars, each clutching an empty attaché case. The students regard the

Easterners respectfully as being the farthest-out of all for they are, reputedly, the drug-takers. Of course all the students smoke pot and experiment with LSD but only a few main-line, and of those few the Easterners, to a man, are thought to be totally hooked.

As a spiritual child of the Forties, I cannot give my imprimatur to this sort of behavior. The drug-taker is a passivist. I am an activist. Yet—to be fair—how can the average person make a meaningful life for himself in an overpopulated world? There is very little of interest for him to do in the way of work, while sex is truly absorbing only for those who possess imagination as well as means. With these young people one has the sense that they know instinctively that there are plenty more where they came from and so why fuss? They'll soon be gone, their places taken by others so closely resembling them that only a mother's eye could tell the difference.

They are an anonymous blur, even to themselves which explains their fitful, mindless shuffling of roles. In the morning Gloria will wear a silver lamé gown complete with Miriam Hopkins cocktail shaker; in the evening her ensemble may consist of leotards and a sunbonnet. It is easy for these young people to be anything since they are so plainly nothing, and know it. Their metamorphoses, however, seldom involve more than a change of clothes and the affecting of certain speech mannerisms, appropriated from Western or Eastern stars of television series, liberally sprinkled with jokes told late at night on television by nightclub comedians.

Mimesis is normal, particularly in youth, and my only demur is that today's models are, by and large, debasing. In the Forties, American boys created a world empire because they chose to be James Stewart, Clark Gable and William Eythe. By imitating godlike autonomous men, our boys were able to defeat Hitler, Mussolini and Tojo. Could we do it again? Are the private eyes and denatured cowboys potent enough to serve as imperial exemplars? No. At best, there is James Bond . . . and he invariably ends up tied to a slab of marble with a blowtorch aimed at his crotch. Glory has fled and only the television commercials exist to remind us of the Republic's early greatness and virile youth.

Of all the students at the Academy, only one has sought to model himself on a Forties star: the sickest of the Easterners is currently playing Humphrey Bogart, and he is hopeless in the part. The rest are entirely contemporary, pretending to be folk singers, cowboys and English movie actors. Needless to say, all attempts at imitating Cockney or Liverpudlian accents fail. For one thing the accents are too much for them; for another, any evidence that there could be a real world *outside* Southern California tends to demoralize our students. Of course they can observe other worlds on television but then that is show business and familiar. Even the Martian landscape of Southeast Asia loses all strangeness when framed by the homey plastic of a television set, while the people involved in that war are quite plainly extras lucky enough to be called upon to fill in prime airtime with the appearance of people dying and living.

Naturally, the Vietnam exercise appeals enormously to the students. "I mean," said one of them, "if we don't stop them there—you know, where they are now—they'll be right here in L.A." To which I answered, "This city could not be worse run by the Chinese than it is by the present administration and, frankly, if the Chinese could be persuaded to take on the job— which is doubtful—I think we should let them."

Since that exchange, Myra Breckinridge has been thought by some to be a Commie, not the worst thing to be known as at the Academy since the students are scared to death of Communism (like, man, they make you *work!*), and so regard any alleged conspirator or sympathizer with awe . . . which I like. As for the theory of Communism, they have not a clue. In fact, the only book any of them has read is something called *The Green Berets*, a jingoistic work written in the spirit of Kipling with the art of Mickey Spillane. Apparently this work is a constant source of sadistic reveries. Time and again have I heard the students speak wistfully of fighting and torturing the Viet-

cong, or rather of other young men fighting and torturing the
Vietcong on their behalf. Not only are the male students drawn
to violence (at second hand), they are also quite totalitarian-
minded, even for Americans, and I am convinced that any
attractive television personality who wanted to become our dictator would have their full support.

As usual, I am ambivalent. On the one hand, I am intellectually devoted to the idea of the old America. I believe in justice,
I want redress for all wrongs done, I want the good life—if
such a thing exists—accessible to all. Yet, emotionally, I would
be only too happy to become world dictator, if only to fulfill
my mission: *the destruction of the last vestigial traces of traditional
manhood in the race in order to realign the sexes, thus reducing population while increasing human happiness and preparing humanity for
its next stage.*

No doubt this tension in me constitutes my uniqueness, and
genius. Certainly everyone senses it. Students flock to my lec-
tures. Craving my attention and advice, they giggle, fascinated
and frightened, at what I say. They sense my power, particularly
the boys who are drawn to it even as they fear it. Of course
these students are not entirely typical of the nation. They are
somewhat stupider than the average, while simultaneously rather
more imaginative and prone to daydreaming. Like most members of the lower classes, they are reactionary in the truest sense:
the unfamiliar alarms them and since they have had no experience outside what Dr. Montag calls their "peer group," they
are, consequently, in a state of near-panic most of the time,
reacting against almost everything. It was Myron who observed
in 1964 that all of the male hustlers were supporting Goldwater
for President. He wrote a fascinating analysis of this phenomenon and sent it to the Americans for Democratic Action, but
received no reply.

II

There is no denying the fact that Mary-Ann Pringle of Winnipeg is an attractive girl and I plainly dislike the fact since I am jealous of all women though I do not need to be. But then envy is the nature of the human beast and one must face that fact, like all facts. For instance, is it a fact that in my Posture class I have been unnecessarily cruel to Rusty, her boyfriend? Yes. I have been cruel. One must never lie to oneself or, for that matter, to others. No truth should ever be withheld. Without precise notation and interpretation there is only chaos. Essentially, each of us is nothing but a flux of sensations and impressions that only sort themselves out as a result of the most strict analysis and precise formulation, as Robbe-Grillet has proposed but not accomplished (his efforts to revive the novel as an art form are as ineffective as his attempts to destroy the art of film are successful). Of course, a *true* naming of things is impossible. Our minds are too feeble and our sensory equipment is too mysterious and complex for us ever to do more than make approximate definitions. Yet we must continue to make the effort, no matter how inadequate the result. In fact,

I have made it a rule that whatever I *consciously* experience, I promptly submit to analysis. Take Mary-Ann Pringle.

I was in my office, just after lunch, looking over my notes for tomorrow's class in Empathy, when there was a timid knock at the door (despite my vow never to make anthropomorphic references in referring to *things* there was no doubt in my mind, even as I heard that knock, that it was the result of a fist striking wood directed by a frightened i.e. timid intelligence).

Mary-Ann entered, wearing miniskirt (bright yellow) and sweater (dark green) and no bra. She is innocent, attractive, young. Her hands are those of a child, rather grubby with broken nails but marvelously smooth, like seamless gloves.

"Miss Myra, I wanted to know could I talk to you just a minute. I'm not disturbing you, am I, Miss Myra?"

As much as I dislike girls, particularly beautiful young ones, I found myself experiencing an emotion which might be called maternal. I promptly stifled it but was kind. "Of course you're not disturbing me, Mary-Ann. My door is always open to you. Sit down. A cigarette? A Coke?"

I realized too late that I was playing Gail Patrick and would have to continue flashing brilliant smiles for the remainder of the two-scene since I seldom abandon a role once I have embarked upon it. Artistic integrity demands consistency, even with the unappreciative Mary-Anns of this world. I would have been much happier playing a sad but compassionate Loretta Young but since I had begun as Gail Patrick I would so remain, grinning doggedly.

After many soft hesitancies, she came to the point: my treatment of Rusty. "You see, he's real sensitive underneath. Oh, I know he doesn't look it being so strong and playing football one year pro and everything, but he's got feelings like anybody else and when you said that he walked 'like an ape with fleas,' well, he was pretty darned upset and so was I."

I looked grave through my smile, not an easy thing to do. "Oh, I'm sorry to hear that. Truly I am. I only wanted to help. And he *does* have terrible posture."

"It's this old football accident he was too shy to tell you about which broke four ribs and when they healed he was sort of ass . . . assy . . ."

"Asymmetrical?"

"That's right, sort of curved to one side. I mean it's not noticeable except when he's nervous and trying to walk straight and you're staring at him and picking on him."

"You make me very, very ashamed, Mary-Ann." I sounded extraordinarily sincere even to my own ears. "He seems like such a strong *confident* young man that I never dreamed he was so sensitive."

"Well, he is about some things. Like that." Mary-Ann looked so forlorn, so touching, so young, so entirely attractive that it was all I could do to keep from taking her in my arms—a gesture bound to be misinterpreted!

Instead I assured her that I would try to curb my natural impatience in the future. Nevertheless, she must realize that in the teacher-student relationship one must always tell the *total* truth. In this case, though Rusty does walk like an ape with fleas, I am duty bound to add that his other bodily movements are often remarkably graceful, the result of a serene and as yet uncompromised old-fashioned virility which seems never to desert him, except in class when I draw attention to his defects. So I will, I vowed, remember in the future to mix censure with deserved praise. She was pleased and grateful. Lovely Mary-Ann. Is she as stupid as she seems?

12

I had just returned from Empathy II when Buck surged into my office; there is no other verb to describe his entrance. Wearing the white Stetson that is his trademark and the well-cut tweeds that reveal his true businessman's identity, Buck entirely filled the room, his smile positively scarring the air, it was so broad, so happy, so ingenuous.

"Well, li'l lady, you lookin' reel good." No, I must not attempt any further phonetic rendering of his speech which, in any case, shifts so rapidly from Cheyenne to Pomona that one could go mad trying to define its actual provenance. "The kids all love you. Honest they do. I've been getting crackerjack reports from them, particularly in Empathy, and I hope once our little business problem is ironed out, you will consider staying on." He sank into the room's only armchair and gave me a conspiratorial wink. "You got what it takes to be a fine teacher and helper to somebody like me, who's ignorant as a yellow dog."

"Not so ignorant!" Two could play at flattery. By the time I'm finished with Buck Loner, he won't have the proverbial pot to piss in or my name is not Myra Breckinridge, at whose feet

40

the proudest men have groveled, wincing beneath the lash of her scorn, whimpering for a chance to hold in their coarse arms her—my—fragile, too lovely for this world or at least *their* world, body. *I am Woman.* "But I will say that after a week of getting to know your students, I realize at last what overpopulation means. The brains have been bred out of the current gener-aration. They are like the local oranges, all bright appearance and no taste."

I meant to wound. I did. Buck sat back in the chair as though I had struck his great golden autumnal moon-face. "Why, that's very, *very* unfair, Myra. Very unfair indeed." He seemed at a complete loss how to begin a defense.

In any case, I did not give him time. "I realize the scandalous state of the public school system in the United States as well as the effect television has had upon the mental processes of those whose childhood was spent staring at the box, and I accept the fact that these young people are a new breed who have gone beyond linear type in their quest for experience—'knowledge' does not seem to be the right word for what they're after; perhaps the 'easy buck' says it all . . . no play on names intended. Anyway I find it extraordinarily difficult getting through to them even the simplest thought, but since I am an American brought up during the great age of film, I want to believe that our culture is still alive, still able to create a masterpiece like *Since You Went Away,* and so I must conclude that what you have assembled here are the national dregs, the misfits, the neurotics, the daydreamers, the unrealists, the—in short—fuckups who form a significant minority in our culture, witness what hap-pened November twenty-second, 1963, at Dallas!"

Well, that took the wind out of those sails. He absolutely shrank into his chair, contracted before my eyes. The huge open face shut tight against my imperious gaze. Frankly I can think of no pleasure greater than to approach an open face and swiftly say whatever needs to be said to shut it. Myron disap-proved of this trait in me but I believed then, as I do now, that if one is right, the unsayable must be said, and the faces that I temporarily shut will, in the long run, be better faces for the exercise.

Buck did not agree. "Those boys and girls are a cross-section of the youth of this country, no better, no worse. What they have got that *is* unusual and which may disqualify them from attending your Business School at Harvard is the overwhelming desire to be in show business, to have their names and faces known to all the world, to see themselves beloved by strangers, and that, believe me, is the only truly gratifying life any human can have, once they get the bug, that is, like I did, and like they have."

"My dear Buck," I addressed him warmly, a husky Jean Arthur note to my voice, "*you* are unusual. Unique. You were—are—a star. You were—and through the reruns of your old movies on TV, you still are, permanently—beloved. Long after these two bodies, yours and mine, have gone to dust and this room is gone, and these boys and girls have all grown old and died and their descendants come and gone, *you will live*. Buck Loner, the Singin' Shootin' Radio Cowboy, astride Sporko, will ride the ranges of the world's imagination. You are for all time. They are not and never can be."

I had him there. My famous one-two, learned from Myron: first, excessive flattery with a grain of truth swathed in cultured nacre; then the lethal puncheroo. His face reflected ecstasy and dismay. Myra's round.

"Well, honey, I see what you mean and it's a real subtle point you got there. I mean, yes, I did make eighteen feature-length oaters, that's true, and that bastard lawyer of mine never put in one word in my contracts about future resale to the TV even though I once said to him, 'Sydney, there is going to be this TV just like there was radio and when it comes the Buck Loner features are going to be worth their weight in solid platinum.' But he paid me no mind and . . . But that's not what we were talking about. No. It was about the kids, yes." He frowned. "Now they are good kids who for the most part come from underprivileged homes across the length and breadth of this country, and they hitchhike to sunny California in order that they might be stars, like me. They get jobs here and there to support themselves while they study at the Academy where we do our darnedest to bring out the creative potential of each and every one . . ."

"Can the brochure, daddy-oh," I said, surprising myself by the Fifties jargon that so amused Myron but rather repelled me. "You're in business to make money, and you do."

He looked genuinely hurt. "Well now, honey, of course I am making money or I should say *eking* out an existence, real estate taxes being what they are in this high-type residential area . . ." Noticing the scorn in my face (and realizing that I am on to his conning), he quickly got away from the ticklish subject of our mutual property.

"Anyway, I genuinely want to see these boys and girls happy because—you may laugh and probably will—I believe in Love and I try to create that sort of atmosphere here where they are as much as possible screened from the harshness of the world, which they get quite enough of working as waitresses in drive-ins and so on not to mention the unhappy often broken homes they come from. I try to give them the glamour and excitement of show business, of fame, of stardom without the pain of failure, the terrible ordeal of real-life show business where so many hearts are broken every day, needlessly, but that's the way it goes. Here at least they are able to perform on our closed-circuit TV and then read the reviews in our school paper which are always good and constructive. They can cut discs which are played on our Muzak-type system. They have special courses in how to give interviews to the press which they can then read in the school magazine. In fact, until it was recently discontinued, our late-night closed-circuit TV talk show was as good as NBC's, with our stars being interviewed by a fellow student, himself a star on the order of Johnny Carson. So with all those things, for a time, within these walls, more than a thousand young men and women with stars in their eyes are happy."

No doubt about it, he was most effective. When he spoke of

hearts needlessly broken (the sort of phrase Myron would have hooted at), I confess tears came to my eyes. For he was paraphrasing Betty Hutton after one of her many failures on television. She never had any luck, that girl. Possibly because she does not realize that she is a true goddess, as a result of all those pictures she made at Paramount during the Forties; films in which she was the demonic clown, the drum majorette of Olympus or, as Parker Tyler puts it with his usual wisdom: "The Hutton comedienne is a persuasive hieroglyph that symbolizes something deeply ingrained in modern morality: the commoner man's subconscious impulse, when a girl evades or refuses a kiss, to knock her out, take it, and have done."

Never was Tyler more on the mark than when he analyzed Hutton's "epileptico-mimetic pantomime," in which he saw straight through the strenuous clowning to the hard fact that American women are eager for men to rape them and vice versa; and that in every American there is a Boston Strangler longing to break a neck during orgasm. Ours is a violent race.

Buck and I agreed to disagree. But though he is a fool, he is also a man of formidable character and persuasiveness and thus a dangerous antagonist. It will require all my genius to destroy him . . . and destroy him I must, for not only has he cheated me of Myron's proper inheritance, he represents all that I detest in the post-Forties culture: a permissive slovenliness of mind and art. It is all like, like, like . . . "like help," as the Californian said when he was drowning. They all use "like" in a way that sets my teeth on edge. Not that I am strict as a grammarian. I realize that a certain looseness of style is necessary to create that impression of spontaneity and immediacy which is the peculiar task of post-Gutenberg prose, if there is to be such a thing. But I do object to "like" because of its mindless vagueness. "What time is it, Rusty?"

"Like three o'clock, Miss Myra," he said, after looking at his watch. He knew the *exact* time but preferred to be approximate. Well, I shall teach him to tell time among other things.

BUCK LONER REPORTS—
Recording Disc No. 715—
5 February

Flagler and Flagler dont seem to be getting much of anywhere with the case they say that Gertrudes will is in order leaving her share of the property to Myron and Myrons will though not made by a lawyer was duly witnessed and will stand up in court leaving everything to his wife Myra so half the property is hers according to law which strikes me as perfect injustice since if it wasnt for me there wouldnt be hardly any value at all to this land even though it is Westwood the lawyers suggest I settle with her for the current going price of these acres in Westwood for land which would be in the neighborhood of two hundred thousand bucks which I am not about to pay also I got a hunch she is out for even bigger game for she has lately taken to making little jokes about what a swell team we make running the Academy I hate that woman and wish to God there was some way to get her out of my hair once and for all Flagler and Flagler are now checking up to make sure she was really married to that fag nephew thats our only hope at this point proving she wasnt married or something mean while I cozy her along best I can period paragraph the taking of drugs is frowned upon by this institution not only is it illegal and injurious to the health but it has been known to be harmful to the performances of those performing while under the influence something along those lines I must write up for the paper before the vice squad gets on my ass any more than they are now its crazy with people murdering each other from one end of L A to the other all our local storm troopers can think of is kids smoking pot which does them a lot less harm than liquor well it is a nutty world and that is for sure period paragraph dont forget to tell Hilda to send me the new French Canadian masseuse on Monday they say she gives a super around the world and also knows about massage remember to pick up chut ney for Bobbie Dean whos cooking curry tonight

13

I have locked the bathroom door. Several people have tried to get in, including Rusty, but I call out to them, "Use the other john," and they go away, doubtless thinking that I am in here with a man when actually I am simply trying to get away from the party.

I feel very odd. I just smoked one entire marijuana cigarette, something I have never done before. In the old days Myron and I used occasionally to take a drag on someone else's joint but never an entire stick. I always thought that drugs had no effect on me but apparently I was wrong.

I feel like crying. The ring around the bathtub, no, the two rings, one light, one dark, his and hers, depress me. What am I doing? I, Myra Breckinridge, Woman, as I proceed in my long trailing robes across the desert. Suddenly I catch sight of my lover, a priest who has given up hope of Heaven for my body. I throw out my arms and run toward him across the silvery sands. . . .

I can hardly write. My eyes don't focus properly but I must put down all my impressions exactly for they are extraordinarily intense and important. The door of perception has swung open at last and now I know that what I always suspected was true is true, that time is space made fluid, that these miniskirts are too short for me; that time is a knee made fluid. That is hell.

14

A terrible hangover, the result of mixing gin and marijuana, though pot is supposed not to leave one with any ill effect, unless of course that is simply a legend cultivated by drug addicts. I am in my office, trying to prepare for the first class of the day. Only with the greatest effort am I able to write these lines. My hands tremble. I feel quite ill.

The party was given by one of the students in the Music Department, Clem or Clint something or other. I had never seen him before but yesterday morning Gloria Gordon (who is in my Empathy I class) told me that he gave marvelous "far-out" parties and that I would be welcome to come last night as he, Clem or Clint, had admired me from a distance.

So Laura came to Petrarch's party, to put it stylishly, and got stoned out of her head. It was too humiliating and yet during those moments when I lay in that empty bathtub with the two rings, staring up at the single electric light bulb, I did have the sense that I was at one with all creation. The notes I made under the influence do not *begin* to record what I was actually feeling, largely because I was forced to break them off when a kind of paralysis set in. Apparently I was not able to move or speak until shortly before dawn when Clem or Clint and Gloria broke the lock on the bathroom door and rescued me from my gaudy reveries.

Fortunately, they took it all as a huge joke, but I am still humiliated at having got myself in such a situation, without dignity and finally without revelation, for in the light of day I find it difficult to believe in cosmic consciousness. In fact, this terrible hangover seems to me proof that the celebrated insights of the mystics are physiological, the result of a drastic reduction of sugar in the blood that goes to the brain. *My* brain, deprived of sugar for some hours last night, now feels as if it were full of an expanding fluid on the verge of seeking desperate egress though the top of a papier-mâché skull.

I did find the party interesting, at least in its early stages. Of those present, I was one of the oldest, which did nothing for my sense of security so laboriously achieved in those long sessions with Dr. Montag. But I was a good sport, laughing and chatting and, all in all, behaving not as a teacher but as just plain Myra Breckinridge, a beautiful woman not yet thirty. As a result, several of the young men showed a sexual interest in me but though I teased them and played the flirt, I did not allow any intimacies to occur or even indicate that they might be welcomed at some future time. I preferred to be Greer Garson, a gracious lady whose compassionate breasts were more suited to be last pillow for a dying youth than as baubles for the coarse hands of some horny boy.

But sex does not appear to be the hangup with this crowd. They wear buttons which, among other things, accuse the Governor of California of being a Lesbian, the President of being God, and Frodo (a character in a fairy tale by Tolkien) of actually existing. This is all a bit fey for my taste. But one must be open to every experience and the young, in a sense, lead us since there are now more of them than there are of us. But they are peculiar creatures, particularly to one brought up within the context of the Forties. They are quite relaxed about sex;

not only do they have affairs with one another, they also attend orgies in a most matter-of-fact way, so unlike my generation with its belief in the highly concentrated sort of love that Leslie Howard felt for Ingrid Bergman in *Intermezzo*. Yet despite all this athleticism, their *true* interests seem to be, in some odd way, outside sex. They like to sit for long periods doing nothing at all, just listening to music or to what they regard as music. They are essentially passive; hence the popularity of pot.

Of course, my generation (chronologically, not spiritually) began all this. We of the Fifties saw the beginning of Zen as a popular force. Certainly our Beats were nothing if not passive in their attitude to life and experience. They were always departing, never arriving. Neither Myron nor I shared their pleasures or attitudes for we were, despite our youth, a throwback to the Forties, to the last moment in human history when it was possible to possess a total commitment to something outside oneself. I mean of course the war and the necessary elimination of Hitler, Mussolini and Tojo. And I do not exaggerate when I declare that I would give ten years of my life if I could step back in time for just one hour and visit the Stage Door Canteen in Hollywood, exactly the way that Dane Clark did in the movie of the same name, and like him, meet all the great stars at their peak and perhaps even, like Dane's buddy Bob Hutton, have a romance with Joan Leslie, a star I fell hopelessly in love with while watching *Sergeant York*. But where is Joan now? Where are all those beautiful years of war and sacrifice and Pandro S. Berman films? None of this will ever come again, except in gray cloudy miniatures on the Late Show, and soon, I pray, in the sinewy prose of Myra Breckinridge as she reworks and completes her late husband's certain-to-be masterpiece *Parker Tyler and the Films of the Forties*.

But what will the current generation think of my efforts? That is the question. I find that any reference to the stars of the Forties bores them. "Who was Gary Cooper?" asked one young thing last night; to which another girl answered, "The one with the big ears," thinking he was Clark Gable! But they all find Humphrey Bogart fascinating and he may yet prove to be my bridge to them.

Conversation from last night.

"Like experience isn't everything, Myra. I mean like you also got to have *it* deep down inside you."

"But what is *it*?"

"What's deep down inside you, that's what *it* is. What you are."

"But isn't what you are what experience makes you?"

"No, it's like what you feel . . ."

Like. Like. Like! The babble of this subculture is drowning me! Although my companion was a lanky youth of the sort I am partial to, I simply shut him out and watched the group that was dancing in the center of the room, a dozen boys and girls gyrating without touching one another, each in his or her private world . . . which is the key to the game of the moment: don't touch me and I won't touch you. While the operative word is "Cool." Like fun? Like crazy!

Of the dancers, Rusty Godowski was easily the most exciting and certainly the most attractive, in his faded chinos and checked shirt, whose top two buttons were missing, revealing a smooth muscular neck at whose base, just below the hollows of the collarbone, tendrils of bronze hair curl, looking as if they would be silky to the touch, unlike the usual male Brillo. Soon I shall know for certain their texture. Poor Mary-Ann.

"He does dance well, doesn't he?" Mary-Ann sat down in the place which the metaphysician had vacated, without, I fear, my noticing his departure. Obviously she had seen me watching Rusty. She is not entirely stupid.

"I was studying him for posture." I sounded colder than I intended, but she had taken me by surprise and I dislike it when people observe me without my knowledge. "I will say he moves very well when he dances," I added with a degree of warmth which encouraged her to smile shyly.

"That's being an athlete. It's just when he walks he sort of lumbers."

"Well, we'll soon take care of that," I said briskly, and indeed I shall, poor bastard.

Mary-Ann chattered away, unaware of my designs. "We've been talking about maybe getting married in June after we finish the course—that is, if we can both get work. Of course I can always pick up a little money modeling. I'm not really crazy about a career, you know. Fact, it's just to be with Rusty that I'm taking this music course, to keep an eye on him. With all these pretty girls around and wild for him, I can't take any chances."

"You make a charming couple." I noticed again how extraordinarily attractive she is, with that fresh unclouded complexion I so love—and envy, for the *texture* of the skin of my face is not all that Helena Rubinstein would desire. In my day I have been too much a sun-worshipper and the skin must pay a price for the spirit's refreshment, and I was certainly refreshed by those long sunny afternoons at Jones Beach and amongst the Far Rockaways.

Rusty's back was to us now and I could not take my eyes off his somewhat square yet small buttocks as they made a slow grinding motion in response to the beat of an electric guitar. Though I tried to visualize what they must look like without the protective covering of cloth, I failed to come up with a satisfactory mental image. Happily, I shall soon know everything!

" 'Course we're both broke. I get a little something from the family in Winnipeg but poor Rusty's only got this uncle and aunt in Detroit who don't like him because he was kind of wild when he was a kid . . ."

"So wild that he was busted for stealing a car." The day that I first noticed Rusty in class, I went straight to Buck's office where dossiers on each student are kept. They are surprisingly thorough. Rusty's three-year suspended sentence was duly noted, as well as the cogent fact that should he ever again run afoul of the law he can be sent up for a maximum of twenty years.

Mary-Ann looked frightened. "I didn't know anybody knew about that."

"Just Uncle Buck and I." I patted her hand. "Don't worry, neither of us is going to tell."

"He's completely changed since those days, he really is. Why, in those days he used to play around with a lot of girls. You should have seen all the photographs he used to have! But after he met me he stopped all that and now he isn't interested in anything except working hard and being a star, which I'm sure he's going to be."

"He's certainly no worse than the rest of them on television." I was perfectly honest with her. "Of course he can hardly talk but neither can they."

"Oh, but he talks awfully well. It's just he has some trouble with *speaking* lines but that takes lots of practice. Anyway what is important is that he comes over so *real*, and of course so sexy. You should have seen him on the closed-circuit TV last spring when he played the part of this crazy gunman. Oh, he was *something!*"

It was at that point that I was given marijuana by Clem or Clint, and the rest of the evening took on a religious tone.

15

Feeling somewhat better, I gave a great deal to my Empathy II class, and though I am now exhausted, I have at least gotten over my hangover.

A letter from Dr. Montag cheered me up. He warns against depressions of the sort I have been prone to since Myron's death and so he proposes, rather obviously, that in lieu of analysis I must keep busy. Little does he dream just how busy I am! Between my plot to entrap Rusty and my efforts to obtain my rightful share of the Academy, I have hardly a moment to devote to my life's real work, completing Myron's book. Fortunately the insights gained during my visit to MGM are bound to add immeasurably to Myron's text. Meanwhile, I have had a marvelous idea for a piece on Pandro S. Berman which *Cahiers du Cinema* ought to eat up. After all, with the exception of Orson Welles and Samuel Fuller, Berman is the most important film-maker of the Forties.

16

I spoke sharply to Rusty in Posture today. He shows no sign of improvement and I'm afraid I was brutal. "You simply cannot walk straight." I imitated his slouching walk which is, in its way, extremely sensual but hardly suitable for the screen.

He looked very angry and muttered something under his breath that I could not hear but assumed was uncomplimentary. Mary-Ann looked more than ever disturbed as she begged me with her eyes to desist.

"I will see you after class, Godowski." I was abrupt. "Things cannot go on as they are," I added ominously.

I then gave the class a series of exercises in how to sit down, something that did not come easily to any of them. All the while observing, out of the corner of my eye, Rusty's sullen face. My plot is working very nicely.

After class, Rusty came to my office and sat on the straight chair beside the desk, listing to one side, legs wide apart. He was not in the least nervous. In fact, he was downright defiant, even contemptuous of *me*, so secure did he think himself in his masculine superiority.

As usual, he wore a sport shirt with two missing buttons. Today, however, a T-shirt hid the chest from view. Faded blue jeans and desert boots completed the costume, and—as I have already noted—it is costumes that the young men now wear as they act out their simple-minded roles, constructing a fantasy world in order to avoid confronting the fact that to be a man in a society of machines is to be an expendable, soft auxiliary to what is useful and hard. Today there is nothing left for the old-fashioned male to do, no ritual testing of his manhood through initiation or personal contest, no physical struggle to survive or mate. Nothing is left him but to put on clothes reminiscent of a different time; only in travesty can he act out the classic hero who was a law unto himself, moving at ease through a landscape filled with admiring women. Mercifully, that age is finished. Marlon Brando was the last of the traditional heroes and, significantly, even he was invariably beaten up in the last reel, victim of a society that has no place for the ancient ideal of manhood. Since Brando, there has been nothing except the epicene O'Toole, the distracted Mastroianni, and the cheerfully incompetent Belmondo. The roof has fallen in on the male and we now live at the dawn of the age of Woman Triumphant, of Myra Breckinridge!

I began pleasantly, disarmingly. "Not long ago Mary-Ann told me that I have a tendency to pick on you, Rusty . . ."

"You sure do . . ."

"Don't interrupt, please." I was stern but pleasant, like Eve Arden. "If I have, it's because I'm trying to help you. I think you have great *potential* talent. How great I can't decide just yet, but unless you learn to walk properly there's not a chance in this world of your ever being a major star."

The reference to his talent pleased him; the prophecy alarmed him. "Hell, Miss Myra, I don't walk that bad."

"I'm afraid you do. And look at the way you're leaning to one side right now. You look like you're about to fall out of the chair."

He straightened up and crossed his legs. "That better?" The

hint of a sneer in his voice excited me. He must be built up in order that his fall be the more terrible.

"Yes. Now I realize that you have a physical problem. Mary-Ann told me about your back."

"I broke four ribs and even so finished the last half." He was inordinately proud; no doubt about it, a confident young man.

"Very admirable. Now I want you to stand up and walk first toward the door and then back here to me."

I could hear him murmur "Oh, shit" under his breath as he lumbered to his feet. Slowly he walked, or rather slouched, to the door and then returned and stood defiantly in front of me, thumbs hooked in his belt. I noted for the first time how large and strong his hands are, hairless with unusually long thumbs.

"O.K.?" he asked.

"*Not* O.K." I studied him a moment. He was so close to me that my eyes were on a level with his belt buckle. "Now, Rusty, I noticed the other night that your problem seems to go away when you dance. So, just as an exercise, I want you to do one of those stationary dances—I don't know what they're called. You know, like the one you were doing at the party."

"Dance? Here? Now?" He looked puzzled. "But there's no music."

"To be precise there never is *music* with those dances, just electronic noise. Nothing compared to the *big* sound of Glenn Miller. Anyway, all you need is a beat. You can keep time by snapping your fingers."

"I feel silly." He scowled and looked suddenly dangerous, but I knew what I was about.

"Go ahead. We haven't got all day. Start." I snapped my fingers. Halfheartedly he did the same and slowly began to gyrate his hips. I found the effect almost unbearably erotic. To have him all to myself, just three feet away, his pelvis revolving sexily. For some minutes he continued to gyrate, the snapping of fingers growing less and less precise as his hands grew sweaty. I then instructed him to turn around so that I could observe him from the rear. He did as he was told. Waves of lust made me dizzy as those strong deep buttocks slowly revolved. Have they ever been violated? I can hardly bear the suspense.

Finally, I told him he could stop. He did so, with obvious relief. When he turned back to me, I noticed the curved upper lip was beaded with perspiration. In his dense masculine way, he too had felt the tension and perhaps suspected, instinctively, its origin and so knew fear. "I can't dance so good without music," he mumbled, as if obscurely ashamed of the display he had been forced to make of himself.

"You did very well." I was brisk, even encouraging. I think I may have a solution to our problem. All you need is something to remind you to stand straight. Where were the ribs broken?"

He touched his left side, below the heart. "Four was busted right here which is why I'm kind of pulled over to this side."

"Let me see."

At first he seemed not to understand the question. "Like this," he said, indicating the way in which he was listing to port.

"No. No." I was brusque. "Let me *see* your back. Take your shirt off."

He was startled. "But there's nothing to see. . . . I mean the ribs are all inside me that was broken."

"I know *where* the ribs are, Rusty." I was patient. "But I have to see the exact point where the muscle begins to pull you to one side."

There was no answer to this. He started to say something but decided not to. Slowly he unfastened his belt and unhooked the top button of the blue jeans. Then he unbuttoned his shirt and took it off. The T-shirt was soaked at the armpits, the result of his strenuous impromptu dance and, perhaps (do I project?), of terror.

For the first time I saw his bare arms. The skin was very white (no one out here goes to the beach in January even though it is quite sunny), with biceps clearly marked though not over-developed; large veins ran the length of the forearms to the hands, always an excellent sign, and not unattractive since the veins were not blue but white, indicating skin of an unusual thickness, again a good sign. On the forearms coppery straight hairs grew. He paused as though not certain what to do next. I was helpful. "The T-shirt, too. I haven't got X-ray eyes."

Glumly he pulled the T-shirt over his head. I watched fascinated by each revelation of his body. First the navel came into view, small and protruding. Just beneath it a line of dark slightly curly hairs disappeared inside the Jockey shorts which were now visible above the loosened belt. The shirt rose higher. About two inches above the navel, more hairs began (I had seen the topmost branches of this tree of life at the pot party, now I saw the narrow roots slowly widening as the tree made its way to his neck). When the chest was entirely bared, his face was momentarily hidden in the folds of the damp T-shirt and so I was able to study, unobserved, the small rose-brown breasts, at the moment concave and unaroused. Then the T-shirt was wadded up and dropped onto the floor.

Aware of my interested gaze, he blushed. Beginning at the base of the thick neck, the lovely color rose to the level of his eyes. Like so many male narcissists, he is paradoxically, modest: he enjoys revealing himself but only on his own terms.

A remark about his appearance was obviously called for and I made it. "You seem in very good condition . . ."

"Well, I work out some, not like I ought to . . . used to . . ." He hooked long thumbs into his belt, causing the smooth pectorals to twitch ever so slightly, revealing the absence of any fat or loosening of skin.

"Now will you please face the wall, arms at your sides, with your palms pressed against the wall as hard as you can."

Without a word, he did as he was told. The back was as pleasing as the front (no hairs on the shoulder, unlike poor Myron, who was forced to remove his with electrolysis). The blue jeans had begun to sag and now hung several inches below the waistline, revealing frayed Jockey shorts. Aware that the trousers were slipping, he tried to pull them up with one hand but I put a stop to that. "Hands flat against the wall!" I ordered in a sharp voice that would not take no for an answer.

"But, Miss Myra . . ." and his voice was suddenly no longer deep but a boy's voice, plaintive and frightened: the young Lon McCallister.

"Do as I say!"

He muttered something that I could not hear and did as he was told. In the process, the blue jeans cleared the curve of his buttocks and now clung precariously to the upper thighs of which a good two inches were in plain view. It was a moment to cherish, to exult in, to give a life for. His embarrassment was palpable, charging the situation with true drama since from the very beginning it has been quite plain to me that *in no way do I interest him sexually*. Since he detests me, my ultimate victory is bound to be all the more glorious and significant.

I studied my captive for some moments (the spine did indeed make an S-like curve and the thick white trapezoidal ligament was twisted to one side). Of greater interest to me, however, were the Jockey shorts and what they contained. But now I knew that I would have to proceed with some delicacy. I crossed to where he stood. I was so close to him that I could smell the horselike odor men exude when they are either frightened or in a state of rut. In this case it was fright.

Delicately I ran my hand down his spine. He shuddered at my touch but said nothing. Meanwhile I spoke to him calmly, easily, the way one does in order to soothe a nervous animal. "Yes, I can see the trouble now. It's right here, under the shoulder blade." I kneaded the warm smooth skin, and again he winced but said nothing while I continued to give my "analysis" of his condition. "Perhaps a brace in this area would help."

Now my hands were at the narrow waist. He was breathing hoarsely, arms pressed so hard against the wall that the triceps stood out like white snakes intertwined, ready to strike.

I felt something warm on the back of one hand: a drop of sweat from his left armpit. "But perhaps the trouble is lower down. Around the small of the back. Yes, of course! The lumbar region—that's just where it is!"

As I spoke, evenly, hypnotically, I gently inserted my thumbs beneath the worn elastic band of his shorts and before he was aware of what was happening, I had pulled them down to his knees. He gave a strangled cry, looked back over his shoulder at me, face scarlet, mouth open, but no words came. He started to pull away from me, then stopped, recalling that he was for all practical purposes nude. He clung now to the wall, the last protector of his modesty.

Meanwhile I continued to chat. "Yes, we can start the brace right here." I touched the end of the spine, a rather protuberant bony tip set between the high curve of buttocks now revealed to me in all their splendor . . . and splendor is the only word to describe them! Smooth, white, hairless except just beneath the spinal tip where a number of dark coppery hairs began, only to disappear from view into the deep crack of buttocks so tightly clenched that not even a crowbar could have pried them apart.

Casually I ran my hand over the smooth slightly damp cheeks. To the touch they were like highly polished marble warmed by the sun of some perfect Mediterranean day. I even allowed my forefinger the indiscretion of fingering the coppery wires not only at the tip of the spine but also the thicker growth at the back of his thighs. Like so many young males, he has a relatively hairless torso with heavily furred legs. Myron was the same. With age, however, the legs lose much of this adolescent growth while the torso's pelt grows heavier.

I had now gone almost as far as I could go with my inspection. After all, I have not yet established total mastery. But I have made a good beginning: half of the mystery has now been revealed, the rest must wait for a more propitious time. And so, after one last kneading of the buttocks (I tried and failed to pull apart the cheeks), I said, "That will do for now, Rusty. I think we've almost got to the root of the problem."

He leaned rigidly, all of a piece, to one side and grabbed the fallen trousers. Had he slightly squatted—the normal thing to do in his position—I might have caught a glimpse of the heart of the mystery from the rear, an unflattering angle which, paradoxically, has always excited me, possibly because it is in some way involved with my passion for "backstage," for observing what is magic from the unusual, privileged angle. But he kept his legs as much together as possible, pulling on clothes with astonishing speed, the only lapse occurring when something in front was caught by the ascending shorts, causing him to grunt and fumble. But then all was in order and when he finally turned around, the belt buckle had been firmly fastened. He was satisfyingly pale and alarmed-looking.

I was all business. "I think this has been a very useful session—yes, you can put on your shirt." His hands trembled as he buttoned his shirt. "I'll have a chat with the chiropractor Uncle Buck uses" (the "Uncle Buck" always works wonders at the Academy) "and we'll see what he can do for you."

"Yes, Miss Myra." The voice was almost inaudible. Nervously, he mopped his face with a handkerchief.

"It is stuffy in here, isn't it? I always turn the airconditioning off. It's bad for my sinus. Well, I don't want to keep you another minute from Mary-Ann. What a wonderful girl! I hope you realize how lucky you are."

"Oh, yes, Miss Myra, I sure do," he gabbled. Then, with the assurance that I had only his interest at heart, I showed him out of the room. It was, in many ways, the most exciting *sensual* moment of my life—so far. But the best is yet to come, for I mean to prove once and for all to Dr. Montag that it is possible to work out in life *all* one's fantasies, and so become entirely whole.

No sooner was Rusty out the door than I noticed he had left his T-shirt behind. I buried my face in its warm sweaty folds, a most agreeable surrogate for skin. The odor was somewhat sharp at the armpits but by no means unpleasant since fresh sweat is the greatest of aphrodisiacs as well as nature's own lubricant.

BUCK LONER REPORTS—
Recording Disc No. 721—
18 February

       Dont know when I have ever come
across a woman as awful as Myra Breckinridge she is wreaking
total havoc with the program telling the students they have no
talent and no chance of stardom which is downright mean not
to mention bad for business so I had a talk with her in the back
of the auditorium where she was holding her Empathy class
which for reasons not clear to me is double the size of any of
the other classes the kids are fascinated by her because of what
she says and she is a sharptongued bitch no doubt of that theres
seldom a class of hers where somebody dont run out crying to
beat the band but they come back for more which is downright
unhealthy as I told her in no uncertain terms you are under
mining all of our work here at the Academy which is to build
up capital c confidence exclamation point paragraph well she
just gave me that high and mighty stare of hers and said you
think lying to people is good for them you think telling somebody

whos got cancer that he is all right and doesnt need an operation
is the right thing to do of course not I said but if he has had the
operation and is a terminal case I think you must keep him as
happy as possible and in a good frame of mind under the cir
cumstances well she said in a voice so loud that the students
on the stage who were pretending to be billboards could hear
her at least you admit that these cretins are terminal cases and
that its curtains for the lot of them no it is not I said wanting
to crack her one against the side of her head just to take that
smirk off of her face no they are carefully selected as possible
candidates for future stardom every last one of them well then
she interrupts with a single swear word delivered in a hiss that
I swear sent shivers down my spine like some mean old rattler
out there in the sagebrush just waiting to sink his fangs into
your leg well I was not about to be put down in my own Academy
and so I said getting real tough you don't talk to me that way
and get away with it you consider yourself warned or else Ill
have you out of here so fast you wont know what hit you to
which she just smiled prettily and cocked her pretty head at me
and said ever so sweet you just try it you motherfucker and Ill
take this whole place away from you lock stock and Empathy
class well I dont think no woman has ever spoke to me like that
certainly no man would dare for fear of getting hisself beat to a
pulp all I could say then was well you watch your step thats all
and as for taking this place away from me I need to know a
whole lot more about you than I do why I dont even know
whether you was ever really married to that fag Myron well I
suppose I did go too far on that one for she hauled off and let
me have it right in the kisser and I saw stars because this wasnt
no girls slap no sir it was a goddam fist with what felt like a roll
of quarters in it I nearly fell over it was such a jolt and the noise
mustve been like a pistol going off for the kids all stopped pre
tending to be billboards and stared at us like we was putting on
a show which is the way she handled it for cool as can be she
said to the kids I quote now that is the classic stage slap delivered
in such a way that though the person being slapped really seems

to be hit hard he isnt its all fake later Ill show you how its done its a trick first used on stage by Miss Patricia Collinge in The Little Foxes so thank you Uncle Buck for the demonstration unquote and with that the bitch went back to teaching her class and I come straight back here to the office and canceled my appointment for massage I am too shook up and then phoned to Flagler and Flagler to ask if theres any report on her from the detective in New York they say the only thing theyve so far found is that Myron really was a fag quite well known in what they call the underground movie set and its thought he killed hisself probably because of Myra about who they cant find out anything except there is no record of her marrying him in New York New Jersey or Connecticut they are meanwhile going to check the other forty-seven states it would be the happiest day of my life if I can find out she really wasn't married to him and put her in the damned hoosegow for fraud on the other hand the three wills are all in order worse luck for me so everything depends now on that marriage license dont forget Bobbie Deans yoghurt with prune whip

17

I am sitting in a booth at Schwab's drugstore in Hollywood where the young Lana Turner was discovered by an agent. Of course the present Schwab's does not in the least resemble the Schwab's of thirty years ago. Today's drugstore consists of two large rooms. The one where I am sitting contains booths while the other is occupied by drugstore, soda fountain and a large display of magazines and paperback books where out-of-work actors and actresses can be seen at any time of day or night furtively reading *Silver Screen,* or searching feverishly through the pages of novels looking for lurid passages whose crude imagery can be calculated to enliven sexual bouts with "loved ones" or, as one hippie said to another after sex, "I'll tell you who I was thinking of if you'll tell me who you were thinking of."

It is curious how often the male (and sometimes the female) needs to think of those not present in the act. Even with Myron, I was always imagining someone else, a boy glimpsed at Jones Beach or a man observed briefly at the wheel of a truck or sometimes (yes, I may as well confess it) a slender blonde girl that used to live in the brownstone next door when we lived at the corner of 11th Street and Ninth Avenue. She studied at the Art Students League and though I never once spoke to her, I was constantly aware of her and learned a good deal about her from the owner of the Ninth Avenue Delicatessen where each of us had an account, ours too seldom paid on time.

Fortunately, I am no longer susceptible to the charm of the female body. Not that a straightforward invitation from the young Lana Turner or the young Ava Gardner might not, as they say out here, "turn me on," but luckily for me there is no longer a young Lana Turner or Ava Gardner and so my lust has taken a different and quite spectacular form since Myron's death.

Rusty has been avoiding me ever since the day of his humiliation. He has even taken to cutting Posture class, which is a serious matter. This morning as I was on my way to Empathy II (held in the auditorium because of the students' desire to be taught by me: the other teachers are mad with envy!), I bumped into Rusty—literally collided with him at the turning of a corridor. I dropped my briefcase, which he swiftly retrieved.

"I'm sorry, Miss Myra." He handed me the briefcase at arm's length as though it contained a ticking bomb.

"You really should watch where you're going." I was severe and he gulped like Gary Cooper, his attractiveness greatly enhanced by a total inability to look me in the eye.

"You've missed two Posture classes in a row. That's very serious, Rusty. Very, very serious. You know how Uncle Buck dislikes that, and how it is bound to count against your final grade."

"But I been real busy, Miss Myra. Working, see . . ."

"The garage?"

"No, with these friends, helping to start this business. Anyway, next week I'll be back in class and that's for sure, Miss Myra." He looked at me with such frightened sincerity that it was all I could do to keep my hands off him right then and there. Gone was the easy masculine arrogance that had characterized him in our early relations. Now he was jittery and profoundly hostile, and all because of *me!* Though the corridor was airconditioned to a polar temperature (like so many fat men Buck suffers from heat), a bead of sweat appearing at the tip of one sideburn reminded me to say, "I still have the T-shirt you left in my office."

Bright red at this reference to his humiliation, he said that he was sorry to be so forgetful and that, if it was all right, he would come around sometime and retrieve the garment. Then the bell rang for class and we parted. I watched him a moment as he ran down the corridor, the buttocks that once I had beheld in all their innocent naked glory covered now by thick corduroy. Soon I shall have occasion to examine them again, at leisure, as his education continues, impelling each of us inexorably toward the last degree.

The class went well until Buck decided to look in. I tolerated his presence. But then when he became critical of me I was forced to take a stern line with him. In fact, after he made a direct challenge to my authority, I struck him. All in all, it was a most satisfying thing to do and it will be some time before that keg of lard dares to cross me again.

Afterwards, in the faculty room (wall-to-wall champagne-beige carpeting, piped-in music, and a color television set), two of my colleagues joined me for coffee from the mechanical dispenser. Apparently "everyone" has heard that there was some sort of contretemps between me and the president of the Academy. But I assured them that Uncle Buck and I could never quarrel about anything. "Oh, perhaps a disagreement or two about how far one should go in telling the students whether or not they really do have talent."

Unfortunately both my colleagues share the Buck Loner philosophy. One of them is a Negro queen named Irving Amadeus. A recent convert to the Bahai religion, he lives entirely on organic foods raised in a series of pots in the backyard of a large house at Van Nuys which he shares with a number of fellow cultists. There are, incidentally, nine Negro teachers but only seven Negro students. Though I suspect that Buck dislikes our dusky cousins, he has done his best to integrate the school at the teaching level, leaning over backwards to give work to almost any show-biz-type Negro who comes his way (the Stepin Fetchit Lecture Series, however, fell through at the last moment, due to a contractual snag). But at the student level, integration has not been easy. A vocal minority are prejudiced, possibly because many young white males fear the Negro cock. Time and again I have observed white youths inadvertently clench their buttocks at the approach of a black man, as though fearful of anal penetration, not realizing that the legend of Negro size is just that—legend. The dozen or so jungle bunnies I have trafficked with were perfectly ordinary in that department . . . in fact, two were hung like chipmunks (Myron, incidentally, was larger than any of them, a fact which, paradoxically, caused him not joy but despair). The physiological origin of the myth was once explained to me by Dr. Montag. Apparently the Negro penis limp is almost the same size as it is when erect, a phenomenon which, though it causes consternation in a shower room, brings no added joy to the bedroom. Nevertheless, uneasy white males still continue to tighten their rosy sphincters at the approach of spooks.

In defense of the Buck Loner philosophy, Irving Amadeus (he pretends to have been Jewish before his conversion to Bahai) spoke of love. "It is necessary to have love for all things, particularly those young people entrusted to our care."

"Love," I said, "ought never to exclude truth."

"But love does not wound." He continued for some time in this vein. Fortunately Miss Cluff, the other teacher, has no interest in love, at least of the caritas sort. She is lean and profoundly Lesbian, forever proposing that we go to drive-in movies together in her secondhand Oldsmobile. Temporarily she is teaching the Bell Telephone Hour Course in Song in order to make enough money to pay for a concert debut in New York.

"Nonsense!" she said to Bahai, cutting him short. "We *must* wound if we are to create artists. I myself am the result of an uncle whom I hated, a teacher of piano who forced me at the age of nine to practice seven, eight, ten hours a day, striking my fingers with a stick whenever I got a note wrong. This was in Oregon." We all recognized the plot of *The Seventh Veil* and so were able to ask the right questions in order to help her complete the fantasy whose denouement was that, in spite of everything, she had come through, become an artist, after the obligatory nervous breakdown, et cetera, and she owed it all to her uncle who had been cruel but *cared*.

I found this conversation pleasing, for I am always happy when people resort to the storehouse of movie myth in order to create for themselves attractive personas. I was not prepared, however, for her next observation. "There is really only one talented student in any of my classes and that is a girl called Mary-Ann Pringle."

I sat up, almost spilling the dregs of my coffee. *Had I missed a trick?* "But I know the girl. I have her in Posture. She is a complete nothing."

"Except," said Black Beauty, "for her connection with Rusty Godowski. I have him in Atavistic Rhythm, and I am here to tell you that that ofay boy has really got sex appeal in spades!" (All in all, not a happy figure of speech, I thought.)

"I know *what* he's got," I said too quickly, and not quite accurately.

"Then you know he is absolutely total man, or, as we in Bahai believe . . ."

"What," I turned to Miss Cluff, drowning out Mother Africa, "is so talented about Mary-Ann Pringle?"

"Her *voice!* It is the pure, the white *bel canto*. Untrained, of course, like a smudged diamond, but a jewel no less. She could be a star of the same magnitude as . . ."

"Kathryn Grayson?"

Miss Cluff is too young to know from experience the Forties and too self-absorbed to attend films seriously. For her the movies are simply a pretext for getting girls onto the back seat of her secondhand Oldsmobile. "She could . . . she *must* sing opera."

But Darkness at Noon saw, perhaps rightly, another fate for Mary-Ann. "As long as that young man wants her she won't have a career. And from what I've seen of him these last two years, he shows no sign of losing interest. Every girl in Atavistic Rhythm has made a play for Rusty, and no dice."

Miss Cluff looked grim. "Women's rights are never won! Never! To think that a girl of her talent is prepared to waste her life —and genius—on a hulk, an oaf, a thing, a man!"

"A mighty *cute* thing," giggled Heart of Darkness, but then recalled himself to add, more seriously, "and talented, too, possessing a natural animal magnetism, and of course highly photogenic as we all of us saw last spring, before Myra joined us, when he acted in a Rod Serling classic on the closed-circuit TV . . ."

Although I usually collect every comment testifying to Rusty's male attractiveness, adding bit by bit to the vivid mosaic that is Rusty the Man (soon to be shattered by me into a million fragments, that I may then rearrange him along other and more meaningful lines), I suddenly found myself morbidly eager to hear about Mary-Ann. Miss Cluff, eager to tell, told. And I believed her. Though mad as a hatter, Miss Cluff is every bit as tough-minded about the arts as I am. And so I am tempted to believe her when she tells me that *Mary-Ann has star quality*.

The columnist Sidney Skolsky has just entered the main part of the drugstore. Everyone stares at him. As well they might! With Louella and Hedda gone, he is Mr. Movies. They say his office is upstairs.

18

I am home now. The blinds are raised and I have been staring for some minutes at the bespangled ten-times-life-size girl as she slowly turns in front of the Château Marmont Hotel. For me she is Hollywood, and mesmerizing.

No further encounter with Rusty. He attended one Posture class but we did not speak and he was more than ever nervous and sullen in my presence. His T-shirt is still in my desk drawer, which now smells of him, a musky disturbing odor that makes me quite weak since, regretfully, I am not able to smell the original, for he keeps half a room's distance between us. I must soon make operative the second phase of my plan.

Meanwhile, to my surprise, Mary-Ann has been unusually friendly. When I told her yesterday that Miss Cluff thought her very talented, she was enormously pleased. "Miss Cluff *is* nice to say that. And I do like singing but, like Rusty says, there's only room for one star in any bed . . . I mean family." She stammered, blushing deliciously at her error, which was no doubt a lovers' joke.

"I'm sure that's what he *would* say. It's the usual male view."

"But I like it. Honestly I do. I think the man's *got* to be boss so a girl knows where she is."

"I'm afraid that's a slightly outmoded point of view." I was careful, however, not to sound too sharp. "Particularly now when the relationship between the sexes is changing so rapidly, and women are becoming aggressive and men passive and . . ."

"Which I just hate!" Mary-Ann was unexpectedly vehement. Good. The subject has occurred to her before. Excellent. "I hate these boys who just drift around taking pot and trips and not caring if—well, if it's a boy or a girl they're with. It's just terrible the way so many are now, and I guess that's why I'm so hung up on Rusty. He's all man."

I thought with some amusement of "all man's" defenseless bottom, quivering at my touch. I have the power forever to alter her image of Rusty. But that is for later. Now I must win her friendship, even love. The plan requires it.

Although Dr. Montag and I write each other at least once a week, I feel somewhat guilty for not having told him what I am up to (these notes will be your introduction, dear Randolph). On the other hand, we do discuss the one topic we most disagree on, the changing relationship between the sexes. Being Jewish as well as neo-Freudian, he is not able to divest himself entirely of the Law of Moses. For the Jew, the family is everything; if it had not been, that religion which they so cherish (but happily do not practice) would have long since ended and with it their baleful sense of identity. As a result, the Jew finds literally demoralizing the normal human sexual drive toward promiscuity. Also, the Old Testament injunction not to look upon the father's nakedness is the core to a puritanism which finds unbearable the thought that the male in himself might possess an intrinsic attractiveness, either aesthetically or sensually. In fact, they hate the male body and ritually tear the penis in order to remind the man so damaged that his sex is unlovely. It is, all in all, a religion even more dreadful than Christianity.

Dr. Montag, however, is a thoughtful man, aware of the damage done him as a child growing up in the household of a kosher butcher whose wife wanted their son to be a rabbi. But even then Randolph was a nonconformist; he chose to be a dentist, that last resort of the rabbi *manqué*. But dentistry soon palled (it was the tongue, not the teeth that interested him) and so he became a psychologist, and his book, *Sexual Role and/or Responsibility*, made a complete shambles of Karen Horney, among others.

Myron and I met Dr. Montag some years ago at a lecture Myron gave on "The Uterine Vision in the Films of the Forties" (this lecture is the basis for the chapter on Betty Hutton and Martha Raye in his Parker Tyler book). Needless to say, the lecture was sparsely attended. Myron was a nervous lecturer and his voice had a tendency to become shrill if he sensed any serious disagreement, and of course there was—is—always disagreement about his work as there is bound to be controversy about the work of any entirely original thinker.

On that famous night poor Myron was forced to shriek his way through the lecture in an effort to drown out the usual hecklers (this particular talk was given, like so many of his best performances, at the Blue Owl Grill on 132nd Street, a place where Happenings used to occur regularly before Happenings were known, and of course poets read). When the lecture was over and the booing had ceased, we were joined by a thickset man with blue jowls. "I am Randolph Spenser Montag," the man said, taking Myron's fragile hand into his own large one. "*Dr.* Montag," the man added but without unction or pride, merely a simple statement, "and I want you to know that you have broken new ground along lines similar to my own."

They talked until morning. I had never before known Myron to be so excited, so energized, so exalted as he was at that moment when he found for the first time in his life a masculine mind complementary to his own. This is not the place to review their joint achievements (as you know better than anyone, Randolph, and it is essentially for you and to you that I write in this notebook, a most liberating activity as well as an excellent way for me to tell you how much I admire you without any of the uneasiness caused by our usual face-to-face encounters, particularly those official ones when I am on the patient's couch and you are striding noisily about the room wheezing and gasping from emphysema). That meeting in the Blue Owl was historic not only for the three of us but for the world, since many of the insights in *Sexual Role* as well as at least four chapters of Myron's Parker Tyler book can be said to have had their genesis in our knowing one another.

But now I am troubled by something in the letter just arrived. Referring to Myron with his usual fondness (do you deliberately want to set me off?), Dr. Montag remarked: "Myron's polymorphism (quite exceptional even by contemporary standards) was coupled with a desire to surrender entirely to the feminine side of his nature, symbolized by you. Yet I cannot help but believe that his masculinity was of great intensity, as you knew best, while the sadomasochistic proportion was quite evenly balanced. That is to say, he was as apt to beat up trade as be beaten up." This is not exactly correct. For all Dr. Montag's extraordinary sensitivity, he remains at heart a dentist of the most conventional kind. Myron's masculinity was, *at times*, intense, but the feminine aspects of his nature were the controlling ones, as I knew best. He wanted men to possess him rather than the other way around. He saw himself as a woman, made to suffer at the hands of some insensitive man. Needless to say, he found partners galore. When I think of the elaborate dinners he used to cook for merchant seamen with tattoos! The continual fussing about the house, so reminiscent of the female bird preparing to lay her egg! The humiliating position he would put himself in when some piece of trade spurned him because he was not able to lay on the requisite bread! Yet, paradoxically, Myron was physically quite strong despite the seeming fragility of his body and, properly aroused, he could beat up a man twice his size; unfortunately, he took no more pleasure in this than he did in the company of lovely girls. He was a tormented creature, similar to Hart Crane, except that while it was Crane's kick to blow those sailors he encountered along the squalid waterfronts of that vivid never-to-be-recaptured prewar world, Myron invariably took it from behind. But though this was a source of great consolation to Myron, Dr. Montag always felt, in his somewhat naïve way, that Myron's obsession involved a certain amount of gratuitous perversity, not to mention just plain waste because Myron's own penis was exceptionally large and much admired (it can be seen briefly in the underground film *Lysol*). Dr. Montag never understood that Myron's sexual integrity required him to withhold that splendid penis from those who most needed it, thus exerting power over them and what, finally, are human relations but the desire in each of us to exercise absolute power over others?

It is my view that the struggle to achieve power is the underlying theme to all of Myron's work, even though he never formulated it clearly. Certainly, *I* was never able to do so until his death clarified so many things for me. At the time I wanted to die, too. But then I entered the next stage: mystical elation. I understood—or thought I understood—*everything!* Myron's restless cruising of bars was the result of a desire to draw into himself, literally, that which men possess for quite another purpose. For him to be able to take from Woman her rightful pleasure—not to mention the race's instrument of generation—became a means of exercising power over *both* sexes and, yes, even over life itself! That is why he was never drawn to homosexuals. In fact, once the man *wished* to penetrate him, Myron lost interest for then he himself would become the thing used, and so lose the power struggle. What excited him most was to find a heterosexual man down on his luck, preferably starving to death, and force him to commit an act repugnant to him but necessary if he was to be paid the money that he needed for survival. At such moments, Myron confessed, he knew ecstasy: the forbidden was his! He had conquered Man, even though to the naïve observer it was Myron who *seemed* to be the one used. But he was almost always user, and that was his glory. Yet like all appetites, the one for power is insatiable. The more one obtains, the more one wants. In the end Myron could not, living, be what he wanted to be, an all-powerful user of men, and so he ended his life, leaving me to complete as best I can not only his masterpiece but the pattern he sought to make, with Dr. Montag's reluctant help.

Yet it is now plain to me that the good Doctor preferred Myron to me, and I cannot at times avoid a certain sense of hurt and rejection. Particularly when I realize that the only way the Doctor could be made happy would be if I were to marry and settle down. Dr. Montag still believes that each sex is intended to be half of a unit, like those monsters mentioned in Plato's *Symposium*. This is the Doctor's Mosaic side overwhelming common sense, not to mention the evidence of his senses. Admittedly *some* are best served when the struggle for power narrows to but one other person and this duel endures for a lifetime as mate attempts to destroy mate in that long wrangling for supremacy which is called marriage. Most human beings, however, prefer the short duet, lasting anywhere from five minutes with a stranger to five months with a lover. Certainly the supreme moments occur only in those brief exchanges when each party, absorbed by private fantasy, believes he is achieving mastery over the other. The sailor who stands against a wall, looking down at the bobbing head of the gobbling queen, regards himself as master of the situation; yet it is the queen (does not that derisive epithet suggest primacy and dominion?) who has won the day, extracting from the flesh of the sailor his posterity, the one element in every man which is eternal and (a scientific fact) cellularly resembles not at all the rest of the body. So to the queen goes the ultimate elixir of victory, that which was not meant for him but for the sailor's wife or girl or simply Woman. Much of my interest in the capture of Rusty is the thought that he is so entirely involved with Mary-Ann. That gives value to what I mean to seize. If it were freely offered, I would reject it. Fortunately he hates me which excites me and so my triumph, when it comes, will be all the sweeter.

BUCK LONER REPORTS—
Recording Disc No. 736—
22 February

        So decision has been made to present for the June jamboree a musical comedy based on the life story of Elvis Presley who will I am sure be present to see this show or better be since he isnt doing all that well box office wise and could use the publicity I dont know who can play the lead but we got a lot of boys capable of singing like Elvis except funnily enough I was surprised to see some objections raised from some of the kids on the ground that Elvis is old fashioned and another generation like Bing Crosby well this made me feel old but I said you got to have some traditional values and respect the show business greats even when they are over thirty years old the girl who will sing the girl lead will be Mary Ann Pringle then there will be two ninety minute closed circuit capital c color TV dramas from the old Playhouse 90 which again brings a lot of criticism down on my head from the hippies who have no respect for the classics of early television well they will learn better anyway we have a lot of speaking parts in both plays and the western lead will be Rusty Godowski who is aimed for stardom if he stays out of the clink write the Governor another letter about the Ronald Reagan festival explaining it was no joke but a serious offer for him to M C the festival and gain good exposure period good news at last from the lawyers about one Myra Breck-inridge who was never repeat never married to my nephew in any one of the fifty United States now Flagler and Flagler will fix her pretty wagon and out she goes on her ass the way she is making trouble around here is like some kind of God damned plague of Egypt telling everybody how lousy they are reminder to stop by Farmers Market and buy okra Bobbie is cooking gumbo tonight

19

Clem Masters grows on one. At that first party when I became hopelessly stoned and passed out in the bathtub, I thought him the creep of the world. But since then I have got to know him and of all the students, he is the only one with something resembling a brain. He comes, needless to say, from the East (Buffalo, New York), and wants to be a singer but will probably settle for a career as songwriter. This morning, after Empathy, I met him in the corridor and he said, "Come on, baby, and let me play you something I just wrote."

"Wrote?" I asked. "Or stole from the Beatles like that last little number you recorded for Pop Tune IV . . ."

"You're a gas, Myra." He was not in the least distressed by my accusation of plagiarism. In fact, of all the students he alone seems not to fear me and since he interests me not at all sexually (he is weedy-looking with thick glasses and a black beard and never washes), I am able to enjoy his irreverence.

Clem took me into one of the music rooms where he promptly fell upon the piano and rushed through several loud syncopated numbers, bellowing banal lyrics at the top of his voice. When

81

at last he stopped, I said the truth, as always, "It's just awful, Clem."

"You crazy mixed-up chick!" He laughed, he actually laughed at Myra Breckinridge! My first instinct was to slam shut the piano cover on his spidery fingers, breaking them all at once. But then I realized that his physical agony would do nothing for me, and so I laughed, too (a good sport like Carole Lombard), and said, "Why crazy? Why mixed-up?"

"Because what you heard is *music,* popular music and I am going to sell the whole mother score, piece by piece, to the Four Skins."

"What score? What skins?"

He looked at me pityingly. "The Four Skins are number four and number twenty-seven respectively in the January *Billboard.* So this score—which is for this life of Elvis Presley big Buck Loner has inflicted upon us—will make me some money."

"In that case, I think your songs are perfectly apt."

"I knew you had taste! Now listen, Myra, in some sick way you appeal to me. No, I really mean it. I dig you and I was thinking why don't we . . ."

"Clem." I was firm yet—how can I deny it?—flattered. After all, I am a woman. "I enjoy your company, you know that. You're the only student I can talk to but I could no more go to bed with you . . ."

"Baby, baby, baby . . ." He interrupted me impatiently. "Not with *me,* baby. I don't want to go to bed, the two of us. That's square. I mean a *party,* like maybe twenty cats . . ."

"*Twenty* men?" Not even my idlest daydreams of Myra Breckinridge, warrior queen, ever included a scene in which I was called upon to master twenty men at the same time. Might it not be too much, psychologically?

"Ten men and ten girls, you nit, or maybe seven of one and thirteen of the other or nine of one and eleven of the other. I mean who's *counting*? Want to make the scene?" Clem looked at me shrewdly through thick spectacles.

I was at a loss for words. On the one hand, the idea was

definitely attractive. Myron sometimes enjoyed the company of four or five men at the same time but he did not believe in mixing the sexes. I of course do. Yet what pleasure, I calculated swiftly, would I extract from such a tableau? My little quirks can only be fulfilled with one man at a time.

I deliberately dithered, trying to make up my mind. "Oh, I don't think I should. Certainly not with people I know, not with the students."

"Not students, baby. I never let those cats in on anything if I can help it. No, you'll meet all five of the Four Skins and some crazy chicks . . . oh, it's your scene, I can tell . . ."

I knew that my hesitation had already betrayed my interest. "Perhaps I might just . . . *watch,* you know, and perhaps help out, in little ways . . ."

"All or nothing. No tourists allowed." He wrote an address on a slip of paper. "Tomorrow night. Ten o'clock." He goosed me, which I detest, but before I could knee him, the door was flung open and Miss Cluff looked in and blushed, for no discernible reason, and said, "Welcome to the Music Department, Myra. We've all been looking for you."

"Clem was playing me his score."

"He's so talented! Mr. Loner wants to see you right away, it's urgent."

Buck was sitting with his feet on the desk and his Stetson over one eye. Since he made no move to sit up, much less stand up, when I entered the room, I was obliged to strike his feet a blow with my stout black leather handbag; they slid off the desk and onto the floor with a crash.

"Stand up when a lady comes into the room, you son of a bitch," I said but with a sweet tone not unlike Irene Dunne in *The White Cliffs of Dover.*

"Lady!" He snorted. I leapt upon him, handbag raised to strike again, but he managed with unexpected agility to get to his feet and put the desk once more between us. "You're nothing but some con-girl pretending to be married to my nephew when I got proof he never married nobody. Here!" He thrust a legal document at me, which I ignored. I knew that I had been careless, and have been found out. My own fault.

"No record of my marriage to Myron exists in any of the United States," I said, "for the excellent reason," I wadded up the document and threw it at him, "that we were married in Mexico."

"Whereabouts?"

"My lawyers will tell your lawyers," I said. "Meanwhile, if that settlement is not made by April first, I will take over the whole shooting match." When in doubt, double the stakes, as James Cagney used to say.

I departed regally, but I was—am—shaken by the interview. I immediately rang my lawyer to assure him that I will be able to produce the marriage license as soon as a new one is issued at Monterrey.

Meanwhile—what a mess! Suddenly I feel terribly alone and afraid. My mood was hardly improved when I learned a few moments ago from a distraught Mary-Ann that Rusty has left town. When I pressed her as to why, she burst into tears and could not or would not say. I have never liked the month of February—even when the sun shines, as it does now, and it is warm.

20

My ground rules for the party were respected. I would wear bra and panties, unless otherwise inspired to remove them. Clem was forced to agree to this after I pointed out to him that in spite of his assurance to me no students would be present, Gloria Gordon was not only at the party but his hostess. My compromise was accepted. Give a little, get a little, as the saying goes.

The party was held in a small house high in the Hollywood Hills. I was driven there by a stocky monosyllabic man who was once a waiter at Romanoff's and could, if he chose, tell a thousand stories about the stars he waited on but instead spoke to me only of the weather and baseball. But then I think that he was probably stoned when he came to pick me up, and not at his conversational best.

When we arrived at the house, the door was opened by Clem, who wore nothing but glasses and a large door key on a chain about his neck. He is extremely hairy, which I don't like, and though he did not have an erection and so could not be fairly judged, his prick is small and rather dismal-looking as if too many people had chewed on it, and of course he is circumcised, which I find unattractive. Naturally, like so many physically underprivileged men, Clem regards himself as irresistible (no doubt some obscure psychological law of compensation is at work). He promptly took me in goatish arms, rammed his soft acorn against my pudendum, and bit my ear.

I stepped hard on his bare toes, and was promptly freed.

"Jesus, Myra!" He hopped on one foot, holding the other in his hand, a ludicrous sight that somewhat aroused me. I was even more aroused by Gloria who came to show me into the changing room. She, too, was nude with a body almost too beautiful for this world, slender and long, somewhat on the order of the early Jinx Falkenburg. As I undressed, it was all I could do not to take delicately in my hand one of those perfect rose-nippled breasts and simply hold it, worshipfully. Although I am not a Lesbian, I do share the normal human response to whatever is attractive physically in either sex. I say *normal* human response, realizing that our culture has resolutely resisted the idea of bisexuality. We insist that there is only one *right* way of having sex: man and woman joined together to make baby; all else is wrong. Worse, the neo-Freudian rabbis (of whom Dr. Montag is still one despite my efforts at conversion) believe that what they call heterosexuality is "healthy," that homosexuality is unhealthy, and that bisexuality is a myth despite their master Freud's tentative conviction that all human beings are attracted to both sexes.

Intellectually, Dr. Montag is aware of the variety of normal human sexual response but, emotionally, no dentist from the Grand Concourse of the Bronx can ever accept the idea that a woman could or should find quite as much pleasure with her own sex as she does with men. Yet many women lead perfectly contented lives switching back and forth from male to female with a minimum of nervous wear and tear. But in the great tradition of neo-Freudian analysis, Dr. Montag refuses to accept any evidence that does not entirely square with his preconceptions. For him it is either Moses or the Golden Calf. There is no middle range. Yet he is often persuasive, even luminous, and for a time Myron fell under his spell just as Dr. Montag has since fallen under mine. Nevertheless, for all his limitations, it must never be forgotten that it was Randolph Spenser Montag who convinced Myron that one ought to live in consistent accordance with one's *essential* nature. As a result, on the Staten Island ferry, Myron acted out a dream of the absolute and like a Venetian Doge married that symbol of woman the sea but with his life, not a ring, leaving me to change the world alone.

Since that traumatic experience for us all, Randolph has been, in some ways, a new man, a changed dentist. How he almost believes those stories his younger patients tell him of parties where sexual roles change rapidly, according to whim and in response to the moment's pleasure, stories he used to reject as wish-fulfillments. Between a beautiful girl and an unattractive man (between Gloria and Clem), I shall always be drawn, like any healthy-minded woman, to the girl, as I was last night when, very simply, I took both of Gloria's breasts in my hands and stooped to kiss the appendix scar just to the right of her navel, for all the world like a delicate dimple, so marvelously had the surgeon done his work.

"Chick, you are turning me on!" Gloria exclaimed as she flung my dress willy-nilly upon the bed with all the other clothes. Then she clutched at my panties, but I restrained her, reminding her of the agreement with Clem.

She frowned and pouted. "Not even for me?" she asked, fingering my lovely breasts already partially revealed through the lacy mesh of the bra.

"Later," I whispered, looking over Gloria's shoulder at my escort who was stripping down. It was evident that what he lacked in conversation he made up for in other ways. Beneath a not unpleasantly curved beer-belly, a large white object sprouted, as inviting to the touch as a well-wrought pitcher's handle.

On his way to the door, my hand snaked out and seized him, causing him to stop abruptly. I held him just long enough to achieve a small but exquisite sense of power (he was not able to move, so powerful is my grasp). Then I released him. Shouting "Crazy!" he vanished into the darkened room where the party was.

Impressions: varied, some pleasant, some not. All in all, *not* my sort of scene. I need one man to break down, not twenty to serve. But visually the scene was appealing. Mattresses spread at random across a tile floor. Towels hung from every lamp, giving a festive look to a room whose only light came from a single Moroccan lamp of intricately chased silver inset with red and blue glass.

Aesthetically, the decor was all that one could have wished and so were the girls; the men had seen to that. In fact, simply on circumstantial evidence, one could tell that a man had selected the guest list, for though there were several attractive young studs in the room (two of the five members of the Four Skins were present), the majority resembled Clem: physically unimpressive males forced to rely upon personality and money to get girls to bed. For my taste, they are exactly the wrong sort to have at an orgy, which, no doubt, is the reason why they are always the leading instigators of what is known locally as the "gangbang."

The party lasted four hours. That is as long as the male can hold out. Women of course can go on indefinitely if they are allowed occasional catnaps between orgasms. At one point Gloria experienced twelve orgasms in as many minutes (supplied her by the ex-waiter from Romanoff's, a really formidable man, capable of quite astonishing endurance and restraint); then she promptly fell asleep with her head in the lap of Clem, whom she had been attending to in an absentminded way. To his great alarm, she could not be awakened. Fortunately, we were able to pry her mouth open and salvage the tiny treasure before serious damage was done. Ten minutes later our Gloria was wide awake and ready for fun. This time Clem provided it. Having strapped on a formidable dildo because, as he said, "You got to have head," he was able to give her maximum pleasure with a minimum of exertion on his part.

My own participation was limited. I watched, and only occasionally helped out: a tickle here, a pull there, a lick, a bite, no more, except for one sudden rude intrusion from the rear which I did not see coming. It was one of the Four Skins, a hillbilly type who explained to me, as he was relieving himself, that he had first committed this particular act at the age of twelve with a sheep and so, to this day, he not only preferred back to front but sheep to goats, or did he say girls? Like the rest of the Four Skins his conversation is as difficult to under-sand as the lyrics they sing. Had there been a pair of shears at hand, I would have made a steer of him on the spot but since there were not I did not, suffering in silence and even, to be honest, deriving a certain perverse, masochistic, Myronesque enjoyment from the unlikely situation of Myra Breckinridge, victorious Amazon, laid low.

Then, having discharged himself, the Skin abandoned me and proceeded on his bully way. I shall of course take my re-venge upon him some day, somehow . . . even if I must wait twenty years! Myra Breckinridge is implacable and pitiless.

These graphic notes are really for your benefit, dear Ran-dolph. Examples of the way that the goyim you especially de-spise behave (of course Clem is Jewish but he has been entirely absorbed by California, that great sponge into which all things are drawn and promptly homogenized, including Judaism). Yet even you, with your prejudices, could not help but be impressed at the ease with which these young people let themselves go, without any apparent fear of commitment or of compromise. The males do not worry about acting out what the society be-lieves to be the man's role (brutal, destructive, vagina-centered); they play with one another's bodies in a sportive way, and seem to have no secret dreams they dare not act out. All is in the open, or as one of them said to me as he rested on the floor between engagements, "After a scene like this I don't need it again for a week. I've had it, and there's nothing left I want, and I never feel so good like I do after a real party." So the Dionysian is still a necessity in our lives. Certainly its absense has made the world neurotic and mad. I am positive that access to this sort of pleasure in my adolescence would have changed me entirely. Fortunately, as it turned out, I was frustrated. If I had not been, Myra Breckinridge could never have existed, and the subsequent loss to the world of Myra, the self-creation, is something we, none of us, can afford at this time.

As I write these words, I suddenly think of Myron making love to Gloria Gordon! Why? How strange . . . just the thought of such a thing makes my eyes fill suddenly with tears. Poor Myron. Yet, all in all, he is better dead.

One must not underestimate the influence of these young people on our society. It is true that the swingers, as they are called, make up only a small minority of our society; yet they hold a great attraction for the young and bored who are the majority and who keep their sanity (those that do) by having a double sense of themselves. On the one hand, they must appear to accept without question our culture's myth that the male must be dominant, aggressive, woman-oriented. On the other hand, they are perfectly aware that few men are anything but slaves to an economic and social system that does not allow them to knock people down as proof of virility or in any way act out the traditional male role. As a result, the young men compensate by *playing* at being men, wearing cowboy clothes, boots, black leather, attempting through clothes (what an age for the fetishist!) to impersonate the kind of man our society *claims* to admire but swiftly puts down should he attempt to be anything more than an illusionist, playing a part.

It is the wisdom of the male swinger to know what he is: a man who is socially and economically weak, as much put upon by women as by society. Accepting his situation, he is able to assert himself through a polymorphic sexual abandon in which the lines between the sexes dissolve, to the delight of all. I suspect that this may be the only workable pattern for the future, and it is a most healthy one . . . certainly healthier than the rigid old-fashioned masculinity of someone like Rusty whose instinct to dominate in traditional ways is bound to end in defeat or frustration, excepting perhaps in his relations with the old-fashioned Mary-Ann . . . relations which are currently at an end, for she has still not heard from him, or so she says. I suspect he has been busted. And just as I was about to make my final move. It is too unfair!

The party ended in an orgy of eating. Delicate girls devoured cold cuts as though they had not been fed in weeks, while spent youths lay snoring among tangled towels that smelled of new-made love. How Myron would have enjoyed all this! Though I'm afraid he would have paid more attention to the boys than to the girls and perhaps imitated my bull-like Skin who, waiting until one young man had assumed the classic position between a girl's legs, leapt upon him and forced his way in, to the obvious irritation of the raped youth who, nevertheless, had sufficient aplomb (and Dionysian abandon) not to break his own stride, as it were—oh, how various are the ways of true love!

BUCK LONER REPORTS—
Recording Disc No. 751—
27 February

Well so far she has got the jump on
me this morning she came into my office and gave me this
Mexican wedding license apologizing for not having got it sooner
but it was mislaid Uncle Buck I tell you when she calls me
Uncle Buck like that Id like to break her neck she is living hell
and theres no doubt about that she also said she was getting
impatient for her share of the estate and she hoped quote mean
old Flagler and Flagler would soon see their way clear to the
half million dollar settlement unquote half million dollar settle
ment I asked it was three fifty that we finally agreed on before
well she says quote that was before but I have been kept waiting
and waiting while your detectives have been trying to get some
thing on me like I was criticizing General Motors or something
and so I regard the extra one fifty as damages for the mental
anguish you have been causing me unquote well I controlled
myself as best I could and said quote now Myra you know what

lawyers are and after all we never did meet before and whats to keep a total stranger from barging in and claiming to be married to my late nephew question mark end quote oh I see your point of view she says in quotes of course I do but you must also see mine and realize just what it is I have been going through since Myron died leaving me entirely alone in the world and broke well we kicked that around the poor defenseless widow number and then she again gave me until April one to pay up or else she goes to court and really gets mean so I do my best to soothe her putting the blame on Flagler and Flagler but the thing is still fishy even though theres no doubt she was involved deeply with Myron because though I didnt know him I sure as hell knew Gertrude and at one point Myra let slip the fact that she personally had always found Gertrude hell particularly the way she used to save worthless things like newspapers and string and keep the icebox jammed with food that had gone bad that she was too damned miserly to throw out well Myra didnt make that up and we both agreed that anybody who had a meal at Gertrudes was courting ptomaine but then when I said Gertrude really loved that boy of hers Myra frowned and said oh no she didnt Uncle Buck she just loved herself well dont we all I said no she said not to that degree unquote but she wouldnt open up any more obviously the two girls did not get on hard to say which is the worst no not hard at all Myra is the worst woman I have ever met exclamation mark paragraph she then asked me if I had had news of Rusty Godowski and I said no but that our students often disappear for a time like that and then show up again like nothings happened but she said she was concerned because of poor Mary Ann being so heartbroken Mary Ann hell Im sure Myras got her eye on that stud like half the girls on campus and is now demonstrating the edginess of a filly in heat anyway I said I would look into the matter of his disappearance beginning by calling up my friend the Sheriff a good Republican and ask him if the boy has been incarcerated in a hoosegow since he was on probation to begin with period paragraph then Myra asks me for permission to look at the medical reports on the students which are kept in my outer office and are private because quote I am doing some research on the I think she said post Rosenberg generation she is probably a Commie along with everything else but I have to handle little Miss Dynamite with kid gloves so I gave her permission after all theres nothing in teresting in any of them reports just a routine physical checkup at the beginning of their academic life we did consider once taking naked pictures like they do at Yale but the girls objected or to be exact the mothers and fathers of the girls objected even though this is the era of the Playboy bunny so that very good idea came to naught period paragraph change masseuses ap pointment from this afternoon to tomorrow as I must go in to town for a conference with Letitia Van Allen the best actors agent in this town for young stars of tomorrow having in her pocket practically her own key to casting at Universal dont forget to pick up sour cream for Bobbies beef Stroganoff

21

I am sitting beside Mary-Ann at the CBS television studio on Fairfax Avenue. Though it is only a caricature of a film studio, the ultimate effect is impressive. So impressive in fact that I am more than ever certain that the movies are now a mere subsidiary to this electronic device for projecting images around the world at, literally, the speed of light. What it will mean, I have not yet worked out. But it is now plain that the classic age of films has ended and will not return any more than verse drama, despite the wonder of the Jacobeans, has a chance of revival.

Of course visual narratives will always be filmed and shown if not in theatres on television. Yet the *nature* of those narratives is bound to change as television creates a new kind of person who will then create a new kind of art, a circle of creation that is only now just beginning. It is a thrilling moment to be alive! And though I yearn romantically for the classic films of the Forties, I know that they can never be reproduced since their era is as gone as the Depression, World War II and the national innocence which made it possible for Pandro S. Berman and a host of others to decorate the screens of tens of thousands of movie theatres with perfect dreams. There was a wholeness then which is lacking now and neither Alain Resnais nor Andy Warhol (the only film-makers of comparable stature today) can give us work which is not hopelessly fragmented. I except always Warhol's *Sleeping Man,* which broke new ground aesthetically and proved a radical theory I had always held but dared not openly formulate: that boredom in the arts can be, under the right circumstances, significantly dull.

I find it altogether too satisfying to be sitting beside Mary-Ann in the audience that has been assembled for the Art Linkletter Show. An M.C. is trying to warm us up with bad jokes. In a few minutes we shall be on the air, performers, technicians, audience, viewers—all made one by the magic of the tube. I find this particular show absolutely unbearable, preferring as I do the *total* electronic effect of, let us say, Milton Berle. But I am here because Mary-Ann wanted me to come and I usually do what she wants me to do for we are now curiously united by Rusty's disappearance. Of course she continues to believe that I dislike him and think him an ape, and I do nothing to disabuse her of this notion. I find almost unbearable the painful sweetness of knowing that I shall one day possess, in my own way, what she believes to be entirely hers, asssuming of course that Rusty ever returns.

Mary-Ann believes that if he is not in prison (the likeliest possibility since a boy with a police record is prone to constant false arrest in the Los Angeles area where only professional criminals are safe from harassment by the local police), he has gone off with some of his wild friends, possibly to Mexico. I do my best to soothe her, and we have long "girl-talks" about men and life . . . and about her career.

Unlike the other students, Mary-Ann could be professional. Miss Cluff is absolutely right and I for one would like to cut a corner or two and present her directly to an agent, instead of waiting until June, the usual time for the students to show what they can do which, traditionally, is not much. Miss Cluff tells me that in the seven years that she has been at the Academy no student has ever got a job on television or appeared in a film. This is a remarkable record. Some do get jobs modeling but that is often just plain whoring.

When I asked Buck about the dismal showing his students make in the professional world, he seemed not at all taken aback. "Honey," he said, knowing how much I hate to be called "honey," resembling, in this, at least one former First Lady, "what matters is making people happy and while the kids are here they are happy. Now there is, I am willing to admit, a real letdown come June when our kids realize that the outside world of show biz is a big cruel place with maybe no place for them. Yes, I admit that's an awful thing for them to find out and I've even toyed with the idea of never allowing any agents or professional people to come to the June exercises but of course if I really kept them away I'd go out of business, so we all have to suffer through the June Letdown which is immediately followed by the Buck Loner July Spectacular which is a series of awards based closely on the actual Academy Awards, with many Oscars (or Bucks as the kids call them) to be given out by some real-life celebrity on the order of Bobby Darin and that, let me tell you, sure as hell makes up for June."

"Yes, but sooner or later they will *have* to go out into the world . . ."

"Why?" The question was straightforward. "As long as they scrounge up enough money to pay the tuition they can stay here for life. Look at Irving Amadeus. He came here fourteen years ago as a student to become a singing star on the order of Paul Robeson and he is with us still, on the staff now as an invaluable teacher with over *three hundred recordings* to his credit. If that isn't as good as being a real star I don't know what is!"

This curiously hateful philosophy has made Buck Loner rich. But then, to be honest, all that I care about at the moment is my share of his wealth. That and Mary-Ann's career which she does not take seriously. "Only one star in the family," she keeps quoting Rusty. To which I invariably reply, "You're the star. He's the garage mechanic."

I have now got Mary-Ann to the point where she will at least audition for an agent before June, and that means I must start making the rounds myself, trying to find the best person to handle her. Although her voice has a classic tone like Jeanette MacDonald (and so of no use in the current market), she also has a second more jazzy voice not unlike that of the late La Verne, the most talented of the Andrews Sisters. I am certain that if she were to develop her La Verne-voice she could, with her remarkable appearance acting as opening wedge, become a star.

Last night I played several Andrews Sisters records for her and though she had never before heard of the Andrews Sisters (!), she conceded that their *tone* was unusual—which is understating the matter! Their tone is unique and genuinely mythic, a part of the folklore of the best years of the American past. They really did roll out that barrel, and no one has yet rolled it back.

Mary-Ann has just nudged my arm. "Really, Miss Myra, you mustn't write like that in public!" She chides me gently, for to write in public in the electronic age is to commit an antisocial obscenity.

To please her, I shall now put away this notebook and listen to the jokes of the comedian as he responds to the sterile laughter of the studio audience of which I am a part, for we are suddenly all of us—such a pleasure—on the air!

22

Just as I expected, seventy-two per cent of the male students are circumcised. At Clem's party I had been reminded of the promiscuous way in which American doctors circumcise males in childhood, a practice I highly disapprove of, agreeing with that publisher who is forever advertising in the New York *Times Book Review* a work which proves that circumcision is necessary for only a very few men. For the rest, it constitutes, in the advertiser's phrase, "a rape of the penis." Until the Forties, only the upper or educated classes were circumcised in America. The *real* people were spared this humiliation. But during the affluent postwar years the operation became standard procedure, making money for doctors as well as allowing the American mother to mutilate her son in order that he might never forget her early power over him. Today only the poor Boston Irish, the Midwestern Poles and the Appalachian Southerners can be counted upon to be complete.

Myron never forgave Gertrude for her circumcision of him. In fact, he once denounced her in my presence for it. She defended herself by saying that the doctor had recommended it on hygienic grounds—which of course does not hold water since most foreskins are easily manipulated and kept clean. What is truly sinister is the fact that with the foreskin's removal, up to fifty per cent of sensation in the glans penis is reduced . . . a condition no doubt as pleasing to the puritan American mother as it is to her co-conspirator, the puritan Jewish doctor who delights in being able to mutilate the goyim in the same vivid way that his religion (and mother!) mutilated him.

I once had the subject out with Dr. Montag, who granted me every single point and yet, finally, turned dentist and confessed, "Whenever I hear the word 'smegma,' I become physically ill." I am sure Moses is roasting in hell, along with Jesus, Saint Paul, and Gertrude Percy Breckinridge.

I was not able to find Rusty's medical report and so do not know whether or not he has been circumcised. I hope not for I prefer the penis intact . . . in order that it be raped not by impersonal surgery but by me!

23

In an alcove at the back of the cafeteria Buck Loner often has lunch with some notable he would like the students to observe at close hand. Today it was the famous agent Letitia Van Allen, and so I joined them, to Buck's ill-disguised fury. Miss Van Allen is a handsome vigorous woman of perhaps forty, with steely gray eyes. We got on famously, to Buck's chagrin.

"Talent is not what Uncle Buck and I deal in, Miss Van Allen," I said, lightly resting my hand on Buck's clenched fist. "We deal in *myths*. At any given moment the world requires one full-bodied blonde Aphrodite (Jean Harlow), one dark siren of flawless beauty (Hedy Lamarr), one powerful inarticulate brute of a man (John Wayne), one smooth debonair charmer (Melvyn Douglas), one world-weary corrupt lover past his prime (Humphrey Bogart), one eternal good-sex woman-wife (Myrna Loy), one wide-eyed chicken boy (Lon McCallister), one gentle girl singer (Susanna Foster), one winning stud (Clark Gable), one losing stud outside the law (James Cagney), and so on. Olympus supports many gods and goddesses and they are truly eternal, since whenever one fades or falls another promptly takes his place, for the race requires that the pantheon be always filled. So what we are looking for—and what you, Miss Van Allen, have *found* time and again—are those mythic figures who, at the right moment, can be placed upon their proper pedestal. For instance, since the death of Marilyn Monroe, no blonde voluptuous goddess has yet appeared to take her place and so, if I were creating stars, I would look for a girl who most filled that particular bill, who could be the lost Golden Girl. In fact, as in any other business, we must begin with market research. This means carefully analyzing Olympus to find out which archetypal roles are temporarily vacant and who are the contenders. At the moment the suave male seducer is in great supply while the befuddled normal man next door, filled with ludicrous fantasies, is a drug on the market, what with at least one and a half Jack Lemmon pictures each year. But the blonde goddess, the dark goddess, the singing girl and the inarticulate hero are each currently in need of someone to make of the divine spirit living flesh as well as eternal celluloid. At this very moment, perhaps in this very room, there are unknown boys and girls destined to be—for the length of a career—like gods, if only we can find and reveal them. That is why you and I, Letitia— I may call you that?—are similar to those Tibetan priests who upon the death of the Dalai Lama must seek out his reincarnation. And so, like priestesses, despite all personal hardship, we must constantly test and analyze the young men and women of America in order to find the glittering few who are immortal, who are the old, the permanent gods of our race reborn."

There was a long silence when I finished. Buck toyed with his icebox cake while Letitia Van Allen simply stared at me. Then she said, "That is the damnedest, truest thing I've ever heard said about this lousy racket. Come on, let's have a drink. Buck, give us a drink in that office of yours, you old bastard!" She took me by the arm. "He's far and away the biggest con-man in the business, but from where I sit it looks like he may have met his match. You've got quite a line and, as a fellow con-girl, I would like to give it some study." I had made, as I intended, an enormous impression.

Over a beaker of Scotch in Buck's office, Letitia told me in no uncertain terms that if I ever wanted to leave Buck there was a place in her office for a go-getter like me.

Buck brightened when he heard this. "Why, honey, that sounds just swell, don't it? This is too little a pond for a talent like yours." To which I replied demurely, "It may be a small pond but it's ours, Uncle Buck, yours and mine (you see, Letitia, I'm a half-owner of the property), and I could never let Uncle Buck down." Buck's face shut with a snap.

Miss Van Allen missed this exchange, for I had just given her some photographs of Mary-Ann Pringle. "Pretty girl. But no Marilyn Monroe." She gave the pictures back.

"It's her voice," I explained. "That's what makes her a possible immortal. She is the Singing Girl Goddess, waiting for the chance to reveal herself."

"They're not making that kind of picture right now. But maybe she could work up a nightclub act or get in the road show of some Broadway musical. Anyway, on your say-so, I'll listen to her—but not now. What about studs?" Letitia, I fear, is a monosexual. Only men arouse her.

"We got some swell kids . . ." began Buck but I cut him short. "There's one—*maybe*. Category: Inarticulate Hero. His name is Rusty Godowski . . ."

"That name has got to go and so do I." Letitia turned to me. "Come see me the first of the week, Myra . . . lunch . . . I'll pick your brains. You Easterners have all the kinky angles that are *in* right now. That's what I keep telling them at Universal: 'Don't be so California, for God's sake! California's square, while the world is full of kinks as yet undreamed of in the Greater Los Angeles Area.'" Then she was gone.

I could not help but rub it in. "Stick with me," I said to the crestfallen Buck, "and maybe some of your students will actually find work in show biz."

Before he could answer, the masseuse arrived: a spectacular Eurasian in a white nurse's uniform. As we parted, I reminded him of our deadline. Either he has paid me my share in full by April 1 or we up the ante.

BUCK LONER REPORTS—
Recording Disc No. 763—
4 March

Things are coming to a head at least
if they dont I dont know if I can stand it much longer with the
new masseuse it took over an hour which is a sign of something
and that something is Myra Breckinridge archfiend Flagler and
Flagler are doing their best they say to get something on Myra
but so far nothing at all they are even bugging her telephone
and just now sent over this tape which may be significant or so
they think of her talking long distance to a New York head
shrinker called Randolph Montag his tape is herewith enclosed
or included or whatever you call it

The Golden State Detective Agency submits the following
unedited telephone conversation with the understanding that
the contents of same are highly confidential and Golden State
assumes no responsibility whatsoever for having obtained said
property.

OPERATOR: Los Angeles calling Dr. Rudolph Moon . . . what's the name again, dear?

MYRA: Montag, Randolph not Rudolph Montag, and why don't you . . .

OPERATOR: Los Angeles calling Dr. Moondog . . . is he there?

VOICE: Mummy [two words not audible] later [three to four words not audible] the cat's sick . . .

OPERATOR: Little boy, could you tell your daddy this is Los Angeles . . .

MYRA: Damn it, Dr. Montag is not married . . .

OPERATOR: . . . Los Angeles calling and . . .

VOICE: . . . threw up all over the floor . . .

MYRA: God damn it, operator, you've got the wrong number . . .

OPERATOR: I hear you, miss, you don't have to shout . . .

MYRA: The number is . . .

OPERATOR: . . . I will redial the number, miss.

ELECTRONIC SOUNDS: heavy breathing of operator and / or Myra.

VOICE: This is a recording. The number you have just dialed is not a working number . . .

MYRA: Operator, please I don't have all day . . .

OPERATOR: Apparently the number you gave me is not a working number . . .

MYRA: Dial it again, damn it! You silly [word not clearly audible].

VOICE: Yes?

OPERATOR: Los Angeles calling Dr. Rupert Moonman, are you him?

VOICE: Yes, yes. This is Dr. Moonman, I mean Montag, who is calling he . . . ?

MYRA: Randolph, this is Myra . . .

OPERATOR: Your party is on the line, Miss . . .

MYRA: I haven't written because I've been . . .

OPERATOR: *Dr. Moon is on the line* . . .

MYRA: I know he is, now will you kindly get off . . .

MONTAG: Who is calling him again?

MYRA: It's Myra Breckinridge, you idiot!

MONTAG: Myra! This is a real pleasure . . .

MYRA: . . . didn't write because so much work to do . . .

MONTAG: . . . so how's the weather out there?

MYRA: . . . need your help . . .

MONTAG: . . . cold here, maybe twelve above zero which is why the ten o'clock patient missed her hour so I can talk . . .

MYRA: . . . about this damned inheritance . . .

MONTAG: . . . how is your dental health?

MYRA: Never been better, as a matter of fact we are on the verge of a real mental breakthrough which should . . .

MONTAG: I meant how are your teeth? That impacted wisdom tooth that was giving us so much trouble . . .

MYRA: For God's sake, Randolph, don't waste the three minutes talking about teeth . . . they're O.K. . . .

MONTAG: Good dental health means good mental health . . .

MYRA: . . . what I want is this: for you to say you were a witness to my marriage, in Monterrey, Mexico. And, God knows, in the truest sense you were and are . . .

MONTAG: At a certain level of course I am a witness and will gladly say so but there's also the legal aspect . . .

MYRA: . . . have to do is come out here and at a crucial moment which may or may not arise say you were present when I married Myron, which you were. . . .

MONTAG: . . . I suppose this all has to do with Gertrude's property . . .

MYRA: . . . swine Buck Loner is trying to do me out of a settlement, and so he wants to prove we were never really married . . .

MONTAG: . . . thinking about poor Myron the other day . . .

MYRA: You might think about *me* for a change. . . .

MONTAG: . . . projecting hostility again, must be careful . . .

MYRA: . . . am in trouble, Myron's dead . . .

MONTAG: Myron was a Christ figure . . .

MYRA: Luckily he found the right doctor with the two sticks of wood and the three nails . . .

MONTAG: . . . need help again. Can't you come back here for a few sessions . . .

MYRA: I'm broke and this conversation is breaking me so will you do what I ask . . .

MONTAG: Naturally only . . .

MYRA: In writing!

MONTAG: Is that necessary?

MYRA: It may have to be. Well? Cat got your tongue?

MONTAG: No, I was lighting a cigar, oral gratification is called for at moments of discomfort . . .

MYRA: Are you uncomfortable?

MONTAG: Naturally, Myra. Who wouldn't be in the spot you've put me in? After all our relationship is a good deal more than that of just analyst and patient. I am also your dentist and have your best interests at heart. Yes, of course I will *say* I was a witness to the marriage with the proviso . . .

MYRA: No proviso unless you want to have your license as a lay analyst revoked in the State of New York for gross malpractice . . .

MONTAG: I detect *a great deal* of hostility, Myra, in your voice . . .

MYRA: . . . then it's a deal. This is costing money . . .

MONTAG: Of course I'll help but . . .

MYRA: Goodbye, Randolph. . . .

End of tape.

BUCK LONER REPORTS—
Recording Disc No. 763—
(continued)

      Something obviously fishy but what question mark Myra probably was married in Monterrey from the sound of what they were saying to each other but why is that doctor so nervous and unwilling to put his John Hancock to any sort of document I will tell Flagler and Flagler to put the heat on this doctor because I must find out the truth or die in the attempt not to mention losing half this place which I built up from nothing period paragraph well I couldve been knocked over with a feather when Letitia Van Allen who I used to boff in the old days and was also a good friend to Bobbie Dean took a shine to Myra who barged in on our lunch in the cafeteria and promptly began one of her endless speeches which drive me up the wall like they say but Letitia who is easily the toughest dame in this town with the key to casting at Universal in her pocket and not one youd think to be taken in by nutty highbrow Eastern talk well Myra did her work and the two girls are now bosom buddies which is not good for yours truly which is why every thing depends now on nailing Myra Breckinridge once and for all question what about framing her with drugs maybe no she would still get the money even in jail God damn it buy chicory for Bobbie

24

Letitia Van Allen has heard the voice of Mary-Ann! And loved it! Yesterday I met Letitia at her offices on Melrose Avenue which occupy an entire Greek revival house, reminiscent of Tara, the late David O. Selznick's trademark. All the rooms are furnished in such a way as to suggest a gracious Southern mansion, not a talent agency. Letitia's private office (we are now on a first-name basis) is a lovely large airy second-floor bedroom-cum-boudoir, a most unusual setting for a famous agent yet somehow entirely suitable for her. Letitia works at a Dutch provincial writing desk in an alcove within view of the four-poster bed at the far end of the room. The effect is enchanting.

The salad and cottage cheese lunch was less charming (I have developed an extraordinary appetite lately and must for the first time in my life worry about becoming heavy). We talked of everything, and found many areas of agreement. She believes I would make a formidable agent and I have no doubt that she is right but I prefer to go my own solitary way as critic and mythmaker, and of course as explicator of the mind of Parker Tyler. Like Myron, I am in the tradition of Mortimer Brewster,

the drama critic in *Arsenic and Old Lace,* a man for whom, as
Tyler puts it so superbly, "the facts of *lunacy, virginity,* and *death,*
the last a mask for *impotence,* are inseparable."

Over a dry martini *after* lunch (Letitia, I suspect, has a drinking problem), we listened to a record of Mary-Ann singing a
number of songs of the Forties, selected by me and arranged
by Miss Cluff. Letitia listened with eyes narrowed. When the
record was finished, she again asked for photographs. I gave
them to her. She studied them for a long time. "O.K.," she said,
"I'll meet her. Make an appointment with my secretary, any
free time next week." Then Letitia put her feet up on a Regency
bench. "Why're you pushing this kid?"

"She has talent. So few people do."

"But according to your theory, that will probably count against
her. Now if you don't mind my asking a personal question, you
aren't perhaps involved with her on a more *personal* level?"

I blushed for the first time in some years. "If you mean am
I a dyke, no. Not at all. Quite the contrary. Actually I'm interested in her because of her boyfriend who happens to have
skipped town and I feel sorry for her. . . ."

"There's nothing wrong with being a dyke, you know." Letitia
blew smoke rings thoughtfully. For an instant I wondered if
perhaps I had not got her range. But she quickly assured me
that my first impression of her had been the right one. "That
bed," she said, indicating the four-poster with a swagger stick,
"has held just about every stud in town who wants to be an
actor. Do I shock you, Myra?"

"How can you shock me when you are just like me? The new
American woman who uses men the way they once used women."

"Jesus, Myra, but you are *quick!* What a team we'd make. Sure
you don't want another martini? It's just water now in the shaker.
Well, then I'll have it." She poured herself a full glass. "Listen,
dear, if you find anything really interesting at that circus of no-
talent Buck's conducting, send him over for a chat with Letitia."

"With pleasure."

"And you come along, too." Letitia flashed a brilliant smile which I answered with one equally brilliant. Two masterful women had met and there is no man alive capable of surviving our united onslaught. Like had been attracted to like from the first moment we met and though it was now plain that she expected me to supply her with studs, I was not in the least distressed at being so used. Women like ourselves owe it to one another to present a united front to the enemy. Meanwhile, as quid for my quo, she will try to find work for Mary-Ann. All in all, as satisfying an encounter as I have had since Dr. Montag first introduced himself to us at the Blue Owl Grill.

25

Is it possible to describe anything accurately? That is the problem set us by the French New Novelists. The answer is, like so many answers to important questions, neither yes nor no. The treachery of words is notorious. I write that I "care for" Mary-Ann. But what does that *mean*? Nothing at all because I do not care for her at all times or at any time in all ways. To be precise (the task set us in the age of science), as I sit here at the card table in my room, wearing an old dressing gown of Myron's, I can say that I like her eyes and voice but not her mouth (too small) or hands (too blunt). I could fill many pages of yes-no and still not bring the reader to any *deep* knowledge of what it is I feel at 7:10 P.M., March 12. It is impossible to sort out all one's feelings at any given moment on any given subject, and so perhaps it is wise never to take on any subject other than one's own protean but still manageable self.

What does Mary-Ann think of me? I could not begin to do more than guess nor, I suppose, could she answer this question even to herself: liking, hostility, attraction, revulsion, self-aggrandizement, self-sacrifice, all mingled together with no clear motif save the desire of each to exert power over the other. That is the one human constant, to which all else is tributary.

Dr. Montag still challenges my theory from time to time. Once he spoke of the maternal instinct as something *not* involving power. But of course it does, in the most obvious way: the teat (or bottle) is the source of life to the baby, to be given or withheld at the mother's pleasure. If there is any more fulfilling way of achieving total power over another human being, I have yet to hear of it. Of course most people successfully disguise their power drives, particularly from themselves. Yet the will to prevail is constant and unrelenting. Take that charming, seemingly unaggressive man who makes apparently idle jokes that cause others to laugh. In a sly way, he is exerting power quite as much as Hitler did: after all, his listeners were not laughing until he *made* them laugh. Thus it goes, at every level. My own uniqueness is simply the result of self-knowledge. *I know what I want and I know what I am,* a creation of my own will, now preparing for a breakthrough into an area where, until Myron's death, I could enter only in dreams. Having already destroyed subjectively the masculine principle, I must now shatter it objectively in the person of Rusty, who has reappeared.

But who am I? What do I feel? Do I exist at all? That is the unanswerable question. At the moment I feel like the amnesiac in *Spellbound,* aware that something strange is about to happen. I am apprehensive; obscurely excited

26

The telephone just rang. It was Mary-Ann. I have never heard her so excited. "He's back! Rusty's back!" I allowed her to think that she was telling me something that I did not know. In actual fact, late this afternoon, Irving Amadeus told me, "That beautiful creature just showed up for Atavistic Rhythm, and here we'd all given him up for lost!"

I went straight to Buck's office and checked with the secretary, who was at first reluctant to give me details, but when I threatened to take the matter up with Buck himself, she told me that Rusty had been arrested with two other young men at the Mexican border and held on suspicion of smuggling marijuana into the States. Fortunately, there was no very compelling evidence against them, and they were let go. Nevertheless, Rusty's period of probation has been extended, and the probation officer has asked Buck to keep an eye on him.

But Rusty had told Mary-Ann none of this. "You see, he was with these wild boys in Mexico and their car broke down and they were too broke to pay even for a bus ticket and so the American consul finally bailed them out, after they were practically starving to death." No doubt about it, Rusty is very much a man of his era: his fantasy life shields Mary-Ann as well as himself from the cruel disorders of reality.

Though I cannot say that the pleasure of others has ever had any effect upon me except to produce a profound melancholy, I was *almost* pleased at Mary-Ann's delight. "You must be very happy," I whispered like Phyllis Thaxter in *Thirty Seconds over Tokyo,* with wonderful Van Johnson.

"And we want to have dinner with you tonight, if that's all right. I told him how simply wonderful you've been to me while he was gone."

"I'm sure you'd rather have him all to yourself tonight. Besides, are you sure he wants to see me?"

There was a slight hesitation, followed by much protestation to the effect that Rusty was really very admiring of me since I had been such a help to him in Posture class.

27

It is now midnight. In many ways, a most exciting evening. I met Mary-Ann and Rusty at the Cock and Bull on the Strip; as one might guess, it is Rusty's favorite restaurant for the food is profoundly hearty. He was unusually exuberant and for once I did not seem to make him uneasy. He improvised freely about his adventures in Mexico, all the while eating scones smeared with raspberry jam. I toyed with a single slice of turkey. I am in danger of becoming fat like Gertrude, who resembled, in her last days, a spoiled pear.

"Then after we left Tijuana, we had to break up because, you see, three guys can't hitchhike together. Nobody would pick up three guys looking like us, with beards and all dirty, though there was this one fruit . . ." Rusty frowned at the pseudo-memory or, more likely, at an actual recollection transposed to flesh out the current fantasy. "He was willing to give us a lift, this funny little Mexican with shiny gold teeth and so nervous those gold teeth was chattering but he wanted us real bad, but we said hell no, I mean who wants to go that route?"

"Many do," I said casually, in such a way that I did not seem to be challenging him. Under the table I gave Mary-Ann's hand a little squeeze which she gratefully returned.

Rusty nodded wisely, mouth full. "Yeah, I know. Why there are some guys—some guys I know right at school—who'll sell their ass to some fruit for twenty bucks, just because they're too lazy to get a job."

"But wouldn't *you* do that, if you needed the money?"

"Hell, I'd starve first, and that's the truth." He pulled Mary-Ann close to him and gave her a kiss. I believed him.

In a sense, Rusty is a throwback to the stars of the Forties, who themselves were simply shadows cast in the bright morning of the nation. Yet in the age of the televison commercial he is sadly superfluous, an anachronism, acting out a masculine charade that has lost all meaning. That is why, to save him (and the world from his sort), *I must change entirely his sense of himself.*

When Rusty had finally completed his story of having been down-and-out in Mexico (borrowing heavily from a recent television drama on the same theme), we spoke of Mary-Ann and the good impression that she had made on Letitia Van Allen. Even the unworldly Rusty was impressed. "Do you *really* think she likes Mary-Ann?"

"Very much."

"Oh, not that much." Although a Kathryn Grayson singing star, Mary-Ann also belongs to the Joan Leslie tradition of self-effacing good-sex woman-wife. For her it is Rusty's career that matters, not her own. "Anyway," she said, "it's all due to Miss Myra. She arranged the whole thing."

"That was a swell thing to do." Rusty's voice was deep and warm and he gave me a level gaze reminiscent of James Craig in the fourth reel of *Marriage Is a Private Affair.* "A mighty swell thing, and we're both as grateful as we can be," he added, carefully putting the two of them together on one side, leaving me alone on the other.

"Who Miss Van Allen should really see is Rusty," said Mary-Ann, predictably, to which I replied, as predictably, "Of course she'll see him, but in June. Don't worry, I've already told her about him."

"That's real nice of you. . . ." He was overcome by sincerity like James Stewart in any movie. Then the large veined hands with the blunt fingers took yet another scone and covered it with jam, and I meditated on the dark journey of those veins inside the jacket as they proceeded up the marbled forearms, coiling about the thick biceps, vanishing finally in the deep armpits.

What would Myron have thought of him? Probably not much. Myron preferred the sinister and vicious, the totally abandoned. Rusty is not only not abandoned, he would not have been available, even to Myron whose technique as a seducer was highly developed. Yet where Myron would have failed I shall succeed.

The fact that Rusty has not an inkling of my plans makes every moment we spend together in Mary-Ann's company exquisite. Also, the deliberate (on my part) manipulation of the conversation was curiously thrilling, affording me an opportunity to observe how something entirely alien behaves in its native habitat: the never-fulfilled desire of the dedicated anthropologist who realizes that the moment he arrives in a village to study its culture, that culture has already been subtly altered by the simple fact of his presence; just as the earthly microbes our astronauts are certain to let loose upon other worlds are sure to kill or change those extraterrestrial forms of life we would most like to preserve in order to understand. But then it is our peculiar fate to destroy or change all things we touch since (and let us never forget it) *we* are the constant and compulsive killers of life, the mad dogs of creation, and our triumphant viral progress can only end in a burst of cleansing solar fire, either simulated by us or thrust upon us by the self-protective mechanism of a creation that cannot for long endure too many violent antibodies within its harmonious system. Death and destruction, hate and rage, these are the most characteristic of human attributes, as Myra Breckinridge knows and personifies but soon means, in the most extraordinary way, entirely to transcend.

Yet the presence of the anthropologist (me) at the wooden table in the Cock and Bull did, eventually, alter significantly the behavior of the two natives as they lost their self-consciousness to the degree that the conversation ceased to be particular and became general, something that almost never happens among the lower orders who are, to a man, walking autobiographers, reciting their dull memoirs at extraordinary length, oblivious to the extent that they bore even others of their kind who, of course, wait impatiently to tell *their* stories.

Somehow the subject reverted to Rusty's proud rejection of the Mexican's advances, and Mary-Ann made it plain that for her part she could never consider making love to another woman. "It just . . . well, disgusts me," she said. "I mean I just *couldn't.* I think, well, a woman should act like a woman and a man should act like a man, and that's that."

"But *how* should a man act?" I was mild.

Rusty knew. "He should ball chicks, that's how he should act."

"But only if he really loves them." Mary-Ann was droll; both laughed at what was obviously a private joke.

"And *why* should he ball chicks?" I continued my gentle catechism.

"Well, because that's . . . well, Christ, it's *natural!* "

"And that's how you get babies," said Mary-Ann sagely. "I mean that's how nature intended it."

"Do you think nature intended you to have a baby each time you make love?"

Mary-Ann looked like a lapsed Catholic, trying to recall what she had been taught. But Rusty was a good Catholic Pole and knew right from wrong. "That's what you're *supposed* to do, yes. That's what we're told in church."

"But you do use contraceptives, don't you?"

Both flushed, and Rusty said, "Well, sure. I guess most Catholics do now, but that doesn't mean you don't know it's wrong."

"Then you basically believe that it's right for more and more babies to be born, even though half the people ever born in the world are now alive, and that each day twelve thousand people starve to death in India and South America?" Oh, the sly Myra Breckinridge! Nothing can escape the fine net of her dialectic!

Rusty frowned to show that he was thinking when actually, as one of the acting-students recently said of another's performance, he was only thinking he was thinking. "Well, maybe those Indians and Chinese and so on should probably practice birth control since their religion doesn't care, if they have one . . ."

"But they do have religions. And they do care. And they believe that for a man to be manly he must have as many children as possible . . ."

"Because so many of their babies die in childbirth." Mary-Ann was unusually thoughtful.

"They used to die," I said. "And that kept the population in a proper balance with the food supply. But now the children live. And starve. And all because their parents passionately believe that to be manly is to make babies and to be womanly is to bear them."

"But we're different." Rusty was dogged. "We got enough food and we also have . . ."

"Family planning." Mary-Ann looked happy. No doubt contemplating some planning of her own.

"Enough food," however, was all the cue I needed. I was brilliant. I quoted the best of the world's food authorities (famine for us all by 1974 or 1984 and forget about plankton and seaweed: not enough of it). I demonstrated that essentially Malthus had been right, despite errors of calculation. I described what happens to rats when they are crowded in too small a place: their kidneys deteriorate, and they go mad. I told how whenever the food supply of the lemmings is endangered, a majority of the race drown themselves in order that those left behind may flourish.

Then I gave statistics for the current world death rate, showing how it has drastically declined in the last fifty years due to advanced medicine. The physically and mentally weak who ordinarily would have died at birth now grow up to become revolutionaries in Africa, Asia and Harlem. As a result of miracle drugs and incontinent breeding, the world's food supply can no longer support the billions of people alive at present; there will of course be even less food for those thousands who are joining us every minute. What is to be done? How is the race to be saved (I did not go into the more profound question of whether or not it *should* be saved)? My answer was simple enough: famine and war are now man's only hope. To survive, human population must be drastically reduced. Happily, our leaders are working instinctively toward that end, and there is no doubt in my mind that nature intends Lyndon Johnson and Mao Tse-tung to be the agents of our salvation. By destroying a majority of the human race, they will preserve the breed since the survivors are bound to be not only wiser than we but racially stronger as a result of cellular mutancies caused by atomic radiation. If I say so myself, I had my listeners' eyes bugging out by the time I had sketched for them man's marvelous if fiery fate.

"But what can we do to *stop* all this from happening?" Mary-Ann was plainly alarmed.

"Don't have children. That is the best thing. A gesture of course, but better than nothing. And try to change your attitudes about what is normal." Then, in quick succession, I delivered a number of anthropological haymakers. Proper womanly behavior for an Eskimo wife is to go to bed with anyone her husband brings back to the igloo. Proper manly behavior for the Spartan warrior was to make love to a boy while teaching him how to be a soldier. I gave a rapid review of what is considered proper sexual behavior in Polynesia and along the Amazon. Everything I said came as revelation to Rusty and Mary-Ann, and they were obviously horrified by the *unnatu*-ralness of what was considered natural in other parts of the world. I believe I planted a seed or two. Mary-Ann of course could never prostitute herself like an Eskimo wife nor could Rusty ever make love to an adolescent boy ("those teeny-bop-

pers give me a pain"); yet each now regards his old certainties
as being, at least, relative. That is progress.

As could be expected, it was Mary-Ann who mounted the
counterattack. "Maybe you're right when you say there's nothing that's really *basically* normal but when everybody tells you
that they want you to behave in a certain way, like marrying
one man and having only his children, isn't that the *right* thing
to do because doesn't the society deep down *know* what it's
doing, and is trying to protect itself?"

Unexpectedly she had made a good point. Not once in all
these weeks have I suspected her of possessing a true intelligence. Obviously I have been misled by her California manner
which is resolutely cretinous as well as nasal. The possibility that
she might one day be a woman I could actually talk to was a
revelation, and by no means an unpleasant one. Naturally, she
could not be allowed to *win* her point. Even so, it will, as we
academics say, count against the final grade.

I challenged her with a simple question: does any society
know how to preserve itself? I then listed a number of civili-
zations that had destroyed themselves through upholding cus-
toms that were self-destructive. For instance, the health of the
Roman state depended upon a vigorous aristocracy but that
aristocracy committed suicide by insisting that their cooking be
done in expensive pots made of lead. The result was acute lead
poisoning which led to impotence and the literal extinction of
an entire class, killed by custom. Then, superb dialectician that
I am, I discussed every society's *secret* drive to destroy itself and
whether or not this was a good thing, taken in the larger context
of the human race's evolution. They were both shocked at the
idea, particularly when I brought it home to them by suggesting
that Rusty's desire to have sex only with girls and Mary-Ann's
desire to have at least four children the world did not need
might be considered proof that our society is now preparing to
kill itself by exhausting the food supply and making nuclear
war inevitable. Should this be the case, the only alternative (and
a most unlikely one) would be for all the Rustys to follow the

Spartan custom of making love to boys while the Mary-Anns, as lovers of women, would at least help preserve the race by bringing no more children into the world. But of course I was playing devil's advocate since I am secretly convinced that we shall soon be purged by a chiliastic fire, and so, in the long run, current behavior will best serve us by hastening our necessary end. Yet efforts must still be made to preserve life, to change the sexes, to re-create Man. There is an off chance that my mission may yet succeed.

Mary-Ann was most depressed.

I took her hand in mine. "Don't worry," I said. "What will happen will happen. Meanwhile, all I ask is that you be happy . . . and you, too, Rusty." I gave him a beautiful yet knowing smile like Ann Sothern in the first of the Maisie films. "But to be *truly* happy, I think you must both begin to think a little bit about changing your sexual attitudes, becoming more open, less limited, abandoning old-fashioned stereotypes of what is manly and what is feminine. As it is, if you, Rusty, should ever find a boy sexually interesting, you might or might not do something about it but whatever you did do or did not do you'd certainly feel guilty because you've been taught that to be a man is to be physically strong, self-reliant, and a lover of girls, one at a time."

"So what's wrong with that?" Rusty gave me a cocky grin.

"Nothing." I was patient. "Except modern man is not self-reliant and as for making love to girls, that is only one aspect of his nature . . ."

"It's my only one. Why, just the thought of boffing some hairy boy makes me sick all over."

"Not all boys are as hairy as you," I said gaily, recklessly. Mary-Ann looked surprised while Rusty looked uneasy at this reminder of our old intimate encounter. I turned to Mary-Ann. "It's positively coquettish the way the top two buttons of his shirt are always missing."

She was relieved. "Men are so vain," she said, looking at him fondly.

"But in America only women are supposed to worry about

their appearance. The real man never looks into a mirror. That's effeminate. . . ." I teased them.

"Well, *that's* changing, I guess." Mary-Ann brought Rusty's hands to her lips. "And I'm just as glad. I think men are beautiful."

"So does Rusty," I could not help but observe.

"Oh, shit, Miss Myra," was the boyish response. Soon. Soon. Soon.

BUCK LONER REPORTS—
Recording Disc No. 777—
18 March

Flagler and Flagler have come up with
dynamite or they think its dynamite but you never know with
that woman apparently the Monterrey Mexican marriage cer
tificate is a phony and there is no record from what they can
find out of her being married down there but weve been burned
before I said to Flagler Junior who is working on the case shell
just go out and prove they lost the records or something and
then that doctor friend of hers will swear he was a witness which
is what it sounded like on the long distance telephone call that
was bugged and what do we do then I ask you question mark
well Flagler Junior seems to think they are on solid ground with
the Mexicans though he admits that our little brown friends are
not only kind of confused in the paper works department but if
Myra thinks of it and shell think of it the bitch they can be
bribed to say that there was a marriage when there wasnt so
meanwhile I am biding my time until tomorrow when there

should be a full final report from Mexico that there really isnt a record of this marriage in question period paragraph Flagler Juniors New York man has already met once with Doctor Montag and his report is on my desk now as I dictate while being massaged by Milly who is the best masseuse in the whole business I mean that Milly you little angel thats right rub good and hard it takes time but when it comes the Buck Loner Special strike that period paragraph interesting conversation with Letitia who thinks that Mary Ann Pringle properly handled could make it as a recording star and she will make some appointments all this is Myras doing she is meddling into everything trying to force the kids out into the cold world when their place is here protected and looked after I know how well I know showbiz and all its heartbreaks and Mary Ann will end up like all the others which is nowhere a waitress some place assuming she doesnt get lucky and marry some guy who will take care of her and cherish her the way Buck Loners Academy does that guy certainly wont be Rusty whos a wild number the Sheriffs office just asked me to keep an eye on him and I told him so yesterday told him that he would have to watch his step or it was the hoosegow for him he was real shook up and asked me not to tell anybody about his scrape in Mexico and I said nobody knows but me and Myra who happened to be checking into his file and read the Sheriffs last letter to me that woman is into everything Rusty seemed upset by this I guess because he thinks Myra will tell Mary Ann well its no business of mine and thats for sure Milly you are the best ever and if you keep that up theres a big surprise coming your way strike that period paragraph Myra asked permission to use the infirmary tonight God knows why I suppose she is mixing up some poison which it is my prayer she takes Jesus Milly dont stop Milly Jesus Milly

28

I am sitting in the infirmary, a small antiseptic white room with glass cabinets containing all sorts of drugs and wicked-looking instruments. Against one wall is an examination table which can be raised or lowered. It is now some four feet above the floor and tilted at a slight angle. Next to it are scales and measuring instruments for both height and body width. I am seated at a small surgical table, making notes while I wait for Rusty.

It is ten o'clock at night. The Academy building is dark. The students are gone. No one will disturb us. I am astonished at my own calm. All of my life's hunger is about to be fed. I am as serene as a great surgeon preparing to make the necessary incision that will root out the problem.

This morning, after Posture class, I took Rusty to one side. He has been friendly and smiling ever since our dinner at the Cock and Bull and now treats me in the confident condescending way that the ordinary young man treats an ordinary girl.

I put a stop to that. His grinning face went pale when I said coldly, "There's been no improvement, Rusty. None at all. You're not trying to walk straight."

"Honest to God I am, Miss Myra, why I even practiced last night with Mary-Ann, she'll tell you I did. I really am trying." He seemed genuinely hurt that I had not recognized his effort.

I was somewhat kinder in my manner, sharp but in the Eve Arden way. "I'm sure you have tried. But you need special attention and I think I can give it. I'll expect you at the infirmary at ten o'clock tonight."

"The infirmary?" He looked almost as puzzled as James Craig in the sixth reel of *Little Mister Jim.*

"I've arranged everything with Uncle Buck. He agrees with me that you need extra help."

"But what *kind* of help?" He was still puzzled but, as yet, unsuspicious.

"You'll see." I started to go.

He stopped me. "Look, I've got a date with Mary-Ann for dinner."

"Postpone it. You see her every night *after* dinner anyway."

"Well, yes. But we were invited some place at ten."

"Then go at eleven. I'm sorry. But this is more important than your social life. After all, you want to be a star, don't you?"

That was always the clincher in dealing with any of the students. They have been conditioned from childhood in the knowledge that to achieve stardom they might be called upon to do *anything*, and of course they would do anything because stardom is everything and worth any humiliation or anguish. So the saints must have felt in the early days of Christendom, as they burned to death with their eyes on heaven where the true stars shine.

I spent all afternoon making my preparations. I have the entire procedure worked out to the last detail. When I have finished, I shall have achieved in life every dream and

29

I must write it all down now. Exactly as it happened. While it is fresh in my memory. But my hand trembles. Why? Twice I've dropped the yellow ballpoint pen. Now I sit at the surgical table, making the greatest effort to calm myself, to put it all down not only for its own sake but also for you, Randolph, who never dreamed that anyone could ever act out *totally* his fantasies and survive. Certainly your own guilty longing to kill the nerve in each of Lyndon Johnson's twenty-odd teeth *without* the use of anesthetic can never in this life be achieved, and so your dreams must feed upon pale surrogates while mine have been made reality.

Shortly after ten, Rusty arrived. He wore the usual checked shirt with two buttons missing and no T-shirt, as well as chino trousers and highly polished cowboy boots. He looked about the infirmary curiously. "I never been in here before."

"That explains why there's no physical record of you."

"Never been sick a day in my life." Oh, he was proud! No doubt of that.

"But even so, the Academy requires a record. It's one of Uncle Buck's rules."

"Yeah. I know. And I've been meaning to drop in sometime and see the Doc."

"Perhaps that won't be necessary." I placed the physical examination chart squarely in the middle of the surgical table. "Sit down." I was pleasant. He sat in a chair so close to mine that our knees touched. Quickly he swung his legs wide so that my knees were now between his and there was no possibility of further contact. It was plain that in no way do I attract him.

We chatted a moment about Mary-Ann, and about Letitia's interest in her career. I could see that Rusty was both pleased and envious, a normal reaction. Then, delicately, I got around to the subject of Mexico; he became visibly nervous. Finally, I told him that I knew what had happened.

"You won't tell Mary-Ann, will you?" That was his first response. "It would just kill her."

"Of course I won't. And of course I'll give a good report to Mr. Martinson, your parole officer."

He was startled. "You know him?"

"Oh, yes," I lied—actually I happened to come across a letter from him to Buck. "In fact, he's asked me to keep an eye on you, and I said I would."

"I hope you tell him that I sure as hell am reformed." He was vehement.

"I will—if you really are, and behave yourself, and let me try to help you with your problem."

"Of course I will, Miss Myra. You know that." He looked entirely sincere, blue eyes round as a boy's. Perhaps he is an actor after all.

"Now then, about your back. I've talked to the chiropractor who will arrange for a special brace. He couldn't be here tonight but he asked me to take an exact tracing of your spine and then he'll know what to do. So now if you'll just slip off that shirt, we'll get to work."

Resignedly, he got to his feet. Automatically his hands went to his belt buckle in order to loosen it but then, obviously recalling our last encounter, he left the belt as it was, pulling off the shirt with a certain arrogant ease.

The belt just covered his navel; otherwise he was in exactly the same state as he had been at the beginning of our first session. I was pleased that my visual recollection of him was so precise. I remembered in exact detail the tracery design of bronze hair across the pale chest, as well as the small roselike inverted nipples.

"Stand on the scales, please." I imitated the chilliest of trained nurses. "Face to the wall and we'll measure you." He put one foot on the scales, when I stopped him. "Take off those atrocious cowboy boots! They'll break the machine."

"Oh, no they won't, why . . ." He started to argue.

"Rusty!" I was sharp. "Do *exactly* as I tell you. You don't want me to tell Mr. Martinson that you've been uncooperative, do you?"

"No . . . no." Standing first on one foot and then on the other, he awkwardly pulled off the boots. He wore white cotton socks; one had a large hole in it through which the big toe protruded. He grinned sheepishly. "Guess I'm full of holes."

"That's all right." The small room was now full of the not unpleasant odor of warm leather.

Obediently he got onto the scales exactly as I directed, face to the wall. In a most professional way, I measured the width of the chest, and then allowed myself the pleasure of running my hand down the smooth warm back, tracing the spine's curve right to the point where it vanished, frustratingly, into the white chinos as they swelled just below my hand, masking those famous inviolate buttocks.

"All right," I said, marking down figures on the physical examination chart. "Now we need your weight which is one seventy-four and your height which is six one and a quarter. The chart's filling up nicely. All right, you can get down."

He stepped off the scales. He was surprisingly at ease: obviously our dinner at the Cock and Bull had given him confidence. "This doctor can really fix me with something that will work?" He was genuinely curious.

"He thinks he can, yes. Of course, he'll have to fit you himself. This is just the preliminary examination which, while we're at it, Uncle Buck said I should turn into an ordinary physical and so kill two birds with one stone, as he put it in his colorful way."

"You mean like height and weight and that stuff?" As yet he showed no particular alarm.

"Exactly," I said, ready now to begin to shake his self-confidence. I took a small bottle. "That means a urine specimen."

The look of surprise was exquisite as he took the bottle. "Go behind that screen." I indicated a white screen in one corner of the room.

"But . . ." he began.

"But?" I repeated pleasantly. Without a word, he went behind the screen which was waist-high. He turned and faced the wall; he fumbled with his trousers. Then there was a long moment of complete silence.

"What's the matter?" I asked.

"I . . . don't know. I guess I'm what they call pee-shy."

"Don't be. Just relax. We've got plenty of time."

The thought of "plenty of time" had a most releasing effect. Water passed into the bottle with a surging sound. He then rearranged his clothes and brought me the specimen which I took (marveling at the warmth of the glass: we are furnaces inside!) and carefully placed on it a white sticker inscribed with his name. The entire affair was conducted without a false note.

"Now then we'll just do a drawing of the spine. Loosen your belt and lie face down on the table."

For the first time he seemed aware that history might repeat itself. He stalled. "Maybe we better wait till I see the doctor."

"Rusty," I was patient but firm. "I'm just following doctor's orders and you are going to follow *my* orders, or else. Is that understood?"

"Well, yes, but . . ."

"There are no 'buts' for someone on probation."

"Yes, ma'am!" He got the point. Quickly he undid the belt buckle; then he unfastened the catch to his trousers and, holding them firmly in place, lay face-down on the table. It was a delicious sight, that slender muscular body stretched full length as sacrifice to some cruel goddess. His arms were at his sides, and I noticed with some amusement that he was pressing the palms hard against the table, instinctively repeating his earlier performance.

I covered his back with a large sheet of paper. Then with an eyebrow pencil, I slowly traced the spine's course from the nape of the neck to the line of his trousers.

"This is going very, very well." I sounded to my own ears exactly like Laraine Day, an all-time favorite.

"It sort of tickles," came a muffled voice. Triceps muscles writhed beneath silk-smooth skin.

"*Are* you ticklish?" This suddenly opened an unexpected vista. Fortunately my program was so designed as to include an occasional inspired improvisation.

"Well, no, not really . . ."

But I had already taken one large sweaty foot in hand (again marveling at the body heat through the thin sock) and delicately tickled the base of the toes. The effect was electric. The whole body gave a sudden twitch. With a powerful reflex, he kicked the foot from my hand, exclaiming "Cut that out!" in a masterful voice, so entirely had he forgotten his place.

I was mild. "Do that again, Rusty, and I will punish you."

"I'm sorry, Miss Myra." He was conciliatory. He looked at me over his shoulder (the tracing paper had fallen to the floor). "I guess I'm more ticklish than I thought."

"Apparently. Or perhaps I hurt you. You don't have athlete's foot, do you?"

"Oh, no. No. Not for a long time . . . in the summer, sometimes . . ."

"We'll just take a look." With some difficulty, I slipped off the damp socks. If I were a foot-fetishist like poor Myron, I would have been in seventh heaven. As it was, what excited me was his profound embarrassment, for he has the American male's horror of smelling bad. Actually, he was relatively odorless. "You must have just had a shower," I said.

He buried his face in the table. "Yeah . . . just now." Carefully

I examined each toe, holding it tight as though I feared that, at any moment, one of the little piggies might decide to run all the way home. But except for a certain rigidity of the body, he did not show, in any way, distress; not even when I examined each pink toe.

"Good," I said, putting the foot down. "You're learning control. Ticklishness is a sign of sexual fear, did you know that?"

A faint "no" from the head of the table.

"That's why I was so surprised at the way you reacted when I touched your foot. From what you said at the Cock and Bull I couldn't imagine you ever being tense with a woman."

"I guess you sort of took me by surprise," was the best that he could think to say. In his present position, he obviously did not want to be reminded of his usual cockiness.

"I'm sorry," I said, deftly sliding his trousers down to his knees.

As I had anticipated, he gave a slight gasp but made no move other than to grip with both hands the sides of the trousers in an effort to keep at least his front decently covered.

On the table before me, like some cannibal banquet, the famous buttocks curved beneath frayed Jockey shorts. Below the elastic, two round holes, like eyes, revealed fair skin. Teasingly, I put my finger in one of the holes. He winced at the touch. "Doesn't Mary-Ann ever mend your clothes?"

"She . . . can't . . . sew . . ." He sounded as if he had been running hard, and could not get his breath. But at least he had steeled himself for my next move.

The total unveiling of the buttocks was accomplished in an absolute, almost religious, silence. They were glorious. Under the direct overhead light, I was able to appreciate physical details that I had missed in the office. A tiny dark mole on one cheek. An angry red pimple just inside the crack where a hair had grown in upon itself. The iridescent quality of the skin which was covered with the most delicate pale peach fuzz, visible only in a strong light and glittering now with new sweat. I could smell his fear. It was intoxicating.

I also noted that although I had pulled the Jockey shorts down to the thighs in the back, he had craftily contrived to hold them up in front, and so his honor, he believed, was only half lost.

Intimately I passed my hand over the hard buttocks, firmly locked to all intruders, and remarked, according to plan, "You aren't feverish, are you?"

"No . . . I'm O.K. . . ." The voice was barely audible. With my free hand I felt his brow; it was bathed in perspiration.

"You *are* hot. We'd better take your temperature. Besides, they want it for the chart."

As I went over to the surgical table and prepared the thermometer, he watched me dully, like a trapped animal. Then I returned to my quarry and, putting one hand on each cheek at the exact point where buttock joins thigh, I said, "Relax now."

He raised up on his arms and looked around at me, eyes suddenly bright with alarm. "*What?*"

"I've got to take your temperature, Rusty."

"But . . . *there?*" His voice broke like a teenage boy's.

"Of course. Now then . . ."

"But why can't you use the other kind, you know, in the mouth . . ." With the back of my left hand, I struck him hard across the bottom. He gasped, pulled back.

"There is more where that came from," I said coldly, noting with pleasure a certain darkening of skin where the blood had been brought to the surface by the force of my blow.

"Yes, ma'am." Defeated, the head returned to its position on the table and once again I put my hands on those firm cheeks.

"Now," I said "relax the muscle." I could feel beneath my fingers the muscles slowly, reluctantly go slack.

I confess I was now trembling with excitement. Gently, carefully I pushed the cheeks apart until everything—secret sphincter and all—was revealed.

Normally at moments of great victory, there is a sense of letdown. But not in this case. For one thing I had half feared to find him not clean—unlike so many anal erotics I am not at all attracted by fecal matter, quite the reverse in fact. Yet had he *not* been tidy, his humiliation would have been total. So I was torn between conflicting desires. As it turned out, his shower had been thorough. The sphincter resembled a tiny pale pink tea rose, or perhaps a kitten's nose and mouth. From its circumference, like the rays of a sunburst, bronze hairs reflected the overhead light. The only disappointment was that he had craftily managed to arrange his scrotum so that it was entirely out of view, only a thick tuft of hair at the juncture of the groin indicating the direction in which it could be found. But sufficient to the moment are the revelations thereof.

I squeezed some lubricant from a tube onto my index finger and then, delicately, touched the never-used entrance. A tremor went through his whole body—the term "fleshquake" occurred to me: so Atlantis must have shuddered before the fall! Carefully, daintily, I applied the lubricant to the silky puckered surface. He held himself quite rigid, again not breathing.

Then I grew bolder. I inserted my finger into the tight hot place as far as it would go. I must have touched the prostate for he suddenly groaned, but said nothing. Then, either deliberately or through uncontrollable reflex, he brought the full force of his youthful muscularity to bear on the sphincter muscle and for a moment it felt as though my finger might be nipped off.

With my free hand, I slapped his tight buttock smartly. "Relax!" I commanded. He mumbled something I could not hear and the sphincter again loosened. I then removed my finger and inserted the thermometer, after first teasing the virginal orifice with delicate probes that made him squirm. Once the thermometer was in, it was completely lost to sight for his buttocks are deep and since the legs were only slightly spread, his cheeks promptly came together when I let them go.

I then took up the chart and read off a list of childhood diseases. Chicken pox, measles, whooping cough . . . and he whispered "yes" or "no" or "I don't remember" in response to the catechism. When I was finished, I said, "All in all, a healthy young boy." My cold cheery manner was calculated to increase his alarm; obviously it did for not once would he look at me, preferring to stare at the wall just opposite, chin pushed hard against the table.

"Now let's see what's cooking." I pushed open the checks and slowly removed the thermometer. He was normal of course but I saw fit to lie: "Just as I thought, you do have a touch of fever. Well, we'll soon take care of that. Now roll over on your back."

He did as he was told, swiftly pulling up trousers and shorts in front; nevertheless, the line of his belt was two inches below the navel and could not, in his present position, be pulled higher. As a result, the timberline of pubic hair was briefly revealed, briefly because he promptly placed both hands over himself in an attempt to hide that quarry from the hunter's approach.

On his back, bare feet pointed and chest streaked with sweat, he seemed smaller than in fact he was, already more boy than man, despite the mature muscularity of the torso. The process of diminishing was well begun. He looked up at me, apprehensively. "Is there much more I got to do?"

"We must both follow the chart." I was enigmatic as I picked up a wooden tongue depressor. "Open your mouth." He obeyed. I pressed down the pink tongue until he gagged, noting, as I did, the whiteness of the teeth and the abnormal salivation that fear sometimes creates. "You take good care of your teeth." I gave him the sort of grudging compliment the stern nurse gives a child. "Your body, too. I was happily surprised to find that you were clean in places most boys your age neglect." Carefully I was reducing his status from man to boy to child to—ah, the triumph! He responded numbly to the progression, blinking with embarrassment.

"Now put your hands behind your head." Slowly he obeyed, aware that I could now see at least a quarter of an inch of dark pubic hair, surprisingly thick and in texture coarser than the fine hairs on the rest of his body. A pulse just above the navel beat rapidly, causing the entire stomach to quiver like some frightened small beast.

I let my hand rest lightly on his navel. Crisp hairs tickled my palm as I in turn tickled them. I could feel the pounding of the blood in his arteries. The sense of power was overwhelming. I felt as if, in some way, it was I who controlled the coursing of the blood in his veins and that it was at *my* command that the heart beat at all. I felt that I could do anything.

"You seem nervous, Rusty." I challenged him.

He swallowed hard. "No . . . no, Miss Myra. No, I'm not really. It's just that it's kind of hot in here . . ."

"And you're not enjoying your examination."

"Well, it's kind of strange, you know. . . ." His voice trailed off nervously.

"*What's* kind of strange?"

"Well, you know. . . I mean having a girl. . . you know, a lady, like you, do all this to a guy."

"Haven't you ever been examined by a nurse?"

"Never!" This reversion to the old masculine Rusty was promptly quelled by the sudden tug I gave to his Jockey shorts; the full bush was now visible, though nothing else for the shorts were stopped at the crucial juncture by the weight of his body.

With great thoroughness, I felt the different sections of his belly, taking pleasure in the firmness of muscles, hard rubber beneath silk. I lingered for quite some time over the pubic area taking the powerful pulse of each of the two arteries that meet at the groin. I could not, however, make out even the base of his penis.

I then took an instrument which resembled sugar tongs, used to test the thickness of the skin's subcutaneous layer. With frightened eyes, he watched as I picked away at the skin of his belly, pulling the skin as high as I could and then releasing it with a snap. "Nicely resilient," I said, pinching hard as I could a fold of his belly and causing him to cry out plaintively, "Hey, that hurts!" The return to childhood was well underway.

"Stop being such a baby!" Delicately I took one of his nipples in the tongs. He shrank from me, but the tongs pursued. I was careful, however, not to hurt him.

With feather touch, I teased the tiny inverted nipple, making him writhe at the tickling pleasure it gave him. Then, suddenly, the nipple was erect. I then teased the other nipple, manipulating the golden aureole of hairs until it, too, ceased to be concave. A glassy look came into his eyes; for the first time an erogenous zone had been explored and exploited (I do not count the probing of his sphincter which, in the context of my investigation, did not arouse him, rather the reverse). I looked at the front of his trousers to see if there was any sudden swelling but I could detect nothing.

"You had better slip off those trousers," I said. "They're getting badly creased, the way you're sweating."

"Oh, that's O.K." His voice cracked again.

"Hurry up! We haven't got all night." Grimly he sat up and pulled his trousers down over his knees. I pulled them over his feet and carefully hung them on a chair.

When I turned back to my victim, I was surprised to find him sitting up on the table, poised for flight. He had trickily used the turning of my back to restore his shorts to their normal position. Sitting as he was, bare legs dangling over the table, I could see nothing of the crotch, concealed by muscular thighs pressed close together while both hands rested protectively in his lap. He was not going to surrender the last bastion without a struggle.

"I didn't tell you to sit up, did I?" I was cold.

"But I thought you were through with me here." The timbre of the voice had become light; he sounded like a pubescent boy trying to escape punishment.

"You're not finished until I say you are. All right. Stand up. Over here. In front of me."

He got to his feet and approached to within a foot of me. There he stood, awkwardly, hands crossed in front of him, torso glittering with sweat, legs as well proportioned as the rest of him, though somewhat overdeveloped in the thighs, no doubt the result of playing football. He was so close to me that I could feel the heat of his flesh and smell the healthy earthlike aroma the young male body exudes.

"Rest your arms at your sides and at least *try* to stand straight."

He obeyed. The target was now directly in front of me, at my eye's level. As I stared straight at the hidden area he clenched his fists nervously, and shifted from foot to foot. The frayed Jockey shorts were unfortunately too loose to reveal more than a large rounded area, without clear definition; they were, however, splotched with fresh urine.

"Look! You wet yourself!" I pinched the damp cloth, careful to touch nothing beneath.

He gave a start. "I guess I did. I was in a hurry."

"Boys are so careless about those things." We had gone from bowel-training to bed-wetting: such was progress! I looked at the examination card. "Oh yes! Have you ever had a venereal disease?"

"Oh, no, ma'am. Never!"

"I hope you're telling me the truth." I was ominous as I wrote "no" on the chart. "We have ways of finding out, you know."

"Honest I never have. I always been careful . . . always."

"Always? Just exactly *when* did you begin with girls?"

"When?" He looked at me dumbly.

"How old were you?"

"Thirteen, I guess. I don't remember."

"Was she older than you?"

He nodded. "In high school. She was a Protestant," he added wildly.

"Did she make the advances?"

"Yes. Kind of. She'd show me hers if I showed her mine. You know, kid stuff."

"And you liked what you saw?"

"Oh, yes." A smile flickered for an instant across the frightened face.

"Did she like what she saw?"

The smile went, as he was reminded of his situation. "Well, there was no complaints."

"Would you say that you were well developed for your age?"

"I guess so. I don't know."

"Did you masturbate often?"

The face went red. "Well . . . maybe some. I guess all guys do."

"What about now?"

"Now? Oh, no. Why should I?"

"You mean Mary-Ann is quite enough to satisfy you?"

"Yes. And I don't cheat on her."

"How often do you come with her in a night?"

He gulped. "That's awful personal . . ."

I took the measuring stick and with a great cracking sound struck his right thigh. He yelled. Fear and reproach in his face, as he rubbed the hurt skin.

"There's more where that came from if you don't answer my questions."

He accepted defeat. "I guess I can go four or five times but mostly we just go a couple times because, you see, we have to get up so early . . ."

"Then you *are* quite a stud, as they say out here."

"Oh, I don't know . . ." He gestured helplessly.

"Would you say that your penis was larger than most boys' your age or smaller?"

He began to tremble, aware of the prey I was stalking. "Christ, I don't know. I mean *how* could I know?"

"You see the other boys in the shower, and you were an athlete, after all."

"I guess I didn't look . . ."

"But surely you must occasionally have taken a peek." I looked straight at the worn cotton which hid the subject of my inquiry. Both of his hands twitched, as though he wanted to protect himself.

"I guess I'm average. I never thought about it . . . honest." This of course was a lie since in every known society the adolescent male spends a great deal of time worriedly comparing himself with other males.

"You're unusually modest." I was dry. "Now I'm supposed to check you for hernia. So if you'll just pull down those shorts . . ."

"But I don't have hernia," he gabbled. "I was all checked out

141

by this prison doctor in Mexico, and he said I was just fine in that department."

"But it does no harm to double-check. So if you'll slip them down . . ."

"Honest, I'm O.K." He was sweating heavily.

"Rusty, I get the impression that for some mysterious reason you don't want me to examine your genitals. Exactly what mischief are you trying to hide from me?"

"Nothing, honest! I got nothing to hide . . ."

"Then why are you so afraid to let me examine you?"

"Because—well, you're a woman and I'm a man . . ."

"A boy, technically . . ."

"A boy, O.K, and, well, it's just wrong."

"Then you're shy."

"Sure, I'm shy about *that*, in front of a lady."

"But surely you aren't shy with all those girls you've—what's that word of yours? —'boffed'?"

"But that's different, when you're *both* making love, that's O.K."

"Baffling," I said. I frowned as though trying to find some way out of our dilemma. "Naturally, I want to respect your modesty. At the same time I must complete the examination." I paused; then I gave the appearance of having reached a decision. "All right. You won't have to remove your shorts . . ."

He gave a sigh of relief . . . too soon.

"However, I shall have to insert my hand inside the shorts and press each testicle as required by the chart."

"Oh." Dismay and defeat.

"I think you'll agree that's a statesmanlike compromise." On that bright note, I slid my left hand up the inside of his left thigh. He wriggled involuntarily as I forced my fingers past the leg opening of the shorts. The scrotum's heat was far greater than that of the thigh, I noticed, and the hairs were soaked with sweat.

Carefully I took his left testicle in my hand. It was unusually large and firm to the touch, though somewhat loose in the sac, no doubt due to his overheated condition. Delicately I fingered the beloved enemy, at last in my power. Then I looked up and saw that Rusty's eyes were screwed shut, as though anticipating pain. I gave it to him. I maneuvered the testicle back and forth until I had found the hole from which, in boyhood, it had so joyously descended. I shoved it back up into the hole. He groaned. Then he gagged as I held it in place. With the gagging, I could feel the entire scrotum contract like a terrified beast, seeking escape. When he gagged again and seemed on the verge of actually being sick, I let the testicle fall back into its normal place and took my hand away.

"Jesus," he whispered. "I almost threw up."

"I'm sorry. But I have to be thorough. I'll be gentler this time." Again my hand pushed past the damp cloth and seized the right testicle, which was somewhat smaller than the left. As I maneuvered it gently about, my forefinger strayed and struck the side of something thick and smooth, rooted in wiry hair. He shuddered, but continued to suffer at my hands. I slipped the right testicle into its ancient place and held it there until I sensed he was about to gag. Then I let it drop and removed my hand.

He gave a deep sigh. "I guess that's it."

"Yes, I think so." I pretended to examine the chart.

With a sigh, he sat down on the chair opposite me and clumsily pulled on one sock, tearing the flimsy material; the toes went through the tip.

"You're very clumsy." I observed.

"Yes, ma'am." He agreed, quickly pulling on the other sock, not wanting in any way to cross me, so eager was he to escape.

"Oh, here's a question we forgot." I was incredibly sunny. "Have you been circumcised?"

The foot he was holding on his knee slid to the floor. Quickly he pressed his thighs together, wadded up his shirt, and covered the beleaguered lap. "Why, no, ma'am. I never was."

"So few Polish boys are, I'm told." I made a check on the chart. "Does the skin pull back easily?"

"Oh, sure!" He was beet-red. "Sure. I'm O.K. Mary-Ann's waiting."

"Not so fast." I was cold. "I didn't give you permission to dress, you know."

"But I thought you were finished. . . ." The deep voice was now a whine.

"I was. But your jumping the gun like that makes me very suspicious."

"Suspicious?" He was bewildered.

"Yes. First, I let you talk me out of giving you the venereal disease examination, and now you're suddenly getting dressed, without permission, just when the subject once more has to do with your penis. Rusty, I am very, very suspicious."

The blue eyes filled with tears as he sensed what was approaching. "Don't be, Miss Myra. Believe me, I'm absolutely O.K. . . ."

"We have to think of Mary-Ann, too, you know. You could make her very sick just through your carelessness."

"Honest to God, I'm O.K. They even gave me the Wassermann test in the jail. . . ." He jabbered nervously.

"I'm sure they did. But what was the result?"

"Mr. Martinson will tell you. I was a hundred percent O.K."

"But Mr. Martinson isn't here while you are, and frankly I don't see how I can omit this part of the examination. Stand up please and put down that shirt."

"Oh, come on, please don't . . ." His voice broke again, close to a sob.

"Do as I say."

On that note of icy command, he stood up slowly and like a man going to his execution—or a schoolboy to his spanking—he put down the shirt and stood dumbly facing me. "Come over here." He came to within a few inches of where I was sitting; he was so close that my knees touched the warm fur of his shins.

"Now let's see what kind of stud you really are."

"Please . . ." He whispered. "I don't want to. It isn't right."

Deliberately I took the Jockey shorts by the elastic waistband

and pulled them slowly, slowly down, enjoying each station of his shame. The first glimpse was encouraging. The base of the penis sprouted from the bronze bush at an angle of almost forty-five degrees, an earnest of vitality. It was well over an inch wide, always a good sign, with one large blue vein down the center, again promising. But another three inches of slow unveiling revealed Rusty's manhood in its entirety, I slid the shorts to the floor.

When I looked up at his face, I saw that once again the eyes were shut, the lips trembling. Then I carefully examined the object of my long and arduous hunt, at last captive. A phrase of Myron's occurred to me: "all potatoes and no meat." Rusty's balls were unusually large and impressive; one lower than the other, as they hung bull-like in the rather loose scrotal sac. They were all that I could desire. The penis, on the other hand, was not a success, and I could see now why he was so reluctant to let me see just how short it is. On the other hand both base and head are uncommonly thick and, as Myron always said, thickness not length is how you gauge the size of the ultimate erection. The skin was dead white with several not undecorative veins, while the foreskin covered the entire head meeting at the tip in an irregular rosy pucker, plainly cousin to the sphincter I had so recently probed.

"I'm afraid, Rusty, that you've been somewhat oversold on the campus. Poor Mary-Ann. That's a boy's equipment."

This had the desired effect of stinging him into a manly response. "Ain't been no complaints," he growled. But as he did, both testicles rose in their sac as though seeking an escape hatch in case of battle, while the penis betrayed him by visibly shrinking into the safety of the brush.

"Next you'll tell me that it's not the size that counts but what you do." I followed verbal insult with physical: I took the penis firmly in my hand.

He dared not move, or speak, or even cry out. The shock had reduced him exactly as planned. I had also confirmed an old theory that although the "normal" male delights in exposing himself to females who attract him he is, conversely, terrified to do so in front of those he dislikes or fears, as though any knowledge they might obtain of the center of his being will create bad magic and hence unman him. In any case, the grail was in my hand at last, smooth, warm, soft.

My joy was complete as I slid back the skin, exposing the shiny deep rose of the head which was impressively large and beautifully shaped, giving some credence to the legend that, in action, its owner (already Rusty had become a mere appendage to this reality) was a formidable lover. He was sweaty but clean (I was so close to him that I could smell the strong but not disagreeable fernlike odor of genitals). Delicately but firmly, I pressed the glans, making the phallic eye open. Not one tear was shed. "Apparently, you *are* all right," I observed as he looked down with horror at my hand which held him firmly in its grasp, the glans penis exposed like a summer rose.

"You're also clean but beyond that I'm afraid you're something of a disappointment." The penis again shrank in my hand. "But of course you're probably still growing." The humiliation was complete. There was nothing that he could say. In actual fact, the largeness of the head had already convinced me that what I said was untrue, but policy dictated that I be scornful.

"Now then, let's see how free the foreskin is." I slid the skin forward, then back. He shuddered. "Now, you do it a few times."

To his relief, I let him go. Clumsily he took himself in one hand as though never before had he touched this strange object, so beloved of Mary-Ann. He gave a few halfhearted tugs to the skin, looking for all the world like a child frightened in the act of masturbating.

"Come on," I said, "you can do better than that."

He changed his grip to the one he obviously used when alone. His hand worked rapidly as he pumped himself like one of those machines that extract oil from the earth, milk from the cow, water from shale. After several minutes of intense and rhythmic massage I noted, with some surprise, that though the head had become a bit larger and darker, the stem had not changed in size. Apparently he knew how to restrain himself. He continued for another minute or two, the only sound in the room his heavy breathing and the soft waterlike sound of skin slapping against skin; then he stopped.

"You see," he said. "It works O.K."

"But I didn't tell you to stop."

"But if I keep on . . . I mean . . . well, Christ, a man's going to . . ."

"A boy," I corrected.

"A boy's going to . . . to . . ."

"To what?"

"Get . . . excited."

"Go right ahead. I'd be amused to see what Mary-Ann sees in you."

Without another word, grimly, he set to work and continued for some time, sweating hard. But still we were denied the full glory. Some lengthening and thickening took place but not to the fullest degree.

"Is anything wrong?" I asked sweetly.

"I don't know." He gulped, trying to catch his breath. "It can't . . . won't . . ." He was incoherent at the double humiliation.

"Do you often have this problem with Mary-Ann?" I sounded as compassionate as Kay Francis, as warm as June Allyson.

"Never! I swear . . ."

"Five times in one night and now this! Really, you young boys are such liars."

"I wasn't lying. I just don't know what's wrong. . . ." He beat at himself as though through sheer force he could tap the well of generation. But it was no use. Finally I told him to stop. Then I took over, practicing a number of subtle pressures and frictions learned from Myron . . . all to no avail.

In a curious way the absence of an erection, though not part of the plan, gave me an unexpected thrill: to have so cowed my victim as to short-circuit his legendary powers as a stud was, psychologically, far more fulfilling than my original intention.

While I was vigorously shaking him, he made the long-expected move that would complete the drama, the holy passion of Myra Breckinridge.

"Do you . . ." He began tentatively, looking down at me and the loose-stemmed rose that I held in my hand.

"Do I what?"

"Do you want me to . . . well, to ball you?" The delivery was superb, as shy as a nubile boy requesting a first kiss.

I let go of him as though in horror. "Rusty! Do you know who you're talking to?"

"Yes, Miss Myra. I'm sorry. I didn't mean to offend you. . . ."

"What sort of woman do you think I am?" I took the heavy balls in my hand, as an offering. "These belong to Mary-Ann, and no one else, and if I ever catch you playing around with anybody else, I'll see that Mr. Martinson puts you away for twenty years."

He turned white. "I'm sorry. I didn't know. I thought maybe . . . the way you were . . . doing what you were doing. . . . I'm sorry, really." The voice stopped.

"You have every reason to be sorry." Again I let him go; the large balls swung back between his legs, and continued gently to sway, like a double pendulum. "In any case, if I had wanted you to—as you put it—'ball me,' it's very plain that you couldn't. As a stud, you're a disaster."

He flushed at the insult but said nothing. I was now ready for my master stroke. "However, as a lesson, I shall ball you."

He was entirely at sea. "Ball *me*? How?"

"Put out your hands." He did so and I bound them together with surgical gauze. Not for nothing had I once been a nurses' aide.

"What're you doing that for?" Alarm growing.

With a forefinger, I flicked the scrotal sac, making him cry out from shock. "No questions, my boy." When the hands were firmly secured, I lowered the examination table until it was just two feet from the floor. "Lie down," I ordered. "On your stomach."

Mystified, he did as he was told. I then tied his bound hands

148

to the top of the metal table. He was, as they say, entirely in my power. If I had wanted, I could have killed him. But my fantasies have never involved murder or even physical suffering for I have a horror of blood preferring to inflict pain in more subtle ways, destroying totally, for instance, a man's idea of himself in relation to the triumphant sex.

"Now then, up on your knees."

"But . . ." A hard slap across the buttocks put an end to all objections. He pulled himself up on his knees, legs tight together and buttocks clenched shut. He resembled a pyramid whose base was his head and white-socked feet, and whose apex was his rectum. I was now ready for the final rite.

"Legs wide apart," I commanded. Reluctantly, he moved his knees apart so that they lined up with the exact edges of the table. I was now afforded my favorite view of the male, the heavy rosy scrotum dangling from the groin above which the tiny sphincter shyly twinkled in the light. Carefully I applied lubricant to the mystery that even Mary-Ann has never seen, much less violated.

"What're you doing?" The voice was light as a child. True terror had begun.

"Now remember the secret is to relax entirely. Otherwise you could be seriously hurt."

I then pulled up my skirt to reveal, strapped to my groin, Clem's dildo which I borrowed yesterday on the pretext that I wanted it copied for a lamp base. Clem had been most amused.

Rusty cried out with alarm. "Oh, no! For God's sake, don't."

"Now you will find out what it is the girl feels when you play the man with her."

"Jesus, you'll split me!" The voice was treble with fear. As I approached him, dildo in front of me like the god Priapus personified, he tried to wrench free of his bonds, but failed. Then he did the next best thing, and brought his knees together in an attempt to deny me entrance. But it was no use. I spread him wide and put my battering ram to the gate.

For a moment I wondered if he might not be right about the

splitting: the opening was the size of a dime while the dildo was over two inches wide at the head and nearly a foot long. But then I recalled how Myron used to have no trouble in accommodating objects this size or larger, and what the fragile Myron could do so could the inexperienced but sturdy Rusty.

I pushed. The pink lips opened. The tip of the head entered and stopped.

"I can't," Rusty moaned. "Honestly I can't. It's too big."

"Just relax, and you'll stretch. Don't worry."

He made whatever effort was necessary and the pursed lips became a grin allowing the head to enter, but not without a gasp of pain and shock.

Once inside, I savored my triumph. I had avenged Myron. A lifetime of being penetrated had brought him only misery. Now, in the person of Rusty, I was able, as Woman Triumphant, to destroy the adored destroyer.

Holding tight to Rusty's slippery hips, I plunged deeper. He cried out with pain.

But I was inexorable. I pushed even farther into him, triggering the prostate gland, for when I felt between his legs, I discovered that the erection he had not been able to present me with had now, inadvertently, occurred. The size was most respectable, and hard as metal.

But when I plunged deeper, the penis went soft with pain, and he cried out again, begged me to stop, but now I was like a woman possessed, riding, riding, riding my sweating stallion into forbidden country, shouting with joy as I experienced my own sort of orgasm, oblivious to his staccato shrieks as I delved that innocent flesh. Oh, it was a holy moment! I was one with the Bacchae, with all the priestesses of the dark bloody cults, with the great goddess herself for whom Attis unmanned himself. I was the eternal feminine made flesh, the source of life and its destroyer, dealing with man as incidental toy, whose blood as well as semen is needed to make me whole!

There was blood at the end. And once my passion had spent itself, I was saddened and repelled. I had not meant actually to tear the tender flesh but apparently I had, and the withdrawing of my weapon brought with it bright blood. He did not stir as I washed him clean (like a loving mother), applying medicine to the small cut, inserting gauze (how often had I done this for Myron!). Then I unbound him.

Shakily, he stood up, rubbing tears from his swollen face. In silence he dressed while I removed the harness of the dildo and put it away in the attaché case.

Not until he was finally dressed did he speak. "Can I go now?"

"Yes. You can go now." I sat down at the surgical table and took out this notebook. He was at the door when I said, "Aren't you going to thank me for the trouble I've taken?"

He looked at me, face perfectly blank. Then, tonelessly, he murmured, "Thank you, ma'am," and went.

And so it was that Myra Breckinridge achieved one of the great victories for her sex. But one which is not yet entirely complete even though, alone of all women, I know what it is like to be a goddess enthroned, and all-powerful.

30

I sit now at the card table. Through the window I can see the turning chorus girl in front of the Château Marmont Hotel; only she is not turning. A power failure? are they making repairs? or is she at last being dismantled? The question takes on symbolic importance since she is, to me, Hollywood. She must never *not* be allowed to dominate the Strip.

Rusty did not appear at school today. I would have been disappointed if he had. But what did distress me was Mary-Ann's absence from Posture. She has never before missed one of my classes.

Discouraged and uneasy, I rang Miss Cluff to see if Mary-Ann had attended the Bell Telephone Hour class. She had not, "I haven't seen hide nor hair of her. But you know how girls are. It's probably her time. . . ." Bell-like laughter from Miss Cluff. Next I rang the girls' dormitory. The matron told me that Mary-Ann had not returned the previous evening, and she had already made a report to Buck.

I confess I was terrified. Had Rusty told her what had happened? I could not believe it. Masculine pride (no matter how damaged) would have prevented him. But he still could have told her *something* which had made her leave the school . . . and me. I had a sudden vision of them together in Mexico, growing marijuana, utterly happy. The thought was too depressing. Also, I reminded myself, impractical since he is on parole and may not leave L.A., much less cross the border.

Matters were not much helped when I received a call from Buck's office to see him at five. I found him looking altogether too pleased with himself. With him was a typical California type: a bronzed empty face with clear eyes and that vapid smile which the Pacific Ocean somehow manages to impress upon the lips of almost everyone doomed to live in any proximity to those tedious waters. It is fascinating how, in a single generation, stern New England Protestants, grim Iowans and keen New York Jews have all become entirely Tahitianized by that dead ocean with its sweet miasmic climate in which thoughts become dreams while perceptions blur and distinctions are so erased that men are women are men are nothing are everything are one. Gentlemen, the desire and the pursuit of the whole ends at Santa Monica!

The typical specimen was Charlie Flagler Junior, lawyer. He gave me the whitest of smiles, the firmest of handshakes and then, at Buck's insistence, he let me have it. "Mrs. Breckinridge, as you know, in representing my client, Mr. Loner, or any client, I—we must of course try to leave no stone unturned in order to—like make it *crystal clear* what their position is."

Buck clapped his hands together, as if in applause. Then he said, "I think, Myra, you should know that Charlie's dad and me have been pals for lo! these many years, ever since he handled me when I had that big row with the Blue Network."

"I guess we value Mr. Loner's account more than almost any single noncorporate account, not only for old times' sake—like Dad says—but because Buck Loner has a *reputation* in this town"—Charlie Flagler Junior's voice became very grave and solemn—"for being like a straight-shooter."

"For Christ's sake," I said, no doubt in the same tone that

Dr. Margaret Mead must have used in trying to extract a straight bit of folklore from *her* Polynesians, "stop gassing and tell me what lousy trick you're up to now."

Buck's face half shut; he looked pained. Charlie Flagler Junior gave me a curious look. I imagined him stretched out before me the way Rusty had been; a satisfying vision except, curiously enough, so complete was last night's experience that any repetition of it would be redundant, even in fantasy. I have accomplished what nature intended me to do and except for one last turn to the screw, I am complete.

"No lousy trick, Mrs. Breckinridge." The young lawyer wanted to appear grieved but the Polynesian face has only two expressions: joy and incomprehension. He looked quite stupid. "I simply must respect my client's wishes and defend his interests which in this case are your claim to like half the value of this Westwood property, due you as the alleged widow of his nephew."

"Alleged?" I was ready for battle.

Joy filled the brown Pacific face, as though a toasted breadfruit had been offered him after a long swim with Dorothy Lamour. "Alleged. The marriage certificate you gave us is an out-and-out forgery."

I was not as prepared to answer this charge as I thought I would be. The game is now becoming most tricky and dangerous. One false move and all will come to a dead halt, like the ominously stationary ten-times-life-size chorine outside my window. "Mr. Charlie Flagler Junior and you, Buck Loner, brother of Gertrude and cheerful thief, I am the heiress to half this property, and I am going to get it. So don't think for one moment you can hold out on me."

"Honey, we're not trying to keep what's yours from you." Buck was plaintive. "That's the last thing on our minds but we've got to make sure you really are entitled to it. I mean you could be some kind of impersonator, saying you are who you are."

"Gertrude gave you two hundred dollars back in Philadelphia when you were twenty years old to pay for the abortion of the daughter of the Rexall druggist you knocked up and refused to marry."

Buck turned white. The Polynesian remained brown. Buck cleared his throat, "I'm not saying you didn't know Gertrude and the boy well. Obviously you did . . ."

"The point is like this," said Charlie Flagler Junior, "you have to *prove* you were married. That's all."

"I shall prove it." I rose to go. The men rose, too, with a new respect. At least they don't underestimate their adversary. "Proof will arrive before the end of the week. Meanwhile, Uncle Buck, I shall list all the loans Gertrude made you over the years, and I shall expect repayment, with interest." I slammed the door as I left.

I have just talked to Dr. Montag in New York. He dithered. I was firm. "Randolph, you owe this to me. You owe this to Myron. I don't want to blackmail you emotionally but you also owe it to the insights we exchanged, the three of us, at the Blue Owl Grill. We made you just as you made us. Now we are at the crunch. . . ."

"The what?" His nervous wheezing often keeps him from hearing what others say.

" 'Crunch' is a word currently favored by the keener journalists. It means the showdown, the moment of truth. Well, this is the crunch, and I am appealing to you, not only as Myron's analyst and my dentist but as our only friend. Fly out here tomorrow."

"But, Myra, I can't. Your appeal reaches me at every level, there's no doubt about that. I am touched in every department from lower id, as your husband used to say, to upper superego, but there is the problem of my other patients. They need me. . . ."

"Randolph." I was peremptory. "I'll cut you in for ten percent of the take."

There was an alarming series of wheezes and coughs at the other end of the line. Then Dr. Montag said what sounded like "Between, Myra."

"Between what?"

"Fifteen!" he shouted from the Island of Manhattan. "Fifteen percent and I'm in L.A. tomorrow."

"Answered like a true Adlerian! *Fifteen it is!*" I knew my man. Many was the night that the three of us used to sit until the Blue Owl closed discussing Randolph's inordinate greed for pastry and money. It was—is—the most likable thing about him. With that taken care of, I can now

31

Life continues to support Myra Breckinridge in all her schemes to obtain uniqueness. As I write this, Mary-Ann is asleep in my bed (I have fixed up the daybed in here for myself). It is three in the morning. We have talked and wept together for five hours. I have never known such delight. Last night with Rusty was religious ecstasy; tonight a rebirth.

While I was writing in this notebook, there was a rap at the door. I opened it. Mary-Ann stood in the doorway, pale, bedraggled and carrying a Pan Am overnight zipper bag. "Miss Myra, I've got to talk to you. You're the only person I can." With that she burst into tears and I took her in my arms, reveling in the full rounded warmth of that body, so reminiscent of the early Lana Turner. In a curious way, though she is so much younger and more vulnerable than I, she suggests a mother figure to me, which is madness since in our relationship I am, necessarily, the one who is wise, the one who comforts and directs. I daresay my hatred of my own mother must have had some *positive* element in it since I am now able to feel genuine warmth for another woman, and a mere girl at that. I must discuss the matter thoroughly with Randolph.

Soon the sobbing ceased, and I poured her a glass of gin which she drank neat. This seemed to steady her.

"Rusty's gone again." She sat on the daybed, and blew her nose. Her legs are every bit as beautiful as Eleanor Powell's in the last reel of *Rosalie*, on those drums.

"Gone where?" I was about to say that any boy on parole is not apt to take a long trip, but I thought better of it.

"I don't know. It happened last night." She dried her eyes.

"Yes?" I was cautious. "You were with him last night?"

She nodded. "We were supposed to have dinner but he said you wanted to see him at ten. . . ."

"A routine chat." I was casual. "I'm sorry I picked such an odd hour and ruined your dinner but I was busy with Miss Cluff and . . ."

She was, happily, not interested in his visit to me. "Anyway he didn't pick me up till after eleven, and I've never seen him in such a bad mood . . ."

"Strange," I added to the official record, "he seemed quite cheerful when he left me. In fact, he thanked me profusely for the help I'd given him."

"I know you were nice to him. You always are—now. Anyway he didn't mention you. He just picked a fight with me, over nothing, and I got angry and then he said maybe I'd better go back to the dorm and not spend the night with him. He said he was . . ." she paused, tears beginning, "sick of me, sick of women, and wanted just to go off by himself. . . ."

"Sick of you or of women in general?" This was a key point.

"I don't know exactly what he said, I was so upset. Both, I guess."

Apparently I had done my work better than I expected.

"On top of that, he said he was feeling lousy and he'd pulled a muscle or something and it hurt him to sit down . . . oh, I don't know, he was just awful. But then I told him about the date I'd made for him, and that cheered him up a bit."

"What date?"

"You won't be mad at me?" She looked so frightened, young,

vulnerable that I wanted to hold her in my arms. "Of course not, dear." I was Janet Gaynor. "I could never be angry with you."

"You *are* a friend." She gave me a dim watery smile. "Well, I had got us both invited to Letitia Van Allen's rustic home at Malibu, in the Colony."

I sat up straight. *I* have never been invited to Letitia's house but then of course I have yet to be of any use to her as a purveyor of studs. Now poor Mary-Ann had fallen unwittingly into Letitia's trap. "Just how did this invitation come about?"

"Well, I was in her office and we were talking about this date she'd made for me with that record company and then, I don't know, the conversation got around to Rusty and she asked to see a picture of him, and I showed her the ones I always carry and she said he was very handsome and had star quality and I asked her if she wanted to meet him . . . oh, I know you didn't want him to talk to her until June . . ."

"It would have been better *after* his closed-circuit TV performance. Anyway the damage is done. So you took him to Malibu last night."

She nodded bleakly. "There were a dozen people there, all so successful and rich. One was a star. You know, the one who's in that television series that was just canceled by CBS, *Riptide*? He was nice but drunk. Anyway Letitia made a big fuss over Rusty, who was rude as could be to her and to everybody else. I've never seen him act like that before."

"Perhaps he had something on his mind."

"Well, whatever it is it was eating him up, for suddenly he gets up and says to Miss Van Allen. 'I got to go. This isn't my scene.' And left just like that, *without me*. I was never so embarrassed and hurt. Anyway Miss Van Allen couldn't have been nicer and said she wouldn't hold it against Rusty and since it was so late I'd better sleep over, which I did, though I didn't sleep much, with that boy from *Riptide* banging on the door all night."

I poured her more gin which she drank. Her spirits improved. "Anyway, today I called Rusty at the place where he's staying and they said he didn't come home last night, and then I called the Academy and they said he didn't go to any of his classes, and then I got scared that maybe he was killed or something so I called the police but they didn't know anything. Then I waited in the dorm all evening for him to call and when finally he didn't, I came here. . . ." Her voice had become quavery again.

"You did the right thing," I said. "And I want you to stay here with me until everything's straightened itself out."

"You're so good, Miss Myra!"

"Not at all. Now don't worry about Rusty. Nothing's happened to him. He's probably in a bad mood because of the situation he's in." Then I told her in detail about Rusty's Mexican adventures. "So you see he's on parole and that means the probation officer must always know where he is. So if Rusty ever really did disappear, Uncle Buck and I would be the first to know about it."

Mary-Ann frowned, still absorbing what I had told her. I gave her more gin which she drank as though it was her favorite drink, Seven-Up. "He promised me he was never going to see any of those boys he used to hang out with."

"Well, he's young. Let him have his fun. As long as he stays out of jail, of course."

She shook her head, suddenly grim. "It's them or me, I told him."

"And of course it will be you." I was soothing as I began to spread and arrange my net. "Don't worry. Now lie down and rest while we chat."

She gave me a grateful smile and stretched out on the daybed. It was all I could do not to sit beside her and caress those extraordinary breasts, made doubly attractive for me since they are Rusty's to do with as he likes, or so he believes. Having raped his manhood, I shall now seduce his girl. Beyond that, ambition stops and godhood begins.

We talked of everything. She is totally in love with Rusty,

though shaken by what has happened as well as by my revelation of his Mexican capers. She has had only three lovers in her life, all male. Lesbianism is repulsive to her. But she did agree, after the fourth glass of gin, that she felt entirely secure and warm with me, and that one woman could offer another, under the right circumstances, great reassurance and affection.

Finally, slightly drunk, I took her into the bedroom and helped her to undress. The breasts are *better* than Lana Turner's in *They Won't Forget*. Smooth and white with large rosy nipples (in a curious way they are an exaggerated version of Rusty's own), their shape is marvelously subtle . . . at least what I could see of them, for she promptly pulled on her nightdress and only then removed her panties, hiding from me that center of Rusty's sexual being in which he has so many times (but never again if I can help it!) spent himself.

The thought that soon I shall know intimately the body *he* knew so made me tremble that I did not dare embrace her good night but instead blew her a kiss from the door, shut it, and promptly rang Mr. Martinson, who was angry at being waked up. But he did tell me that Rusty had decided to leave the Academy and take a permanent job with a firm that sells foreign cars on Melrose Avenue; however, when I asked where Rusty was staying, Mr. Martinson told me that it was none of my business. Needless to say, I told him where and how to head in, and hung up.

Now I must find some way of breaking the news to Mary-Ann. This will be tricky because under no circumstances must they be allowed to resume their love affair. That is at an end.

A miraculous omen! I just looked out the window at the enormous woman and she is again turning gaily upon her axis, beautiful and omnipotent, the very image of deity!

32

Dr. Montag is sitting on the daybed reading my description of the conquest of Rusty. I sit at the card table, writing these lines, waiting for his comment. Tomorrow we meet Buck and his lawyers. The showdown.

Randolph is wheezing through clouds of pipe smoke. He is frowning. I suppose he disapproves. Yet of all people he should understand what it is that I have done. He looks simply God-awful. He thinks he's in Hawaii. He is wearing a flowered short-sleeved shirt that hangs outside his shiny black rabbinical trousers and

33

Randolph has returned to his motel for a nap; he is still not used to the change in time and wants to be at his best for tomorrow's meeting. We have prepared two lines of attack; at the worst, one will succeed.

The description of my life's triumph did not entirely please him which, naturally, does not please *me,* and that is what matters.

"Am I to understand all this really happened?" Ashes fell upon the page which I snatched from his hand. Randolph's pipe often produces cinders as well as smoke, for he has a tendency to blow through the stem when ill at ease.

"Exactly," I said. "At least you'll have to agree that I've got him down in black and white, once and for all, every detail, every hair, every pimple."

"You've got his *outside,* yes." Judiciously he arranged a screen of smoke between us. "But that's just Rusty's skin, you haven't shown his inside."

"I haven't shown his inside, dear Randolph, because I don't know it. And, if I may say so, it is presumptuous for anyone to even pretend he can know what another person's interior is really like, short of an autopsy. The only thing we can ever know for certain is skin, and I now know his better than he does himself."

"Possibly. Possibly." Randolph still appeared distressed.

"In fact," I improvised, "nothing matters except what is visible to the eye. For me to write, as I shall when you go, that you *looked* distressed at this moment could very easily be a projection on my part, and misreading of your mood. To be accurate, I should simply write that while you were reading my notes there was a double crease between your brows, which is not usual, since . . ."

"It is *not* a projection to say that I am distressed. And up to a point we can, more or less, assume that we know what others are feeling, at least at the more accessible levels of consciousness. At this moment, I am feeling a certain distress for that young man, a certain male empathy. After all, it is a most unpleasant thing to be assaulted anally and I think we can both assume that he was not happy, no matter how mute the skin."

"I agree and that's why in my review of what happened, I not only recorded his conversation but tried to give what I believed were his feelings when he spoke. Yet I realize that at best my interpretation is entirely subjective, and perhaps false. Since I wanted to frighten and humiliate him, I chose to regard his groans and grunts as symptoms of fright and humiliation."

"Which, no doubt, they were. Although we must never rule out the possibility that he was enjoying himself."

"If that is true, my life's work has failed." I was very grave. I have never been more serious.

"Or succeeded in ways you do not yet undersand. In any case, his girlfriend is living with you, isn't she?"

"Yes, she came to me. Of all the people she knows, I am the one she turned to. The irony is perfect." So is my delight!

"Does she know what you've done?"

"Of course not."

"What will happen if she finds out?"

"I have no intention of telling her. As for Rusty, I don't think either of us needs a degree in psychiatry" (Randolph looked momentarily unhappy; he has only an M.A. in psychology) "to know that he will never tell anyone what was done to him."

"Perhaps not." Randolph's pipe went off again. One bright cinder burned a hole in the carpet. "But aren't you afraid he may want compensation for what you did, particularly if he is as healthy and 'normal' as you think?"

"What sort of compensation?"

"He might take *physical* revenge on you. Do to you what you did to him."

"Rape? Not very likely. He's much too terrified. No, I've heard the last of him, except in connection with Mary-Ann . . ."

Randolph listened carefully as I told him how I planned, with every appearance of love and affection, to possess Mary-Ann in order that the cycle be completed.

"What cycle?"

"The justification of Myron's life." I was prompt. I have intellectualized everything, as I always do, to the despair of Randolph, who is, despite all his modish pretensions and quibbling subterfuges, entirely emotional, in many ways a dead ringer for Jean Hersholt. "By acting out what was done to him, I exalt him—the idea of him, anyway—and also avenge him . . ."

"*Avenge* him? In what way? The Myron I knew was hardly a victim. Rather the contrary."

"No, he was victim. I know that now. But no matter what he really was . . ."

"A marvelous man . . ."

"How you enjoy throwing that in my face!" I was stung and deeply hurt, as I always am, by reminders that Randolph worshipped Myron and cannot, at heart, bear me.

"Now, now you must not project. When I praise Myron, I praise *him*. I don't denigrate you."

"*You* are the one projecting now. But, in any case, once I have completed my seduction, I shall be free of all guilt toward Myron and for Myron. I shall be a new woman, literally new, something unique under the sun."

"But who and what will you be?"

I answered vehemently, at length, but said nothing, for, as usual, Randolph, in his blundering way, has touched upon the dilemma's horn: I have no clear idea as to my ultimate identity once every fantasy has been acted out with living flesh. All that I do know is that I shall be freed of obsession and, in this at least, be like no one else who ever lived.

Randolph then departed for his nap to be followed by a trip to Disneyland. So here I sit, making these notes. Suddenly ill at ease. Why? The telephone rings

34

That was Letitia. She came straight to the point. "Rusty's living with me. He's down at the beach house right now."

"Letitia!" That was the best I could do. Not even in my wildest dreams had I ever connected the two of them, particularly after Mary-Ann's description of Rusty's rudeness to Letitia on the famous night.

"All I can say, Myra, is you sure know how to pick 'em. That is the best Grade A stud I have ever had, and as rumor hath doubtless had it here at the heart of the Industry, Letitia Van Allen has made many a trip to the old corral."

I could think of nothing but Rusty's soft rose wobbling childishly in my hand. "Is he really the *very* best stud of all?"

"The very best, and I've you to thank for it. When I saw how you had conned that girlfriend of his into bringing him to my house, I said to myself: Myra Breckinridge is a *pal!*"

I was startled but delighted at being given full credit for maneuvering Rusty into Letitia's orbit. "Of course I knew you'd enjoy meeting him." I was neutral, not wanting to betray the fact that it was Mary-Ann I had wanted Letitia to help, not Rusty.

"He's *everything* I like!" Letitia roared into the telephone. "In fact, the moment I clapped eyes on him, I said, 'God, Letitia, but that's it!'"

"But Mary-Ann told me he behaved abominably at your house."

"Natch! That's what I like. He was sullen, sneering, raging inside . . ."

"I'm sure he was." I purred with secret satisfaction.

"But I knew by the way that he insulted everybody and stormed out of the house that I'd soon be seeing him again. And I did. The next day he came to the office and apologized, still sullen, of course, but wanting to make up . . . said he'd had a fight with the girl, as if I didn't know, and could I get him work. So I said you bet I can, and signed him to a five-year representational talent contract. Then I rang up Maddox Motors and got him a job as a mechanic. He was grateful, and showed it, right then and there, on the old four-poster. That chenille bedspread will never be the same again."

"And it was really marvelous?" I was genuinely curious to see how Rusty would perform after my disciplinary session.

"I thought, Myra," Letitia's words were measured and awed, "that he would *kill* me. I have never known anyone so masterful. He threw me on the bed and struck me repeatedly. Yes, *struck* Letitia Van Allen who *never* goes that route but did this time. I'm still black and blue and totally happy, all thanks to you!"

"You exaggerate." Rusty's compensation with Letitia for what he had suffered at my hands will fascinate Randolph. "But did he . . . well, say anything about leaving school, about me?"

"Not a word, except that he was sick of being treated like a kid and wanted to get to work. He won't talk about you at all. Did you ever lay him?"

"Not in any classic way, no. But what does he say about Mary-Ann?"

"That's why I'm calling you. He feels guilty. I can tell. Now, let's put our cards on the table. I want him all to myself as long as possible which won't be very long, since once he starts making a living he'll be off with the cute young chicks, leaving poor old

Letitia to her Scotch and casting couch. But for now I'm hanging on to him for dear life. So what do we do to keep Miss Pieface out of our lives?"

I told her exactly how it could be done . . . and will be done tonight! Thanking me profusely, and vowing eternal friendship, Letitia hung up.

35

Three in the morning again. Joy and despair, equally mixed, as I watch, hypnotized, the turning statue, and think for the first time how lonely she must be out there, ten times life-size, worshipped but not loved, like me.

As soon as Mary-Ann returned from school, I suggested that we drive down to the beach in my rented Chrysler and watch the sunset. She seemed to like the idea. Though she was plainly fretting over Rusty, she did not mention him once, as we drove along the Pacific Highway, bumper to bumper with the rush-hour crowd as it crawled slowly between the dull sea and the brown crumbly hills of fine shifting dust, forever dropping houses into the sea. This coastal region is quite inhospitable to man. What we have done is colonize the moon, and so are lunatic.

To amuse Mary-Ann, I acted out the entire plot of *Marriage Is a Private Affair*. She was very much amused, particularly when I quoted Parker Tyler to her. We both agreed that his explication of that paradigmatic wartime film is altogether wonderful.

Just as the red-smog sun was vanishing into the olive-drab

sea, I turned casually into the private road of the Malibu Beach Colony, a number of opulent beach houses jammed together between road and sea; many are occupied by stars of the first and current (if that is not a contradiction!) magnitude.

"But this is where Miss Van Allen lives!" Until then, Mary-Ann had been indifferent to her surroundings, doubtless conducting some inner dialogue with Rusty even as I spoke of James Craig and the great days.

"Really? Where?" In fact, I did not know which was Letitia's house. Mary-Ann indicated a gray clapboard Provincetown-style house. "Then why don't we drop in and say hello?"

"Oh, no! I couldn't. Not after last time. Not after the way Rusty talked to her. I'd be too uncomfortable."

"Nonsense." I parked in front of the darkened house. The light from the sea was now very faint. "I'm sure she's forgiven him. She's used to artistic temperament. After all, that's her business."

"But he was so awful, and I looked so silly."

"Don't be a goose!" I took her hand and led her to the door and rang the bell. "Besides, this will be good for your career." To this argument, the only response was acquiescence.

From inside the house I could hear a Benny Goodman record (Letitia belongs in fact to the generation to which I belong in spirit). No one, however, answered the doorbell.

"She's out." Mary-Ann was relieved. "Let's go."

"But I hear music. Come on." I opened the front door and led the reluctant Mary-Ann into a large darkened room that looked onto the sea. Silhouetted against the last light of the day, two figures were dancing, intertwined.

According to plan, I switched on the light. Rusty and Letitia leapt apart; they wore bathing suits (marvelously reminiscent of Garfield and Crawford in *Humoresque*).

"What the hell!" exclaimed Letitia, simulating anger.

"Darling, I couldn't be sorrier!" I simulated alarm.

Both Rusty and Mary-Ann were genuinely shocked; but where she was hurt, he was truculent.

It was Mary-Ann who made the first move. "Where," she asked him in a quavering voice, "have you been?"

But Letitia did not allow him to answer. "Come on, children, let's all have a nice drink!" She crossed to the sanctuary of the bar at the end of the room opposite the plate-glass window, black now from the light within.

Rusty simply stared at Mary-Ann. Not once did he look at me.

". . . Then," said Letitia comfortably, "we can sit down and discuss this like adults." (Bette and Miriam in *Old Acquaintance*). "Who wants what?" But no one answered her.

Then Mary-Ann repeated, "Where have you been all this time?"

To which Rusty responded in a clear hard voice, "What are you doing with *her*?" And he gave me a look of absolute hate.

"Myra's my friend." Mary-Ann's voice was faint.

Letitia gargled some Scotch and then said hoarsely, "Rusty's been staying here while I get him launched over at Fox with this new series. You sure you don't want a drink, honey? Or you, Myra?"

"Are you *living* with this woman?" Mary-Ann was still unable to comprehend the situation.

"Now, dear, don't get upset." Letitia was soothing. "Rusty and I do have a great deal in common but neither one of us would want to hurt you for the world." She gave Rusty a shot of whiskey which he gulped, eyes still on Mary-Ann. "In fact, he was all for telling you this morning but I thought we should wait. Anyway now that the cat's out of the bag . . ."

"It's all my fault, Letitia." I was humble. "The whole thing."

"No, dear. Don't blame yourself. It's probably for the best. Personally I like everything in the open. That's the way I am. And that's why I'm here to tell all the world that I'm proud to be in love with Rusty, and proud that he loves me!"

With a wail, Mary-Ann fled back to the car. When Rusty started to follow her, Letitia's arm darted out and held him back. "She'll be all right. She's got Myra." That stopped the young man. He made no further move to follow the girl.

Then Letitia crossed to me. She was thrilling, every inch of her a great actress on the order of Frances Dee or Ann Dvorak. She took my hands in hers and kissed my cheek. "Be kind to the girl."

"I will, Letitia. You know I will."

"When she's older, she'll understand how these things just happen and that we are all of us simply putty in the hands of the great potter." The metaphor was mixed, but the delivery was bravura. "Rusty and I need each other. That's all there is. A man, a woman . . . What else? It's Kismet." She let go my hands. "Good night, Myra."

I said good night and followed Mary-Ann into the darkness. She was in the car, weeping. I comforted her as best I could which was hardly at all since I am a nervous driver and need both hands on the wheel when driving through traffic, particularly along Sunset Boulevard at night.

Back at the apartment, Mary-Ann recovered sufficiently to finish the bottle of gin. But her mood did not improve. She is shattered. She cannot understand why Rusty has deserted her or what he sees in Letitia. This was of course my cue to point out that for an ambitious young man like Rusty to be taken up by Letitia is a sure way to stardom.

"But he *swore* he'd never do anything like that. He's just not that kind of a boy . . ."

"Apparently he is. I mean, let's face it, he is *living* with her." Since this brought on more tears, as I intended, I took her in my arms. She wept into my neck. Never in my life have I felt so entirely warm and contented.

"Forget him," I whispered into a soft pink ear that smelled of Lux toilet soap.

Suddenly she sat up and dried her eyes. "I could murder him!" Her voice had gone cello with rage.

"Now, now you mustn't be angry with the boy." I was supremely anodyne. "After all, that's the way he is. You can't change people. Just think how lucky you are to have learned all this *now* instead of after you were married, and had children."

"I'll never marry! I hate men." She got shakily to her feet (she was quite drunk), and made her way to the bedroom.

I helped her to undress—for once she really needed help. She was grateful for my attentions which I managed to make discreet, despite the turmoil caused in me whenever those marvelous breasts are unveiled. Then she threw herself onto the bed, and as I pulled off her stockings she pointed her feet like a ballerina. But before I could remove her panties, she pulled the sheet over herself and said, "I'm so tired. The room's spinning around. . . ." Her eyes shut.

I turned out the light and got into bed. Shyly, I put out my hand beneath the sheet and touched the nearer breast. She sighed in her tipsy sleep. "Oh, Rusty . . ." That was chilling. I took the other breast in my hand, and she woke up. "Oh, Myra! You felt just like Rusty." But she pushed my hand away. "He's gentle, too."

"Gentle?" I recalled what Letitia had said. "I thought he was violent!"

"Whatever gave you that idea?" She mumbled, still half asleep. "It's because he was so gentle I loved him. He never grabs you like other boys. . . ."

If nothing else, I have changed at least one young man's sexual performance, and for the good—at least the good of Letitia. From now on Rusty will continue to take out his hatred of me on other women, never realizing to what extent he is really pleasing them. It is ironic what I have inadvertently accomplished. Wanting to tame for all time the archetypal male, I have created something ten times as masculine in the classic sense as what I started with. All in all, not the desired effect but perhaps, like Columbus, I have stumbled on a new world.

I caressed Mary-Ann's breasts, which she allowed . . . but only for a moment; then she turned away from me. "You are an angel, Myra, and I really love you, I do. But I just can't . . . you know . . ."

"Of course I know, dear." And I do; yet I am still profoundly hurt at being rejected.

174

"If only you were a man or there was a man like you, I'd really fall, I would—but not like this, even with you."

This froze me, turned me to stone.

But why should I care? After all, the silkiness of her body, the tautness of the skin, the firmness of the flesh is neither more nor less appetizing to me than Rusty's body since, in the final analysis (where I am now marooned), a girl is neither more nor less attractive than a boy and I have, God knows, possessed the boy. Yet taking all this into account, there is something about Mary-Ann's wholeness that excites me. There is a mystery to be plumbed, though whether or not it is in her or in myself or in us both I do not know. I did extract a certain pleasure from stroking the body that Rusty had loved, but that victory has already begun to pale. He no longer exists for me. Only the girl he loved matters.

Fortunately, she was compassionate enough to allow me to cradle her in my arms until she fell asleep. Then when she began softly to snore, obedient to her wishes, I got out of bed and returned to the living room where now I sit at the card table, drinking gin and tonic, writing these lines, too disturbed for sleep.

My head is spinning with fatigue. I must have Mary-Ann but only if she wants me, and that is impossible as things are now. I've just tried to ring Randolph but he gave instructions to the motel operator that he was not to be awakened until morning, the bastard! He knew that I would need to talk to him tonight. Obviously Disneyland was too much for him.

36

Buck's office. I sit at his desk. Randolph sits in the big chair beneath the portrait of Elvis Presley. Buck and his lawyer have gone into the next room to take a telephone call from New York.

As soon as they were out of the room, Randolph wanted to talk but I motioned for him to be quiet. The room is bugged, like everything out here. So Randolph now sits wheezing softly, chewing the stem of his pipe and staring out the window. I write these lines for something to do.

We've shaken them, no doubt of that. But I'm still not certain whether or not they will call our bluff.

Randolph presented them with a signed affidavit, duly notarized, swearing that he had witnessed my wedding to Myron in Monterrey, Mexico. Up until the very last moment I thought I would have trouble with Randolph. Fortunately his greed finally convinced him that he should do the right thing, despite the risk involved. Nevertheless, he is nervous as a cat. So am I.

Buck was true to form. "It was a real nice gesture of your'n, Doc, to come out here and help out this li'l ol' gal." More than ever was Buck, revoltingly, the Singin' Shootin' Cowboy, so inferior in every way to Hoot Gibson. "Naturally we want to do the right thing by her."

"Then cut the cackle," I said firmly, "and hand over the three hundred fifty G's which all of our lawyers now agree is my adjusted share of the property."

"Certainly, Mrs. Breckinridge," said Charlie Flagler Junior. "Just as soon as we get final word, any minute now, from our New York office which will like clear up one final detail, it's all yours because," he turned to Randolph, "we are not about to question the probity of such a well-known person and author like Dr. Montag."

"Thank you," I answered for Randolph, who looked gloomy as he always does when someone praises him (his father withheld all praise during Randolph's formative years and so today he can never accept any compliment without suspecting that it is loaded, as this one of course was).

"Right here," said Buck, holding up a check written on the Bank of America, Beverly Hills Branch, "I've got the check, all made out to you and everything."

Both Randolph and I felt a good deal better at the sight of the loot: three hundred and fifty thousand dollars is more than enough to finance me for the next few years while I finish Myron's work and begin my own. Yes, I have decided to make an investigation in *depth* of the problem of communication in the post-McLuhan world. Each day that I spend in the company of the students makes me more than ever aware that a new world is being born without a single reliable witness except me. I alone have the intuition as well as the profound grasp of philosophy and psychology to trace for man not only what he is but what he must become, once he has ceased to be confined to a single sexual role, to a single person . . . once he has become free to blend with others, to exchange personalities with both men and women, to play out the most elaborate of dreams in a world where there will soon be no limits to the human spirit's play. As I have been goddess, so others can be whatever they want in this vast theatre we call the world where all bodies and all minds will one day be at the disposal of everyone, and no one will read books for that is a solitary activity like going to the bathroom alone (it is the proliferation of private bathrooms, which has, more than anything else, created modern man's sense of alienation from others of his kind: our ancestors bathed and shat together and, all in all, relished the sharing of their common natural functions) or like making love alone if there are others available to share the body's pleasures. I see this new world whose prophetess I am as clearly as I see this page on which I scribble random notes while waiting for Buck and Charlie Flagler Junior to return from their telephoning in the next office.

I have made up my mind to continue teaching here, if Buck will have me . . . which I doubt. Yet I must make the effort to charm him, if it is not too late, for not only am I able to observe and learn from the students but they in turn profit from me. Without the Academy, I would have to invent an equivalent, a place in which to shape the minds of the young, particularly the boys who crave discipline. Yet, oddly enough, since that night of nights in the infirmary all my desires to dominate the male have been—if not satisfied—in abeyance, a true breakthrough, according to Randolph, though he still believes that I went too far and may have damaged Rusty's capacity to love women, to which I responded, "That is exactly what I wanted to do, to teach him fear."

"But why? Why not teach him love?" There are times when Randolph is singularly dense.

"Because only through a traumatic shock, through terrifying and humiliating him, could I hope to change his view of what is proper masculine behavior. To keep him from breeding, and so adding to the world's overpopulation, I was forced to violate everything he has been taught to regard as sacred, including the sanctity of his tiny back door. . . ."

Randolph looked suddenly queasy. "Please, Myra, you know how any *explicit* reference to the anal upsets me. The fault is mine, or weakness I should say," he added quickly, anticipating one of my sharp rejoinders. "But tell me, is there any evidence that your tormenting of him has had any effect at all, good or bad?"

"He quarreled with Mary-Ann . . ."

"A passing fit of ill-temper . . ."

"Not passing. He's left her for Letitia Van Allen." Candid as I always am with Randolph, I have not yet told him the entire story of my maneuvering to keep Rusty and Mary-Ann apart. There is evidence that Rusty is still in love with Mary-Ann. Fortunately she will not, in her present mood, have anything to do with him and I am certain that as long as she is with me I can prolong that mood for quite some time. Also, the fact that Mary-Ann is living with the woman who raped him will unconsciously identify her with me in Rusty's mind; if nothing else, this connection should help to maintain the current distance between the lovers. "And from what Letitia tells me, his lovemaking has been dramatically improved as a result of what I did to him."

"How would you know? He never made love to you."

"Mary-Ann has told me that he was always extremely gentle with her . . . she has a childhood trauma and cannot bear rough lovemaking and so, in time, will be drawn to women who are gentle. But with Letitia, he is a rampaging bull, knocking her about and otherwise getting back at me through her, to her delight of course."

"Interesting" was all that Randolph had to say on the subject. But I can tell that he is impressed at what I have accomplished even though, being a Jew and a dentist, he can never wholeheartedly accept my new order for the human race since the *fluidity* which I demand of the sexes is diametrically opposed to Mosaic solidity. Yet I am right, for it is demonstrably true that desire can take as many shapes as there are containers. Yet what one pours into those containers is always the same inchoate human passion, entirely lacking in definition until what holds it shapes it. So let us break the world's pots, and allow the stuff of desire to flow and intermingle in one great viscous sea. . . .

The door just opened. I keep my head down, continuing to write, pretending to be occupied and not at all eager. From the corner of my eye I can see two human sections approach. One section is brown (Buck) and one is blue (Charlie Flagler Junior). I don't look up. Buck says: "Myron Breckinridge is *not* dead."

BUCK LONER REPORTS—
Recording Disc No. 808—
1 April

        Oh God I dont know if I can stand it
dont know if I can go on its just not worth it reminder cancel
masseuse for rest of week period paragraph they just left I dont
know what to do not that theres anything I can do caught by
the short hairs by the fickle finger of fate we thought we had
them when this detective in New York came up with absolute
proof that that fag nephew of mine was not dead because there
never was any death certificate issued and New York City is a
place where you cant screw around with that sort of thing unlike
down old Mexico way well Myra who had been sitting at my
desk pretending to write letters sat up real smart and said quote
I say hes dead and that means hes dead to which statement
Charlie Flagler Junior replies thinking he has got her over the
barrel at last not knowing its his turn inside the barrel quote its
not what you say Mrs Breckinridge its what the police and the
city records say and they say your husband is alive and so his

will cant be probated unquote well she smiled this funny smile and says quote the body was never found thats true but he was drowned while cruising the Staten Island ferry unquote there is says Flagler Junior not one iota of evidence he is dead so we are not paying you one single penny until your husband shows up to collect his share of Mrs Gertrude Percy Breckinridges estate unquote then Myra looks at that fat Jew doctor who is blowing ashes all over my brand new wall to wall carpeting and she says I quote Randolph I guess this is the moment of truth unquote and he nods and allows that maybe shes right and then so help me god she stands up and hikes up her dress and pulls down her goddam panties and shows us this scar where cock and balls should be and says quote Uncle Buck I am Myron Breckinridge unquote period paragraph I like to have fainted at the sight not to mention the news Flagler Junior just stood there his mouth wide open then Myra or Myron says quote Randolph can testify to all this because he was my analyst before the operation which killed Myron and gave birth to me Myra unquote the Doc agreed saying I quote I should also add that I never approved of this operation but Myron was my friend as well as patient and so when I saw that there was nothing I could do to talk him out of this extreme gesture I arranged for the best surgeon in Copenhagen to perform the operation two years ago this spring unquote by then Flagler Junior had got back some of his cool I dont he said quote believe one word of this story so whoever you are you may have been a man once but how do we know that that man was Buck Loners nephew Myron question mark unquote well that bitch was ready for that one she opens her handbag with a smirk and says I quote we had two plans Uncle Buck one was to get you to accept me as Myrons widow the other was to prove to you that I used to be Myron here are Myrons fingerprints from the FBI when he was fingerprinted as a small boy while visiting the nations capital with a Boy Scout troop you are free at any time to check these prints with my own unquote well thats the ball game I said to Flagler Junior who still made noises about how did we know the prints were the same and not just another bluff so I said I accept the fact that this is my nephew Myron with his balls cut off like a year old steer God help us all end quote why Uncle Buck said that thing quote I am going to kiss you unquote and Buck Loner who has never been kissed by a man except by Leo Carrillo in a flick and is all male as the East West Home Massage Service can almost daily testify allowed himself to be kissed by that goddam thing that creep that capon oh screams Myron after he has got his goddam lipstick all over my ear I knew wed be great friends one day ever since I used to see every single picture you ever made and wrote you all those fan letters yes I said I sure remember those letters and I told Gertrude that you were ob viously bright as they come so now Myron no no no it says to me Im Myra Myron is dead as a doornail why when I lost those ugly things it was like a ship losing its anchor and Ive been sailing ever since havent I Randolph free as a bird and perfectly happy in being the most extraordinary woman in the world un quote well what can you say to that question mark I said nothing but just handed her the check which she put in her handbag Ill cash it this afternoon he she said oh he she was bright as can be all smiles now that the moolah has been handed over but then on top of that she delivers the whammy quote you know Uncle Buck we make a wonderful team together you and I and so I thought if you didnt mind that Id just keep on teaching here for the rest of the year after all youve got to admit that Ive done well and now that Letitia Van Allen is my best girl friend I can help the students achieve real stardom end quote well I tried to be as polite as possible under the circumstances and so I said quote Myron Myra that is a wonderful thing of you to offer me your services here and theres no doubt about it but that youre a crackerjack teacher a little strict maybe and sometimes maybe a mite too sharp in what you say but all in all youve been a real asset to the Academy as I am the first to admit only thing is weve got two former teachers returning who have like tenure and one wants to take over Posture and the other Empathy well she was not about to be conned I quote apparently what youre trying to say Myra said in this awful low voice she sometimes uses that now I recognize is a mans voice quote is that you dont want me here at all end quote now Myron Myra I said thats not true only with these two coming back but I was interrupted again when Myron came up to me and grabbed me by the collar that little bastard is strong as they come ball less or not listen Buck he says tough as nails quote if you dont give me a job I am going to announce to the world that Buck Loners nephew became his niece two years ago in Copenhagen and that will fix your wagon in this town unquote thats blackmail says Flagler Junior but nobody paid him any mind OK Myra I said you win end quote then she was all smiles again I knew youd do the right thing Uncle Buck and I can help you I really can Jesus God what am I going to do now with this mad freak taking over my life and running the Academy that I built up on dreams and hopes which she believes in destroying by telling everybody whats wrong with him if I could get away with it I would kill her strike that period paragraph

37

Tomorrow is moving day. I have rented a house just above
Santa Monica Canyon. A superb view of the Pacific Palisades
somewhat compensates for the inevitable view of that despicable
body of water, drowning the horizon to the west and all Asia.

So now I sit for the last time looking out upon the giant
turning woman who holds her sombrero like a benediction over
those who pass beneath her on the Strip.

I am not at all certain what to do about Mary-Ann. I know
that I want her to live with me always. I know that I want to
possess her entirely, body as well as mind; yet I puzzle myself,
and Randolph has been no help at all. He has, incidentally,
decided to stay on for one more week but of course that one
week will become a lifetime. He is made for Hollywood and
Hollywood is made for him, particularly now that he has discovered the Will Wright Ice Cream Parlors.

This morning Randolph again challenged my theory of sex.
He maintains that the desire to possess another person's body
simply as a means of achieving power is only one part of an
infinitely complex response. To a point, I agree with him. It is

of course true that, power aside, a certain amount of tenderness
is necessary in human relations. Myron never understood this
and it is possible that no man really can. Yet we women are
instinctively tender, even when we are achieving total dominion.
As a woman, I was touched by Rusty's tears. I even experienced
a maternal warmth while tidying up his poor bloody bottom.
That is woman's role, to make the wound and then to heal it.
Not for nothing do the earliest of myths depict us as Fate itself,
attending the male from swaddling clothes to winding sheet.
But there has been nothing in my experience which has quite
prepared me for Mary-Ann. Of course she is unique in her
charm, her beauty, her womanliness. I have never known a girl
who could arouse in me so many conflicting emotions. Even the
uterine mysteries, so deplored by Myron, are now for me the
be-all and end-all, the center to which one must return and not
simply in search of Rusty's phallic track but for the sake of the
journey itself to the very source of life.

We had dinner tonight with Letitia at Scandia, an excellent
restaurant on the Strip where Scandinavian food is served to a
most elegant clientele, among whom I counted four bona fide
stars of the Forties.

It took me an entire day to talk Mary-Ann into having dinner
with Letitia, whom she regards as "the other woman." She only
agreed when I assured her that Letitia was the one being used
by Rusty, not the other way around. Letitia and I had agreed
on this approach when I saw her briefly this afternoon at the
office. The poor woman's arm was in a sling but otherwise she
was in splendid form. "*He* sprained it last night!" she exclaimed
fondly. "I thought he was going to break every bone in my
body!"

"And you really enjoy that?" It seemed to me incredible
that a fellow goddess could endure such treatment from a
mere man.

"I never knew what sex was until that little bastard moved
in. Four, five times a night on the floor, on the beach, in the
damned bathtub!" She looked misty at the recollection. My own

experience of that small limp rose was obviously not the entire truth.

Then Letitia congratulated me on my appointment as co-director of the Academy. The announcement appeared in all the trade papers last Monday and so I am now, to my amusement, a figure in the world of show biz—which of course has only the most shadowy of connections with the world of mythic films.

"Yes, Uncle Buck and I seem to be getting on better." Buck has, in fact, completely surrendered and for the past week I have been running the Academy. As a result, morale is infinitely higher at every level. Even Dark Laughter found creative some of my suggestions for including Dionysian elements in his Atavistic Rhythm class. Morning, noon and night I am Rosalind Russell, efficient girl executive, and the students are the better for my constant brisk encouragement.

I came to the point. "As you know, Mary-Ann is living with me. Now don't smile like that, nothing dykey has happened or will. But I do feel responsible for the poor kid. And that's why I'd like to know just what Rusty is going to do about her."

"Not a damned thing if I can help it." Letitia was hard as nails. "I'm hanging onto that stud for as long as I can."

"That suits me. But what about him?"

"Mr. Martinson!" Letitia gave a laugh which started out to be tinkling but quickly became not unlike the minatory rattle of a leper's bell. I should have known that Letitia would be as clever as I. She, too, has Rusty by the balls. "We're on good terms, Mr. Martinson and I, and he thinks if anybody can make something of the boy it will be me."

"So if Rusty decides to stray . . ."

"Mr. Martinson will bring him back." Letitia sighed contentedly. Then she frowned. "But there's no doubt about it, he's still interested in Mary-Ann, even though he can't get over the fact that she's living with you. He absolutely hates you, darling. Why? He won't tell me."

"And never will." I daresay I looked as pleased as I felt.

"Anyway, that's all in the past. Now I want you to have dinner with Mary-Ann and me and I want you to convince her that Rusty was just using you and that now he's off with someone else."

Letitia wondered if this was a wise tactic. I assured her that it was, and I was right. Our dinner at Scandia was a success. Mary-Ann got tiddly on snaps and, all in all, we were like three schoolgirls on the town. Mary-Ann soon forgave Letitia. "I understand what you must've felt. I mean, he's the most wonderful boy there is and I don't suppose any woman could resist him."

"I tried," said Letitia solemnly, stroking her sprained arm in its sling. "God knows I tried."

"I guess it was too much for me to hope to keep him." Mary-Ann was close to tears but we both did our best to cheer her up, assuring her of future boyfriends not to mention the prospect of stardom which Letitia dangled before our eyes, a dream made all the more palpable by the sudden appearance of a major television personality who embraced Letitia and complained, "You never call me!" Mary-Ann and I were duly impressed by this public display of Letitia's greatness, and flattered that we are now her friends.

After saying good night to Letitia, Mary-Ann and I came back to the apartment. We are both a little sad at the thought of leaving our first home together. But we are also excited at the thought of the new house, particularly the soundproofed music room where Mary-Ann will practice. She has become, suddenly, grimly ambitious. She means to be a major star and if she does not attain at least the magnitude of Susanna Foster my name is not Myra Breckinridge. In fact, according to Miss Cluff, there is a thrilling new quality to Mary-Ann's voice which "I'm sure staying with you and receiving a *woman's* love and guidance has given her." Miss Cluff giggled despite my coldness, for I do not want her—or anybody—to think that either of us is one of *les girls*. I must protect Mary-Ann. I must also protect myself since I can never rule out the posssibility that some day I shall find that perfect man who will totally resist me and so win my love, and hand in marriage.

I find that lately I've been prone to the most sickening sentimental reveries, usually involving Mary-Ann though sometimes a faceless man is at my side and we live together in an enchanted cottage filled with the pitter-pat of little feet or I should say paws since I detest children but have lately come to adore dogs. First thing Monday, Mary-Ann and I are going to the kennel and buy two wirehaired terriers, "Hers" and "Hers"—in memory of Asta, that sweet dog who was in the *Thin Man* series with William Powell and Myrna Loy.

Tonight our love took on a new dimension. Mary-Ann now undresses in front of me. She then lies on the bed, eyes tight shut, lovely breasts fallen back upon themselves; and as I trace their contours with a finger, causing them to tighten visibly, she sighs with pleasure which is the signal for me to begin with my hand the exploration of that pale dimpled belly which curves its secret way to the blonde silky thatch so often penetrated by Rusty but still forbidden to me. In fact, every time my hand approaches that secret and for me so beautifully enticing and *central* reality, the cave of origin, she turns away and whispers, "No."

But tonight she was subtly changed. I don't know whether it was the snaps at Scandia or the cold bright charm of the powerful Letitia or the knowledge that Rusty would never be hers again but whatever it was, she allowed my hand to rest a long moment on the entrance to the last fantasy which is of course the first reality. Ecstatically, I fingered the lovely shape whose secret I must know or die, whose maze I must thread as best I can or go mad for if I am to prevail I must soon come face to face with the Minotaur of dreams and confound him in his charneled lair, and in our heroic coupling know the last mystery: total power achieved not over man, not over woman but over the heraldic beast, the devouring monster, the maw of creation itself that spews us forth and sucks us back into the black oblivion where stars are made and energy waits to be born in order to begin once more the cycle of destruction and creation at whose apex now I stand, once man, now woman, and soon to be privy to what lies beyond the uterine door, the mystery of creation that I mean to shatter with the fierce thrust of a will that alone separates me from the nothing of eternity; and as I have conquered the male, absorbed and been absorbed by the female, I am at last outside the human scale, and so may render impotent even familiar banal ubiquitous death whose mouth I see smiling at me with moist coral lips between the legs of my beloved girl who is the unwitting instrument of victory, and the beautiful fact of my life's vision made all too perfect flesh.

When at last she pulled away from me, she seemed almost reluctant, as though she wanted me to continue and achieve for her that orgasm which tonight I could sense was near. "Myra, don't. It spoils it."

"Darling, whatever you want." I have learned restraint, unlike Myron who could not be deterred from the object of his lust by even a teeth-rattling fist in his poor face. But Myron was tortured by having been attached to those male genitals which are linked to a power outside the man who sports them or, to be precise, they sport the man for they are peculiarly willful and separate and it is not for nothing that the simple boy so often says of his erection, partly as a joke but partly as a frightening fact, "He's got a head of his own." Indeed *he* has a head of his own and twice I have punished that head. Once by a literal decapitation, killing Myron so that Myra might be born and then, symbolically, by torturing and mocking Rusty's sex in order to avenge Myron for the countless times that he had been made victim by that mitred one-eyed beast, forever battering blindly at any orifice, seeking to scatter wide the dreaded seed that has already so filled up the world with superfluous people that our end is now at hand: through war and famine and the physical decadence of a race whose extinction is not only inevitable but, to my mind, desirable . . . for after me what new turn can the human take? Once I have comprehended the last mystery I shall be free to go without protest, full of wisdom, into night, happy in the knowledge that, above all men, I existed totally. Let the dust take me when the adventure's done and I shall make that dust glitter for all eternity with my marvelous fury. Meanwhile, I must change the last generation of man. I must bring back Eden. And I can, I am certain, for if there is a god in the human scale, I am she.

And so, unlike Myron, I am able to be loving and gentle. I am able to hold Mary-Ann in my arms as a mother cradles a child or as I hold a fox terrier puppy who has taken my fancy.

"I love being with you—like this," she said tonight, eyes shut, smiling.

"I love it, too." I was simple. "It's all I want, making you happy." I squeezed her bare shoulders; our breasts touched, teasingly. Mine are even larger than hers, filled with silicone, the result of a new process discovered in France and not always successful in its application (recently a French stripper died when the silicone was injected by mistake into an artery). I was fortunate, however, and no one, not even a trained physician, can tell that my beautiful firm breasts are not the real thing.

Shyly, Mary-Ann once said, "They're just super, Myra! I bet the boys were really after you in high school." An amusing thought since, in those days, it was I who was after the boys. At fourteen Myron vowed that he would, in one way or another, extract the essence of every good-looking boy in school and he succeeded in one hundred and one cases over a three-year period, a time in his life which he used to refer to as the Scheherazade phase, the hundred and one nights—or possibly "flights" is the better word to describe what he did with those birdlike objects whose thrust so fascinated him but so disgusts me, for I have got past that crude *obvious* instrument of procreation to the deep center where all is veiled, and purest magic.

But Mary-Ann is making progress; her admiration of my body is not entirely aesthetic . . . but then the body in question is, if I may say so, unusually lovely, the result of the most dedicated of plastic surgeons who allowed me, at my request, to remain conscious during all stages of my transformation, even though I was warned that I might be seriously traumatized in the process.

But I was not. Quite the contrary. I was enthralled, delighted, fascinated (of course the anesthetic had a somewhat intoxicating effect). And when, with one swift movement of the scalpel, the surgeon freed me from the detested penis, I amazed everyone by beginning to sing, I don't know why, "I'll be seeing you" . . . hardly a fitting song since the point to the exercise is that I would *not* be seeing it or any of its equivalents, except for that of the tortured Rusty, ever again; at least not in the way Myron saw such things.

Nevertheless, I was elated, and have not for one moment regretted my decision to be unique. That my plans have lately gone somewhat awry is the sort of risk one must take if life is to be superb. For instance, I had always believed that between the operation, on the one hand, and the rape of someone like Rusty on the other, I would become Woman Triumphant, exercising total power over men as men once exerted that same power over Myron and still do over the usual woman. But the very literalness of my victory deprived me of the anticipated glory. To my astonishment, I have now lost all interest in men. I have simply gone past them, as if I were a new creation, a mutant diverging from original stock to become something quite unlike its former self or any self known to the race. All that I want now in the way of human power is to make Mary-Ann love me so that I might continue to love her—even without possessing her—to the end of my days.

Imagine my consternation when, once again, she said what she truly felt (and what I have known all along but refused to let myself admit even to myself): "If you were only a man, Myra, I would love you so!"

Of course the shock of the anticipated is always more intense than that of the unexpected. I let her go, as though her cool body had turned suddenly to flame. "Love is not always a matter of sex," I said weakly.

"Oh, I know. And I do love you, as you are. I even like it when you touch me, up to a point," she added judiciously, "but it's really only with a boy I can let myself go. That's the way I am."

"Rusty?"

She shut her eyes, frowning with recollected pain. "No. That's finished. But someone like him." She sighed, "And there aren't many."

"Not many!" I was tactless, and harsh. "The garages of America are crowded with Rustys."

She shook her head. "No. He *is* special. Most boys grab. He doesn't. He's so sweet in bed, and that's what I like. I can't stand the other. I never could. That first boy almost turned me off for good, in high school. He was like a maniac, all over me!" She shuddered at the memory. "In a funny way," she said, "you remind me of Rusty, the way you touch me."

As I write these lines at the card table, facing the Château Marmont and the solemnly turning chorine, I feel the tears rising. What am I to do?

Randolph has been useless. This morning I met him at Will Wright's on the Strip, near Larue's. He was already halfway through a double chocolate burnt-almond and pistachio sundae, gaining the sort of oral gratification that, were he not a puritan Jew, a cock might have provided, with far fewer calories. But he is hopeless. His first and only marriage ended after one year and though he has not confided in me what went wrong, I suspect that he was inadequate if not impotent. Since then, as far as I know, only the theory of sex interests him; the real thing causes him a profound distress which he relieves with food.

"You must tell her everything, if you love her," was his profound advice, as he munched on three maraschino cherries.

"I can't."

"Why not? You wish to exert power over her . . ."

"Only that she may exert it over me . . ."

"So power is intransitive as well as transitive? Then you are clearly moving into a new phase."

"Whatever the phase, I don't know what to do. If I tell her that I used to be Myron, I destroy Myra . . ."

"Not a bad idea."

I was furious. "You always preferred Myron to me, didn't

you?" I let him have it. "And I know why. You were in love with him, you God-damned closet-queen!"

But in my fury I had misplayed my hand for this is exactly the sort of scene Randolph delights in. Carefully he put down his spoon, licked his chops and said, "That's very interesting, what you say. Now tell me exactly: why do you feel that friendship must invariably have an *overt* sexual connotation when your own experience . . ."

"Darling Randolph, why don't you go fuck yourself? It would be an act of some mercy, and therapeutic, too."

There is nothing more satisfactory than to be at last entirely free of one's analyst, and I am rid of mine. The end occurred when I found myself deeply resenting having to pay him forty-two thousand five hundred dollars for perjuring himself when, as things turned out, I didn't need his help at all.

Unfortunately Randolph chooses to interpret my harsh dismissal as a new symptom of neurosis. "We're making splendid progress," he exclaimed, pig's eyes gleaming with excitement. "Now let's go back a moment. The emotional trigger, as usual, is your fear that I preferred Myron to you . . ."

"Look, I couldn't care less who or what you prefer. Your feelings are your own problem. My only concern in this world is not you and your gluttony (a sex life must be ruled out), but Mary-Ann . . ."

"Wonderful! This is the big breakthrough we've been waiting for! By saying that I have no sex life . . ."

". . . is apt to leave me if she knows that I used to be a man . . ."

". . . you must be able to visualize . . ."

". . . and I couldn't bear that. Yet if I don't tell her . . ."

". . . me having sexual relations with Myron. Now then, how exactly do you see me in the act? Active or passive . . ."

". . . I'll lose her to the first light-fingered stud who comes her way . . ."

". . . would I be oral in my desires or anal or . . ."

"From the way you eat, oral! Randolph, you disgust me, you really do!" Like all analysts, Radolph is interested only in himself. In fact, I have often thought that the analyst should pay the patient for allowing himself to be used as a captive looking-glass. "I take it all back," I said curtly. "I didn't mean a word of it."

"*Consciously* this may be true, but to have made the accusation you did reveals . . ."

I left him and crossed the street to where my car was parked, nearly getting myself run over by one of those maniac drivers who make walking so perilous in the Greater Los Angeles area. But then the pedestrian is not favored hereabouts. In fact, the police are quick to stop and question anyone found on foot in a residential district since it is a part of California folklore that only the queer or criminal walk; the good drive cars that fill the air with the foul odor of burning fossils, and so day by day our lungs fill up with the stuff of great ferns and dinosaurs who thus revenge themselves upon their successors, causing us to wither and die prematurely, as did they.

As I watch the Las Vegas chorine turn and turn, I find myself thinking, not unnaturally, of *Turnabout* (1937), with Adolphe Menjou, Carole Landis and adorable John Hubbard; and I ponder that brilliant plot in which husband and wife exchange personalities through the magic of the talking film (he speaks with her voice, she with his) and, as Parker Tyler puts it so well, we have, as a result, "a realization of ancient magical belief in the guise of modern make-believe, and the same ambiguity and ambivalence of spiritual essences are revealed that modern psy-chology, especially psychoanalysis, has uncovered in present-day civilization."

My worn copy of Tyler's *Magic and Myth of the Movies* is always open before me when I write, and I constantly search the fa-miliar text for guidance. But tonight I can find nothing more comforting than Tyler's suggestion (referring to *Turnabout* and the Warsaw Art Players' film *The Dybbuk*, which also deals with the idea of possession) "that by *imitating* the female the male believes that he *becomes* the female, thus automatically and un-consciously practicing the imitative variety of sympathetic magic." Of course magic is involved at the beginning of my quest. But I have since crossed the shadow line, made magic real, created myself. But to what end? For what true purpose have I smashed the male principle only to become entrapped by the female? Something must soon be done or I am no longer triumphant, no longer the all-conquering Myra Breckinridge ... whisper her name! Sympathetic magic must be made. But how?

38

I must record my situation exactly. They say that I am under sedation. That means I have been drugged. They are holding me against my will. But I shall outwit them.

The one who calls himself Dr. Mengers has already fallen into my trap. When I asked for this notebook, he granted my wish. "Excellent therapy," he said, assuming a bedside manner that even a child could detect was false. He is with the CIA. They all are. He pretended to take my pulse. "Much better today. Very much better. It was touch and go for a while, you know. But you've pulled through with flying colors!"

I played my part with magnificent cunning. I fell in with the game, pretended that I had been ill, made my voice even weaker than it is. "Tell me, Doctor," I quavered, "how long have I been here, like this?"

"Ten days. Out cold," he said with all-too-obvious satisfaction.

For ten days they have held me captive! But now for reasons of their own, they are bringing me around, and that is their mistake for when it comes to a contest of wills, I am bound to win, even in my present hallucinated condition.

"When can I get up?" I whispered.

"Not for a week at least. As you see, you are in a plaster cast from neck to ankles. But your arms are free." He pinched me hard above the elbow. "Does that hurt?"

He is a sadist, too. I refused to give him the satisfaction of crying out. "Certainly not," I said, and he frowned and made a note in a little black code book. Obviously I am a tougher nut to crack than he thought. Yet what I fear is not torture but the various drugs and serums that they have obviously been giving me from the look of my arms, which are blue, black and yellow with bruises and punctures. Not even a woman as brave and unique as I can hope to withstand an all-out chemical assault upon the brain and nervous system.

What have I told them? Did I reveal the secret of human destiny to the enemy? I pray not. But only a careful questioning of my captors will be able to set my mind at rest. If I *have* told all, then there is no hope for the coming breakthrough. They will do to me what they did to Mossadegh in Iran and Arbenz in Guatemala.

We were then joined by the "nurse." Even for the CIA she was a poor actress, obviously recruited at the last minute, assuming that she is not the mistress of some Pentagon bureaucrat. She approached me with a thermometer as though she were uncertain as to how to go about placing the object in question in my mouth. She was plainly nervous and ill at ease. But then the thermometer was drugged and it is possible that she was experiencing a momentary twinge of conscience, quickly dispelled by the "doctor," who had been watching her with ill-disguised irritation.

"Go on, take the temperature. Please," he said in an irritable voice.

"But he bit my finger last time," she said plaintively, as I allowed the thermometer to be placed beneath my tongue.

"But Mr. Breckinridge was delirious at the time. Now he's quite normal."

"What do you mean *Mr.* Breckinridge?" I asked, suddenly aware of the shift in sex, and nearly swallowing the thermometer in the process. They exchanged a conspiratorial look, much like the one Oswald gave Ruby on television seconds before he was struck down by his supposed friend and accomplice.

"Of course, *Miss* Breckinridge," said the "doctor" soothingly, readjusting the thermometer. I made no further complaint although I prefer the honorific title of Mrs., to which my uniqueness entitles me.

"I still have an ugly scar," said the "nurse," holding up a bandaged hand in an effort to engage the "doctor's" sympathy. I was pleased with myself: apparently I had fought hard to retain my mind's integrity so rudely violated by these drug-administering agents of imperialism.

"Now, Nurse, we must try and understand what he . . . what she has had to go through these last few days."

"What *we've* had to go through," grumbled the "nurse," at the very least the mistress of an Assistant Secretary of Defense, so cheeky is she.

Her superior was coldly unsympathetic (obviously a division in their ranks; one that I shall exploit). "I suggest we tend to our job, Nurse, and take the rough with the smooth."

"Yes, Doctor." She tried to sound chastened but failed. Then she withdrew the theromometer and said, "Normal," and looked disappointed. It is quite evident that they want me to die of what appear to be natural causes. Fortunately, my body will no more surrender to their poison than my mind has. I shall outwit them all, and prevail! If they mean to kill me they will have to take direct action, and so leave clues.

"Good news!" The charlatan beamed, writing in his code book. "We've passed the danger mark and I'm pleased as all get-out!"

Get out, I thought, smiling bravely, like . . . what's her name in . . . my memory seems to have left me. The drugs must have been enormously powerful. Or did they use electroshock treatments? That would explain my condition like who was it in . . . I can't recall that film's title either. Whole sections of memory are missing. But I shall regain them: it is simply a matter of will. Meanwhile, they are certain that I can find no way of getting a message to the outside world but in this, as in everything, they underestimate me.

They are gone now. I am sitting up in a metal bed placed at the center of a small cell disguised as a hospital room. There is even the awful odor of disinfectant to lend verisimilitude to the otherwise ridiculous decor. Any fool can see that this is a prison, not a hospital. Why else are the venetian blinds shut?

I am encased in what appears to be plaster of Paris from neck to ankle. Inside this carapace I can hardly move. My legs feel as if they had just been asleep and now, tingling, are coming to life again. I can wiggle my feet: that is something, and my poor arms, though discolored, are intact and I suppose, in time, I shall be able to peel off this plaster strait jacket . . . unless of course they keep such careful watch over me that any attempt at freeing myself will be thwarted. For the moment, it is my intelligence upon which I must rely.

I cannot recall the name of Lana Turner's first film! Something *has* been done to my brain. I know that I am Myra Breckinridge whom no man may possess, but what else? Film titles are lost to me. The past is a jumble. I must not panic.

What's the last thing I can recall before they captured me? This is difficult. Santa Monica. The mesa? No. Not mesa. A word like it. Canyon. The Santa Monica Canyon. A winding road. Sun in my eyes as I drive. Alone? Yes, alone. No one is in the car. A dog? Yes, a wirehaired fox terrier puppy. Sitting on my lap. Sun in my eyes. That means it was late afternoon and I am coming *from* Hollywood to the sea—oh, the mind of Myra Breckinridge can never be broken or too long deranged, even by the CIA!

I park the car in front of a small house, green with white shutters, overlooking the ugly ocean. Fortress? Canal? Pilings? Palisades . . . that's it: Pacific Palisades are visible. It's our house. Ours? Who else? No. I'm going too fast now and my head is throbbing. Sodium pentothal obviously.

I park the car on the main road. I get out of the car. I stand and wait for the dog to jump out. The dog does. He runs up the driveway. He stops at the door of the house. I start to follow then

39

Struck by a hit-and-run automobile, I have been unconscious for ten days. I sustained twelve broken ribs, one cracked femur, one fractured shin, a dozen torn and bruised ligaments, as well as a concussion of the brain. Only my powerful *physical* organism was able to save me, according to Dr. Mengers, who has been an absolute saint during my ordeal.

"Frankly we didn't think you were going to make it," he said earlier this evening. "But the first moment I saw you I said to myself: that one's going to put up a good fight, and you did. The night nurse is still home, convalescing."

"Night nurse? What did I do?"

"Bit her arm to the bone."

We had a merry laugh about that. Then I spoke seriously. "I'm worried about my memory, Doctor. For instance, I can recall the stars of *The Uninvited* (Ray Milland, Ruth Hussey, Donald Crisp) and I know that Charles Brackett produced the film for Paramount in 1944 but who . . . *who* was the director?"

"Lewis Allen." He did not pause to think.

I was momentarily distracted from my own problems at finding a doctor who knew so much about movies. Apparently he too had seen every film made between 1931 and 1947. He was even, for a short time, Roland Young's physician. We exchanged movie lore excitedly, and as we did, I found myself recalling more and more details which I had thought were forever lost to me. But not until I listed every film that Edith Head had worked on did Dr. Mengers show his delight. "You see? You *can* remember. It's just a matter of practice. Nothing serious has happened to your mind. With the sort of concussion you sustained, it is like having the wind knocked out of you . . . takes time to catch your breath. Don't worry. You're doing fine."

I was relieved, to say the least. I have every confidence in this marvelous doctor who is to me now more friend than physician. So close do I feel to him that I am able to confide in him. I did this evening, though not without a degree of embarrassment.

"Dr. Mengers, I realize I'm not looking my best, what with this turban which is not exactly flattering to my delicate features, and being all bruised, but there is one thing that does alarm me. I seem to be . . ." I could hardly get the words out. "I seem to be growing a beard."

He became immediately evasive. Why? In the vaguest of terms, he told me not to worry; he even suggested that I *shave!* To which I responded, rather sharply, that a woman who takes a razor to her face may as well say farewell to her femininity. "What I plainly need," I said, coming to the point, "is a massive shot of female hormones."

"I'm afraid that's out of the question in your present condition. Such an injection would interfere seriously with the healing process. Later, perhaps." But though he was soothing, I detect something very odd in his manner. Is it possible that my first impression was correct? That there is indeed a plot against me? I must be on my guard at all times and not allow myself to be lulled into a sense of false security by a man who *claims* to be a doctor but knows altogether too much about films.

Apparently Mary-Ann has been trying to see me. She comes to the hospital every day, the adorable girl! I told Dr. Mengers to tell her that I love her dearly and when I am looking less ghastly I will see her. Meanwhile, I talk to her twice a day on the telephone.

"You don't know what I've been through!" she exclaimed when she first heard my voice, and promptly burst into tears of joy. I'm afraid I wept, too, at the sound of my darling's voice. In any case, all is well at the house. The dogs are almost house-broken though there are still occasional accidents, particularly on the new curtains in the living room. Mary-Ann continues her singing lessons and attends the Academy where I am much missed. Buck inquires daily about my health and Dr. Montag is coming to see me tomorrow.

The driver of the car that struck me has not yet been apprehended. The police hope for me to give them some clue but I cannot. I have no memory of anything once the dog ran up the garden walk. Apparently I was struck from behind.

Was it an accident, or was it . . . who? Rusty? Buck? I am suddenly filled with suspicion. Two weeks ago I was almost run over in front of Larue's. A coincidence? Well, if either of those sons-of-bitches did this to me I will have his God-damned head or my name is not Myron Breckinridge!

40

The room is filled with the smell of Randolph's pipe. Across the floor, burnt-out cinders indicate his various maneuvers. He was in good form. So am I, despite constant headaches and the odd sensation that my legs are filled with burning pins. Fortunately the cast will be removed tomorrow.

To my surprise, Randolph did not think me paranoid when I told him my suspicions.

"It crossed my mind, too," he said, sucking at his pipe. "It could very well have been Rusty's revenge."

"Or Buck Loner's. He would do anything to remove me from the Academy. Even murder."

Yet as I gave voice to my suspicions I cannot, in my heart of hearts, really believe that anyone in his right mind could wish to remove me from a world so desperately in need of me. I prefer to have faith in my fellow-man. I must even have a certain tenderness for him if I am to change, through example as well as teaching, his attitude toward sex. There was a time in our evolution when hate alone was motor to our deeds. But that age is ending, for I mean to bring to the world love of the sort that I have learned from Mary-Ann, a love which, despite its intensity, is mere prelude to something else again, to a new dimension which I alone am able to perceive, if dimly. Once I have formulated it, the true mission will begin. But for now I must be cryptic and declare that nothing is what it seems and what nothing seems is false.

"I would suspect Rusty more than Buck," said Randolph, plunging his thick paws into the huge get-well basket of fruit sent me "with love" from Uncle Buck and Bobbie Dean Loner. Randolph crushed a peach against his jaws. I looked away. "The motive in the case of Rusty is more profound psychologically." Randolph's teeth struck the peach's pit with a grating sound that sent shivers along my spine.

"Well, it's done and past. And I'm willing to forgive whoever it was."

"Are you really?" Randolph sounded surprised, not prepared for the new me.

"Of course. Suffering ennobles, doesn't it?" I had no desire to confide in Randolph, particularly now when I am assembling an entirely new personality with which to take the world by storm. "But I do wish you'd talk to Dr. Mengers and ask him to give me a hormone cocktail. I'm sprouting hair in all directions."

Randolph wiped his lips free of peach juice with a banana which he then unpeeled. "Yes, he told me about your request. Unfortunately, it's medically dangerous at the moment."

"But I can't let Mary-Ann see me like this."

"I'm sure she'll understand."

Before I could remonstrate with Randolph, he was launched upon one of his monologues whose subject, as usual, was Randolph Spenser Montag.

". . . office in Brentwood, a quiet neighborhood. Many of my patients live nearby which makes things easy for them if not for me. I've already made the down payment on the house, which is Spanish-style ranch-type, and so I should be ready for business in a few weeks. Culturally the Los Angeles area is far richer than I had dreamed, with many extremely stimulating people . . ."

I was spared Randolph's rationalizations by the sudden opening of the door and the nurse shouting, "Surprise, surprise!"

The surprise was an incline board on wheels which the nurse rolled backwards into the room, to my amazement. Was I expected to get on it and be wheeled about like a sacred relic or Pharaonic mummy? The mystery was solved when, with a flourish, the nurse spun the thing around to reveal Letitia Van Allen in a neck brace, strapped to the board.

"Darling!" Letitia was exuberant, despite the strangeness of her position. "Thank God, you're conscious! We were so worried!"

"I'm Dr. Montag," said Randolph gravely, never one to be kept for long out of a conversation. I made the introductions.

"Sorry I can't shake hands." Letitia was intrepid. "My neck is fractured and two spinal discs have fused. Otherwise I'm in a great shape."

The nurse agreed. Obviously she worships Letitia. "Miss Van Allen is just *bursting* with energy. It's all we could do to keep her in traction."

"How long have you been here?" I asked, suspecting what had happened.

"Two days after your accident, I took a header on the stairs at Malibu, and here I am, getting the first real rest I've had in twenty years."

"Except she's a naughty girl and not resting at all." The nurse was adoring. "She has moved her whole office into the hospital. You should see her room. It's a madhouse!"

"Sweetie, will you mix us a nice martini? Beefeater gin, no vermouth, on the rocks, with just the tiniest dash of rock salt."

"Oh, Miss Van Allen, you know hospital rules . . ."

"And a glass of champagne for yourself. Hurry up now! Letitia is parched."

The nurse departed. Letitia beamed at us. Then she frowned. "Angel, what's wrong with your face? It looks like you're . . ."

". . . growing a beard." I sighed. "Well, I am. A result of some sort of hormonal imbalance caused by the accident. Isn't that right, Doctor?"

Randolph blew sparks at Letitia and agreed, at convincing quasi-scientific length. All the while, Letitia was studying me with a thoughtful look. I cursed myself for not having used a thick foundation makeup.

"You know," said Letitia, when Randolph had wheezed into silence, "you would make a marvelous-looking man. Really, Myra, I mean it."

"Don't be silly!" I grew hot with anxiety, as well as rage at Dr. Mengers for not having done more to prevent this dreadful, if temporary, reversion to my original state.

"Darling, I didn't mean it as an insult! Quite the contrary. In fact . . ." Letitia apologized at length as we drank the martinis the nurse brought us and watched Randolph break open a large pineapple and tear at its tallowy flesh.

After what seemed an age of small talk, Randolph finished the pineapple and, with many a puff and wheeze and groan, got to his feet and said good-by.

The moment the door shut behind him, Letitia flew across the room on her incline board, coming to a full stop beside my bed. "It was perfection!" She roared happily. "Total perfection! I have never in my life known such absolute and complete happiness. Such a . . . no, there are no words to describe what I went through. All I know is that I am now *entirely* fulfilled. I have lived and I have loved to the fullest! I can at last give up sex because anything more would be anticlimax."

"Not to mention fatal." I must say Letitia's happiness depressed me mortally. "Just what did Rusty do to you this time?"

"What did he *not* do!" Her eyes became glazed with memory and gin. "It all happened the day he signed the contract at Fox. You know I got him the lead in that series with top money, special billing, participation, the works. Anyway, after the signing, we went back to Malibu to celebrate." Her voice was dreamy. "It began upstairs when he tore my clothes off in the closet.

Then he raped me standing up with a metal clothes hanger twisted around my neck, choking me. I could hardly breathe. It was exquisite! Then one thing led to another. Those small attentions a girl like me cherishes . . . a lighted cigarette stubbed out on my derriere, a complete beating with his great thick heavy leather belt, a series of ravenous bites up and down the inner thighs, drawing blood. All the usual fun things, except that this time he went beyond anything he had ever tried before. This time he dragged me to the head of the stairs and raped me from behind, all the while beating me with his boot. Then, just as I was about to reach the big O, shrieking with pleasure, he hurled me down the stairs, so that my orgasm and the final crash with the banister occurred simultaneously. I fainted with joy! Without a doubt, it was the completion of my life."

"And here you are, half paralyzed." I could not resist being sour.

"Only temporarily. But I agree, one more go and I'll be dead, which is why we've agreed not to see each other again, except in a business way."

"He no longer needs you, so he drops you."

"You are a case, Myra!" Letitia tolled a great bronze laugh. "Actually the opposite is true. Since he's going to be a star he'll need me more than ever, in the business way. No, these things run their course. Frankly I don't think I shall ever again need sex. Once you have known the kind of perfection that I obtained at the moment of collision with that banister, anything else is too second-rate to be endured. I am a fulfilled woman, perhaps the only one in the world."

I must say I can only admire (and perhaps envy) Letitia. Not since the early Betty Hutton films has female masochism been so beautifully served. But I have my own problems. I came straight to the point. "Will Rusty go back to Mary-Ann?"

"Never. He's playing the field now. He's taking a bachelor pad with that young stud who was just let go by Universal— John Edward Jane."

"So you think he'll settle down to a life of promiscuity." I was relieved.

"After me, where can he go? Don't worry. He's lost all interest in your girlfriend."

This was said gaily. Even so, I felt shame, not so much for myself as for Mary-Ann.

"She's *not* my girlfriend. She has a horror of Lesbianism."

"That you don't share. Oh, come off it, Myra. You can tell your pal Letitia. Why, we've all gone that route one time or another—it can be a lot of laughs, two girls and one dildo."

Nevertheless, I continued to protest our innocence, while Letitia, getting more and more drunk on gin, described in some detail how, many years before, she had been seduced by Buck Loner's wife Bobbie Dean who then, no doubt filled with remorse, got religion one day while buying Belgian endives at the Farmers Market and gave up dyking on the spot to become a Jehovah's Witness. The story is not without its inspirational side.

But I am more concerned with Mary-Ann's reputation, and our relationship which means more to me than anything in this world.

I talked to Mary-Ann a few minutes ago, shortly after the dead-drunk Letitia was wheeled back to her room. Mary-Ann sounded happy. She can't wait for me to come home. I told her what the doctor told me just now: the cast comes off tomorrow and I will be able to go home by the end of the week. Unfortunately he refuses to give me a hormonal injection and my face looks a fright, with strange patches of beard. I also dread the removal of the bandage since, according to the nurse, all my lovely hair has been cut off. I hope Mary-Ann can bear the gruesome sight. I hope I can.

41

Where are my breasts? *Where are my breasts?*

42

What an extraordinary document! I have spent all morning reading this notebook and I can hardly believe that I was ever the person who wrote those demented pages. I've been debating whether or not to show them to my wife but I think, all in all, it's better to let the dead past bury its dead. As it is, neither of us ever mentions the period in which I was a woman and except for my agent, Miss Van Allen, we deliberately avoid seeing anyone who knew me in those days.

For over three years now we have been living in the San Fernando Valley on what they call a ranch but is actually just a few acres of avocado and lemon trees. The house is modern with every convenience and I have just built an outdoor barbecue pit which is much admired by the neighbors, many of whom are personalities in show business or otherwise work in some capacity or another in the Industry. Ours is a friendly community, with many fine people to share interests with.

At present I am writing a series, currently in its second year on ABC. I would of course like very much to do feature films but they are not that easy to come by. Miss Van Allen, however, keeps submitting my name so who knows when lightning will strike? Meanwhile, the series is a good credit and I make good money.

While cleaning out the attic, I came across this notebook along with all the manuscripts I wrote back in New York. Frankly I can't make head or tail of them. I certainly went through a pretentious phase! Luckily everything is now stabilized for me and I have just about the best wife and marriage I know of. Mary-Ann still sings professionally from time to time as well as appearing locally on television with her own children's program five days a week in the early A.M. She is quite a celebrity with the small fry in the Valley.

It's been a long time since I've seen Buck Loner but he's doing O.K. with the Academy, I gather, and every now and then one of the students actually gets a job in show business. So my work wasn't entirely in vain. The most famous alumnus is Ace Mann who used to be Rusty Godowski. After mopping up in that television series, he promptly inked a multiple non-exclusive contract with Universal and is now the Number Four Box Office Star in the World, according to *Film Daily*. He is also, I'm sorry to learn, a complete homosexual, for which I feel a certain degree of responsibility and guilt. But Dr. Montag, whom I ran into last week outside Will Wright's on Santa Monica Boulevard, said he thought it was probably always in the cards for Rusty and what I did to him just brought his true nature to the surface. I hope he's right.

Dr. Montag seems happy, although he now weighs over three hundred pounds and at first I didn't recognize him, but then he didn't recognize me either. Well, none of us is getting any younger. I am now almost entirely bald, which I compensate for by wearing a rather dashing R.A.F.-style moustache. Needless to say, it is a constant sadness that Mary-Ann and I can never have children. But ever since we both became Christian Scientists we tend to believe that what happens in this life is for the best. Although I nearly lost my mind and tried to kill myself when I learned that my breasts had been removed (Dr. Mengers had been forced to take this step because my life was endangered by the silicone which, as a result of the accident, threatened to enter the bloodstream), I now realize that it was the best thing that ever happened to me if only because once Mary-Ann realized that I was really *Myron* Breckinridge, her attitude toward me changed completely. Two weeks after I left the hospital where I spent my long convalescence and rehabilitation, we were married in Vegas, and so were able at last to settle down and live a happy and normal life, raising dogs and working for Planned Parenthood.

Incidentally, I noticed a quotation scribbled in one of the margins of the notebook. Something she (I hate to say "I"!) copied from some book about Jean-Jacques Rousseau. I don't suppose it's giving away any secrets to say that like so many would-be intellectuals back East Myra never actually read books, only books about books. Anyway the quotation still sort of appeals to me. It is about how humanity would have been a lot happier if it had kept to "the middle ground between the indolence of the primitive state and the questing activity to which we are prompted by our self-esteem." I think that is a very fine statement and one which, all in all, I'm ready to buy, since it is a proven fact that happiness, like the proverbial bluebird, is to be found in your own backyard if you just know where to look.

MYRON

I

I don't know where I am but wherever it is that I am I have to get out of here pronto!

As the late sodomist and film critic Myra Breckinridge used to say, if you keep notes about where you are, you can always figure out sooner or later where it is in relation to other things. Naturally, I don't usually feature her advice or views on anything, as they are repellent to me as her successor and *true* self but I think that maybe in my present situation she had the right idea, as I am confused repeat confused not to mention upset by what just happened to yours truly Myron Breckinridge.

Now then—easy does it. One, to the best of my knowledge I am caught inside the movie *Siren of Babylon*, starring Maria Montez and Bruce Cabot, a picture made at Metro in 1948 and released in 1949 and one which I have seen, oh, maybe thirty times on the Late Late Show, where I was watching it again last night with this account book on my knees, trying to make sense of my wife and better half Mary-Ann's entries of income and outgo in our "San Fernando Chinese Catering to Your Home Service."

We had been watching the movie together downstairs in the rumpus room when around the sixth commercial, the one for Turtle Oil Cosmetics, Mary-Ann said she was going up to bed, and I said, "O.K., honey. I'll be up just as soon as I've added up these old digits." And she said, "You hurry up now," and tossed her head the way Marilyn Maxwell used to do in the film clips they used in the Empathy class at the Academy of Drama and Modeling where I met her six years ago when I was not myself but one of the teachers known as *Myra* Breckinridge, a woman whose career I prefer to forget and do forget except sometimes when I sit down with ball-point in hand to write a letter to the Van Nuys local paper on behalf of capital punishment or against smut and suddenly find that something very like Myra is trying to get out of the tip of my ball-point.

I'd be a fool if I didn't know that she was lurking somewhere inside me, but since that hit-and-run accident just as I stepped out of the car in Santa Monica Canyon which knocked Myra and her famed knockers to bits, I have been *me*, my real self, a straight shooter, living with Mary-Ann the sort of American life that has made this country great, with our Chinese Catering Service and of course the silky terriers we breed. Like the President says, the American dream has been won for most of us who work hard and support our country and various community churches and organizations throughout this great land of ours in spite of the heavy burden of the people on welfare that we are forced to carry on our shoulders as a result of the crushing tax burden we have inherited from earlier, socialist-minded administrations.

You must forgive this digression but I am, as you can tell, trying to keep my sanity by deliberately reminding myself of the U.S. of A. and the San Fernando Valley and my wife Mary-Ann and everything that is normal and American because at about one-oh-seven this morning I leaned over to the TV to turn down the volume and fell or was pushed—if so, by whom—who?—into *Siren of Babylon* at the point where the Priestess of the Sun, Maria Montez, wearing a golden metal bra and with this tall golden crown on her head, appears at the top of a flight of stairs with these big plaster horses with wings on either side of her and these priests in white old-fashioned nightgowns, some holding spears, others holding and banging drums.

2

Myra Breckinridge lives! Like World War II hero General Douglas MacArthur, "I have returned." Yet colorful as corncob-pipe-sucking dugout Doug was, his panache was nothing compared to that of the second husband of his first wife Louise, the immortal Lionel Atwill, who stunningly out-acted Errol Flynn in *Captain Blood* (1935). It is a curious coincidence that when Errol Flynn made his tipsy way to the john on a certain sad day in 1959, he echoed Louise Atwill's husband when he declared to his bibulous chums (amongst them, legend has it, the nubile Beverly Aadland), "I shall return!" But Errol did not return. An hour later he was discovered on the bedroom floor, cold as a mackerel.

No mackerel Myra, cold or otherwise! For six years, since that terrible moment in front of my house when I was shattered by a mysterious car, I have bided my time, gathered my resources, prepared an agenda which, very simply, will restore me to my former glory and the world to its golden age: 1935 –1945, when no irrelevant film was made in Hollywood, and our boys—properly nurtured on Andy Hardy and the values of Carverville as interpreted by Mickey Rooney, Lewis Stone, Fay Holden and given the world by Dream Merchant Louis B. Mayer—were able to defeat the forces of Hitler, Mussolini and Tojo.

Since 1948 it has been downhill all the way. It is—again—no coincidence that the accident which put me out of commission in 1967 was directly responsible for the presidency of Richard M. Nixon, the current energy and monetary crises and the films of S. Peckinpah. I do not exaggerate: *All these disasters are the direct result of my removal from a scene which I was on the verge of transforming entirely.* Proof? Without me everything has gone haywire. Fortunately, I am back in the saddle again, ready to save the world at the eleventh—twelfth?—hour.

I will not dwell on my own private tragedy. Suffice it to say that being trapped inside a Chinese caterer in the San Fernando Valley, with, admittedly, a big restructured phallus between his legs but no scrotal sac, is not my idea of a picnic. But self-pity is not box office. Enough to say, I have come through!

Yes, it was I who *pushed* Myron Breckinridge into *Siren of Babylon*. After twenty years as a film critic, there is nothing I don't know about how to break into the movies.

3

I must've passed out or something from nervous exhaustion, because when I came to, sitting at this table in this hotel room where I am, I was numb in both legs from having sat sound asleep for what my watch says is one hour.

A funny thing. Someone has been writing something very funny in this account book. I can't read a word of what they wrote, as it is backwards-looking. I held it up to the mirror just now but I still couldn't read it. Anyway, so many crazy things are happening to me that this, at this point in time, is the least of my worries. Where was I? Even more to the point. Where am I? Well.

One minute I was fiddling with the volume knob of the TV and then suddenly there was this awful pushing and sucking sensation and there I was on my fanny about a yard away from Bruce Cabot, who is commander of the Babylonian royal guard as well as the rightful king of Babylon though he does not know yet that his rightful place was taken from him in childhood by Louis Calhern, who plays Nebuchadnezzar on whose dining-room wall God is going to write a pretty tough message in a later reel just before destroying Babylon.

At first I just couldn't believe that I had gone from the middle of the night in our TV and rumpus room to outdoors where the sun was shining real hot and all around me those extras in Babylonian costumes and technicians were wandering about. In front of me was this tall staircase made of wood that was painted to look like marble. Just off to my left was Bruce Cabot, who was smoking a cigarette and picking his nose. I just sat there in the dust wondering if I was dreaming or not. Well, I am not dreaming I have now decided, having been here for several hours.

I must've sat there for maybe five minutes or so, with all these extras and other people acting as if I wasn't there. The movie that you see on the TV was sort of stopped from where I sat. That is, I wasn't really *in* it just on the *edge* of it but while it was still actually being made like twenty-five years ago, and the scene I've seen so many times on the TV was about to be made. A director or somebody shouted from somewhere behind me, "O.K., people, pipe down. We're going to start rolling."

Then somebody else said, "Cue Miss Montez," and then a makeup man came up to Bruce Cabot (born Jacques de Bujac in Mexico—how do I know that?) and said, "You've got a bit of shine, Mr. Cabot."

"Yeah, I'm sweating like a horse in this fucking blanket," said Bruce Cabot, as the makeup man powdered Mr. Cabot's face —all this just a few feet away from where I was sitting, out of my mind.

Sitting there on the ground in the hot sun, I decided that I was not in a dream but on the back lot of Metro-Goldwyn-Mayer, which I recognized from earlier visits when I was Myra Breckinridge. Just outside what they call the sight line of the movie, which is the picture that you see on the screen, were all these permanent and unpermanent sets: a railroad station next to this big water tank, and in front of some real woods off to one side there were maybe fifty different staircases set side by side—some straight, some spiral, going from nowhere to no-where like the one in front of me—lined with costume extras in their nightgowns, down which Maria Montez is about to come.

"O.K.!" a voice shouted from behind me. I turned to see where it came from, but saw that where the camera and the director and so forth ought to be there was nothing but this milky gray-blue square of nothing—sort of like the glass of your TV set when the light is on but there is no picture.

"We're starting to roll. Quiet on the set. Miss Montez, Mr. Cabot. Ready."

Then another voice—the director?—shouted. "It's magic time, children! Camera! Action!" And everybody got real quiet, even the technicians outside of the sight line.

The extras on the staircase began to bang their drums while these trumpeters at the bottom of the stairs blew this terrific blast. Bruce Cabot got rid of his cigarette and started to look very worried, which is what the scene calls for. I guess I know the picture by heart.

I got to my feet, still surprised that nobody had noticed me. "Civilians" like they call us who are not, thank God, in the movie industry are seldom welcome during the making of a picture, except of course on those special Universal City guided tours which Mary-Ann and I take at least three times a year when the in-laws are in town, and never get tired of.

Suddenly at the top of the stairs appeared Maria Montez. I'm afraid my heart just stopped. In spite of my predicament and my overall dislike of the movies, I was overwhelmed to be able to actually see this great star in the flesh.

For a moment Maria Montez just stood there at the top of the staircase, looking proud and disdainful, and everybody stared back at her with awe, including me. I can tell you it was a really funny feeling to be able to see the original of a scene I have seen so many times on the TV in actual three-dimensional real-life color as well as from a different angle, since I was able to look all around the set in every direction except where the director and the camera are.

Maria Montez is fabulously beautiful in real life, despite what looked like a coat of spar varnish on her face. She was the idol of my mother Gertrude the practical nurse who actually took me once years ago to see Maria Montez in the flesh when I was a kid and had been going through this sort of breakdown and for several weeks was out of my head, though I don't remember anything except Gertrude saying, "You were nuttier than a fruitcake." Anyway, Maria Montez was the first star I ever saw in the flesh and seeing her jolted me back to life, so Mother claimed, at the opening of Penney's in L.A.

Awful as the fix I am in is, I have to admit that it was a privilege a little while ago to see Maria Montez descend that staircase, her hips moving in this suggestive way as the priests banged those drums.

About halfway down the staircase Miss Montez stopped and said in this loud voice with a sort of Puerto Rican accent, "Hail, oh, commander of our farflung armies!" I was so overcome that I started to go over to where she was standing and ask—I don't know what. Maybe for the nearest exit.

"Out of the sight line, stupid!" a voice hissed in my ear.

I turned to see this fat small man with a big, bald pug-dog head and a damp-looking face like Peter Lorre with the same sort of damp-sounding voice that could make Chinese mushrooms grow even in your driest attic.

"Call me Maude," the small man Maude said, "and *get out of camera range.* Not that you'd show up in the movie as anything except a mike shadow, but the rules are the rules."

I was too stunned to say anything, much less understand a word he was saying, and so I let him steer me to the edge of the set where I could see the steel scaffolding behind the so-called marble staircase. Behind the set there were a half dozen extras and a dozen or so technicians all reading the racing forms. They paid no attention to us because, Maude told me later, *they aren't able to see us.* This place is awful. But first things first.

Bruce Cabot pushed out his chest and walked to the foot of the staircase and said, "Hail, Priestess of the Sun. I come to high Babylon to make sacrifice to the oracle."

"Yea, you do well," said Maria Montez in her magical voice.

It's funny, but I guess that over the years I have, without knowing it, learned all the dialogue by heart. Even so, it's scary hearing it like this from inside . . . inside *where?* We'll get to that.

Then Maude pulled this small worn-out-looking booklet from his pocket and began to flip through the pages as though he was bored to death. This booklet is titled "Orientation of New Arrivals to *Siren of Bablyon.*" Maude confesses to a bad memory and always has to look at what's written down when somebody new arrives.

Maude started rattling instructions. But I couldn't really take them in.

"I guess this is a dream," I said.

"No, sweetie, it's not a dream. You're one of us now and you've made a *classic* entrance! Everybody who really matters comes in during this scene. It's fun and it's chic. We keep a twenty-four-hour watch and today it was my turn to greet the new arrivals and tell you that you must learn to stay out of the picture frame or what we call the 'sight line' when the camera is actually rolling. Then, let me see . . . Oh, yes, the farther back you are from the camera and the action, the nicer it is because . . . Hold on tight, sweetie! We're about to *FADE TO BLACK!*"

FADE TO BLACK is a movie term which means the scene you're looking at is going to fade out until it is black and then start over again fading into the light of the next scene. Well, this is O.K. when you're *watching* the movie but when you're caught *inside* the movie it is just horrible. I tell you I have never felt anything like that first *FADE TO BLACK*. I still can't get over it. Suddenly everything starts to go dark all around you like when you're about to faint. Then for what seems like forever you're surrounded by the blackest black you ever saw and you feel this awful weight pressing in on you from all sides like when you're deep under water and can't breathe.

Then just like when you come up to the surface for air, you suddenly *FADE TO LIGHT* and there you are in the next scene, which in this case was a section of the Temple of the Sun where there is this hole in the floor out of which comes steam from a block of dry ice that you don't see in the picture, naturally, but I was able to see from where I was standing. Beyond the hole is an altar on top of which stands Maria Montez in a different dress with a tiger-skin pattern and these huge earrings.

Bruce Cabot approaches her. "Oh, Priestess, I come to hear the oracle and learn the fate of our expedition in the land of ice and storm." Mr. Cabot was always a much underestimated star, as was Maria Montez, whose untimely death just three years after making *Siren of Babylon* in a hot paraffin bath at Elizabeth Arden's after taking too many reducing pills caused Myra to think seriously about the idea of becoming a Roman Catholic so that she could wear a mantilla and offer prayers for Maria's soul in St. Patrick's Cathedral, New York. Myra was like that. She would try to upstage even Miss Montez in death.

Why am I writing so much about Myra when my surgeon and mental-adviser Dr. Mengers and everyone is in agreement that I must simply block out that awful period of my life? I guess it's being here in this movie that has got me to thinking like they say at the think-tanks the unthinkable.

Shaken up as I was, I still wanted to watch the rest of the scene, but Maude had my arm in a tight grip and before I knew it, we were outside the set, heading away from the production.

"At least you didn't get sick." Maude sounded very pleased. "The first *FADE TO BLACK* is quite an experience. Some of the toughest studs you ever saw throw up all over Bruce Cabot and sometimes they cry for days afterwards. As a matter of fact, *your* eyes look red." Maude gave me a suspicious look. I think he was wearing eyeliner and is a fag, an element I do not mind when they keep to themselves and do not prey on minors or solicit straight people like yours truly. Or hold these parades down Hollywood Boulevard and talk about Gay Lib.

I told Maude I was not about to cry. "You see, I've been watching first the Late Show and then the Late Late Show and that's why my eyes are red. Now if this isn't a dream, then where are we?"

"Well, let's put our thinking cap on, shall we? Isn't it pretty obvious that you've just joined our little colony inside *Siren of Babylon*, which is currently being filmed on the back lot of Metro the summer of 1948."

Maude took a quick peek at the booklet. Maude is something of a scatterbrain. "Oh, silly me," said Maude. "I can never remember all these facts and Mr. Williams fusses so if the newcomer is not thoroughly briefed." Maude's high voice became official-sounding. "Our little colony dates all the way back to 1950, when *Siren of Babylon* was first shown by special arrangement with Metro on TV because it bombed so badly at the box office. As of 1948—this year—Metro is over six million dollars in the red but Dore Schary has now taken over the studio and he will save the day or so the locals back here in 1948 think."

My head was going around. "Stop. Wait a minute. You mean that there are a lot of other people here who got caught in the picture like me?"

"Tons! What year is it back where you come from? 1972?"

"1973. But . . ."

"Hang on to my arm, sweetie! Here comes a *CUT TO!*"

Watching your average movie you hardly notice the CUT TO which is simply one scene taking the place of another real fast without a *DISSOLVE* which is a slow fade or a *FADE TO BLACK* which is just hell. Well, the *CUT TO* was like being flung across a room by a giant hand or swung about in one of those dodgem-cars at the fun-fair.

Suddenly we were dumped down outside the black walls of Babylon where the enemy army is standing. I can't get over the way you go from scene to scene in the picture just the way you do when you're watching it, only in this case *you're in it*. Maude takes all this for granted and pays no attention to the movie.

"I got here in 1961," said Maude. "Which makes me one of the old settlers. I don't mind telling you there was quiet a stuffy group running things when I got here, but in the last few years we've been getting some really—what's that wonderful new phrase?—'groovy cats.' "

Just then a small fat old man of fifty or so with a full head of wiry gray hair and wearing a sort of white apron came running toward us. "Cocksuckers!" he shouted at the soldiers in front of the painted canvas brick wall of Babylon. "Not one of you has the guts to stand up and fight a real man!" He started bobbing and weaving like a prizefighter who is punch drunk or in this case just plain drunk, which he turned out to be. The soldiers ignored him because they can't see him or any of us. That's one of the rules I will get to presently.

"I spoke too soon!" Maude moaned. "In every Eden there is a snake. That's ours. Whittaker Kaiser. He's a cook from Philly, and you know how cooks are! All those hot stoves, all that frying, all those flambés! This one is a perfect menace."

Whittaker kept on dancing and shadowboxing around the dozen soldiers, his large cook's bottom wobbling like a bale of live cats.

"He's only been here a few weeks and we all hope to God he starts to cool it soon. Sweetie, what's your exact date of arrival by the way?"

"April 16, 1973," I said. "No. It was after midnight, so it must be April 17." I confess that that drunk cook was making me nervous because cooks always carry knives somewhere on their persons.

"You'll get an identity disk when we get to the Strip."

"Bastards!" shouted Whittaker to nobody in particular. "Let me out of here!"

"I must say that shit-heel is driving us all straight up the wall with his flabby machismo. If it wasn't for this lady back at the Strip, who every now and then beats him up, we . . . Oh, God, here he comes!"

Whittaker came toward me, head down like a drunken heifer. "They're all fags in this picture! Like you! You're both fags!"

"Oh, shut up, Whittaker!" Maude sniffed. "And stay out of the sight line. One of these days you're going to be seen by the director of this picture and we'll all be in the soup."

"I can certainly outact and outfight and outfuck Bruce Cabot." Whittaker's eyes are small, with this glazed look that all your cooks have. I know, since I am in Chinese Catering and must deal with cooks day in and day out. Admittedly this cook is all shaken up over having got caught in this old movie, but so am I and so are we all but that's no reason for him to carry on like some kind of loon.

"Of course you can, sweetie. You're the tops!" Maude gave me a wink. "But the rules are *stay out of the camera frame.*"

"Where," I asked, "*is* the camera?"

"There isn't one. That's the joke around here." Whittaker was dancing around me, making little boxing jabs and feints. But that stopped when we hit a *DISSOLVE TO*, which is almost as unpleasant as a *FADE TO BLACK* because during the worst part of it you're in two places at once: the scene you were just in outside the walls of Babylon and the next scene which happened to be the banquet hall of Nebuchadnezzar.

Luckily Maude had maneuvered us some distance away from the set, so that the *DISSOLVE TO* was not as painful as it is when you're at the edge of the action and are forced to go through the movie at the same rate it takes to unreel, which in the case of the TV version of *Siren of Babylon* is one hundred minutes of which twenty-two minutes are commercials and station breaks in which everybody freezes on the set and if you want to you can walk around on the set because everyone is frozen stiff and the camera isn't recording.

Important point: if you stand on the *camera* side of the action you have this entirely different sense of time, because you really are back in 1948 when the picture is being made and since it took eight weeks to make the picture I guess you could stay on the camera side the full eight weeks and see the whole thing being made. Anyway, for the record, that was where I first arrived—the camera side. Then Maude got me to the *other* side and I started to go through the picture as it plays until Maude, finally, got us out of the action. Apparently the farther away you get from the filming the more slowly you go through the picture, until about halfway across the back lot you are out of the movie altogether though you can still see it slowly, slowly unwinding back to front because you're now behind it. From the far end of the back lot the picture looks like a big drive-in movie screen hanging there in the sky.

"How do you know there's a camera?" I said, thinking of what Whittaker had just said. "I can't see one."

"Because . . . What's your name, sweetie?"

"Myron. I'm in Chinese Catering in the San Fernando Valley."

"You're not a cook, are you?" Maude looked alarmed until I explained about my business and Mary-Ann and the dogs. God, how I miss them! While I was talking, Whittaker kept eyeing me. Finally he said, "My cock is bigger than your cock."

"Whittaker!" Maude shrieked with delight.

"I doubt that," I said coolly, knowing what a remarkable thing Dr. Mengers was able to make for me after I was run over by that car and lost forever, I am happy to say, Myra's silicone breasts and so was able after the auto accident to be restored to my original manhood, except of course that I had had my male organs removed some years ago in Denmark when I was Myra and so it took all of Dr. Mengers' genius to roll a sizable cylinder of skin and flesh from the inside of my left thigh. "You dressed on the left originally, did you not, Mr. Breckinridge? Then you will do so again, thanks to Miracle Mengers!"

This large artificial phallus was then attached to what had been my—or rather Myra's—vagina, and all, or nearly all, your usual blood vessels and odds and ends were hooked up by one of the finest surgeons it has been my good luck to meet in the greater L.A. area. The fact that I had a certain amount of hair on the inside of my thigh meant that at first my *membrum virilis* was sort of furry and funny-looking. But then electrolysis came to the rescue and I am now clean as a whistle.

The result is extremely decorative and I am a sensation in the shower room at the Y, even though, to tell the truth, I do not have much feeling in this new part except for a bit on the underside where sensitive skin from my wrist was grafted. But as Mary-Ann says, love is all in our heads anyway, and it is true that we have a perfect marriage and one day when our joint workload lessens somewhat I will have Dr. Mengers make me a set of testicles.

"Of course, they will only be for show, Mr. Breckinridge," said Dr. Mengers. "They won't work. But you'll find the overall effect is much dressier and good for morale. I guarantee that you will never regret the money you invest in a Miracle Mengers' Scrotum, the perfect gift for the man who has nothing!" Dr. Mengers is very witty for a surgeon.

"Ah'm gonna knock the shee-it out of yee-ooh," said Whittaker, suddenly talking like some sort of hillbilly. He then pulled a bottle from his pocket and took a drink of whiskey.

"You're drunk," said Maude.

"There's a lot to be said for being drunk."

"Must you say it all, sweetie?"

Whittaker was looking very mean, even for a cook. This place has clearly made him crazy. After three hours here I can see why.

For absolutely no reason Whittaker lowered his head and charged at *me*. I stepped to one side and he fell over a bush just as we *CUT TO* the wharf at Tyre where Bruce Cabot is about to set sail for Ultima Thule.

"We *know* there's a camera," said Maude, returning to the subject at hand, "because we can *hear* the director's voice from time to time."

"It's a trick!" Whittaker was on his feet again; he had dropped the hillbilly accent. "They just *pretend* there is a director."

"There *has* to be a director, sweetie, because we've all seen the movie and we've all read the credits over and over again and we know that this picture was directed by Benjamin R. Laskie. So out there, somewhere"—Maude gestured at the blue-gray horizon—"Benjamin R. Laskie in June and July of 1948 is shooting *Siren of Babylon* on the back lot at Metro."

"You *think* he's out there. Well, I happen to know that he's not out there, fagola."

Maude drew himself up. "Whittaker, I am reporting you for trying to break frame. Come, Myron. We've got to get you registered."

We left Whittaker trying to get on board the false ship where Bruce Cabot was standing looking out to the sea which was painted on a large piece of canvas and hung from a derrick. Every time Whittaker would try to crawl up onto the boat, a heavy-set man would pull him off. No one else paid any attention to him.

"The big fellow is Luke. He's on duty during this scene."

"Why can't the actors see Whittaker?"

"Because nobody can see us who's actually in the movie. In fact, we're invisible to everybody in this part of the back lot, although Mr. Williams . . ."

"Who?"

"*Our* director. He was the first arrival. Mr. Williams insists that even so we must be very, very careful not to break frame —you know, get in range of the camera—because sometimes we're apt to show up as shadows or smudges, especially in the background shots. I must say, thinking about it makes my head ache. So I don't. I suggest you do the same. Just 'ride with the film' like we say on the Strip."

Maude and I were now at the halfway point between the movie and the end of the back lot. "Pretty isn't it?"

Maude turned to show me for the first time the movie unreeling in the sky. It is quite a sight. Half the sky at this point is filled with the movie, while there is this thin bright line all about whatever is being photographed at the moment and shown on your TV. Sometimes the line just makes a square around Maria Montez's face in Technicolor. Then the square will show you the hills of Mesopotamia in the summertime. It is really scary, that bright line forever forming these squares against that funny-looking blue-gray sky which hides where the camera is, where all the people are who are sitting at home tuned in to the Late Late Show courtesy of Dade-Freakness Used Cars, not knowing that they are watching some real people like Maude and Whittaker and me, smudges and shadows though we may look to you, as we try to get out of camera range, try to get out of this movie. Because that is the name of the game around here as I see it. Out!

4

So that asshole Myron thought that he had destroyed me once and for all! Sooner destroy all memory of Helen Gahagan in the title role of *She* as obliterate from the face of the world— *this* world of holy celluloid—its one and only begetter, the arch-creatrix herself who rises now as inexorable as Baron Franken-stein's creation when it emerged from beneath the fallen timber of Universal's Transylvanian castle, as minatory as the Karlov-ian hand of the mummy when it first twitched beneath that dusty millennial unguent-soaked wrapping, as poignant as Bela Lugosi when he drew from his heart the wooden stake, as ca-thartic as Lon Chaney, Jr., when he gouged from his furry chest the silver bullet!

Now let the enfolding night ring once again with the cries of the vampire bat, with the ululations of the werewolf, with the monster's moan and hiss as he takes the flower from the little girl beside the twilit tarn! Because Myra is back in the saddle —without a wardrobe, I fear, and with insufficient control over the mutilated body I am forced to share with Myron Breckin-ridge. Happily, I have arranged for his demise in a matter of hours . . .

5

What's wrong with me? It's happened again. I passed out again
and there is more writing I can't read in this account book. I
guess I am going crazy, but who wouldn't go crazy after the
last few hours, I ask you?

Anyway, whoever is writing in this book better watch out, as
I am in a mean and desperate mood. So where was I before
the blackout? Out? Yes, *out*. Out is the name of the game.

Maude enjoyed being my guide through the back lot, putting
away the booklet and chattering about all the interesting people
caught like me inside the movie. Maude also showed me the
different permanent sets. Some of them I dimly remembered
from those awful years when I was Myra.

Just past a Swiss Alpine village street was the fence and gate
to the back lot of Metro which is now (1973) about to be a
housing development but now (1948) is still pretty fascinating
because Hollywood is at its peak.

What Myra would have given to see the back lot the way I
am seeing it! And how she would have cut her wrists if she
could see what has happened to Hollywood in the five years it's

been since "*She* left us," as Mary-Ann sometimes says, with a shudder, during which period of time the Kerkorian-Aubrey management has all but stripped MGM to the bone in order to build a colossal-type hotel in Vegas.

The guard at the gate was reading the *Hollywood Reporter* and paid no attention to us as we passed through. "He's used to us by now," said Maude.

"I thought nobody can see us."

"The dividing line is halfway into the lot. From the gate to the middle of the lot, they can see us. After that, they can't. If they did, we'd all be in pictures, wouldn't we? And of course we weren't."

At the time Maude might as well have been talking Latin for all the sense he was making to me at that moment.

Beyond the studio gate is the Strip—Thalberg Boulevard— which extends to left and right in a straight line as far as the eye can see, which isn't too far because after what looks to be maybe a quarter mile in either direction of the studio gate there is a glassy mirage effect like on a hot day when you see lakes and puddles in the highway that aren't there from the sun. That's the end of the road for us "out-of-towners"—as we are known to the 1948 people, who are known to us as the "locals."

Across from the gate is the Irving Thalberg Hotel, a pink-stucco four-story Spanish-style building with oleanders in the front yard and a red neon sign in which the word "Irving" does not light up. On either side of the hotel there is nothing but vacant lots filled with tin cans, remains of cars and a large billboard advertising *The Three Musketeers*, a Pandro S. Berman production—I seem to recall Berman was a favorite of Myra —starring Gene Kelly with Van Heflin, Gig Young and Robert Coote.

"That's home for most of us." Maude indicated the hotel. Cars sped past. Funny-looking old cars. Just past the vacant lot where the billboard is, is a Texaco gas station and just past that are two bungalows with neat gardens in front, with morning glories growing on trellises and hollyhocks by the door, the kind of garden Mary-Ann likes so much and has made for us in the Valley as a setting, she likes to say in a joking way, for her plastic Seven Dwarfs from Disneyland.

"Some of our groups live back there, on the lot. Others board at those houses down the road or at the Mannix Motel. The Mannix is low-life, sweetie, but fun!" Maude's small paw indicated some tacky wooden cabins in the opposite direction from the Texaco station. Each cabin has a spindly wooden porch in front. On the crabgrass lawn in front of the main building of the Mannix Motel and Café a faded sign says *Vacancy*.

" 'There's always room at the Mannix' is an old saying around here. But what's really maddening is the movie house down there. See?" Beyond the motel cabins is the wall of a medium-sized picture palace entirely covered by a huge sign advertising Henry Hathaway's *Call Northside 777*.

"Well, by some strange coincidence none of us has ever seen *Call Northside 777* and we can't see it now because the entrance to the theater is just past the end of the road—*our* end, that is—and there's no way we can get in from this side without blasting a hole in the theater, which of course Mr. Williams won't allow, since the first rule around here is never interfere with the locals. But I'm sure I told you that, didn't I?" Maude looked uneasy; a very forgetful-type queen.

All in all, my mind was absolutely blown by Maude's revelations. Up to a point I can see how you might *think* yourself inside a movie. People wander around doing that all the time at Buck Loner's Academy of Drama and Modeling where Myra used to teach Empathy, but it is totally demoralizing to find that you have thought yourself or been thought by somebody else into a place where there is a road which ends, just *ends* completely as far as you and the other out-of-towners are concerned even though this very same road keeps right on going for all the cars that whiz by and for any of the 1948 people who want to stop, say, and see *Call Northside 777*.

"Maude, I'm going to be sick." For a moment I thought that the trip through the movie had really done me in, particularly the knocking about you get during the *CREDITS* when all those names keep jerking past you and the MGM lion comes on, roaring and scaring the shit out of you because you can smell him, thirty times life-size.

"Sweetie, don't! You've made it this far. We're almost home." The nauseous feeling, thank God, passed. So I just belched and had a feeling that I had had this conversation before: what Myra used to call in French *déjà vu* because there is no English way of saying what it's like to be talking to a fat bald hairdresser called Nemo Trojan who wants to be known as Maude because he took over Chez Maude, a hairdressing establishment in White Plains from which, on the night of January 2, 1961, he fell into *Siren of Babylon*—and have the sense while talking to Maude on the edge of Thalberg Boulevard that I had had this exact conversation before.

Normally I would think that I was dreaming except that in your usual dream you can't read anything at all no matter how hard you try and I can read with no trouble "Thalberg Hotel," *Call Northside 777*, "Mannix Motel and Café," *The Three Musketeers*, not to mention the license plates on the passing cars which all date from 1948, the plates, that is. Some of the cars themselves ought to be in museums.

"Who," I asked Maude as we crossed the highway, "is this Mr. Williams you keep referring to?"

"I told you, sweetie. *Our* director. The first arrival." Maude was staring at the sky above the motel just as the sun suddenly went behind some dark stormy clouds. Maude shuddered. "I hate this time of day. Come on in and we'll get you registered."

It's funny, but it wasn't until I stepped into the lobby of the hotel that I realized for the first time that I am really and truly stuck in the year 1948, a year I have already lived through once as a ten-year-old and now have come back to, through no fault or wish of my own, as a thirty-five-year-old caterer who should be living in the Valley a quarter of a century later, happy as can be with a great wife, only he's not because I have got somewhere caught in a year which I didn't like at all that much the first time around because I was ill most of the time.

I don't know why but the musty, dusty cleaning-wax smell of

the lobby of the Thalberg reminded me suddenly of the way houses used to smell when I was a kid. The calendar back of the reception desk which said June 14, 1948, was pretty depressing as was the red plastic jukebox in one corner where the latest oldies are constantly played very low as the guests do not like loud music.

On a big table beside the door to the dining room there are magazines like *Collier's* and *Saturday Evening Post* and local newspapers and not one is dated later than June 14, 1948! I know. I checked. You can never rule out conspiracy in this day and age of revelation about the surveillance of—and even by—Federal officials, which is why, even now, I still don't rule out the fact that I have been drugged and that this is all a put-up job.

Back of the reception desk is the manager's office, where the radio was playing. A newscaster was telling all about how there is a new president of Czechoslovakia as well as trouble in Korea. I guess the Korean War over there hasn't begun yet. I wish I could remember more current events than I do but I don't have much of a memory for such things because Myra was always going to the movies in those years. In fact, from about the time I was, oh, twenty years old until I was thirty and got run over on Sunset Boulevard I was not myself but Myra Breckinridge. Mary-Ann who knew both of us says she can't really believe that Myra ever existed. Neither can I, thank God. That part of myself is gone with the wind like they say, starring Clark Gable, Vivien Leigh, Leslie Howard. Funny, there I go again, remembering movies.

"Mr. Myron Breckinridge," said Maude to the tall man behind the desk. "He's one of our party."

The tall man shook his head and frowned even though he never stopped smiling the whole time. He was actually born in California, I later learned. "I never seen *anything* like the business this time of year! Never! Not that I'm complaining! Just sign here please, sir."

I signed.

"I guess he'll be staying until . . ."

"Until July 31 when the picture stops shooting." Maude sounded rehearsed.

"Then what happens?" I asked.

"Why, we start all over again. You see, there are eight weeks of shooting beginning June 1 and ending July 31, 1948."

"Does *he* start all over again?" I lowered my voice, as I referred to the manager whose back was to us as he looked for my room key.

"Sweetie, say anything you like in front of him about our situation because whenever any of us talks about all *that*, we might as well be talking gibberish as far as the locals go."

As if to prove Maude's point, the manager turned around and showed us a lot more of his upper plate and an even deeper scowl as he said, "There you go again! It's been going on for two weeks now, all you out-of-towners coming here and talking this funny language. Well, just so long as it's not Russian, I say!" He laughed like he had made this little joke before.

"I'll be in the bar, sweetie."

Maude vanished into the back part of the hotel while Mr. Van Upp, which is the manager's name, took me to the second floor and gave me a room looking onto the back yard. Just below my window was a kidney-shaped swimming pool, a bit scummy-looking but even so a number of good-looking girls in one-piece Jantzen bathing suits which show the shape but not the skin were lying around the pool, taking sunbaths though the sun was now gone behind the dark stormy ugly sky and it must, I thought, be about seven in the P.M.

"Won't they get wet?"

"That's what the pool's for, Mr. Breckinridge."

"No, I mean it's going to rain from the look of that storm."

Mr. Van Upp nodded like he had a secret. "Looks like rain to you, don't it?"

"Well, yes."

"You all say that. It's my guess—now, mind you, I don't want to pry—that you are all some kind of Masons with secret passwords, and so on. I was going to be a Mason once but my mother was a lapsed Catholic and you know what they're like. Mr. Williams is picking up your bill." Then he was gone.

I am suddenly absolutely miserable, sitting now in the middle of this small hotel room that smells of Dutch Cleanser and knowing it is the summer of 1948 when just a few miles away, over the hills, is my own house and wife—except the house isn't built yet and Mary-Ann isn't born yet and I am back in New Jersey aged ten except I'm not really. I'm really in the Thalberg Hotel.

I don't know what I'm going to do without my water pick for thorough dental hygiene. Must buy dental floss if it has been invented in this frame of time.

The phone just rang.

"This is Mr. Williams." The voice on the telephone was very high class and English like Claude Rains. "I trust you are comfortably lodged."

"Well, yes, sir, I am, but I have a wife and a business and just how long am I going to be in this place?"

"Until the last day of shooting. That will be in about six weeks."

"Six weeks! But Mary-Ann, she's my wife, she'll . . ."

"We must accept our situation, Mr. Breckinridge. We are inside *Siren of Babylon*. That is the principal fact of all our lives. The link, as it were, between us."

"But I want to get out."

"You will find your identification disk and orientation booklet at the desk. A small allowance will be paid you each Saturday by Mr. 'Rooster' Van Upp. Each Thursday you will stand guard at the Great Staircase—where you met Mr. Nemo Trojan formerly of Chez Maude—to greet anyone who may be joining us. You will bring him here as you were brought here. We shall be in communication, Mr. Breckinridge."

"But, Mr. Williams, I'd like to sit down and chew the rag with you about all this, man to man."

"An appointment can be made at the desk. Write your name in Mr. Van Upp's book. And now good . . ."

"But . . . but . . ." I am desperate for any information I can get, not to mention any human contact. "When did *you* get here?"

"In 1950, Mr. Breckinridge. *Siren of Babylon* was one of the first new pictures to be sold to television. I watched it, as a novelty. Good evening." Click.

Possible ways to get out of here.

One: why not thumb a ride from one of the cars? Or if they won't stop for fear of muggers, go to the service station and pay somebody to drive me in to Hollywood. Of course, it would still be 1948 . . . or would it? Must find out. If it's still 1948 I could at least find my mother Gertrude the practical nurse and get to see myself at the age of ten years old and we could work something out.

Two: go back into the picture and try to get out the other side where the camera has got to be. Since that is the way I came in, that will probably be the best way to get out.

Three: . . .

I was interrupted and now I've forgotten what three was and it was important, I remember thinking, when I first thought of it.

The door to my room opened and this strange-looking girl with hair piled high on her head in front but hanging down her back in the back with a short dress and square shoulders and no stockings but wearing wedgies came into the room without any invitation and said, "I'm Iris. You're new. I saw you register. Let's have a roll in the hay."

The voice was throaty like Kay Francis but without the lisp and she was wall-eyed like Norma Shearer . . . I don't know why but something about this place is making me start to think about movies like Myra used to do. *I have got to cool it.* I have got to be careful because all this is behind me. Myra is dead. And Myron lives . . . only I am living twenty-five crazy years ago!

"*Why* do you want to have a roll in the hay?" I played for time. She got down on the bed beside me. I saw that her thin lips were smeared with orange Tangee like Gertrude my mother the practical nurse. For an awful moment I thought maybe this *was* Gertrude my mother at age thirty, but of course in 1948 Gertrude was in Red Bank, New Jersey, with yours truly.

"I love all of you. I *want* all of you. Because you're different. You know something we don't." She took off her blouse. She was wearing a very elaborate bra just like Gertrude's. "Unhook me," she commanded. I unhooked.

The left breast was only half the size of the right—and I was reminded suddenly of the proud perfectly matched pair of breasts shaped for me—for Myra—by the best surgeons in Europe, who pumped golden silicone into me in order to create those twin glories that were destined so rudely to be deflated and drained as a result of that mysterious hit-and-run accident. Thank God, of course.

Iris started grabbing at me but I was firm and fought her off. Unlike your average Oedipus, I could never make love to anyone who looked like Gertrude. Besides, I did not exactly go for those ill-matched tits with, I swear, one pink aureoled nipple and one brown!

Most important of all, I am true to Mary-Ann. Partly because Mary-Ann is the only girl in the world for me and partly because I have never looked forward to having to explain to some strange woman, no matter how sexy, how I never got around to ordering new balls because I have been too busy these last five years. Besides, Mary-Ann has been so happy with the unusually large weenie Dr. Mengers rolled for me from the skin from inside my left thigh that she has never really insisted on my investing in a set of Miracle Mengers testes.

"I don't appeal to you." Iris pouted when I pushed away her hand after first letting her get a good feel of Dr. Menger's handiwork. "You're a pansy, I'll bet."

"No, Iris. I am a married man, that's all. A happily married man. Your tits don't match," I heard myself say without meaning to.

"Only a pansy would've noticed!" Iris was turning ugly, not to mention red in the face, as she struggled back into her old-fashioned bra.

"What year you from?"

"1973."

"Nineteen Lady Me! Hey, that's close. At least I got the nine-teen. You realize I *almost* dug you, solid sender? Rooster says that's the question to ask."

"You couldn't hear what I said?"

"You think I'm deaf? Of course I heard you. But like all you out-of-towners you make no sense. Can I blow you?"

"No, Iris. Thanks. But no thanks." Old films are beginning to fill up in my head as do things which were once a part of Myra's mind. I am very definitely getting uneasy.

"I blew Mr. Louis B. Mayer." Iris gestured toward the studio across the road. "When I was under contract a few years back. It was in his office during the lunch break. He had a hot pas-trami sandwich at his desk while I was underneath. He spilled some mustard in my hair and said, '*Mustard-yellow!* That's the best color for you, Rose.' He kept calling me Rose. I only saw him the once. Since then I model. Rooster is an old pal. He was under contract, too, but he saved his money. He was in *Thirty Seconds over Tokyo*. Now he does real well with this hotel. At least this summer. He says he's never seen anything like all you out-of-towners, acting so strange. You know, the sheriff came by once to investigate because the people at the gas station are from Oklahoma and think your group are Communists and so they told the sheriff, who had a long talk with Mr. Williams and never came back."

"Have you met Mr. Williams?"

"Not really. He was the first to check in. I remember it was the first day of shooting that new flick they're making now with Maria Montez and Bruce Cabot. I'd like to blow Bruce. I like him in pictures. He was really swell in *Sundown*. Did you see *Sundown*? Really nifty. You're certainly well-hung, Myron, I could feel."

"Thanks, Iris. But I just can't."

"Well, if you change your mind . . . I always like to strike while the iron is hot because when you people first get here there's something real different about you. I don't know what it is but it really sends me. Then after you're here a few days you get more or less like everybody else."

Food for thought: Rooster Van Upp knows more than he lets on. Mr. Williams, too. As the first arrival, Mr. Williams must know what this is all about.

One more point: on the last day of shooting we go right back where we started from. But where is that? Home, I hope.

6

Myron's will is more powerful than I suspected. He must be broken. Soon. Because, frankly, I cannot take much more of this seesawing back and forth, this coming and going—particularly the going—when I have work to do!

A few minutes after the ill-groomed Iris left the room, I was able to replace Myron at the controls. But there was a struggle. In his cretinous way, he, too, shares the Breckinridge genius. But in the end of course he will be no match for me—nothing human is (or *non*-human for that matter, as I shall presently demonstrate).

Just now I went to the window. Took a dozen deep breaths of 1948 non-polluted ozone and started to tingle from top to toe; became giddy; almost drunk with joy.

Beneath my window, shadowy figures cavort beside the pool. As the boxer-trunked boys and Jantzened girls sunbathe in the dark, they look exactly like some of those extras I have so often glimpsed in the background of Esther Williams films—are they the very same boys and girls? It is perfectly possible. After all, we are next door to MGM and off-duty extras must cavort somewhere.

Despite the darkness, I was able to detect, here and there, an ominously bulging *pullulating* set of trunks. Involuntarily, I shuddered. The enemy has been sighted. *Operation Myra* now goes into phase one.

My moment of euphoria passed when, foolishly, I removed my—Myron's—clothes to get a good look at the work he has done to what was once, very simply, the body of the most beautiful woman the world has known since that tragic day when Vera Hruba Ralston hung up her ice skates at public request. *Hair* grows down my—no, not my: *his* ugly chest.

Worst of all, between my still gorgeous legs, within that sacred precinct where the finest of Scandinavia's surgeons once fashioned a delicate vagina as cunningly contrived as the ear of a snail, that son of a bitch Myron has not only removed the delicate honeypot of every real American boy's dreams but replaced it with A Thing! A ghastly long thick tubular object which must look to the casual onlooker—if such there be in my case!—as if it were some sort of vegetable in the order of *The Thing* (1952), a curiously religious film written by clever funster Charles Lederer, the nephew of Marion Davies; and starring James Arness, my *assiette de thé* if there ever was one, all six feet six of him, now lost to television.

This cock has got to go! For one thing the overall effect is ghastly, since Myron was obviously too cheap to buy a pair of balls.

My once and future exquisite body has been hideously hacked and butchered by one Dr. Mengers, formerly Nurse Mengers, whom I always suspected of treachery even in the heyest of my days. The once and future glorious breasts have been deflated. Livid scars beneath each dull masculine nipple bear mute witness to those astonishing twins which for too brief a time made glorious the Hollywood of the late sixties.

I sit at this table (fully clothed—I cannot bear the sight of me—him!), and begin now to weave my web, to create my universe. And the first strand of this astonishing creation that I have in mind will be a proper wardrobe—not to mention wig, eyelashes, silver detachable fingernails, etc.

Then once and for all, Myron must be suppressed. I had thought that I could obliterate him simply through the exertion of my will over his. But nut-wise he is harder to crack than I thought. So I must now resort to my old stand-by that never fails, the hormone cocktail. But has it been invented yet? If not, I think I recall enough of the formula to whip up a batch that will get this hair off my chest and Myron out of my skull.

Removing the pseudo-phallus will be more of a problem, but I am sure that there are a dozen friendly surgeons in the area who will do the necessary snip-snip under hygienic working conditions. The rebuilding of my glorious boobs, of my delectable cunt will take more time, but have I not time enough to spare, since this world is mine and all things in it?

To work! First, I shall save MGM at the most crucial moment in the history of the motion picture industry when, thanks to television, the studio system is about to go down the drain, taking with it Andy Hardy, Maisie, Pandro S. Berman, Esther Williams—everything, in fact, that made America great, that made it possible for our boys to destroy Hitler, Mussolini and Tojo.

I shall personally take charge of all MGM production during the coming crucial weeks, supporting the beleaguered Dream Merchant Louis B. Mayer against the interloper Dore Schary, whose sponsorship of *The Boy with the Green Hair* (1948) marked the beginning of the end of the golden age of the movies. By August 1 Schary will be out on his ass and L. B., guided by me, will restore Metro's product to what it was before the release of *The Boy with the Green Hair* and the advent of television's Milton Berle and Snookie Lanson.

It is important that I save not only Hollywood—the source of the best of our race's dreams since those brutish paintings on the cavern walls at Lascaux—but the United States. For in a nation inspired by the values of Andy Hardy's father, good Judge Hardy as played by Lewis Stone—still alive and kicking as I sit in this dingy hotel room (I am home! home!)—the current age of darkness through which we are passing (1973) would never have taken place, for the simple reason that Richard M. Nixon could never have been elected President, while the films of S. Peckinpah would not have obtained financing from a major studio even with the return of block-booking, and block-booking is high on my agenda because the studios must own their own theaters again; so to hell with the Sherman Anti-Trust Act!

Once I have restored Hollywood to its ancient glory (and myself to what I was!), I shall very simply restructure the human race. This will entail the reduction of world population through a complete change in man's sexual image.

7

I knew it was you all along, you bitch Myra! I was just leading
you on, pretending I couldn't read that dumb disguised writing
of yours which has to be read in a mirror but *upside* down, which
is the way you see everything in your perverted way.

Well, you are not about to take over yours truly Myron Breckinridge, any more than you are going to take over MGM, which
is a big laugh. Who over there will listen to you, you drag queen
freak? Yes, that's what you are, and as for hormone cocktails,
two can play at that party. By the time I finish taking *male*
hormones I'm going to be covered with hair like a tarantula,
with a voice way down in my balls when I buy them which will
be soon, you can bet your sweet ass. Then *you* are going to be
finished once and for all. Kaput.

Meanwhile, I am getting out of here pronto because I am,
like they say at the touch-and-feel sessions Mary-Ann and I
used to attend in Encino, *highly motivated*. Get that, Myra? I have
the best wife in the world and eight terriers and my catering
and no crazy-type mad woman is going to keep me away from
them. Warning. I am eating oysters tonight. That will put lead
in my pencil like they say, and if I can find any prairie oysters

I'll eat them and vitamin E, too, if it's been thought up yet. You've had it, Myra.

After writing this message to Myra, I went downstairs to the bar which is cozy with two glass doors that open out onto the patio where the pool is and where, even though it is dark, there are still people splashing around. Of course, it's a fairly hot evening, I thought in my innocence, and looked at my watch which said it was only five o'clock. I thought, having found out that it was Myra who got me into this picture and is now trying to take over, that I had learned the worst. Well, I hadn't. I was in for some pretty awful surprises, as I will recount.

In the bar there were half a dozen local people sitting at these round tables drinking beer and listening to Perry Como on the red and green plastic jukebox. It's funny, but you get so you can tell right away who is local and who is an out-of-towner. The locals if they are girls look like Iris with funny hair styles and short dresses with these squared-off shoulders. So far I have only seen one with a long dress on and she made everyone go buzz-buzz and talk about The New Look, whatever that is. The local men have short hair and wear wild-looking Hawaiian-style sports shirts with wide baggy trousers which totally disguise their baskets.

Maude was sitting with a lady in black who greeted me with "August 11, 1969." Good form in our group is to say on first meeting your date of arrival and the place you left from: "Plandome, New York." And your name: "Miranda Bowles. Mrs. Connally Yarborough Bowles."

I said my piece.

"Sit down, sweetie," said Maude. "Look what I've done with Miranda's hair with only this *ancient* equipment!"

"Maude has a gift," said Mrs. C. Y. Bowles, whose flame-colored hair had been teased into a beehive, suitable for 1961, the year that Maude left the real world.

"Bartender. A daiquiri for me with plenty of ice, and now—get this, sweetie—a full jigger of rum *on the side*." Maude turned to me. "Have one, too." So I had one and so did Mrs. C. Y.

Bowles. Maude I'm afraid was a little tipsy. "You know I'm a Paganini of hair!" Maude yelled after the second swallow of what must've been his third daiquiri.

"There's nothing I can't do with hair, no matter how dry or how thin or how frazzled at the ends. Doris Duke used to say 'Maude, you are supreme.' I also do the Duchess of Windsor when she's at the Waldorf."

"I thought your business was in White Plains."

"I'm *sent* for, sweetie. A talent like mine only comes once in a generation. Everybody wants Maude to *bend* their hair. Mr. Kenneth hates me but I don't give a hoot!" hooted Maude.

"It is odd, Mr. Breckinridge," said Mrs. C. Y. Bowles, "but I actually went to Maude some years ago at the recommendation of a dear mutual friend. Now deceased. From Plandome. Little did I dream that one day we would meet *here*. I am a widow," she added for no particular reason except she likes to keep adding these bits of information.

"Miranda's husband was a judge in New York."

"With the Appellate Court. Connally died July 4. I have a lime tree in the garden. The only one in Plandome. It must be taken in during the winter."

"Wowee!" Two adolescent boys, one tall and skinny and one short and skinny with hair plastered down from water and wearing boxer-type swimsuits, came running in from the pool.

"Angels!" cried Maude. "You're dripping water all over everything!"

"Screw you, Maude!" said the short one in a saucy way and then the Filipino bartender chased the two of them out of the room.

"Ill-bred," sighed Mrs. C. Y. Bowles.

Maude giggled and rolled his eyes. Then said to me, "Those are Rooster Van Upp's two sons. The oldest one is the smallest one and he's known as Chicken."

"Why," I asked, "were those two kids swimming this late? And why are all those people still sitting around the pool in the dark?"

"Oh, dear!" Mrs. C. Y. Bowles looked distressed. She turned to Maude. "You didn't brief him?"

"Sorry, Miranda!" Maude looked guilty and kind of worried. "You know I have no memory except for hair, where I have ninety-eight-percent perfect recollection."

Maude got up. "Come outside," said Maude to me. Gripping ahold of my arm with a hand like a hot starfish, he took me out to the pool where I could see fairly well even though the sun had gone down. *Except that the sun hadn't gone down.*

"Those people are locals," said Maude, pointing to a dozen or so young men and women who were lying about the pool or splashing around inside its kidney-shaped form. "They are swimming and sunning themselves. Because it's only five thirty in the afternoon."

"Maude, it's later than five thirty. It's at least seven o'clock because it's dark outside—unless I am going blind like Bette Davis in *Dark Victory*." I have got to watch out for these movie references which mean that Myra is getting ready to pounce and take the controls away—and I had a dozen oysters for dinner. Must see a doctor tomorrow about hormones. Maude says vitamin E isn't invented yet.

"No, sugar, you're not going blind. It's just that we can't see the sun and they can. They are also getting nice tans. Particularly that sexy lout over there jumping up and down on the diving board. Look at those big white varicose veins, will you? They really—what's the new phrase?—turn me on!"

"Maude, why is it dark for us and sunny for them?"

"Because the sun has gone down for us but it's still up there in the sky for them." Then Maude pointed one of his starfish fingers at the middle of the darkness just opposite us. "What do you see, sweetie?"

"I don't see anything because it's dark, because it's night."

"*Try* to see. Maybe I should get you some carrot juice."

I squinted and stared until, finally, I made out a huge round shape, darker than the rest of the sky and hanging up there in space like some kind of dead planet. "I see this big round thing,"

I said, "and I see, well, I don't know what I see. There are these strange sorts of spirals and things in the sky."

"That's it, sweetie. Only it's not the sky you're looking at. *It's the back of the inside of the television set.*"

I guess I must've looked pretty dumb even in the dark because Maude proceeded to spell it all out for me and I thought my mind would just break open like a watch does when you drop it hard.

"The local people see the sky and the sun on this side of the Strip because they're home where they belong in 1948. But we can't see the sky and the sun because though we're here, too, we're also inside the set. Oh, really! Don't look so gloomy. Cheer up. It's fun! It's montage-time in Dixie, sweetie!"

Maude left me standing there in the darkness with the sun-bathers in front of me and back of them the enormous workings of the television set that filled half the sky.

As my eyes grew accustomed to the gloom, I saw to the left of the sky what looked like this huge letter "W."

For one crazy desperate minute I thought that there was a message for me up there.

So, squinting and staring hard as I could, I was able to make out next to the "W" the letter "E."

Well, I got the message loud and clear all right. "Westing-house."

8

Myron is asleep. Poor Myron. Nothing can save you. Not even the dozen oysters you just ate and which I have just sent on their merry way down the john after a tickle or two of the old gullet.

So we are inside the television set. Well, why not? Unfortunately, I only heard part of Maude's explanation. But then, it is with greatest effort that I am able to look out through Myron's eyes, to tune in on what he hears. It is a bit like being at the bottom of a well when Myron is at the controls, and it takes the most intense concentration on my part to supplant him. Yet each time I return I find the trip easier; his resistance to me less. Soon he will be permanently at the bottom of the well, tastefully attired in a cement overcoat!

From the moment of my arrival I knew instinctively that Maude would be an ally. So while Myron slept or thought he was sleeping, I took control, vaulted into the saddle like Ella Raines (*Tall in the Saddle*, 1944, with John Wayne) and stole out of our room.

It was about midnight. Want to know what I did, Myron? Then try to crack *this* code, you dumb asshole!

MYRON

I am now using the same code that the Japanese used in World War II, a code which was finally broken by American intelligence, making it possible for our Navy to shoot down Admiral Yamamoto. Nevertheless that special Kamikaze Kode still remains the best of all possible codes, as I discovered while writing what many people thought was the masterpiece of the *first* Myron Breckinridge: "The Banality of Anality or *Thirty Seconds Over Tokyo*: The Gunner's View."

This startling essay did *not* appear in *Cahiers du Cinéma,* thus establishing for an entire generation the uniqueness of the original Myron's genius. Let me note in passing that I still have a sneaking fondness for the first of my metamorphoses as he slithered from art house to art house, from one 42nd Street triple-all-night feature to another. After all, out of those fructifying years came the amusing monograph "Penny Singleton and Sally Eilers: The Orality of Florality" which not even *View* would publish: proof once again that Myron's seminal—in every sense—work *had hit,* slightly to derange a metaphor, *the nail on the head.* The first Myron was also a connoisseur of the subway tearooms, and between films he could usually be found in one or another of the IRT rooms (he had a passion for the IRT), pouring.

Trial and error brought me to Maude's room on the floor above mine.

I rapped on the door.

"Come in, Harold," said Maude.

I went in, and there was Maude in a fascinating Chinese dragon gown, surrounded by a hundred wigs on plaster heads. The walls of the room are covered with photographs of celebrated women's heads with the hair highlighted.

"Who the fuck is Harold?" I asked gently, all woman despite my appearance.

Maude gave me a sneaky look and giggled, "Ask me no questions . . ." Although I still don't know who Maude's swain is, we did let our hair down and had an old-fashioned hen-fest.

As I suspected, Maude is a sexual degenerate. But I make no moral judgment. Besides, fags have their uses. Were it not

for the fags, man would never have flown. The fag Leonardo
da Vinci created the idea of flight, while two fag siblings (Orville
and Wilbur Wright) got the human race off the ground at Kitty
Hawk (a name known to every dyke). So to the fruits belong
the sky! Of course, they are second-class citizens. But in my
universe it is better to be second-class than to be barbarian—
to be beyond the pale like those sinister heterosexuals who *breed*.
Happily, by the time I am finished with them, incontinent
breeding will be a thing of the past (as of 1973). After all, that
is why I have returned.

For the moment I shall not divulge my master plan even in
Japanese code. (I have reason to believe that the Filipino bartender is not a Filipino bartender but a Nisei spy.) I merely
note in passing that I have not returned to 1948 simply to save
Hollywood and the United States, amusing (and easy) as those
tasks are. No, I am here to save the human race through change.
For I am, let us face it once and for all, the Embodiment of
Necessary Mutancy on the verge of creating a superrace, in my
image.

"But first I need a wardrobe, Maude. Wigs. Eyelashes. Fingernails. Foundation garments. Adrian dresses."

Maude hooted in a most disagreeable way and it was all I
could do not to smack his fat, slightly rouged cheeks. "Myron,
I never knew! You're so square, yet you're—you're a drag queen!"

"Maude." I was stern as my fingers casually wrapped themselves loosely about Maude's plump toadlike neck. I saw terror
in his eyes. Most suitable. "*Never* use that word to me, because
I am *all woman*. Or was."

Maude gulped. "Sorry, sweetie. Do let go of my neck,
Myron . . ."

"Call me Myra." I let go of his neck.

"Myra? Well, I must say this *is* a surprise . . . Myra, sweetie."

"We're going to be great friends." I was Kay Francis in *Four
Jills in a Jeep*, warm, gracious; I even lisped slightly in a throaty
voice as I graciously jilled.

"Natch," said Maude. "And I'll try to rustle up some duds
for you. What size?"

Maude noted down my measurements.

"Now then, Maude, for the time being this is our little secret."

Maude looked puzzled. "But how can it be a secret when you're going to *wear* these clothes? Or are you just going to put them on in the closet and stay there?"

"No, shit-heel," I jeeped at him severely. "I will appear on the Strip exquisitely groomed from time to time *but* in total disguise."

"Word will get around, sweetie."

"I know. And I must take that chance. Meanwhile, there are those who must *never* know." This was awkward in the extreme. How to tell Maude that Myron must never know without telling Maude too much? Thinking hard, I tried on one of Maude's wigs in front of his special makeup mirror surrounded by electric light bulbs—perfect middle-period 20th Century-Fox. I felt like June Haver but I looked, I fear, like late-period ZaSu Pitts. Hormones! Hormones!

"Maude, I am, at times, not myself."

"Then who are you?" Maude was teasing one of the wigs nervously, copying a photograph of a society queen circa Camelot.

"I have these—dizzy spells. I was having one when we met. I go on and on about how I am *Myron* Breckinridge who lives in the Valley . . ."

"Yes, sweetie, you do go on and on."

"Well, when I am in one of those 'fits,' I don't want you to mention a word to him—that is, to me—about Myra or about my wardrobe, which I am going to keep in here for the time being, if you don't mind being such an angel!" I jilled gloriously. Maude is now my slave.

We agreed to meet day after tomorrow before dinner in his room where he will have my new wardrobe assembled. I insisted on giving him Myron's gold signet ring as payment. "But you don't have to," said Maude, pocketing the ring. "We get a nice allowance once a week from Mr. Williams."

"Pawn it. I want the best, Maude. Good night, angel." I started to the door.

"Are you going to wear that wig to bed?"

"Silly me!" I jilled. I had forgotten that I was still wearing the fright wig. "By the way, who *is* Mr. Williams?"

"Such a nice man!" Yet the way Maude said that phrase I felt something was being held back. "He has a suite upstairs on the top floor."

"I shall see him tomorrow."

"Oh, I wouldn't count on that. Well, see *you* tomorrow." Maude was eager to meet his beau Harold and so I came back to this room, tripping on air. I have begun.

9

Myra has a new code, well, I will crack this one in time, too, except there will be no need as I expect to be out of here by the weekend.

So far I've got to admit this place has me stumped. For instance, this morning after breakfast I took a stroll along the highway as far as the Texaco filling station.

I said "Howdy" to the attendant and his son, who are large pink-faced men with big bellies and laugh a whole lot but you can see that they are suspicious of all of us "out-of-towners," as if everybody in California wasn't an out-of-towner including these two porkers from Drake, North Dakota.

"Howdy, pardner," said the son to me as he introduced a hose full of Texaco into the rear end of what proved to be a Hudson of the kind that the Smithsonian would give a fortune for. I have, incidentally, seen *two* Kaiser-Frazer four-door sedans in apple-pie condition.

"Hi," I said and just sort of stood idly by while the porkers serviced the Hudson, all the while eyeing me as if I was about to gun them down for the contents of their dusty old-fashioned cash register.

The driver of the Hudson was a businessman-type with a flowery tie and trousers wide enough to hide the shape of your average elephant's legs.

We fell into conversation of the usual California kind, though I made a mistake by asking about the smog-rate on the freeway that morning and of course he didn't know what I was talking about as the air back here in 1948 is just about crystal-clear and every day you can see Catalina Island if you want to look that way.

The upshot of our conversation was his agreeing to drive me into the center of Culver City where his realtor office was. I was pretty thrilled.

The Drake, N.D., porkers looked kind of sly when I got into the front seat beside the realtor, who revved up his Hudson which is a fine car I have always been told by those who really know. I would've given quite a few bucks to look under the hood for a while.

"The Commies," said the realtor, "are not going to stop unless we drop the big one on 'em and I say let's drop it before *they* drop it on us."

I am familiar with this conversation from having lived five years in the Valley and though I think we ought to sooner or later drop the big one on them, it is hard to do this when for all we know our President or our Vice-President or any one of a number of other good Americans might happen to be visiting in Peking or in Moscow at the time the big one went off. Of course, this is hard to explain to a realtor in Culver City back in '48. As it is, it's not easy to explain to the Young Republican League of Orange County, California, now in '73.

I agreed with the driver wholeheartedly and as we passed the two bungalows and the billboard with Gene Kelly and the three other musketeers on it, I said, "Of course, co-existence is just a dream indulged in by Com-symps . . ."

I never finished the sentence because before I knew what was happening, there was the Hudson up ahead of me, driving off into the distance, and there was I, sitting in the middle of the highway. A pickup truck which had been following us swerved to one side and the driver yelled at me to get my ass out of the road, which I did.

What had happened? Well, speaking technically, at the moment the Hudson crossed the barrier from where we are inside the TV to where the rest of the world is outside the TV and *Siren of Babylon*, he kept on going and I stayed where I was. That is what happened.

I brushed off my clothes and then walked as far as I could along the road toward downtown Culver City, which was not very far. First there was this glassy mirage-like effect which I have mentioned before where you can't really see anything but a sort of shining lake in the road. Then you stop. There isn't any wall or plate glass in your way. There just isn't *anything* ahead of you and you can't move an inch forward even though the locals whiz back and forth in and out of the mirage and for them there is obviously no barrier of any kind.

I was pretty depressed by all this even though it was a nice morning and the air is fresh back here and the dark clouds that are really the back of the inside of the TV set are hardly noticeable until a bit past noon when the sun drops behind the back of the TV and half the sky starts to look gloomy and shadowy and creepy—for us, that is. The locals don't notice it. I am getting to hate them.

The porker at the filling station gave me a wise look. "Decided to come on back, did you now?" The son winked at the father.

I pretended not to hear them. But I am suspicious of them and of everybody else around here. I mean, how much do they really know? Everything *looks* so normal, like the people and the cars even though they are old. Even the back lot of Metro looks perfectly O.K. with people coming and going who at a distance you can't tell if they are local or out-of-towners except sometimes the clothes will give them away.

"Hi!" On the porch of one of the bungalows was a nice-looking girl with long hair like Ann Sheridan, the Oomph Girl in *Nora Prentiss*. I've got to stop this thinking about and remembering old movies like Myra. Must also try to remember my International Code Book to see what she is up to in this phase of time.

"Hi," I said.

"You're from out-of-town, aren't you?"

"No." I was getting tired of being taken for granted by the locals. "I'm from the Valley. Near Van Nuys."

"Funny. You look like one of the people who're staying at Rooster's hotel."

I knew it was my narrow trousers and not the identification disk that I wore on the chain inside my jacket, and out of view. "Yes, I'm staying at the hotel."

"Come on in. We take boarders, you know. I'm Suzy."

So I went up the steps to the morning-glory-trellised porch where I found a fellow out-of-towner seated in a rocker, drinking beer. "This is Mr. Telemachus," said Suzy.

I introduced myself. Mr. Telemachus is a Greek and about thirty years old, with a deep voice and a long dead-looking face like John Carradine's: "April 1, 1968, and no jokes about April Fools' Day."

I gave my date and Suzy was delighted. "I knew you were an out-of-towner, even if you are from the Valley."

"I guess you're the latest arrival," said Mr. Telemachus. "Look forward to hearing from you tonight. There's a general meeting called. So it must be for you."

Before I could make sense of this, Suzy asked, "Would you like a beer?" She is very gracious, I'll say that. I soon learned that she hopes to get a job in wardrobe at Metro where her mother used to work as an assistant to Edith Head before her gall bladder was removed. Suzy's mother's gall bladder, that is, not Miss Head's. If the studio hadn't lost so much money last year Suzy would've been hired "but luckily this year everything looks wonderful for the studio because Mr. Mayer has hired Dore Schary who is the best there is to take over production and he's really doing a job. I know." Suzy looked proud and kind of cute in a Jean Arthur way. "I had an under-five-line part in a picture he's shooting now which is going to be a block-buster."

"It's called *Intruder in the Dust*." Mr. Telemachus chuckled in a disagreeable way.

"Oh, Mr. Telemachus, really! How can you judge a picture before it's finished?"

"Oh, it's *finished*, Suzy."

"Now don't start talking that funny double-talk with me. *I* read the script, the whole thing, and it's about intolerance, which is a powerful subject and sure-fire box office like *Gentleman's Agreement* last year."

Suzy went for my beer. Mr. Telemachus laughed. "I know the grosses of every picture they're currently lensing at Metro. And are they ever in trouble!"

"You're in the Industry, aren't you?"

Mr. Telemachus nodded. "I was with daily *Variety* for six years. Then I was an executive at Four Star until I came here, with a copy of world grosses for all pix between 1930 and 1968 in my back pocket." He showed me this worn-looking book which he carries in his pocket at all times. "A tome worth its weight in gold to the locals, since it tells just what is going to happen box-office-wise to the product now lensing or prepping."

"So why don't you show it to them and get the gold?"

Mr. Telemachus' laugh was real hollow like someone pounding a drum. "When I first got here I showed it to Suzy. I was green. She couldn't read a word. Part of the rules around here. We're not allowed to interfere. That's rule one."

At this interesting point we were interrupted by Suzy and my beer and then before we could really settle down for a visit we were interrupted again by Mrs. Connally Yarborough Bowles, who was chasing Whittaker Kaiser with a swagger stick in her hand. "Rapist!" she roared. "Foul rapist!"

For a fat man Whittaker moves very clumsily and for a frail-looking woman Mrs. Bowles is amazingly strong, but then, she is a karate brown belt as well as an expert with the swagger stick which she proceeded to use on Whittaker's fat head. He was roaring like a heifer at slaughtering time and I am sorry to say that it did us all a lot of good to see her beat the shit out of him for having taken a liberty, as she put it, with one of the maids in the hotel who had run weeping from Whittaker's room shortly after he had tried to commit an act against nature on her Mexican person early this A.M.

I didn't learn much of anything from Suzy and Mr. Telemachus except that when Mr. Williams first came here he made a lot of money on the stock market out of which our allowances are paid each Saturday. Mr. Telemachus says that though he's talked to Mr. Williams on the phone he's never met him and only Rooster Van Upp is on a first-name basis with him. Suzy remembers seeing him once when she was a little girl and she remembers him as being bald and wearing a white suit and a panama hat on the order, I suppose, of Sydney Greenstreet. Stop it, Myra!

That was a close call. She almost took charge. I was dizzy for a moment but then came to.

It's about five o'clock and I am in this awful room with the lights on though it is as dark outside for me as it is broad daylight for the Van Upp boys who are yelling and splashing in the pool below my window.

The telephone just rang and it was Mr. Williams and the conversation went about as follows.

"I trust I do not disturb you." He was very ceremonious and so was I as I told him that his trust was not in vain as I was doing nothing but staring at the wall and going crazy trying to figure out how to get the hell back home.

After some more "daresays" and "I trusts," he said, "I hope in the future you will not attempt to leave our little world by motorcar. It is not possible."

"So I found out."

"And it is demoralizing for the locals who suddenly find themselves alone in their vehicles once the barrier is passed."

"I wonder if you could have a talk with me about where we are, Mr. Williams, you and I man to man?"

"But *you* are the one who must talk to us, dear Mr. Breck-inridge." Oh, he's a smooth one. "Tonight, in fact, you will address our full group in the rumpus room. That's in the basement of the hotel. Mrs. Connally Yarborough Bowles will chair the meeting and I will of course be listening in on the intercom."

"But talk about what?"

"You are the latest arrival. It is customary for the 'new boy,' as it were, to report on what has been happening since the last arrival, who, I fear, was Mr. Whittaker Kaiser. *His* report to our group was disappointing. I am sure that yours will more than compensate."

"Report on what?"

"You arrived April 17, 1973. Mr. Kaiser arrived February 9, 1973. Specifically, we would like you to tell us all that you can remember that happened in the 'other' world between February and April. You will find much interest in the sordid affair at the Watergate and a certain skepticism about Mr. Nixon's pro-testation of peace with honor in Vietnam."

"I happen to believe that Mr. Nixon is probably the greatest American President . . ."

"Dear Mr. Breckinridge, please! We are non-partisan. Non-sectarian. Do tell it—what is the new phrase?—*like it is*. As *you* see it. Also add any details about the arts, high fashion, cuisine. Anything, in short, that you think would amuse our group."

"How many are there?"

There was this slight, this very slight, pause on the line. "Ac-tually we are not certain. I have kept as careful count as possible, since I am, after all, the first arrival. But a number of out-of-towners prefer making do for themselves on the back lot or in the film itself, going on and on from reel to reel. We seldom see these people. But those who do live on what we call, col-loquially, the Strip, some eighty ladies and gentlemen, will be in the rumpus room at nine sharp to hear your report."

"Mr. Williams, when do we get out of here?"

"Mr. Breckinridge, what is *when*?"

"Now look here, Mr. Williams . . ."

"And where, Mr. Breckinridge, is *here? Au revoir.*"

Well, at nine o'clock the rumpus room began to fill up. Rooster Van Upp and his two sons, the tall one is fourteen and the short one is sixteen and very well-hung . . . No, Myra. You're not coming back because I had *two* dozen oysters during the day and kept them all down though I have a feeling you did get back for a few minutes during dinner when I had this funny blackout with Maude and Mrs. Connally Yarborough Bowles in the hotel dining room.

Between the oyster cocktail and the fruit-cup dessert I have no memory of what we ate or what I said except that when coffee arrived Mrs. C. Y. Bowles was staring at me with a funny expression and Maude said, "Sweetie, you are really wound up, for a Chinese caterer in the Valley." What did I say? Do? I shudder to think. But at least *she* was back no more than twenty, thirty minutes.

My eighty or so fellow prisoners of *Siren of Babylon* were all sitting on folding chairs when I went down to the rumpus room, which has no windows as it is in the basement and has overhead fluorescent lights of the same blue-gray as the television screen. By the way, the one thing we all have in common around here is missing television. Rooster keeps saying he will buy a set from Dumont, but of course even if he does there isn't anything worth watching on it and won't be for a couple of years. Meanwhile there is radio, which most of us put up with as second-best.

Otherwise there is nothing that our group has in common with each other other than our all being in this same boat together inside the TV. They are all ages, from this seventeen-year-old girl with braces on her teeth to this old man from St. Augustine, Florida, who claims to be a hundred but is probably older.

Mrs. C. Y. Bowles called the meeting to order. She then read the minutes of the last meeting which was obviously a disaster, as Whittaker Kaiser had said and perhaps done a number of violent and probably obscene things.

Mrs. C. Y. Bowles looked very grim as she reported on the meeting and everybody clucked and shook their heads and read between the lines. Whittaker looked angry but cowed—probably because Rooster Van Upp and his two boys were standing behind his chair as though ready with a series of rabbit punches to keep him in line.

Then I was introduced.

Well, I did my best to try to recall what Walter Cronkite has been telling us the last few weeks and I was surprised at how much I was able to remember. A lot of people asked questions about the Watergate and I defended our President from a number of allegations of the sort that I can't imagine any American who loves his country would allege or countenance. It is as plain as the nose on his face that he knew nothing about those people who broke into the Democratic headquarters nor did any of his close advisers know or condone what happened. I am convinced of this.

Unfortunately, there is a small but vociferous group of radicals in our group and for a while I thought they would get out of hand but Mrs. C. Y. Bowles kept a firm leash on their emotions, and Maude's questions about hair soon relieved the tension as I did my best to recall the latest styles for fashionable women in Brentwood as glimpsed by me in the supermarket there where Mary-Ann and I sometimes shop for special things.

I also reported on the work those of us in Planned Parenthood are doing and how the young son of our neighbor in the Valley Sam Westcott Junior has just won the Nobel Prize for inventing this easy-to-take-no-side-effect-permanent-style contraceptive. Sam Junior is the savior, they say, of the Third World.

Well, after these comments the meeting was warming up very nicely and Whittaker Kaiser was under control, muttering to himself but no bother to anyone, when I guess I made the gaffe of the century or of the movie anyway by saying, "Naturally I will pledge myself to help this group not only make a better America where the American dream is realized for everyone regardless of color or creed but to help each and every one of us find a way out of this movie and back home to our loved ones."

I thought this pretty rousing. Certainly I spoke from the heart with the image of Mary-Ann and the silky terriers in front of me like a vision.

Well, there was dead silence in that room. One of Maude's hairpins, if it had dropped, would have sounded like a tray of dishes.

I noticed Rooster Van Upp exchange a quick glance with his oldest and smallest son, Chicken. Whittaker Kaiser nodded drunkenly. The rest just stared at me and said nothing, nothing at all, like they hadn't heard me.

"Thank you, Mr. Breckinridge, for an excellent presentation covering those crucial weeks immediately prior to April 17, 1973, which is of course a happy date for us because *you* arrived!" There was a round of applause at the end of this very kind little speech on the part of Mrs. C. Y. Bowles and the formal part of the meeting broke up.

Rooster and sons passed around cola drinks and cookies and all sorts of people came up to me in a very friendly way to say hello and how glad they were to have me aboard and anything they could do for me they'd do and if I wanted to play bridge or poker or join the Film Discussion Society or the *Siren of Babylon* Club or whatever I was welcome to join this group or that. I must say they were very friendly except for Whittaker, who said, "You're as dumb as they are, shit-heel."

I don't know how dumb I am but I do know that I was pretty mystified by the attitude of everybody. When I asked Mrs. C. Y. Bowles if I had said something wrong, she was vague. "No, no. Certainly not. A beautiful presentation. Of course you are not yet acclimatized. That takes time. You perhaps miss—how shall I put it?—the nuances. But they will come. In good time. After all. As we say. Here. Babylon was not built. In a day." This was not much use.

Mr. Telemachus just chuckled in his bass voice: "You should do field work. Get into the movie more often. Ride the *DIS-*

SOLVES, the *FADES*, the *CUTS*. Learn the dialogue. The secret's there, if there is one."

I mingled for a while and got to know some pleasant people of the sort that Mary-Ann and I know in the Valley and I suppose, all in all, I could hack it like the President says pretty well here for a while but only for a while.

Yet I can't help but feel that there is also something pretty strange going on. I mean even stranger than being inside *Siren of Babylon*. There is something nobody's willing to tell me.

At midnight Iris came to my room and I told her how I lost my balls in the Marine Corps at Iwo Jima. After all, I did see *Sands of Iwo Jima* a half dozen times when I was eleven, and know all the ropes.

"I don't care," she said. "Whatever's left I want."

So I gave her what was left and she went right out of her mind. Dr. Mengers has certainly done well by me. "You make Rooster look like a chipmunk!"

"That was not my intention," I said, not wanting any trouble through arousing envy of the sort that Myra's beautiful boobs used to do. But I'm afraid the word will now spread pretty fast about Dr. Mengers' handiwork and I expect I will have quite a following among the fair sex if I am so minded, which I am not, as I wish to be, as much as possible, true to Mary-Ann.

By the way, girls in 1948 are—if Iris is a good example—a bit more gamy than they are in 1973 what with Mary-Ann's geranium vaginal spray. I don't think deodorants have been invented.

This is a long time ago.

10

Post Coitum Myra!

Oaf that he is, Myron collapsed after his engagement with the tacky Iris, and as he lay snoring on the bed I was able to take over the controls. You might say he blew those oysters—psychically if not physically.

It is late at night and I am in a pensive mood. For half an hour I lay on the bed whose sheets still reek of Iris's tidal process and, eyes shut, I concentrated furiously, opening one by one the attic cupboards where *my* memories are stored like so many spools of celluloid.

I played a scene here—a scene there. But soon stopped. The process was exhausting, for mine has been—I suddenly realize—a tragic life.

I realized that somber fact as I lay on the bed, fingering my flat hairy chest, trying not to look at that grotesque thing which has been so ineptly sewed to what was once, literally, the symbolic center of the universe.

I confess (but only to this page) a moment's weakness. Yes, I confess to tears for all that was lost. Only by an effort of will—and will power does remain to me in vast and comforting quantities—did I throw off melancholy by forcing myself as therapy to recall the plot of Henry Hathaway's *Call Northside 777*. Then a review of Hathaway's credits swiftly brought the roses to my electrolycised cheeks.

Thank God, no hair grows on my perfect face, while unwanted body hair will presently be banished either through hormones or—but sudden uneasy thought: do they have electrolysis back here in 1948? I seem to recall that my mother Gertrude the practical nurse removed her unwanted facial hairs with *wax*! Well, if I must endure pain in order to be beautiful, then I shall willingly dance the tarantella in my iron Maidenform bra! Perfection is all. I have never settled for less. And so to bed.

Like the phoenix, I rose from Myron's bed. I am still me. I peeked in the mirror and noted with delight that despite the inadequate frame of hair, my face is as minxlike and saucy as Kathryn Grayson's before she is contractually obliged to open her yap and give with those ear-rending high notes.

Humming to myself, I put on Myron's clothes—steeled myself to looking like a caterer by imagining that I was really Dietrich or Garbo in a butch mood circa 1933. Then I took to the Strip.

No words can describe what it is like to be back in 1948!—except my words, and I see no reason to deploy them on this page, for I have other work to do. Method is the key to all creation.

In the hotel lobby I asked Rooster Van Upp where Maude might be found and he gave me a hard look and said, "Mr. Nemo Trojan is out by the pool."

"And fuck you, too!" I jilled and saw in his eyes fear as he realized that Myron the schmuck had been replaced by a force of nature capable of devastating Culver City with a single epithet.

Sitting beside the pool, guzzling daiquiris, Maude was regal-

ing several ladies with scurrilous tales of the famous people he
says that he has known. I fear Maude is something of a mytho-
maniac—which explains his popularity on the Strip. Lie and
the world lies at your feet!

Beside the pool lounged several youths, ranging from well-
to ill-hung. I shall get to them presently, one by one—if not,
two by two.

I was brisk. "Maude, I want to talk to you privately."

"Sweetie, I was just telling the girls what Jackie said to me
when she asked me to come stay two weeks at the White House
and de-kink her hair after what Mr. Kenneth did to her."

"Do they know *who* you're talking about?"

"We're all post-1960," said one of the ladies. "Fact, we have
a Post-Sixty Club and if you'd like . . ."

A phrase or two—nothing worth recording—and the girls
fled, leaving Maude with that look on his face I have come to
know so well. It is like that of Miriam Hopkins when she first
gets a gander of Frederic March as he turns into quaint, crusty
Mr. Hyde.

"So it's you, Myra," said Maude. "Well, I got most of your
wardrobe."

"You angel!"

"I must say it's very funny, the way you're two people."

"One and a half, Maude. And Myron is the half that is about
to go."

Clothes-wise Maude came through splendidly.

"The quality is not the best," I said, arranging the snood to
cover my auburn wig, which consists of a high pompadour in
the front with a long Ann Sheridan fall in the back. "But the
overall effect is"—I rolled my eyes like Ann Dvorak—"devastating!"

"Sweetie, you have to be seen to be believed!" Maude was
even more thrilled than I at the transformation in front of his
middle-period 20th Century-Fox mirror.

"Now all that we need do is rebuild my bosom and cut off
this hideous penis."

"Oh, Myra, not that!" Maude's greedy—and highly unbecoming—interest in Dr. Mengers' Frankenstein-monster forced me to be sharp. "Look but don't touch," I said sternly. Then when I saw Maude's face crinkle with disappointment, I relented. "If you like, I'll give it to you when it's been removed."

Maude shuddered. "Myra, you couldn't? You wouldn't! You *mustn't*!"

But I was already looking up plastic surgeons in the Culver City yellow pages. Apparently there are only two. One did not answer. The other was on vacation at Lake Arrowhead but will be back in a few days. "Next June 1—in three weeks—when the picture starts shooting again, I shall have the operation performed right here in the hotel."

"Sugar, no plastic surgeon worth his salt is going to make a house call."

But I know all the difficulties and will, as always, surmount them. I have a hunch that silicone has not yet been invented, but fortunately, *I remember the formula*. Incidentally, there is no reason why I cannot make a fortune back here where there must be thousands of transsexualists longing to be properly boobed. By cornering the market in silicone . . . No! I have more important work.

Maude suggested that we have a drink at the Mannix Motel bar. "A sort of trial run, sugar. To see if you're recognized. Also, there are usually some really super studs at the Mannix."

"Maude, you are an insatiable pervert!" I jilled, amused at Maude's passion for males of the lower order.

The Mannix bar was—how shall I describe it? Funky. Smelling of beer and pre-filter cigarette smoke and that funny odor that is 1948 and perfectly indescribable in the vocabulary of 1973. The inevitable jukebox played "Sentimental Journey." The locals can never get enough of that oldie.

We sat at the booth farthest from the jukebox and ordered one of Eddie Mannix's special Sazerac cocktails (this Eddie Mannix is no relation to Eddie Mannix the top-flight Metro executive). As I suspected, there were no super studs or even studs in the bar; a luckluster group of locals with a sprinkling of out-of-towners. No one recognized me. Not even Whittaker Kaiser, who actually gave me the eye—if that tiny red oyster so like to an infected buttonhole could be said to have any *interpretable* expression. He shall be dealt with in good time.

"Maude, I've got to get onto the Metro lot."

"Sweetie, just fly across the Strip and there you are!"

"No, I want to go to the front office. I want to meet Louis B. Mayer and Dore Schary." I did not tell Maude that I have decided to become, briefly, for the experience only, a movie star, on my own terms of course. A half mill up front. A percentage of the gross. Terms that are unknown back here but I am by definition *avant-garde*, particularly in the past.

"You have got to be kidding, sugar. Even if they were to put you under contract, there's no way of your getting from here to there."

"Then we must work out a compromise." I was all sweet reason and lovely logic in perfect Virginia Bruce balance. Virginia must now, even as I write, be filming *Night Has a Thousand Eyes*. Did she find happiness with that Turk she married? And why, if she was mad for Turks, didn't she marry adorable Turhan Bey, now a photographer in Vienna? Questions, questions!

"The studio chiefs can always come *here* for conferences. Have you met any of them, by the way?"

"Met them? Sweetie, I've done Mrs. Dore Schary's hair a dozen times. She rings me from their palatial Bel Air mansion and says, 'Maude, my hair needs bending,' and I say, 'Come right over, Miriam,' and as I tend to her in my room we discuss her paintings—she's *talented*! And of course we talk about all the problems between Dore and L. B. which are, let me tell you, coming to a head . . ."

I was suddenly aware in the midst of Maude's deliciously spontaneous lie (he no more knows Miriam Schary than I do) that a young man of extraordinary allure had come into the bar. "Gimme a brew!" he commanded.

Beneath my half-lowered beaded lashes, I took inventory:

old checked shirt, Levis faded to no color, a silver Indian belt, worn moccasins, dingy white socks of the sort affected by working-class youths in every generation. Gray eyes, black hair, bronzed skin, whilst at the denim crotch a hornet's nest of sheerest menace to the future. He turned his back to me. Oh, those globes. No! Those gorgeous hemispheres, crying out to be wrenched apart in order that one might create the opposite to Plato's beast by substituting that dumb Greek's trendy ideal of the unnatural whole to my truer vision of forcibly divided and forever separated parts. No monist Myra!

"Hey," said the youth to Maude. Apparently he is half Cherokee Indian—the upper half, Maude swore to me, since the lower half of your average brave need not cause mother to sprint to the letter box for news of what is seldom more than a darkling shrimp despite that race's heroism at Wounded Knee best represented by the superb mimesis of Jeff Chandler as Cochise in *Broken Arrow*.

Half-Cherokee is a lineman with the telephone company and according to Maude strictly "jam," a word new to me but much in use back here to describe those males so addicted to heterosexuality that they will not drop their drawers for another male no matter how high the price—under twenty dollars, that is. During my formative pre-Myra years, as Myron the First, I came to the cynical conclusion that every working-class youth has his price, which varies from practically nothing at all for the release of seminal fluids in a friendly moist orifice to a fair chunk of cash if the fudge to be stirred is his.

Half-Cherokee plainly dislikes Maude and fags in general, but as for me . . .

"I gotta tell you, Myra, I never seen a woman like you before." His sinewy thigh was jammed against mine under the table, his moccasined foot was delicately tickling my ankle straps; he was so close that I could smell his rich, slightly musky odor, like Romanoff caviar newly spread on a Triscuit with a dash of lemon juice, a soupçon of onion.

Maude was delighted and, perhaps, just the tiniest bit jealous of my success with Half-Cherokee. "He's never been with a fag, have you, Butch?"

Half-Cherokee finished his beer with a provocative long suck. "No, sir, and I ain't startin' now. Hell, in the Marines at Pendleton, they was selling their asses for ten bucks a throw—but not yours truly! I was always saving up for a good broad. Like you, Myra."

"I hope there's plenty in the bank now!" I fear that I allowed my voice to take on the tonality of the sinister Mae West.

"I reckon I could drown you," he said quietly, again pushing his thigh against mine, to which I responded by reaching under the table and taking into my hand his entire posterity (the meat was mashed in with the potatoes). He looked shocked. Before he could wriggle away, I gave a powerful squeeze. He choked, as though the wind had just been knocked out of him, which, symbolically at least, it had.

"Jesus!" He gaped at me.

"What's the matter?" Maude had seen nothing.

"I'm just teasing Half-Cherokee." I was Joan Leslie winsome.

Poor stud, he did not know what to make of my sudden assault. Yet still he wants me even though pain is obviously not his bag; nor is it mine for that matter, except as catharsis, as a means of revelation. It was then that I had *my* revelation.

As I sit in this depressing hotel room (a cabin at the Mannix is plainly in the cards) I realize that once again fate has been my patsy. Half-Cherokee will be my first creation!

When I was Myra Breckinridge, the goddess of the late sixties and symbol of all that was best in Hollywood, I began, blindly, I confess, my restructuring of the sexes. Through the anal penetration of what that son of a bitch my uncle Buck Loner used to call your average hundred-percent all-American stud, I shifted the self-image of one Rusty Godowski (boyfriend to the dread Mary-Ann) from bull to heifer. With a single gesture I was able, once and for all, to shatter the false machismo of the American male. As the world now knows, my total victory over Rusty, et al., put an end not only to the American conquest

of Asia but to the previously undisputed primacy of the com-
bustion engine.

Unhappily, my creation of Unisex proved to be no more than
a stopgap. I did not go far enough (except with myself and,
mea culpa, I humbly confess that when I made myself Myra
Breckinridge, I did so simply in order to be unique). I realize
now that in my petty selfishness I was deliberately denying
others what I was so quick to claim as my own *re*birth-rite.
Worse, it is now evident that I have doomed the entire human
race to death from famine and pestilence as the result of overpopulation because, thanks to my efforts, the American male
now lacks the arrogant sexual thrust to conduct those wars that
in the past were so necessary to population control through the
playful use of antipersonnel weaponry. Yet the American male
—like all males—still continues mindlessly to reproduce. I made
him spiritual heifer but not *total* heifer. In a nutshell, I *un*-
manned the American male when I should have *de*manned him.

Sitting there in the Mannix bar, my hand squeezing Half-
Cherokee's generative organs (in which I could feel a billion
Half-Cherokee spermatozoa writhing in their eagerness to make
a billion Quarter-Cherokees ready to eat up the last of the
world's diminishing food supply), I realized what I must do. *I
must remove those organs—darkling shrimp, too.*

But obviously that is only the beginning. Something new,
vital, must take the place of this sturdy lineman once he is rid
of his lethal genitalia. Therefore, I shall, solemnly, share with
him my glory—with the whole world, for that matter. I am in
a *giving* mood! I shall pump silicone into Half-Cherokee's tiny
breasts and introduce female hormones into his bloodstream.
Then, after a crash course in makeup and skin care, I shall
present him to a grateful world as a gorgeous, fun-loving, sterile
Amazon, an Indian princess made for good times but not for
breeding.

A few press conferences, perhaps a lecture tour of the major
cities, a documentary film and my fun-loving sterile Amazon
will be the ideal of every red-blooded American boy. Something

to emulate. Population will then decrease at such a rate that by 1973 we should see the human race in perfect harmony with the environment, while, best of all, we shall be living in a joyous world dominated by fun-loving sterile Amazons, at peace with one another and the Arab emirates.

I have just sent President Truman a telegram saying that the Korean War must be called off. It will not be necessary, as I am about to stabilize world population. Naturally, a small cadre of unrestructured men and women will be allowed to breed. The rest of the men, however, will be re-created in my image! If I may say so, selflessness on this scale is unique in human history, and smacks of the divine.

Tomorrow I shall buy the basic ingredients for silicone, as well as a book on surgery. The whole thing could not be simpler. Three quick slices, tie up the loose ends and start pumping.

But, first, physician, heal thyself!

II

I got up early this A.M. to find that my face was covered with makeup and that Myra had gone to bed wearing these god-awful false eyelashes which I have flushed down the toilet. Also, Myra has *tweezered* my eyebrows! You cunt, if I ever get my hands on you it will be murder, justifiable homicide as any court would agree.

Today is my day to get out of here and I think the way out is somewhere around where I came in.

At breakfast in the hotel Mr. Telemachus happened to come in and offered to show me around the back lot. "Some interesting people are living there. Might give you a few ideas."

"Morning, Mac," said Mr. Telemachus to the guard at the gate who was reading another *Hollywood Reporter*.

"Morning, Abner," said the guard and motioned us through.

"Is that your name—Abner?" I asked.

"No. But that's what he thinks it is."

"He sees us, doesn't he?"

"He sees something but maybe it's not us. Maybe it's Abner." This was all pretty obscure. Mr. Telemachus likes his little mystery, which I don't.

Beyond the gate to the lot there is a street which used to be used for the Andy Hardy movies. It is a wide curving street with real lawns in front of the false-front houses and real trees. Every day real gardeners tend the lawns and prune the trees and the bushes as though this were all part of someone's private estate.

"That's Judge Hardy's house." Mr. Telemachus showed me the sights but I couldn't've cared less since all I really want to know is where the nearest exit is.

"How," I said, sounding as casual as I could as we wandered along the Hardy street, "do you—uh, get out of here? You know, back to where we came from?"

Mr. Telemachus acted like he hadn't heard me. "The last Hardy film," he said, "was released last year. It bombed."

"No." I surprised myself—well, not really. Myra's down there sending me all sorts of god-awful messages. I couldn't stop myself from saying, "They'll make one more in 1957."

I also couldn't stop myself from remembering the marquee blazing with *Andy Hardy Comes Home*, and me standing under it with, I'm sorry to report, this heavy eye makeup and bee-stung crimson lips and a trench coat like Marlene Dietrich. It was the start of Myra, really, that year when I was Myron first time around—a fag, I guess you'd have to say—and sent my first essay to André Bazin at *Cahiers du Cinéma* on Garbo's teeth and how dramatically they had changed after *As You Desire Me*. André Bazin died before he could write back his views on this subject.

"They'll lose their shirt, too. Nobody wants that crapola any more." Mr. Telemachus gave me from memory the disastrous worldwide grosses of Metro's last Hardy movies as well as the grosses of all films the studio is currently (1948) making. "Biggest bust of all will be *Siren of Babylon*. Domestic gross one million two. Negative cost one million three."

The back lot is a pretty big place, a good many acres of woods and streams and sets—city streets, French villages, old mansions, with these tourists riding in funny sort of trolley cars, seeing the sights sort of like they do now at Universal City. Yet all the while, back of everything, there is this giant screen hanging like in a drive-in movie against the blue-gray sky with the figures of Maria Montez and Bruce Cabot slowly acting out *Siren of Babylon* backwards from where we are. We out-of-towners see it. The locals don't . . .

12

Curious that Myron cannot get the point to where we are. He even misses the point to time and its simultaneity. Well, I shall not explain it to him—even if I could, which I cannot.

The bastard flushed my eyelashes down the toilet! He will pay for this. I confess, however, if only to this Kamikaze Kode, that I am somewhat disturbed at Myron's recuperative powers. *He keeps coming back.* Although his search for hormones has been as fruitless as my own (I have a lead, however, in Brentwood), he simply will not stay put. My terror is that he will blunder onto the exit, so clearly marked. If he does, I will kill him rather than face a life in the San Fernando Valley with Mary-Ann, Watergate, recession and Peckinpah. Call it suicide, I don't care.

Meanwhile, I have been active on a number of fronts. I have bought (or acquired on the back lot) disinfectant, a scalpel, a hypodermic needle, sutures. The components for silicone are now nicely jelling in a bucket in Maude's closet.

"What on earth do you want all those *sinister* things for?"

"Ask me no questions . . ." I jilled a reprise of Maude's favorite line. Actually, if Maude would tell fewer lies people would ask him fewer questions.

So far I have been able to come and go pretty much unnoticed in the hotel, though I can see that Rooster is puzzled to have observed, on at least two occasions, a strange and wondrously beautiful girl coming downstairs from the bedrooms. Luckily, each time I was in the company of Maude, who is above suspicion in that department.

Even before tonight—this marvelous evening—I had decided that the time had come to take a cabin at the Mannix Motel: a *pied-à-terre*—a home away from Myron. Also the isolation of one of the Mannix cabins will provide an ideal operating room for the Culver City surgeon—and for me!

"Hello, gorgeous!" It was Eddie Mannix himself who greeted me. Old, randy, drunk, Mannix is a true Californian from New York. I threw the full voltage of my charm at him.

"Gorgeous yourself, you hunk of man! Victor Mature has nothing on you, big boy!" I should note that a day or two ago while examining Myron's memory bank—soon to be in the hands of the receivers—I was saddened to find that Victor Mature (whose photograph taken unaware in the altogether during his heroic service in World War II helped defeat Hitler, Mussolini and Tojo) acted not long ago in an *Italian* film, directed by a one-time bad actor and neo-realismo director, with a script by a Broadway jokester. Worse, in the course of this travesty, the *image of Victor Mature was deliberately mocked*! I am certain that with some judicious tinkering back here, I shall be able to save Victor from his subsequent decline into camp even though, as I write these lines in Japanese, Victor has been taking a wrong turn in his career, collecting "kudos," as Mr. Telemachus would say, for such "serioso" products as *"I Wake Up Screaming."* Admittedly, Victor is currently lensing *Samson and Delilah*, a film in which his breasts will be revealed to an astonished world as larger and more significant than those of co-star Hedy Lamarr —a cataclysmic reversal of the expected which presaged my own subsequent—and still unfinished—realignment of the sexes.

Unfortunately, in the pre-Myra world, Victor's triumph in *Samson and Delilah* proved to a one-shot affair. Post-Myra, Victor must now play the title role in the remake of *Ben-Hur*. If he does, I guarantee that in the seventies he will be a star greater than *Last Brando in Paris*, with or without the two fingers up his anal canal (question to ask the makers of that deeply sentimental film [closer to *Snow White and the Seven Dwarfs* than to, say, *The Egyptian*]: were the fingernails of the poodlesque girl *actually* trimmed? Of course, I have only Myron's recollection of the film to go on, and perhaps there are essential points he missed, as usual).

"Big boy," I addressed Eddie Mannix with moistened lips half ajar like poor Veronica Lake now working as a luncheonette hostess and barmaid, glorious platinum locks long since shorn. "I may want to move over here, to be close to *you*."

"Any time, sweetheart." Mannix pinched my right hip and it was all I could do not to throw him through the window. In this world of her creation, it is Myra Breckinridge who pinches. But by playing it cool, I was rewarded with the key to Cabin 9—the most isolated cabin of all, he assured me with a wink. Then I went into the bar.

Half-Cherokee was sitting by the jukebox, arms back of his head, moccasined feet on a chair, eyes shut, listening to "Sentimental Journey," a beer in front of him—the picture of masculine contentment, ready to be altered entirely by the hand of the master potter.

As I joined Half-Cherokee, he gave me a long look—and I could not help but think how beautiful those gray eyes will look with false eyelashes and the thick brows that grow together in a straight line plucked.

"Have a brew, Myra."

I had a brew. I was enchanting. Seductive. Infatuating. Frilly, yes, and feminine in the pre-Lib way. Everything a manly boy would want a girl—*his* girl—to be.

I encouraged him to talk about himself. "I just broke up with this girl. Pussy. Yeah, that's her name, believe it or not. She's

Irish and real fair like you. But she wants to marry and settle down and me I want to like play the field. Not that I'm against getting married. I'd like that when I'm getting old like thirty. Yeah, I'd like it then. To settle down and have five or six kids."

With some effort I contained my disgust. If ever anyone was needed, I am needed at this crossroads in human history. As we sat there, I could almost hear the cries of the nearly sixty babies born every minute on this crowded globe as of 1948. Today (1973) it is closer to two hundred a minute unless I succeed in getting to the root of the matter. Whether I prevail or not—and I know that all the prayers of the human race are with me, and thank you all—I can guarantee that at least one Half-Cherokee will not add to the starving billions of the seventies.

I softened him up. Then heated him up in order to string him along—but cautiously (I thought) since I am not yet fully equipped to re-create him. Half-Cherokee's lust, however, was so great that I was tempted to play with him as matador does with bull. I fear I was naughty.

"Why don't we go up to your place, Myra?" Under the table a strong hot hand held my upper thigh.

"Oh, I couldn't. Not at the Thalberg! Think of my rep! That's all a girl has."

"You got a key to one of ole Eddie's cabins. I saw you take it."

"What sharp eyes you have!"

Half-Cherokee was now seriously aroused. I was seriously amused and thought, oh, for heaven's sake, you silly billy! What have you got to lose? If he becomes too forward, you have the means to bring him to heel.

And so I committed my near-fatal error. I left the bar. Ten minutes later he left the bar. One minute later we were together in the cabin farthest from the road, and from help.

I was not prepared for his crudeness, his violence.

No sooner had Half-Cherokee locked the door behind him than I saw an expression on his face which, I confess, I did not like. Gone was the hot pleading boy of only eleven minutes earlier. Instead there was the contorted face of a man with rape on his mind.

Roughly he grabbed me. Oh dear, I thought wearily. Has it come to this? I asked myself, echoing James Mason as he played the Emperor Franz Josef in the Terence Young remake of *Mayerling*, a film that has, I gather, delighted hundreds of long-distance jet-travelers, amongst them Myron.

"Baby, I gotta have it. And I gotta have it now!"

"Please," I whispered, gently pushing at his hard chest which was jammed against my Maidenform bra stuffed with latex. But his only response was to slam his hornet's nest (considerably enlarged) against my crotch.

I struggled. He held my arms close to my sides. He was very strong, I noted. For one weak but delicious moment as I inhaled the clean sweat of his body, I weighed the pros and cons of surrender. But when his greedy lips began to ravish my ear and I realized that my wig might fall off, I wrenched free of him.

"Come here," he commanded.

"No, no!" I fluttered away. "I'm saving myself for Mr. Right."

"Honey, *I'm* Mr. Right." He started toward me, an ominous figure.

"But I don't *know* you. I mean let's not hurry this, darling. This is only our first real date. Petting, yes, but not . . ."

He grabbed at me. I leapt behind the bed.

"Shit!" He swore. "Come here, bitch!"

"Darling, no. Please. I want you to respect me." To my joy I realized that vocally I had, for the first time, achieved the dark throaty Margaret Sullavan quality. Transfixed by the sound of my own magical voice, I fear I let down my guard.

Half-Cherokee dove across the bed and tackled me. Yes, tackled *Myra Breckinridge*, a goddess, true, but also a woman, tender, frail. I was stunned by his force; horrified by his brutality; saddened that he did not respect me.

For a confused moment he held me pinioned in his arms,

my back pressed against the radiator which left me—I just noticed—with a black and blue derrière. I looked up; saw a satanic smile. "I'm gonna fuck you, bitch." Those carven boyish lips were like a satyr's, no, like a carnivore's.

"Don't, please!" Without difficulty I summoned a tear to my eye. After all, Margaret Sullavan's voice was coming from *me*.

"You white bitches are all alike, cock-teasers."

I was bemused by the adjective. It was not *me* he wanted—beautiful and vulnerable as I am. No, it was a *white* woman that he wanted to humiliate. He wanted to avenge Wounded Knee in *my* body. At that instant, I fear, the lad lost my sympathy if not my interest.

As he started to rip at my dress, I gave him my special Giant Moth karate blow to the belly. He doubled up, unable to breathe. Then a well-aimed twist and push (coordinating right shoulder with left leg), dropped him to the floor with a crash.

Before he knew what hit him, I was seated on the small of his back with his left arm twisted behind him so that the slightest pressure of my forefinger on his wrist would cause the most excruciating pain.

"Christ!" he grunted. "What the fuck do you think you're doing?"

"Protecting myself from rape—darling."

"Rape, shit!" he snarled into the floor, still unbroken. "You want it. You know you want it."

"Not—perhaps—in the way you think." Delicately I pressed my forefinger on his wrist and was rewarded with a yelp.

"Stop that!"

"Only if you promise to be a good boy."

"What're you? Some kinda freak? A lady wrestler or something?" He looked at me over his shoulder. For the first time I detected the beginning of fear. But I had—have —no desire to hurt him. I want only to rebuild him in my own image. I also knew that if I were to frighten him too much he would never return.

"Foolish goose!" I gave him a sweet smile. "I just learned a few little tricks to keep from being all mussed up by purse-snatchers and by rapists."

"But you want it, Myra. I know you do. Hey, come on. Let me up, and I'll show you a good time."

"That I'd like to see, darling. But I think you better cool off a bit." I made myself comfortable on his firm rubbery buttocks. He looked remarkably appealing with his head twisted around so that he could see me like the new moon over his left shoulder, the straight black hair all tousled. I noticed that in our scuffle he had lost his moccasins.

One associative thought led to another. "You called me a white bitch."

"Well, you are. I mean you're white."

Pressure no greater than a feather's fall on his wrist. "Don't!" He yelled.

"Say you're sorry for calling me a bitch, darling."

"I'm sorry."

"That's a good boy. You hate white people, don't you?"

"No. Hell, I'm half white."

"Let's see which half."

He stared at me blankly.

With my right hand I took his right ankle and bent his leg back so that the large square foot in its dingy white sock was almost level with my eyes. I peeled off the damp sock.

"What're you doing?" He tried to straighten his leg but pressure on the wrist made him change his mind. He groaned. Then shuddered as I examined the calloused olive-tinted sole of his foot.

"Looking to see what color you really are. Darkies have pink soles."

"I ain't no nigger," he muttered.

"No, but the bottom of your foot is lighter than the rest. You're definitely two-toned, darling!" This was quite true. He was not, literally, a redskin—more light brown with yellowish tints. I noticed that the hairs on his ankle were sparse, black and fine.

"Come on," he said, embarrassed as I playfully tickled his toes. "Let me up. Let's call it a day. I'm sorry what I did."

I was now tickling the other foot, and he began to shudder. "Hey, stop! I'm ticklish."

I stopped. "Let's see if you're two-toned everywhere." I reached under him and got his belt buckle in my hand. He tried to roll away from me. This time I gave him sufficient pressure to make him scream.

"Darling, there must be no secrets between us." I changed my position; sat on his shoulder blades.

"You're breaking my arm," he whined.

I was also pushing his jeans down to his knees with my foot. He wore no underwear. The smooth coppery buttocks glistened sweatily in the bright glare of the single overhead Mazda.

"Well, well," I said significantly.

"Well, well . . . what?" He squeaked, nervously clenching his buttocks tight together.

I ran my hand lightly over the silky moist surface; it was like a hard Goodyear rubber tire. "Relax, darling." My hand was at the juncture of buttocks and legs, a dark, velvety Maltese cross that marked the spot, as it were: the center of the male, the sacred anus.

"I *am* relaxed. Listen. I better get going."

I gave his bottom a little smack. "Open for Myra."

"For Christ's sake . . ."

Pressure on the wrist; a cry; the buttocks went slack. I pushed at them; made them jiggle. Although at present his musculature is typically masculine, I could see how, once his male organs are removed and his system fortified with female hormones, the broad pelvic region would be truly ravishing.

Absence of unsightly hairs on his back (except for a single black tuft at the beginning of the anus) is also a definite plus. Looking down at what will soon be a woman's superb thighs, I could not help but think how one day some man—no, a host of men!—will be forever in my debt when they hold in their arms the luscious woman's body of Half-Cherokee, my creation.

But I still have my work cut out for me. "Spread your legs wide, darling."

"Shit!" He moaned but obeyed. There on the floor, vulnerable yet somehow impressive, were his large black hairless testes.

"What a nice bean-bag!" I sounded like Marie Wilson in a Ken Murray sketch. I gathered the two balls in my hand, and again was appalled at nature's terrible mindless fecundity. "Just think of all the billions of little Half-Cherokees swimming around in there, waiting to get out."

"Not now they aren't." (I had broken him.) "Come on. Let me up."

"But maybe I've changed *my* mind." I teased him. "Maybe I want it now."

"I don't think I can."

"Some stud! Anyway, you need relief, darling. All rapists do." I got off him suddenly. "Stand up, darling."

Warily he got to his feet. He looked frightened and angry, as what would-be rapist would not with his trousers about his ankles and his shirt hiked up to his armpits?

"You can relieve yourself, darling," I said, pointing to his dark long penis which curved in a baroque line over the loose-hanging scrotum. He was not circumcised. I was also pleased to note that except for a silky black mustache at the base of the prick, his front was as hairless as his back. I was particularly satisfied by the nipples: they are small, brown and for a male unusually protuberant, almost a quarter inch in length when excited. I know, for I proceeded to tickle him as he stood there dumbly, unable to believe what was happening to him.

"There's many a girl who would love to have boobs like yours."

"I ain't got boobs."

I slapped the hard flat pectoral muscle with my hand. "But, darling, you do have beautiful, exciting, excitable nipples." As I played with him I studied the veins near his armpit, trying to recall which is the one that will take the silicone. I must get the old anatomy book out and do my homework.

As a reward for Half-Cherokee's new cooperativeness, I al-

lowed him to masturbate in front of me. At first he was shy;
even hostile. But with a sharp word or two I was able to persuade
him to do what I wanted him to do.

During the milking process, my thoughts were somber. Three
times in forty-two minutes I forced him to shoot into the world
billions of Half-Cherokees. "Jesus, I can't do it again this quick,"
he whimpered after the second full flooding that hurtled toward
the bed where I was sitting, falling to the floor like a thick deadly
white rain.

"I can't . . . any more." His breath was coming in great gasps;
his face and armpits were streaked with sweat. He held tight
his balls in one hand as though to protect them from me (I
have already decided where the first incision will be in his groin).

As I write, I can imagine the joy I shall experience when I
detach that dark lethal bag from the beautiful and *sterile* Amazon, the Indian princess who is waiting for me to bring her
into the world. I shall christen her Minnehaha.

It is plain that nature and I are on a collision course. Happily,
nature is at a disadvantage, for nature is mindless and I am
pure mind. Wanting to preserve our species, nature idiotically
made us able to breed at much too early an age and in too vast
quantities. As a result of nature's mismanagement, any male in
his lifetime can personally produce 43,800 children, using a
different woman of course for each child. With the use of artificial insemination, a healthy male could double the world's
population after a few hours of idle handwork of the sort I
required Half-Cherokee to perform.

This must stop.

The balance between population and food supply is now un-
done. Starvation has begun in the Third World. According to
FAO, if all the world's arable land were properly farmed and
the food was then equally distributed, there would be sufficient
calories for the three billion people now alive *but* there would
be insufficient protein per capita. Result? Malnutrition for all.

I alone can save the human race. Knowing what I know, and
given this miraculous opportunity to begin the reduction of

population in 1948 by creating a new and exciting human image, one that every healthy boy will want to imitate, I shall be
able in one generation to reduce the world's population to *minus*
zero growth—and all in the name of metamorphosis and of joy!

As Half-Cherokee toweled his body and then cleaned up the
mess he had made on the floor, I stared at him with half-shut
eyes, saw him as a woman, saw the thick musculature of arms
and thighs reduced by hormones to soft suppleness; envisaged
tender breasts like those of one of Gauguin's native girls (the
suicide of George Sanders was an act of self-definition equal to
my own; and all honor to one who found it better to be dead
than bored); while the dark dangling threat to the race's future
would be sliced away, and buried deep—*you'll* get no child, oh,
mandrake root!

I am already planning the press conference we will hold. Half-
Cherokee—beautifully groomed by Edith Head—will address
the members of the fourth estate, explaining to them the whys
and wherefores of the metamorphosis—with perhaps a modest
phrase or two from me. Then Minnehaha will offer herself as
a living solution to the problem of overpopulation (not to mention this century's restless search for sexual identity), and together we will open a clinic, no, a thousand clinics all around
the world in order to create an entire race of beautiful, sterile,
fun-loving Amazons.

In no time at all, Half-Cherokee had put on his clothes; had
run to the door, as though fearful I might stop him. But how
could I—when I was suddenly June Allyson, twinkling my eyes
and husking my voice?

"I have great plans for you, darling."

"I bet." His shaky fingers fumbled with the doorknob.

I stepped toward him; he jumped backward, one hand protecting his crotch, the other his face. Poor boy! I fear he has
overreacted to me.

"Don't be afraid, darling." I touched his cheek to make sure
that he has no beard. Except for a bit of stubble under the chin,
the boy's face is as smooth as Dolores del Rio's. I fear that I am

already half in love with my raw material. "Next time I'll have a wonderful present for you."

"How about that?" He was shaking in his moccasins. I patted his cheek.

"Sayonara," I husked, and let him run off into the night. Two minutes later I heard his motorcycle revving up. A blast. He was gone.

I note in the mirror that my eyes are luminous with the power that has begun to concentrate in me. Yet in my victory I am, as always, pensive, self-critical. It is not for my sake but for that of our dying race that I must now, quite simply, bring nature to her knees in order that there be sufficient food and space for those who wish to live with dignity on this turning green globe whose protectress I am.

I shall now move all my equipment into this motel cabin, where, I pray, Myron will never set foot. He will remain in his digs at the Thalberg Hotel. I at the Mannix, where, as Maude would say, "There's always room."

13

O.K., Myra, so you are taking over for a day or two at a time now but it's the war not the battle that matters and I am winning the war though I can't say I like waking up every morning with my face smeared with inches of makeup. When I find your drag, you bitch, I am going to tear it to pieces.

Rooster Van Upp's oldest boy Chicken brought me coffee this morning after I had cleaned up my face. Chicken was wearing blue jeans and Keds and a Hawaiian shirt. He has a crewcut which looks like golden fuzz on his round thick head. As he put the tray down I could see inside his short sleeve where the armpit is, and the hairs in there are just as golden if fewer than the ones on his head and beaded with these tiny drops of sweat. "Hot day," says Chicken.

Now why did I keep on staring at Chicken like that when I am not a fag but straight as a die with the best little wife in the Valley? I know why. It is because Myra is all over the place. This is going to stop. You hear me?

Thank God, we were interrupted by Maude, who came in the room with this package and when Chicken saw Maude he skedaddled out of the room. Flaming queens like Maude often have that effect on impressionable adolescents in Southern California who even when they like getting blown by said queens are terrified of a daiquiri-tasting tongue landing in their ear or up their . . .

I am getting double vision as I write these lines. It's like being caught in one of *Siren of Babylon*'s lap-dissolves. There. Now it's gone.

"Good morning, sweetie!" Maude was in a very good humor. "You don't look so good. What you need is some action. Like Chicken Van Upp maybe?" Maude leered.

"You must be crazy, Maude . . ." I began.

"Well, I got you a different wig. And more clothes." Maude undid the package and there inside was this complete forties hooker outfit, consisting of a flashy short dress with the Adrian shoulders, ankle-strap black patent leather stiletto-heeled shoes, foundation garments of the sort which make any normal man hard as a rock, and a black wig.

"What the fuck," I asked, "is all this?"

"Sorry, Myra," Maude stammered, "I mean *Myron*. It's nothing at all. Forget I ever came by." Maude swept the clothes display back into this bag.

"You thought I was Myra, didn't you?" I was mean as all hell. "You're in cahoots with that bitch."

Maude sniffed. "Myra is a good friend, and I won't hear a word against her from the likes of you."

"You keep her drag for her, don't you?"

"Ask me no questions, I'll tell you no lies." And Maude was out of the room.

I got dressed and headed for the back lot. I am going, all by myself, back to the beginning. Back to where I came in. I am getting out of this movie.

14

Myron took control for half a day in which, I gather, he managed to antagonize everyone. He also went onto the back lot but, thank God, did not manage to find the exit. Sooner or later of course he will, as it is plainly marked, according to the Fire Laws. I must move fast.

I met Maude in the bar of the Mannix, where we had an apéritif as we waited for Half-Cherokee. At last I was ready for him.

I have converted my cabin into an operating room. Ready are the scalpel, the sutures, the clamps, the book of anatomy (belonging to Eddie Mannix, who is a darling but something of a hypochondriac) and of course a gallon of Lysol. The silicone has jelled nicely in its plastic bucket and I now have more than enough to jug Half-Cherokee to Marie Wilson proportions. I have also obtained four sets of handcuffs (lifted from the Police Station Set on the back lot), as well as a tin of ether used by the housekeeper at the Thalberg to clean rugs.

I have not yet made up my mind whether or not Half-Cherokee should be conscious or not during the operation. It would be a vivid experience for him to say *aloha* to his old sex and *ciao* to his new sex. After all, I was given nothing stronger than Demerol when I underwent transformation in Copenhagen, and not only did I feel no pain, I experienced ecstasy as I watched the longed-for removal. But I fear that Half-Cherokee is the sort of sensitive young rapist who would burst into tears at the slightest prick, so I shall probably have to put him to sleep.

"I think," giggled Maude, "that Myron is gay."

"I dislike that word, Maude." There was a threat of jeep in my voice that was plainly Carole Landis' to any aficionado.

"You may not like the word, Myra, but I saw the *way* Myron was staring at Chicken Van Upp."

"Myron is much too dull for anything so interesting. Not that the lobotomized Chicken is exactly interesting except as a morbid example of how California grows its boys like navel oranges, only instead of lacking pits they lack wits."

"I heard that, Breckinridge." It was Whittaker Kaiser, who has, somehow, learned that I am, on occasion, the monster Myron.

Whittaker was half-drunk and all-cook as, uninvited, he sat down at our table, clutching a bottle of beer in his hand.

"Look at you!" he snarled.

Since I knew that I had not looked so lovely since I lost that which I shall soon regain, I gave him a madonna smile and said, "Fuck off, Whittaker."

But he was not about to go. He proceeded to make us a drunken speech in which he affected a peculiar Southern accent somewhat like that of the late Lyndon Johnson, whose own performance was a mere shadow of Gene Autry's.

Incidentally, I have just learned that during my five years' absence not only has President Johnson left us but also Jeffrey Hunter, born Henry H. McKinnies, whose memorable starring role in *King of Kings* was the last important Hollywood film—though I have not yet become acquainted with the latest product since Myron has seen almost nothing but TV commercials. Jeff suddenly died in 1969, aged forty-two. How? Why? I had a good cry over that; and suspect foul play.

"Look here, Breckinridge, this is a man's country because no woman can do a fucking thing except break balls, and never will be able to! I know. I had 'em all. Every kind. Every type. Crying for it. Begging for it, they were. Including the libbies from Women's Lib who're really the lesbies. Get it? You got it? Good. Because I got it. And they know I got it. Their number, that is. But you have to hunker down to beat 'em, the way I do. In every department including the kitchen. I can cook any woman's ass off, do you hear me, Breckinridge? And stop screwing up your mouth like that. And get out of that drag outfit. Act like a man, Breckinridge, a real man like we all used to be before the ball-cutters got loose and we were turned into a bunch of under-glass capons—at least the few of us who didn't fight it. You got that, Breckinridge? There's still *a few of us* who're fighting to be all-men. To be tough. To kill if we have to. Because that's what it is to be a man, Breckinridge. It's to kill. To stick that breadknife in a woman's cunt and make the blood come gushing out! That's what being a man is, Breckinridge. That's what the orgasm is all about. Murder is sex, sex is murder."

I listened to this crazed harangue, delivered in a cornpone accent picked up in that mess hall of the quartermaster corps where Whittaker spent his war years, frying things in lard for hungry hillbilly boys who are really sweet as lambs except for a tendency, in an offhand way, to beat up lard-asses like Whittaker Kaiser. Then, too, there is nothing so dark or so violent as the soul of a cook. According to police statistics, cooks are responsible for more acts of violence than are the members of any other profession except that of the police themselves.

I dealt cooly with Whittaker; yet ready at a moment's notice to introduce him to the Lotus-in-the-Northwind karate-twist which would fling his fat soft cook's body over my left shoulder and into the jukebox.

"Sex," I said, *ex cathedra*, "is sticking a cock not a knife into a woman's cunt."

"You're sick. You're a sick fruit."

"Shut up!" I smiled at Whittaker, preparing for the knockout. "Sex is the union of two things. *Any* two things whether concave or convex or in any combination or number in order to provide more joy for all or any concerned with the one proviso that no little stranger appear as the result of hetero high jinks. So life not death is the Big O. Write that down, Whittaker. Tattoo it on your fat ass. Drop the news into that frying pan of a brain of yours sizzling with greasy dreams of murder to be served up like McDonald's French fries with real blood for ketchup. A yummy dish for the typical hardhat soft cocksman like you . . ."

With a scream, Whittaker charged me.

I threw the Lotus-in-the-Northwind at him but it misfired. Apparently the Breckinridge reflexes have been slowed down from too much TV-watching in the Valley. Fortunately I was able, easily, to get out of his way. As he crashed into the wall, I picked up my handbag, swung it three times about my head to gain maximum velocity, then connected with Whittaker's head and knocked that tedious chef out cold.

Eddie Mannix and the bartender carried Whittaker from the barroom. The patrons applauded. I smiled shyly my Joan Leslie smile.

But I fear that my victory was spoiled. Half-Cherokee did not come. In fact, he has—according to a blowsy hooker—pulled up stakes and moved permanently to Stockton. I was stunned; broken-hearted. Like a Zoë Akins heroine, I sat there in the lurid light from the jukebox—a dazzling smile upon my lips, a tinkling laugh and a gay word for all; yet in my eyes there was a darkness which only the magic of George Cukor's Brownie could have captured.

How easily broken is a woman's heart! Now I must find another stud.

15

I had it out with Maude this afternoon when he started talking about "our" last-night adventures.

We were in the lobby of the hotel and so had it pretty much to ourselves, for Rooster Van Upp was busy showing to her room a shook-up lady who got into the movie early this morning and can't stop crying. Rooster, I must admit, is very soothing.

"There is something, Maude, I think you better understand about me and that is that I am not who you think I am or was last night." I think I straightened Maude out without going into too much detail, leaving out the surgery bit and just keeping my story to plain old-fashioned schizophrenia, like Dr. Jekyll and Mr. Hyde starring . . . No! Every time I think of an old movie it means that Myra—you bitch!—is trying to push her way back up into my head. Well, I'm not playing ball. So forget it.

Of course Maude naturally had to have his little joke about which was Dr. Jekyll and which was Mr. Hyde, since he plainly preferred that drag queen of last night to the company of—I don't deny, am proud of it—a square member of the silent majority who honors the flag and is in Chinese Catering.

"Where by the way does Myra keep her drag outfit?"

"You'll never know, sweetie. Her wardrobe is my sacred trust."

"What has Myra told you about me?"

"All she said was that sometimes she has these sort of fits and becomes the crashing bore she was when I first met her—no offense, sweetie, I am just quoting, and you know how she talks."

"Well, you can tell her from me that if I find that outfit of hers I am going to burn it and meanwhile I am devoting my every waking moment to getting the hell out of here and back to Mary-Ann, my wife, and our analyst who will soon set me straight, maybe with a hormone cocktail."

"Myra's not too eager to go back," said Maude mischievously.

"We'll see," I said, not feeling at all confident about anything.

"In fact, she wants to stay. Why, just yesterday we were looking through the yellow pages together for a plastic surgeon in Culver City who could pop over here and cut off your whang. Such a pity, too! Because I dig what you've got, Myron, even if my girl friend doesn't. Anyway, the only plastic surgeon in the book is on vacation at Arrowhead, but when he gets back —*snip!*"

At that moment Rooster Van Upp appeared at the desk, smiling and looking very serious. I got up and said, "Could I talk to you a second, Rooster?"

"Certainly, Mr. Breckinridge."

Rooster and I went into his office, which is a cubbyhole back of the desk with a brand-new old Dumont TV set. "I can't get it to work," said Rooster. "I've tried and tried but all I get is what looks like this blizzard and I know how much you out-of-towners like watching video."

"Rooster, you know what's going on, don't you?" I took the bull by the horns. Rooster never stops smiling his celluloid-teeth smile even though his small red eyes never look at yours and he has a permanent frown. A tricky customer. "Well, Myron, I've heard a few rumors, yes. For instance, I've heard that for three nights running you've been seen at my good friend and colleague Eddie Mannix's bar in women's clothes, raising hell."

I must've turned purple. For some reason Myra's activities never seem to have anything to do with me until somebody says something. "I can explain that," I explained but actually I wasn't about to and he didn't seem to care.

"Live and let live is our motto on the Strip. Just play it cool and keep your hands off, say, minors, and your average local Culver City cop will lay off as he is paid to lay off by me among other innkeepers and bonifaces along the Strip." I blushed this time for myself, thinking of sixteen-year-old Chicken's dewy golden armpit.

"It's all a game I—we—Maude—I mean Mr. Trojan and I are playing. To fool the locals, you might say."

"Well, the Mannix Motel is a wide-open establishment and if you think you really want to—uh, keep up this sort of game I think Mr. Eddie Mannix will be happy to let you have one of his cabins."

I could not believe my ears! I am apparently well on my way to being a person non grata at the Irving Thalberg Hotel. Well, it's not my fault. Unfortunately there's no way I can explain that to Rooster so I just changed the subject.

"I have wanted for some time, in fact ever since I got here"—I looked at the Varga girl calendar behind Rooster's desk—"thirteen days ago—to talk to Mr. Williams, but whenever I get him on the phone which is not as often as I'd like and ask him for an interview, he tells me to write my name in that book at the desk, which I've done, and still no answer. I've *got* to see him."

"Well, Myron, I can see that things may be coming to a head and at our next powwow which will be day after tomorrow I'll tell Mr. Williams that I think it's like urgent for you to sit down and chew the rag with him."

That was the end of that.

Outside the hotel Mrs. Connally Yarborough Bowles gave me a frosty smile. I guess word of Myra's high jinks has spread.

"There will be a presentation tomorrow, Mr. Breckinridge. A new arrival. I hope you'll attend. In the rumpus room. At nine. A gentleman. From Washington, D.C. The nation's capital."

"Oh, yes, ma'am." I overdid the good "Chinese Catering to Your Home" manners. But I need allies in the war with Myra. Not to mention in the coming showdown with Mr. Williams. "I wonder if you could put in a word to Mr. Williams that I would like a word with him."

"Oh, but I haven't seen him in ever so long! Not in a coon's age. In his charming suite. On the second floor. With the reproductions of the old masters. The first editions. And all the sets of beautiful books in their fine Heritage Club bindings. Read, read, read, that's Mr. Williams. From Albany originally. Of an old River family. I will convey your request. Of course."

This afternoon was to be my afternoon on duty at the Grand Staircase of Babylon set where I was supposed to wait around in case there were any new arrivals.

So I decided to cross over early to the lot and work my way by slow degrees back into the movie. It still takes me time to get used to the DISSOLVES and CUTS without getting sick.

Just inside the gate who should I see but Whittaker Kaiser with a bandage across his swollen nose and the beginnings of a black eye.

When Whittaker saw me he scowled and automatically crouched down like an overweight chimpanzee and then waddled toward me in a way he thinks is threatening. It was lucky for him I'm not Myra.

"So how's it going, old buddy?" I asked, real nice. Well, Whittaker became very old buddy himself and started grinning in what I guess he thinks is a boyish way and said, "Boy, you sure pack some wallop, Myron. You really laid one on me in the bar. The doc says my nose is fractured."

"Sorry about that, Whittaker, but . . ."

"Hell, Myron. Let's let bygones be bygones."

I was relieved that he had dropped the Lyndon Johnson cornpone talk and now sounded sort of breathy and nervous and solemn like Richard M. Nixon our President when he's really got something difficult to explain to us on the TV and knows that he is surrounded by enemies who will later try to distort his every word in the interest of an alien philosophy.

"I guess I was drinking pretty heavy in the bar last night and then of course I always see red—now don't get mad—when I see a guy carrying on like a woman when it's bad enough for a woman to be carrying on like a woman. No offense intended," he added quickly, afraid of Myra's quick repartee and knee to the groin.

"Well, Whittaker, what can I say? It just so happens that I see myself as your average John Q. Citizen who's kind of a bluenose about these things."

"That wasn't the way you were acting in the bar."

"Well, I have this . . . uh, comedy routine I do. Sort of like Milton Berle, remember? On the TV? In the lady's hat?" I improvised fast and not too well. So far I have no defenses against the inroads Myra is making on my reputation not to mention on my mind where she is fighting for control at this very minute and will break through one of these days once and for all if I don't get some hormones soon along with friendly counsel from the family analyst. I am certain it is basically a matter of diet. I have noticed that there is altogether too much refined sugar being eaten here in the forties and un-enriched bread.

"Look, Myron, I got great respect for you." Beware of a cook bearing grease! "I can tell we got a lot in common. We both want to get out of here. That's the most important thing. And of course I've got these crazy drives, too. Who hasn't? I mean what red-blooded all-male-man hasn't got these urges? But, Myron, you got to fight those other impulses. Of course women are shit. Of course sex with women is a steaming, sickening mess, but God damn it, Myron, the real man goes through with it! And if he can't get it up because the woman is loathsome, he's got to keep trying, front, back, sideways. *Somehow* he's got to do it because that's what makes him a man! Even if he has to take a knife to her to get it up, he's got to or he won't be a man but a fag who has given up, surrendered, taken himself out of the only game there is, getting women away from other men—from other women, too—and at the risk of losing his sanity sometimes, he's got to plow deep into that swamp, that awful sickening place . . ."

Whittaker was very worked up. Also, I noticed that he had started pronouncing swamp "swaw-yump" which meant he was going overboard again and into his Lyndon Johnson hillbilly Genghis Khan number and I would soon be forced to continue the work that Myra has begun and really break his nose.

But Mr. Telemachus and Iris—of all people—came strolling toward us and I shouted "Hi," and they started to come over and I said, "Whittaker, if you hate women so much, why don't you leave them alone? Get yourself a boy or something."

"I explained it. You weren't listening." Whittaker was getting very white around the mouth. "I guess it's the way I use language that is difficult for some people with no attention span to dig. Look, every man wants to make it with another man but the *real* man is the one who fights this hideous weak fag self and takes one woman after another without the use of any contraceptives or pill or diaphragm or rubber, just the all-conquering sperm because contraception of any kind is as bad as masturbation and because the good fuck makes the good baby . . ."

And so on for a reprise which didn't end until Mr. Telemachus and Iris joined us.

Whittaker gives me the creeps. But I think Iris likes him and for her sake I hope he stays away from the old kitchen knife in the coming days. I introduced them all around, and then proceeded on my way alone into the picture and my lookout station at Shot 128.

Along the way, feeling sort of tired, I sat down behind a lilac bush in front of a Chinese pagoda left over from *The Good Earth* and got a load off my feet. Since it's a real nice day, I just sat awhile, not even making any notes in this book. So while I was just sitting there, suddenly I saw coming toward me these two men who were dragging this third man between them. One of the two men was the big hulk I saw my first day, Luke. The other was a dapper-looking Negro in a white suit and wearing a white Panama hat. The man they were kind of holding up and dragging between them was wearing one of those rubber Richard M. Nixon masks that you can buy in the novelty shops and are in such bad taste.

The three men didn't see me as they walked past the Chinese pagoda. I was just about to say "Hi," but thank God, I didn't or I would not be almost home as I am now.

What stopped me from saying "Hi" was the man with the rubber mask who was saying in a funny quavery kind of voice, "Actually, there's no . . . uh, hurry. I mean I thought I might look around for a place to stay. Nothing fancy. Of course, I'll need your latest electronic equipment. That's in the interest of national security. As is your best authentic redwood wind screen, and some of those ornamental shrubberies, and one of your jumbo-size electric ice crushers. Also a ceramic tile shuffleboard. That's a must."

The Negro was very polite and sounded just like a white man when he said, "I'm afraid, sir, that won't be possible."

Well, when he said that the man in the rubber mask sort of struggled a bit but the Negro and Luke had a good grip on him and just as they passed me and I was about to step forward the Negro said, "We're sending you home, sir. It's our duty. It's *your* duty."

"No. No. Going home, that would be the easy way. That would be a cop-out."

Home! *Boing.* This light went on in my head. *They were on their way to the exit to send this man home!* Well, I sneaked along behind them, hiding behind bushes and trees, overhearing some but not all of their conversation.

The man in the mask sounded very upset at having to leave. "I mean I'd hoped for a longer visit. Like . . . uh, five years.

Statute of limitations. We had this checked out very carefully.
It was my responsibility, let me say right off. To keep the cap
on the bottle. First I sent Claypoole of the FBI . . ."

The Negro said, "We have our quota, sir, and Mr. Claypoole
is it. Or will be it when he arrives on schedule. As for yourself,
feel free to apply again in a few years . . ."

"That will be too late. At least let me take this expletive deleted
mask off."

The Negro looked at Luke, who said, "We're past the point
where the locals can see us."

"You may remove the mask, sir."

Well, I guess you could've knocked me over with a feather
because under that rubber Richard M. Nixon mask was Richard
M. Nixon, wearing heavy makeup and sweating like he had
been in a Turkish bath. Now let me make one thing absolutely
clear. I don't rule out conspiracy and that this *might* have been
a double except that no double could sweat like our President
or *sound* that much like him when he's sweating.

I'm afraid I didn't listen to what our President was saying as
carefully as I ought to have because I was waiting for one of
the other two to say something about where the exit is, which
Luke did which is why I am here, waiting for them because I
ran as fast as I could in order to get here first which wasn't
hard since they are walking very slowly and every now and then
Mr. Nixon wants to sit down and rest.

But some of what I heard went like this. "Spiro . . . Mr. Ag-
new, the Vice-President and one of the finest men I have ever
met in public life." Amen to that, I said to myself. "When you
look him in the eye, you know he's got it . . ."

"True, true," said the Negro in a snotty way.

"Spiro would take over. We would have this announcement.
Something simple. Saying that for reasons of . . . uh, health, I
have gone back to this year, to 1948 . . . one of the best years,
let me say, in the best country in the history of this nation, and
I have taken up residence inside *Siren of Babylon*—a really great
film, which is also great entertainment *for the whole family*. What

else? I mean I certainly would not want to *see* much less *live* inside of an X-rated movie *because it would be wrong*. That's for sure."

"True, Mr. President. But I fear that in this hour of peril your country needs you. Watergate needs you . . ."

"How does a million dollars grab you? It would be wrong but . . ." Well, the President went on and on like that, making absolutely no sense to me. I suppose that he was like always being devil's advocate which means you try to give both sides of a knotty moral issue in order to find out what the right thing to do is.

Then Luke said something about the exit being just opposite the Grand Staircase and that they'd better hurry up and that's when I sprinted off just as Mr. Nixon was, as usual, examining carefully all his options by asking, "Is there an extradition treaty between 1948 and the future?"

I am now sitting near where the exit is soon going to be. Just now I saw the three of them on the other side of the set. Mr. Nixon seems to be putting up some kind of struggle which I don't quite understand as he has so many good things going for him back in the White House. Well, in a minute he and I are going through that gate . . .

16

It was touch and go for an instant. Five minutes before Mr. Nixon was shoved screaming through the exit, I took possession of the Breckinridge psyche, preventing Myron from getting even so much as a glimpse of where the exit is and how it is made to open.

There *was* an awkward moment when the dinge and the mountain of gristle known as Luke saw me a few scenes later, but I put on one of Myron's truly cretinuous expressions and said that I had just arrived in the film and was waiting to take up my post at Shot 128. Convinced that I had seen nothing untoward, they hurried out of the film.

But let us forget the trivial Mr. Nixon, who will, in any case, never be elected President as a result of what I am now doing! Let us contemplate the truly important.

Siren of Babylon!

17

The joy of actually being inside the film of *Siren of Babylon* is beyond description!

Right off, I could hardly believe that there, only a few yards away from me, was Bruce Cabot—handsome, virile, masterful if a bit paunchy, for he is now forty-four years old and fifteen years of good living have passed since Bruce was the glorious pith-helmeted youth of *King Kong* fame (1933).

As I watched Bruce swirling his cape at the foot of the Grand Staircase, waiting for Maria Montez to descend, I found it almost unbearable to think that two years ago (1971) he died, and even worse, that this handsome if somewhat corpulent swashbuckling romantic star of Mexican extraction who gave me such delight for many an afternoon (no, for an entire lifetime!) will in almost no time at all become the bloated character actor in Sam Spiegel's *The Chase* (1966), a film whose only distinction was the hair-styling of the late Miriam Hopkins.

I almost screamed when I got my first glimpse of Maria on the Grand Staircase. It is so different actually being inside the picture! So much more vivid, more real—even though one can see that the actors are sweating under their heavy makeup and that the sets are just painted canvas. Also, I am able to see the technicians beyond the set. Yet no matter how hard I try, I cannot see the camera which is seeing us or the director behind the camera or anything, in fact, past the frame of the action except a blue-gray void.

Experimentally I moved toward the void—careful to avoid the exit.

At a certain point I discovered—nothing. As usual, I have found the right word. One feels nothing; one sees nothing; one simply stops. It is the end of wherever we are but *my* beginning because I could happily spend eternity examining just this one film, frame by frame, reveling in the dialogue, the lighting, the makeup.

Most delicious of all, I am able to study the actors in close detail during the commercial and station breaks when the action stops and the actors freeze.

One of the interesting ground rules: if you stand just past the frame of the action on the side where the camera ought to be, you are in the quotidian. That is, the movie is being made right then and there, with all the takes and various hazards of union overtime. But if you step into the frame of the film from the opposite side, you are, literally, *in the picture*, exactly as it is shown on television with all the station and commercial breaks. This is known as "breaking frame" on the Strip. One of the taboos that I have now shattered.

Since some of the commercials go on selling cars for ten minutes at a time, I am able to circulate on the set and actually touch the players. Yes, it is possible to *feel* the characters in *Siren of Babylon* even though the stars are dead and I am sure that half the extras must be dead, too, or in the old actors' home.

Creepy but exciting to be able to go up to Maria Montez— how tall she is!—with her glamorous makeup and golden crown, and pass one's hands in front of her obsidian black eyes and see no response in them save a reflection of one's own hand, as though it had been for an instant engraved upon some dark negative of the soul.

Does her mind unconsciously retain a picture of me? Inhaling her divine aroma (perfume with a gardenia base) and feeling, let me confess, with hungry curiosity, her beautiful breasts beneath the gilded breastplate she wears in the banquet scene. Let me note for posterity that her breasts, though fine, did not in life approach in magnificence those that I have lost but will one day regain.

Maria *must* see me, and if she sees me she must remember me. But of course she cannot retain much memory because for her on a June day in 1948 all this is *continuous* action while for me (in 1973 *and* in 1948) the action has been frozen by the Used Car Dealers Association of Van Nuys. What is five minutes eight seconds for me is a meson of time for her: a brief shadow across the face, a mote in the klieg lights.

When the action starts again, I am *pulled* from the frame of action. No other verb will do. Since this "pull" is not a powerful force, I suspect it comes from inside oneself and not from, say, the director of the film or from the management of Loew's Incorporated which pulls *all* the strings at Culver City under the able leadership of company president Nicholas M. Schenck in New York.

Almost delirious with joy, I went through the film not once but twice. I even enjoyed the buffeting one gets during the *CREDITS*! This is Hollywood! This is magic!

I had also never realized what a splendid actress Maria Montez was. "Oh, foul King Nebuchadnezzar," she says with spitfire intensity to Louis Calhern, who plays that ill-starred monarch just before the writing on the wall appears, the work of a special-effects man from Disney.

"You who have debauched thousands and listened to evil councillors, now will you listen to the voice of the One True God?"

Every time Maria says this line I shiver and want to pee and am covered with gooseflesh. Her air of Puerto Rican majesty combined with a Santo Domingan accent result in a performance which is, voice-wise, superior to that of Loretta Young as Berengaria in *The Crusaders* (1935) when Loretta said so movingly to her husband Richard the Lion-Hearted, "Richard, you gotta save Christianity," and equal to that of Lana Turner's portrayal of a priestess of Ba'al who is stoned to death in *The Prodigal* (1955): a performance which was, very simply, the high point of 1940's movie acting in a 1950's film.

Luckily no one joined us from outside the movie or I would have proved to be poor Virgil to any TV-watching Dante as I allowed myself to be hurled deliriously from scene to scene, over and over again, learning by heart the dialogue, detecting new glories in the décor, getting to know not only the stars intimately but the extras as well.

Yes, *extras!* I am not a snob. Far from it. As I moved among the Babylonian army during the commercials, I lifted a good many of the skirts the soldiers wear (designed by Travis Banton) and delighted in the variety of anachronistic undergarments— dance belts, Jockey shorts, white World War II navy drawers with the name of the owner stenciled in black across the seat, olive-drab army shorts, jockstraps.

Needless to say, I amused myself by going to the root of each young man's—not to mention the world's—problem. In the process, I discovered to my amazement and horror that two thirds are circumcised. This is a great blow to me, for these young men costumed as Babylonian soldiers are the very same young men who only three years earlier as American soldiers, sailors and marines defeated the Axis powers, and it was always my understanding that the youths of that heroic era had *not* been criminally mutilated by the surgeon's knife and so, foreskins intact, they had been able to conquer the world. Now I must revise my notes on the golden age or do more work in the field.

I do not rule out the possibility that those young men who are destined to be movie extras must suffer mutilation not only psychically—that goes without saying—but *physically* in order to make them amenable to direction without billing and so members in good standing of the Screen Extras Guild. This could be a major insight and the *donnée* of an important essay for *Films and Filming* now that the *Cahiers du Cinéma* is strictly Stalinist. Certainly I am in an amazing position, able to report on the genitals of several hundred extras in an MGM film of 1948. It is like being present at the siege of Troy. I also cannot help but think how different the world would be if I could *remove* all those superfluous tubes and knobs! As it is, in twenty-five years time these three hundred-odd male extras will have contributed 2.3 children apiece to our burgeoning population. In turn these 690 new citizens will produce 1,597 by the year . . . Monstrous, monstrous nature! It was all I could do not to start hacking away then and there.

Quite by accident I discovered that it is possible to alter *Siren of Babylon*. In the scene where Maria Montez summons four soldiers to her presence and gives them orders to kill Bruce Cabot (there has been a rift between the lovers), I was very taken with one of the soldiers, a tall youth of perhaps twenty with bright red hair hidden beneath a Babylonian helmet and swarthy makeup. I was not aware of his true coloring until I lifted up his skirt and with a now practiced hand scooped my hand inside the sweaty jockstrap and let fall free as fine a set of boyish baubles as ever adorned a member of the Screen Extras Guild—a snow-white penis decorated with the most delicate blue veins and, best of all, heroic! That is, uncircumcised. The added glory of bright gold-red pubic hair so entranced me (against my better judgment, let me say: although I am aware of the lethal nature of these machines I am also, let me confess, a mere woman, susceptible to atavistic impulses old as the race) that I lingered too long. As the off-camera pull began, I hastily relinquished my grip on the redhead's whang and the skirt fell back into place . . . almost.

Two hours later when I had returned to the same scene, I noticed that *the skirt did not fall free:* the elastic of the jockstrap had caught the material of the costume, baring two inches of white unpainted and definitely unBabylonian thigh. The fact that the audience's attention is entirely on Maria at this moment means that only a few film buffs will ever note the slightly unkempt look of one of the Babylonian soldiers.

The possibilities, however, of *intervention* are fascinating. But are they limitless? Presumably the editor of the film will catch any important change that I make. Yet he is long since dead or retired as of now (1973). It is all very puzzling. I am both now and then. The makers of the film are entirely then. Presumably what they made *then* cannot be altered *now*, yet I have slightly changed one scene, and for at least one showing on television in the San Fernando Valley area my alteration was detectable. Somewhat alarmed at the possibilities, I decided to undo what I had done the next time I came to the scene.

I also decided to play a little trick on the red-haired extra. I took from my pocket one of a half dozen Chinese fortunes which that schmuck Myron is in the habit of stuffing into cookies for the delight of his rustic clients. This one said "You will meet your one true love."

On the back of the thin rice paper I wrote "Mannix Motel Bar Saturday June 30 9:00 P.M. love Myra." During the station break I hurried onto the set, lifted the soldier's skirt and took in my hand the long cock which still hung rather uncomfortably outside the right jockstrap (he is suffering, I noted, either from prickly heat or jock itch—strawberry blotches in the hot rosy crotch). Deftly I pulled back the loose foreskin to reveal a shiny mauve-tinted head. I then wrapped the Chinese fortune around the neck of the head and restored the foreskin to its usual protective position. As I scooped the whole floppy apparatus back into the jockstrap, I yanked hard at one of the red curls that sprang out on either side of the tight elastic. The curl came free: a souvenir! I straightened the boy's skirt and withdrew from the scene.

One reel later Mr. Telemachus arrived to take my place at the Great Staircase scene. "Anybody come through?"

"No," I said, playing it like Myron. "It's been real quiet."

We chatted for a few scenes. Mr. Telemachus told me that he never watches the movie anymore. "I know it by heart."

"But there is so much to see. To learn."

"Glad you're getting with it. You should. You're new. I used to be the same. Now it bores the shit out of me. But then, I'm in the Industry."

I confess that anyone who has ever worked for *Daily Variety* excites me, and Mr. Telemachus was no exception.

We talked of various matters during the army mutiny scene in which my redhead distinguishes himself—unaware that twenty-five years later Myra Breckinridge, battered but unbowed, not only has sent him a message in a most provocative way ("meet cute" is the first law of the classic Hollywood film and I am proud to say that I have not transgressed this primal commandment), but next Saturday will initiate him into delights undreamed of since Pasiphaë surrendered to Minos the holy maze king.

While chatting of this and that, my unconscious mind was at work restructuring the universe—starting with Red. Looking at him, I suddenly realized that with the telephone lineman I had been barking up the wrong tree. True, Half-Cherokee would have made a perfect Indian princess but there would also have been, I realized suddenly, innumerable *ethnic* complaints as well as unjust charges of genocide aimed at the original American. Anyway, Half-Cherokee has skipped town.

Watching Red, I *knew* that I had stumbled upon the perfect subject. With a bit of work, Red would make a totally luscious Amazon on the order of Rhonda Fleming, currently (1948) lensing *A Connecticut Yankee in King Arthur's Court*. In fact, if Red's vocal quality is sufficiently nasal, there is no reason why he could not take over some of the roles that Rhonda, more interested in domesticity than filming, turned down during the fifties, depriving the world audience of the only bona-fide Amazonian redhead since the advent of color.

"You still want to go back, Myron?"

"Well, I don't know." I played it like Myron. *Go back!* I would rather go direct to the Forest Lawn Slumber Room than ever again live as Myron in the Valley! Wild producers could not drag me from the Strip, from *Siren of Babylon!*

I am where I want to be, and of how many people can this be said? The only thing that stands in my way is Myron (and *his* thing) but I do not for an instant doubt that I will win this battle as I have won all the others in my quest for uniqueness. I am a self-creation both perfect and complete. Yet, paradoxically, protean and still evolving toward . . . Not even I know *exactly* what but I suspect. The enormity of the role that I am now required to play humbles, exalts me.

"Because, Myron, what we've got here is a fine way of life, as everyone who has come onto the Strip agrees."

"I've got a real nice way of life back home." I played the part of a homesick Chinese caterer to the hilt.

"I don't think there's much chance of any of us getting out anyway."

"I guess not," I said, sounding sad. To my knowledge there has never been a movie star more convincing than Myra Breckinridge when it comes to acting both behavioral and technical. Certainly my work is superior to that of Joanne Woodward whose performance in *The Three Faces of Eve* is but the palest carbon of my own story. Yet for the Dixie Duse's mild exertions in Nunnally Johnson's film, *she* was given the Oscar! On that downward sliding scale, I deserve at the very least the Nobel Peace Prize!

"If there was a way out Mr. Williams would've found it," said Mr. Telemachus.

"How could he if he spends all his time in his suite, reading *books*?"

"Not all the time. According to the grapevine he often holds confabs on the blower with Louis B. Mayer."

"Then it *is* possible for us to ring the front office?"

"Why not? But will they call back? That's where the heartache comes in show biz."

"They will call *me* back, Mr. Telemachus."

On this powerful note, I left the film, enjoying to the fullest the last slow buffeting in the *CREDITS*.

It was growing dark as I walked on air down Andy Hardy's street—so lovely and folksy and American in the gloaming.

Fireflies hovered in the rosebushes. I could almost smell the apple pie Fay (Mom Hardy) Holden is baking for our boy.

Just as I got to the Strip, I felt faint as Myron made a desperate effort to seize control, hoping that I had been weakened by the *CREDITS*, but I am made of stronger stuff than any mere caterer. I hurled him to the bottom of our mutual well. Now—full speed ahead! Operation Myra: Phase Two!

With a heart full of gladness for all mankind, including Red, for whom I have my little plans, I went straight from the Thalberg Hotel to my hideaway cabin at the Mannix, collecting Maude on the way.

Maude was, I fear, down in the dumps.

"Do you realize, sweetie, that here it is 1973 and I still don't know what Mr. Kenneth is doing? I haven't had any real word since that girl from Vidal Sassoon's hairbending parlor in New York arrived two years ago. I'm cut off from the world!"

"Don't fret, Maude. Think of all you have going for you in this marvelous place."

"Oh, I'm not ungrateful. It's just that it seems very strange that for two years absolutely no one who knows anything about hair has come through, that's all."

During this, I was putting on my clothes, transforming myself from drab Chinese caterer to glittering Myra Breckinridge, the siren of 1948, a year whose fashions fit me to a T (like all the other important stars I ignore the New Look and its hideous leg-hiding skirts).

Even Maude was forced to admit that given the sleaziness of the materials he has rustled up for me, the ultimate effect was stunning, particularly with a drop or two of belladonna in each eye to give me that gleaming vulnerable little-girl-lost look so reminiscent of poor Gail Russell. "I've known many a drag queen in my day, sweetie, but you're the tops."

I could not let that low blow go unparried. "Maude," I said, achieving that very special vocal quality which has been known to make the marrow of the cockiest stud turn to water. "I am not a drag queen. Repeat: I am not that most ridiculous of creatures. I am Myra Breckinridge. Admittedly damaged, mutilated but, Maude, *unbowed!* The anomaly, the imposter, the travesty is *Myron* Breckinridge."

I think Maude got the point.

As we crossed to the bar for our evening apéritif, I saw an open convertible slowly passing by, apparently headed for the Texaco station. In it were two young men. Note how calmly, how simply I record this information. It is as if St. Paul were to start telling *his* tall tale with the casual remark that "while making good time one morning on the road to Damascus, I happened to see this funny-looking specimen standing on the side of the road—a hitchhiker, I thought."

Well, those two young men in that open convertible were none other than William Eythe and Lon ("Bud") McCallister. I confess that when I recognized them, I screamed.

They looked around; and beneath the feigned alarm on their legendary faces, I could detect admiration, yes, even *lust* as their eyes focused on me.

But then I am afraid that I started to *run* after their car. Yes, I lost my head! I kept calling out their names and this I fear was simply not cool of me, for they did not, after all, stop at the Texaco station. In fact, William gunned the motor of his "wheels" as they used to call their jalopies back in those—these days and in a cloud of exhaust they were gone.

Maude was much amazed. "Sweetie, you've got to get used to movie stars. They drive along here all the time."

"But . . . but . . ." That was the extent of my eloquence. For once I was silenced by emotion. How could I ever express to this Paganini of hair—to anyone—what it is that I feel about those two mythic youths now seen by me in the actual flesh at the height of their glory and *in the round*—an effect so far not truly possible in the movies despite various attempts like *House of Wax*, where one was obliged to hold up cardboard spectacles containing red and green celluloid in order to get a sense of the third dimension whose absence—and one must face this fact squarely—has *made* the art of cinema unique and glorious, for in its very flatness celluloid is as complete and final as the walls of the Sistine chapel or of the Radio City Music Hall. Yes, as two-dimensional and triumphantly flat as a page of the *Divine Comedy*. To give either the movies or the pages of a classic actual depth would be to mar perfection, to make confusion where all is now clarity. Yet, I confess, that for me to see *in person* movie stars of yesteryear *in* yesteryear is something else again, and creates euphoria.

Like Carole Landis, William Eythe had no back to his head; each died young. He of a liver complaint; she a suicide. But Lon ("Bud") McCallister lives on, I am told, doing well with his many business enterprises in and around Malibu, and though one is happy for him today (1973), he is of course no longer the boy who broke your heart in *Stage Door Canteen*, playing Romeo to Katharine Cornell's gracious Juliet nor can he ever again go home, except on the Late Show, to Indiana.

What a beautiful couple they were this afternoon! But William will soon be dead, still a boy. My eyes are full of tears (not to mention Maude's vile belladonna) as I write these lines in my cabin at the Mannix Motel, where I have moved officially and with the blessing of Mr. Williams, whom I spoke to on the telephone earlier this evening.

Mr. Williams was polite. I was polite, and firm. "I believe, Mr. Williams, that all things considered, it is best for me to transfer myself to the Mannix Motel where I find an atmosphere more to my taste, more congenial in every way."

I gave Mr. Mannix a wink (we were in his office) and he seemed pleased despite a face as expressionless as that of Virginia O'Brien, though hardly as cute. Incidentally, I think Metro never used Virginia correctly. But then even without hindsight it is plain to me that Hollywood is responding to television in the wrong manner. Instead of increasing the "pure" Hollywood product, Dore Schary is trying perversely to "upgrade" the product, poor bastard, because when the day of reckoning comes eight years from now (1956) he will be out on his ass and MGM—which is Hollywood—will go into permanent eclipse.

Fortunately my master plan requires that *I* take over the company. Knowing what I know of past films plus what I know of the disasters in preparation at this very moment (1948), I have every confidence that I can, with the cooperation of the various guilds and unions and of those organizations and individuals who have made the Industry great, continue the golden age of Hollywood for another decade, and perhaps indefinitely. Who knows?

Mr. Williams knows. Or suspects. "Of course, Mr. Breckinridge, if you are happier at the motel . . ."

"Please," I interrupted, all sourness and dark. "Not *Mr.* Breckinridge, *please*. Call me Myra, and I'll call *you* Mr. Williams!"

There was a sound of coughing at the other end. "Of course—Myra. Did you enjoy your first day on duty in the film?"

I could tell that the dinge and Luke had reported to him that I *might* have observed them giving Tricky Dick the old heave-ho but I played it more gelid than usual.

"More than I can say!" Roz Russell could not have played the scene more briskly or with greater sincerity.

"I'm pleased that you are no longer—uh, restless here in our little family."

"Quite the contrary."

"I must remind you, however, Mister—I mean Myra—of that essential rule which we are all obliged to observe for the privilege . . . and I think we agree that it *is* a privilege to be here?"

"Oh, yes!"

"Which is: *never* interfere with the locals."

"But surely, Mr. Williams, carefree friendships of the casual sort . . ."

"Naturally, naturally, one is not a prude. Of course. No, I meant we must never, never *change* anything. On the Strip or on the set."

Was I observed? Does he know? Obviously I must be more careful. "I certainly understand the ground rules. But then, how could we change anything when the locals can't understand us whenever we talk about the future?"

"One can never be certain how much they pick up from us." Oh, he was smooth! It's plain to me that he and Rooster are in cahoots. After all, how could Mr. Williams have made that killing on the stock market using *future* knowledge if he had not been able to communicate with Rooster, or with a broker at the very least? But in the interest of my threefold master plan I was willing to "play dumb," as they say, and on a genial note we signed off.

First and foremost, I must destroy Myron. As soon as that plastic surgeon returns from Arrowhead, I shall remove Mary-Ann's grotesque pacifier and have my *poitrine* restored. Meanwhile, I have put in an order at a nearby pharmacy for the ingredients necessary for the making of a hormone cocktail.

Once Myron is eliminated I shall, gradually, insert myself not only into *Siren of Babylon* (where certain plot changes are absolutely necessary) but into the higher councils of MGM itself. I realize that this will not be easy. After all, there is no way for us to get from the back lot to the administration building or to the sound stages, but there is still the telephone, and of course the directors, actors, executives can always come here to the Mannix Motel, to confer with their—and I use, as always, the right word—*savior*, for I—and I alone—have been chosen to save Hollywood at this crucial moment when television is about to steal some ninety million worshippers from the gorgeous temples of Loew's, of Paramount, of RKO and of Pantages.

Finally, I shall reduce the population of the world by the sexual transformation of Red. Properly presented by the media, I know that I can make the sterile fun-loving Amazon the ideal identity for every red-blooded American boy. Naturally, I realize that a few boys will object to transformation but I am sure that the American Mom will join with me in "persuading" those oddballs to conform. Meanwhile, sperm banks will be set up in every community and pre-transformation boys will be obliged to make monthly deposits in order that non-sterile Amazons (*born* women, that is) may be inseminated artificially *but rarely* because population in the United States must be reduced by two thirds before the new century begins—my century. Century? How modest I am! Myra's *millennium* is about to dawn.

Sitting with Maude in the Mannix bar, I noticed several keen-looking men with crewcuts, all drinking beer in a quiet boisterous way. Maude said, with a sniff (Maude is the total snob), "They're *technicians*, sweetie, working on *Siren of Babylon*. They're in most every evening. So square. They go home to their wives."

I was intrigued. "Do many people from the picture drop in?"

"Oh, my, yes! During the lunch break we get quite a few."

"Maria? Bruce? Louis?"

"Not the *stars* of the movie, silly! Though Maria did come here once." Maude frowned. "But just for a minute. She was very strange. She knew all about *me*, of course." Maude is such a liar that I discounted this story automatically. "But the grips! We're big as can be on grips and cameramen and extras. Oh, and John Wayne did come in one night with a bunch of cronies and someone at the bar over there, someone drunk, said, 'Hi, Marion!' " Maude giggled. "I nearly fell out of my chair, sweetie. I mean I never *knew!* John Wayne, so butch!"

I was severe. "It just happens, Maude, that John Wayne's real name is *Marion* Michael Morrison."

Maude looked disappointed. "Then I guess I missed the point. Anyway, there was a row because the drunk was a war veteran who said, 'Tell us, Marion, why, when we was having our asses shot off in the Pacific, you was making *Flying Tigers* in good old Hollywood and never lifted a finger for your Uncle Sam?' "

"That was cruel," I said, trying to be fair. "But we must take the long view. By arranging so wisely to stay out of the Second World War, John Wayne was able to make not only *Flying Tigers* but *They Were Expendable* and those two pictures did more to defeat Tojo than all of General Chennault's air raids on the enemy."

"I hadn't thought of it like that, Myra." There was awe in Maude's voice.

"Of course you hadn't—sweetie." But I was benign. Maude will be a useful accomplice in the exciting days ahead.

Above the rickety table on which I write these notes hangs a calendar. It is Thursday. Will Red come here on Saturday? I am certain that he will if the day on which he was working in that scene with Maria Montez *precedes* this coming Saturday. But it could as easily have been shot *after* this Saturday, in which case I shall have to keep a lookout every Saturday until the picture ends. Of course, he might be frightened when he reads the message. Or he might simply wash it away without bothering to look. Or, somber prospect, not wash at all. But, no, he was clean if sweaty. He will come on Saturday and through him I will work my way not only into the film but into the decision-making process of Loew's Inc. That is a solemn vow.

In the weak lamplight the gold-red curl gleams on the palm of my hand. What surprises are in store for him!

Locked in my bureau drawer is silicone. A scalpel. Lysol.

18

All right, Myra, so you got back into the driver's seat just as I was heading for the exit with our President, but don't think you'll be able to stop me next time now that I know that (a) there is a way out of here and (b) I know more or less where that particular exit is through which our President, I guess, went as he is no longer here—and I don't dare let on to anybody that I ever saw him as Luke and his Negro friend will then try to keep me away from the exit—which just doesn't make any sense. I mean here I am being forced to stay here where I don't want to be while our President who wanted to take a much-needed vacation in this neck of the woods was made to go back to the White House. Anyway, as far as I can tell, nobody here knows about Mr. Nixon's brief visit except for the Negro, Luke, me and Myra.

Maude avoids me whenever I am myself. "Oh, you're in one of *those* moods, are you?" He says, "Well, you'll never find Myra's drag. Never!"

Although I wore a sort of raunchy cowboy outfit I bought last week and was careful to walk like some kind of bear with arthritis to show how deeply and sincerely butch I am, I am afraid a snigger was heard from several people among them Chicken Van Upp who blushed bright red when I looked at him hard and tough. At least Myra has scared the boy-element among the locals.

Myra has also pretty much ruined me, if not herself, with the other out-of-towners. I have no idea how they take to her when she is all dressed up. I suppose she compels attention like always. I sure Lord God don't.

Anyway, Whittaker Kaiser approves—the other skunk nobody likes. "You look good, Myron," he said in his thick cook's voice. "You're fighting this thing."

"Yeah," I said, dropping my voice a couple registers. "I'm trying to beat it once and for all."

"Just remember you got to be absolutely ruthless because that's what kills them, finally, the cunts that are cutting our balls off."

"Amen," I said, meaning it, too. That is just what I am going through now in a way that that dumb cook could never understand.

Whittaker asked me if I cared to hoist a brew with him at the Mannix bar and I said why not, since no one else was being friendly.

As we walked down the Strip, the old cars tearing past us just like they were new and the sign *Call Northside 777* at what is the end of the road for us, Whittaker gave me his views on politics: "It's all part of the same thing. The Watergate. The FBI. Us being caught here."

"I don't see how what's happened to us has anything to do with anything."

"The connections are all there, all right. Look at that cunt Mrs. Bowles." The fact that the lady from Plandome has three times beaten up our tough cookie has not done his not-very-good-at-best disposition much good. "She's in with the FBI scum. And *he's* in with Mr. Williams who is a fag. Sorry, Myron."

"You got the wrong end of the steer, Whittaker," I said,

getting ready to bust him. We were now at the door to the Mannix bar.

"Don't take no offense. It's just that there are some times, you got to admit, when you're . . . well . . ."

In a fairly friendly way we hoisted a couple brews together, with me all the while trying to treat coolly Myra's friends and she has a good many in that low bar, including the owner old Mannix himself who leaned over me as he passed and said, "Hey, gorgeous!"

Well, I gave him a look which if you could wrap it around your average Mafioso hood would have anchored him to the bottom of Lake Arrowhead until the cows came home. But Mannix had moved on to serve a table of tough-looking characters with their cheap whores. God, I miss Mary-Ann and the silky terriers.

"Myron," Whittaker was rumbling in my ear, his voice just on the verge of losing its natural, mild Philadelphia scrappleness for the hillbilly tone that always means he is getting ready to pick a fight that he always loses except sometimes with dizzy girls like Iris who though they could handle him with one arm behind their backs are excited by the brutal way he comes on and forget how soft and fat he is and how, as Iris said to me just before I came back to my lonely cabin tonight where I write these notes, "That buddy of yours can hardly get it up, all two inches of gristle that looks like it'd been trimmed from a roast by some crook butcher with his thumb on the scale or maybe it was the thumb he cut off by accident and that's Whittaker full length."

Iris has a bloody kind of imagination when she gets going. "Now, I think you're something pretty special, Myron, even though you are not absolutely *complete* down there but I got to confess that when you get yourself up in drag you are the best fun I've had around these parts in a long time. You undergo *a personality change*, did you know that?"

I said yes, I knew that, feeling pretty low. Anyway, to get back to earlier, to before Whittaker went to sleep with his head in the jukebox, he said, "The only way we-all's gonna git outta hee-yuh— You lisn'in, boy? You mindin' what Uh say?"

"Yes, Whittaker."

"—is to break in on that fruit Mistuh Williams an' hole a knie-yuf to his throw-yut till he shows us thuh way to git home."

If I am game and not a coward, Whittaker plans to pull this caper tomorrow, at sundown. We will break into Mr. Williams' hotel suite with two kitchen knives which Whittaker will get from the Mannix Motel Café kitchen where he is currently working half-time deep-frying things.

I said I'd sleep on it, and not wanting any trouble with Whittaker, I sounded like I was interested and of course maybe I am, for things are a lot more desperate for me than they are for anyone else around here. I mean how many oysters can a man eat?

19

You don't know the half of it, buster!

But good news first. Yesterday one J. D. Claypoole formerly of the FBI hit the Strip—saved by *Siren of Babylon* from what I am certain would have been an indictment for his part in the Watergate scandal so wittily foretold by Preston Sturges' *The Great McGinty* (1940). According to Claypoole (who read the good news in the *Star*) Lon Chaney, Jr., at the age of sixty-eight, has made an excellent recovery from beriberi, an illness he contracted some years ago, thus explaining the absence from the silver screen of one of its finest, most deeply American presences: the monster as square. I am almost tempted to ring up Mr. Chaney right now and congratulate him! Except that his number is sure to be unlisted and of course he has not yet caught beriberi.

And then of course we must not interfere! Ha ha! Mr. Williams will not recognize 1948 by the time I get through with it. As I change for the better this holy year, future time will be affected. Or, if I may resort to witty metaphor, as one domino is picked up and set erect, so will the next and the next be restored to an upright position.

331

I intend to make 1948 the hinge of history. I shall split human history in two parts to be known henceforth as *pre-Myra* and *post-Myra*. Do I need to repeat that in the post-Myra world sordid scandals like Watergate will not take place because Richard Nixon's presidency will not take place?

My fellow Americans both before and after, saved and unsaved, cut and uncut: central to my vision is the street in Carverville on the Metro lot where Andy Hardy once lived and will live again. If I succeed in this great enterprise, I vow to you that the moral rot at the center of the United States will be nipped in the bud by a society which (post-Myra) will be informed throughout by the wisdom of good Judge Hardy as played by Lewis Stone.

At the moment Lewis Stone has only five more years (pre-Myra) before translation to the big studio in the sky; yet during the half decade that currently (1948) remains to Lewis Stone he could make at least five more Hardy films and, who knows, revived in his career he might not want to cool it, aged seventy-four in 1953 (pre-Myra). But if Lewis Stone does die according to the old pre-Myra schedule, then I have a replacement ready. Hang on to your hats: Mickey Rooney will become the new Judge Hardy!

Mickey will be thirty-one in 1953 and with a bit of the old Perc Westmore in the Gray-Hair-and-Crowsfeet Department, Mickey can succeed to his father's judgeship, thus sparing future (pre-Myra) generations Mickey's truly excruciating imitations of Japanese waiters on television, a minor art form that will be dedicated (post-Myra) to the glorification of Hollywood's product while continuing to make its small yet exquisite contribution to the (pre-Myra) culture, the creation of ever longer and more inventive commercials.

Meanwhile, I have begun my work. Oh, how I have begun! This is Saturday, or was. I sit in a filmy pink chiffon negligee, writing it all down in my book. Need I say I am not alone? But I shall come to that in due course.

I found out about Lon Chaney, Jr., from J. D. Claypoole, who stopped in at the Mannix bar for a drink just before noon.

I was dressed in an amusing slit-skirt affair with tiger-lily design. "Wow," said J. D. "You're some looker! You live around here?"

"I'm an out-of-towner, too." I gave him my siren voice and we kicked the old ball around for a while, and it was then that I learned—after a good deal of probing—about Lon Chaney, Jr.'s recovery. "Noticed it in the papers just before I landed here."

"Lucky you."

"They got nothing on me, baby."

I simply gave him a slow slightly crooked smile like Joan Fontaine six reels into *Rebecca* and *all the way* into all-time movie greatness, unlike her sister Olivia de Havilland, whose career has been one of sad decline since *Anthony Adverse* (1936). With dedication and luck Olivia might have been a second Beulah Bondi; as it is, she must forever be known as Joan's lackluster kid sister.

When J. D. tried to pick me up in a crude way, I said, "I never thought I'd be propositioned by a G-man! I guess that makes you a real maverick, doesn't it? Sort of odd-man-in, if you get what I mean."

"And what is that that you're implying?"

"I'm implying that I thought all G-men who were loyal to J. Edgar were fruits, too."

J. D. turned blue about the mouth. "That is a Commie lie!"

"Well, it's all academic now, J. D." I got up from the bar stool, my sturdy handbag ready for action. *"De mortuis,* as we Latin bombshells say. Anyway, let's hope J. Edgar's having a ball or two up there in the biggest closet of them all, making it with Dillinger, a plaster cast of whose whang I am told your leader used to keep under his pillow."

J. D. lunged at me. I stepped lightly away. He fell with a crash off the bar stool. "See you in the movies," I trilled, with an Ann Rutherford wrinkling of my nose; and so headed for the back lot.

Did I wonder whether or not Red would show up tonight? Was I fearful that he would not? Of course I was anxious, edgy, not myself. Although I am the creatrix of this world I am also, at heart, a mere woman. One who wishes to love and be loved. To hold out my hand to a masterful man, to let him draw me close to his powerful chest, to feel strong arms about my beautiful if not entirely re-equipped-for-action body, to look up into his strong face and say, "I love you!" And then fuck his ass off. Yes, I, too, am vulnerable, tender, insecure.

Just past the gate there is a train station where died Anna Karenina, played by one Greta Garbo, whose allure was *not* truly Hollywood as a comparison with, say, her contemporary Lana Turner would quickly demonstrate and to Miss G's disadvantage.

I crossed the tracks; stepped around the real locomotive as an equally real trolley packed with tourists comes into view. "Watch it, miss," said the driver. Obviously we locals are still visible to the out-of-towners as far into the lot as the railroad station.

Just back of the station there is a pleasant bosky dell with tall trees and thick bushes and birds twittering—and on the greensward I stumbled upon these two guys making it. Their shirts were off; their blue jeans were down to their ankles and they were lying one on top of the other rubbing back and forth like a pair of nine-year-olds.

"Well, this is a pretty how-de-do!" I thundered, handbag at the ready.

"Get lost," said the dark-haired one on the top. But the fair-haired one on the bottom knew the voice of authority when he heard it and pushed the other one off him and then they quickly pulled up their pants, allowing me a pleasant glimpse of turgid, nay, tumescent, nay, *nothing* powers: a pair of standard American rosebuds, but then, to be fair to the American rosebud, like a Christmas present, it is not the actual tiny gift but the thought *behind* the erection that counts.

"We were just taking it easy," said the dark one, giving me a look of hate.

"You won't tell nobody, will you, lady?" The blond was nervous. "I mean we're really straight."

"Save that for the Blue Parrot." This was a shot in the dark but it connected. Myron—the original Myron—used to know a group of slightly older queens in Manhattan who all swore that right after the war the bars of New York were filled with beauty, particularly along "the bird circuit" as it was then known; and of these legendary aviaries, the Blue Parrot on the East Side was always the most brilliantly stocked with our feathered friends.

"Are you from New York too, lady?" The blond one wanted to be friendly, fearing an indictment for an act against nature as nature is defined in the unnatural state of California.

The two young men are from New York. The dark one, Mel, is going to Columbia where he plays football, he says, and the other is his buddy Gene, a carhop, and they are traveling about the country while school is out. "We dig the road, lady," said Gene, the con man of the pair.

"You dig each other."

"Hell," said Mel, "I'm just a kind of *come on'er*, that's all."

"Come on *him* is closer to the mark, buddy."

I don't know why I thought at first that they were out-of-towners but they proved to be locals. It was exciting, I confess: two genuine sweaty 1948 youths, smelling of sex, as they talked of bop music, of hipsters, of smoking tea . . . tea! That dear old pre-mainline word! They were, they said, *beat*. Yes, that word was born in the bosky dell of Metro's back lot or at least revealed for the first time to me as though for my blessing, which I gave.

Mel said, "I guess you might say that I am—that we're both—sort of beat with life, with everything."

"Not Hollywood surely."

"L.A. is shit," said Gene. "We been holed up on South Main where the police bust you every two minutes and the women is all whores."

"Not all of us." I was, I fear, revoltingly saccharine but something about those two studs touched me. After all, I was witnessing the dawn of Beat.

Mel was conciliating. "You're a right beautiful woman, ma'am," he said respectfully. "But what we're after is this pure thing that's beyond sex. You dig Céline?"

"I do *not* read novels." I was suddenly hard. "The only words that I care for are dialogue. Get it? High-priced Metro dialogue is all I need words-wise, so you can take your Céline and shove his collected works all the way up that long journey to the end of the night in your asshole."

Well, that had the effect of inspiring terror and awe. They both started trembling and, though swathed in denim, their rosebuds were plainly contracting to acorn proportions. As is my policy, after the whammy, the softening up. "I confess that in my day I have studied the enemy, contemplated the strategies of fiction if only in order to find new ways to destroy the art form whose only distinction is that it prepared the way for the movies, much as John the B. prepared the way for the big J. C. And of course I will never deny the importance of *any* novel which has been used to inspire a work of celluloid. We are all permanently indebted to James Hilton, Daphne du Maurier and W. Somerset Maugham, whose names head the golden list. Yet at best their works are no more than so much grit beneath the studio's shell: mere occasions for masterpieces, for cinema pearls."

I could see that I had completely overwhelmed them; and was pleased. Unfortunately (for him), Mel still had a little starch left in him. "But I don't think that's true, ma'am. I mean words, wowee, that's all we got, my buddies and me with these long talks we have about perception and really *seeing* just what it is this cosmos-thing sees and all the beatness of it, the beatitude, yeah, that's the word for all the words we say, for all this yakking we do."

"Stop!" I commanded. I had had a sudden vision—like Jennifer when she saw Linda in *The Song of Bernadette*—of the post-Myra world which I now realize that I must devise a *precise* blueprint for. To date, I confess, I have been creating the future in an inexcusably haphazard fashion, but in my defense I must note the extenuating circumstance that I lack not only a well-trained staff but mobility. "Mel, you must write all this shit down."

"Shit?" whined Mel, but Gene stopped him, muttering, "Don't get the lady mad. Watch out for that handbag. There's lead in it."

"Like in your pistol, Gene?" I was jocose. Buddy buddy. I needed them. "Yes, write it down. make a book of it. Call it a novel, if you like."

"But I thought you said I was to take all the novels and shove them . . ."

"Please, Mel. That is an offensive image to use in the presence of a lady. I mean that I can predict absolute success for your work at this time. *But* you must beat—that word again!—Kerouac to the punch."

"Who?"

"If you do as I say, Mel, your name will be up there on the screen, and *his* will be unknown. Can't you see it, Mel? *Based on a novel by Mel American Rosebud . . .*"

"But that's not my name."

"Because—this year—I promise that Metro, *my* studio"—I indicated the Thalberg Building, which I cannot see but they could—"will begin a series of films about hipsters, hot-rodders, lovers of boogie-woogie, not to mention belly-rubbing . . ."

"Belly-rubbing?" This blew Gene's mind.

"What do you think you two pro-crypto fags were doing just now?"

"But we dig the broads," squeaked Gene, jumping to avoid the handbag with which I had intended to reduce to an ounce of attar his tiny rosebud.

"Of course you do! You're part of my vision for this studio. And—now get this—if we can have your story on the screen by 1950, as a vehicle for Van Johnson and Peter Lawford, camera work by James Wong Howe and directed by any one of our staff directors, though I might bring in Irving Rapper from Warner's, I will be able to start a cycle of profitable pix that will knock the quiz shows out of the box and off the tube and fill the movie houses of the world with a new sort of film, more wondrous than anything as yet dreamed of even by Herbert Yates. A *beat* generation is what I will give the movie audience first. But a beat generation that is well groomed, exquisitely lit, and acted by major stars in perfect frames. Here is my card." I had—as always—written my name on the back of a cocktail napkin and stuffed it in my purse just in case.

I gave it to the stunned Mel.

"Now mop the come off your jeans, boys. Mel, you dictate into the nearest recorder that tome which, I promise you, Irving Lazar will see is bought by my studio for a sum in the high six figures. Gene, you will be inked, too, as tech. adviser."

They fled me, grateful for the vision I had given them of a new world. We shall hear from Mel, I am sure of that.

So, Mr. Williams, I have begun to alter this year of grace, *my* grace, and if I can film a photoplay with a title that has Beat in it—*On Beat, Beat Me Daddy Eight to the Bar, The Beat Years of Our Lives, The Beat Man, Beat Your Meat*—I will anticipate and torpedo an entire "literary" movement of the pre-Myra fifties when the so-called Beat writers, howling their words at random, helped distract attention from our Industry's product and made it possible for Charles Van Doren to dominate through television the entire culture, answering questions whose answers he had been given in advance—a twenty-one-inch corruption that was directly responsible, first, for the death of Marilyn Monroe at the hands of the two Kennedys and, second, for R. M. Nixon's current subversion of the government. Fortunately I—and I alone—can turn America around. It is a great responsibility and one to which I intend to rise, humbly of course but inexorably.

Meanwhile, right in front of me, there is something else for me to turn around. I shall, in a few minutes, create the first fun-loving sterile Amazon. Ether, scalpel, Lysol, sutures, Mercurochrome, clamps, silicone, needle and thread are ready. So is Red, who arrived at nine-oh-five in the bar of the Mannix Motel.

I am half in love with Red—or should I call him Steve Dude, his acting name? Stark naked, Steve is on his tum-tum, hands and feet handcuffed to the metal headboard and footboard; a pillow beneath his tum-tum not only makes for added viewing pleasure but, according to the medical dictionary, it is the classic position for the removal of unwanted testes. I have not of course told him what I have in mind for him. I am in a mischievous trick-or-treat mood.

Steve is looking at me, as I write, and I detect in his round blue eyes not only true passion but tenderness of the sort I have needed all my life. Once he is not Steve but Stefanie—my best girl friend—we will be inseparable pals, like Constance and Norma Talmadge.

The gag which I made for him using an old bra and one of his socks has slipped down to his chin, revealing the full sensual lips of a second Maureen O'Hara . . .

20

Jesus Christ, Myra is going to get me killed or put in jail on a sodomy rap for life and *she* would damn well deserve it though I am innocent, I swear.

Suddenly just now I find myself sitting at this table in this motel cabin dressed in a slinky dressing gown with a padded bra underneath and holding a pencil in my *left* hand which maybe explains why I can't read what she writes in this notebook because I am right-handed while handcuffed to the bed is this naked red-haired kid.

I just sat and stared at him and he stared at me, obviously scared out of his wits as who would not be if he's fallen into Myra's clutches? It took me, oh, maybe five minutes to get it together in my own head.

As per usual I tried to see into Myra's mind and as per usual I got nowhere at all. Whatever she does or thinks is just a blackout for me. Each time I come back I pick up where I left off last time—not to mention having to pick up the pieces *she's* left lying around and, let me tell you, Steve Dude is about the biggest piece of all so far and I am still stunned even shook up by the enormity of Myra's crime against this boy's nature not to mention my own.

"What's your name?" I asked in my normal voice.

"Steve Dude like I told you, Myra." The voice cracked as if Steve was your average teenager though he is at least twenty-one—that is, I pray to God he is twenty-one and not a minor with all the problems I would then have to face like twenty years in Alcatraz.

"I'm sorry about this Steve."

"Oh, that's O.K. I really didn't mind. Sincerely, Myra."

He was lying and willing to say anything to get the hell out of there. How Myra had managed to overpower this six foot two one hundred eighty pound stud is something I do not want to think about. Any more than I want to know what she was going to do with him. The sharp knife I found in the top bureau drawer I took and buried behind the cabin and the Lysol and the ether I poured in the sink. I couldn't open the bottom bureau drawer which is locked. Anyway, I am certain she couldn't've wanted to do what I think she wanted to do.

"Where did she . . ." But then I decided it would be too complicated to explain to Steve my situation. He seems sort of dumb, with a Texas accent like Whittaker likes to put on only Steve's is for real since he is from Beaumont.

"I seem to've forgotten where I put the keys." I pointed to the handcuffs. He looked up at me as if he thought I was about to turn into Charles Manson or something.

"I reckon they're still in the pocket of your robe, Myra, where you put them."

So they were. I took a deep breath and crossed to the bed, keys in hand. What I was about to do was pretty risky. Though no man is a match for Myra, who does know a bit of judo and has the strength of ten, I am just your ordinary guy with the strength of one who is getting kind of out of shape in the Valley particularly since the Vic Tanney Studio down the road shut down a few years back. Steve could do me a lot of damage if he was in a bad mood.

Well, I decided that I would just have to take that chance and rely on his memory of whatever it was that Myra did in the first place to get him in the fix he was in and be too scared to do anything violent.

I undid the handcuffs first from his ankles (how did Myra manage to get ahold of handcuffs in the first place?). Modestly he put his legs together even though he didn't need to because no power on earth could have got me to look at his spread cheeks. I did not want to know anything, *repeat* anything, about what that monster did.

"I'm sorry about this," I said and I really meant it as I unlocked the handcuff first from his left then from his right wrist. "I really am. It's just that I get sort of carried away sometimes."

"Oh, that's O.K." The relief on his face was like the sun coming up over the prairie. I stood back from the bed, automatically crouching down just in case he threw a punch in my direction, but Myra had really done her work whatever it was.

Steve just lay there a minute or two on the bed, rubbing his wrists. Then he rolled over and sat up on the edge of the bed, modestly crossing his legs and putting his hands in his lap but not before I had a look at his very large equipment (thank God, undamaged) and also took in the fact that all his pubic hair had been shaved away.

Steve blushed when he saw where I was staring and said, "You really give a clean shave, Myra."

Why had Myra shaved him? And why . . . ? No, I don't want to know. "So it seems," I said, pretty embarrassed too.

"Well," said Steve, "I guess I better be on my way."

"I guess so," I said, suddenly wanting just to lie down and go to sleep until I get out of this nightmare and am home again.

"Can I put my clothes on now?"

"Oh, yes, Steve. Yes. Please." I was flustered and probably more upset than he was if that was possible.

Quickly Steve pulled on an old army shirt, wrinkled chinos,

white sweat socks, one of which had been used to gag him with, and desert boots.

"Well," he said, ready to leave, "I guess there's a first time for everything."

Of course I didn't know what he meant though of course I really did know or could've made like they say at important press conferences an educated guess. "So it was really your first time?" I heard myself say from far off. I am developing a sort of echo chamber in my head.

"Jesus, couldn't you tell? Anyway, I'm sorry about yelling the way I did. I mean that sincerely."

My heart skipped—is skipping beats. My hands are still clammy. "I guess she—I guess I wasn't very gentle."

"Could I see that thing you used? The dill—what do you call that thing?"

"Dildo." I croaked the word and knew then just what it was Myra had done. She had pretended to sodomize Steve with a dildo when, in fact, she had actually used Dr. Mengers' powerful tool which is almost too large for your average experienced female or male much less for a boy who is a virgin in that department which Steve is, or was, poor bastard.

I stammered something about how what with the damp night air and all I had locked the dildo up for the night, all the while wondering why Steve didn't turn violent and beat the dickens out of me. Myra sure has it coming to her. But I guess Steve was still scared to death of Myra and, craziest of all, he's still very much intrigued by her from what he had to say before he left. "I just hope you won't have to do that again. I mean I'm really, like you say, broken in now, and I mean that sincerely."

"Oh, never, never again!" This was from the heart.

"Because to tell the truth I didn't really feature it too much."

"I understand. I really do!"

"I mean I've cornholed a few li'l ole gals in my time and I always believed 'em when they *said* it was O.K. and didn't hurt too much though I'm a fair-sized man, you know."

"I know you are, Steve."

" 'Course I never in my wildest dreams dreamed any li'l ole gal would ever come along and cornhole *me*."

"Well, live and learn." I was just gabbling anything that came into my head.

"But I tell you one thing. If any guy ever did that to me, why, I'd track him down to the end of the earth and I'd kill him. I sincerely would and that's a promise." Steve looked mighty mean when he said this which is about as mean as they come since in his clothes he looks like quite a lot of potentially tough guy, very different from the scared boy I first saw on the bed with his wounded tail wide open to every breeze that blows.

"Well, Steve, we girls"—how I hated having to put on that act but I am not about to get killed for Myra's crimes—"like our little games."

"I'll say. You know it was kinda like an enema with a blow-torch."

"But it wasn't so awfully bad, was it? I mean you did like *some* of it, didn't you, Steve."

"Myra, I hated every last minute of what you did, and that's the absolute truth so help me God, sincerely."

"Sorry" was the best I could do, as I sort of edged him out of the cabin.

"I still don't know why you shaved me like that."

"To . . . uh, to control your prickly heat, dear."

"Well, I'll be waitin' for your next message, Myra. Will it be . . . uh, sent like the other one was?"

What other message? What was he talking about? "Yes, yes," I said, anything to get him out of the cabin.

"Jesus H. Christ!" Steve said and shaking his head he jumped into his Plymouth convertible which was parked beside the "Vacancy" sign and drove off into the night while I came back in here and sat down to write in this book only to notice that pressed between the leaves of an earlier section were quantities of Steve's red hair from his crotch which I just now got rid of.

When I came back from the bathroom who should be sitting

on the bed but Whittaker, half plastered and looking for trouble which I was not in the mood to give him having been, let me say, shocked and shook up by the whole Steve Dude business.

"Look at you!" Whittaker pointed at my wig, makeup, dressing gown.

I'm afraid I was every bit as disgusted as he was but I was not about to pick a fight. "Get lost," I said quietly.

"And what were you doing to that man in there? Why was he screaming?"

"So you're a wiretapper as well as a ptomaine peddler."

"You don't need no electronic bug to hear what I heard."

"Why don't you get your ass out of here, Whittaker?"

"You forgot what night this is?"

I could no more have told him what night it was than I could get into the movie house down the road and see *Call Northside 777*. For all I knew, Myra might've been at the controls for weeks.

Well, I learned that she hasn't been around all that long and that tonight is the night when Whittaker and I were supposed to break in on Mr. Williams and force him to get us out of here. "He's got this place under his thumb. He knows every entrance *and* every exit."

I didn't tell Whittaker that I know more or less where one of the exits is but I don't think I'm going to be able to find it on my own and I don't expect Luke or the Negro will be very helpful. Anyway, I don't want to tangle with them, particularly Luke.

Whittaker kept rambling on. "If we stay here much longer it's cancer."

"Cancer?"

"Yes, you dumb queen! Can't you tell? This place is giving us all cancer. This is where it all started. I got it pinpointed to right after the war when all the cancer-causing agents got loose in spite of Saran wrap. Those food additives. And television. The hormones in the chicken and beef. Myron, we're in cancer gulch."

Whittaker went on making this crazy connection between

cancer and food and what he calls his existential vision of the last big connection which is between lard, I think he said, and sex but by then he had lost me and I kicked him out with a promise to reconsider the plan to kidnap or threaten to kidnap Mr. Williams in order to get out of here because if I don't get out of here soon and back under the care of a good physician I will not only lose all control to Myra who will never leave this place if I know her, not to mention probably getting killed by one of these 1948 local boys who are tough war veterans and not like the soft youth of America today who, due to the coddling they got as babies from Dr. Spock and other Communist sympathizers, were unable to stem the rise of Communism in Southeast Asia and so let down our President in his quest for peace with honor, forcing him to abandon the democratic and *freely* elected government in Saigon to the mercies of Hanoi, and to the yellow hordes of Central Asia, thus explaining the fact that he looked very unwell the other day when he was here, particularly when he took off his Nixon mask.

Next day.

Dressed in my denim cowboy-style duds and nervous because I know that I am now thanks to Myra your average pariah on the Strip, I went into the lobby of the Thalberg Hotel where Mrs. Connally Yarborough Bowles was playing canasta with three out-of-town ladies from the mid-fifties when that game was all the rage.

I'm afraid the ladies pretended not to see me as I went on over to the desk where Chicken was in charge. He looked kind of pale when he saw me, the usual effect Myra has on young males, and even though I am Myron and straight as a die I guess it shows through, her terrible lust, her desire to take over everybody, everything in the world, and in this case I was truly sorry because I could image a real sort of palship between Chicken Van Upp and yours truly, consisting of us two fishing for trout in one of your nearby streams, skinny-dipping together in the old swimming hole the way it used to be when a man and a boy and a dog, too, sometimes, could have a real relationship without your real boy like Chicken ending up stuffed from behind like an olive with a pimento like Steve Dude.

"I'd like to talk to Rooster, Chicken," I said.

"Pa!" yelled Chicken; and skedaddled.

Rooster entered the lobby from the office, smiling and frowning at the same time like always. "Mr. Breckinridge—I presume?"

"Yes, you presume right. I want to see Mr. Williams."

"Write your name in this book . . ."

"I've written my name in that book ten times. Now I want to see him or there will be real trouble around here." I noticed something odd then. There is a mirror behind where Rooster was standing and in the mirror I could see the canasta players. Well, Rooster looked over my shoulder at Mrs. C. Y. Bowles and she gave him a nod and a high sign—that is, made a circle with thumb and forefinger.

"O.K., Mr. Breckinridge. I'll do my best. Come this way."

I followed Rooster up to the first floor and down the corridor to a door with a metal plaque on it which said *Mr. Williams*. "That's a pretty old plaque," I said, pointing to the tarnish on the brass and how the letters are getting a bit dim from too much polishing over the years.

"Mr. Williams brought it with him." Rooster was smooth. "And we put it up in June when he got here. We think the world of Mr. Williams around here." Rooster peered at the plaque. "Needs a bit of elbow grease. You're right." Then Rooster rapped on the door and Mr. Williams said, "Come!"

Rooster opened the door a crack; put his head in. "It's Mr. Breckinridge. Mayday! Mayday!"

"I read you, Rooster. Carry on."

Rooster stood back and I went into the sitting room of Mr. Williams' so-called luxurious suite and it was really pretty swell-looking with bookcases packed from floor to ceiling with thousands, I'd guess, of books and a crystal-type chandelier in the center of the ceiling and a big gold desk just under it and a big chair near the window that looks out onto Thalberg Boulevard and, yes, a telescope at the window through which Mr. Williams obviously keeps track of us out-of-towners.

The door shut behind me and the key was turned in the lock.

I was alone with Mr. Williams, who turned out to be the Negro who had been so snotty to our President. Mr. Williams is as black as the ace of spades and looks just like old photos of Father Refined I think he was called, who was short and stocky and bald with a gold-toothed smile and used to give away fried chicken at his Heaven in Harlem during the Depression, serving even honkies like my mother Gertrude the practical nurse who went there when she was broke.

"Do come in, please. Sit down." Mr. Williams was graciousness itself and I responded in kind although I cannot say I have been too happy about the prospect of a black mayor of Los Angeles, a current (1973) possibility. What with property values already seriously endangered by taxes together with having the coloreds start to move into the various neighborhoods would further depress the sole capital investment of many middle-income *completely* tolerant people like me who happen to be white and who oppose busing just on practical and not, I repeat *not*, on racist grounds.

I sat down in the chair opposite the big leather chair where Mr. Williams had been reading *The Federalist Papers*, something from school I recall. Within easy reach was the telescope. He smiled when he saw what I was looking at. "Yes, I must keep an eye out for new arrivals. Our people don't always catch them, you know, at the usual entrances. Might I offer you a cordial?" If you shut your eyes you'd think from listening to Mr. Williams that he was white.

After he had poured us two small shots of something pretty awful, I said, "Well, I guess you probably know why I'm here . . ."

"Concerned all of us who are good Americans." Mr. Williams was talking right through me as if he hadn't heard me. "It is my view, Mr. Breckinridge, based on the latest reports, particularly the valuable presentation of J. D. Claypoole Friday night, that the President will be forced by events and by world opinion to resign."

This was about the last subject I had on my mind which is filled with nothing but homesickness for Mary-Ann and the dogs and fear of Myra and Steve Dude though if I could go fishin' with Chicken—no, cancel that last. It is now inoperative as it could be misinterpreted because something basically fine and noble would look suspicious to anyone who associated Myron who is a straight shooter with that monster as who couldn't help doing on the Strip?

Nevertheless I rose to the defense of *our* President. "Mr. Nixon has not been in any way directly connected with the break-in at the Watergate or with the later attempted cover-up by certain of his highly motivated associates who in their love for America and our institutions perhaps went too far in ensuring the re-election of what, after all, has proved to be a winning combination Dick, Pat, Tricia, Julie, David, Cox . . ."

Well, I had a lot more to say to Mr. Williams who even though he *sounds* like he's white when you shut your eyes is black as the ace of spades when you open them and so is naturally opposed to our President who has put his people—Mr. Williams' people—on notice that until they stop their crime in the streets and having children on welfare and start to make for themselves the kind of strong family structure which is essential in a true democracy they will continue to enjoy the benign neglect they deserve. I happen to have read up at length on this problem in *Reader's Digest*.

"I fear we must agree to disagree," said Mr. Williams. "Now your problem, I gather—"

"In one word is O-U-T. I want out, Mr. Williams."

"So do we all."

"No. You've been here twenty-three years—I saw that name plate outside, it's about worn thin—and you've got a good thing going just like all the others, living the same eight weeks in the summer of '48 over and over and over again, no wonder you're all nuts."

" 'Nuts'?" Mr. Williams looked real polite and snotty at the same time. "Mr. Breckinridge, if you will forgive me, I don't believe that the behavior of any member of our little band can compare for sheer *eccentricity* to your own."

Well, that was score one for your high-toned nigger and I didn't have much of a comeback, not knowing how much he knows about Myra's activities—not knowing myself. "I have these moods," I said, trying to sound as offhand as possible. "Comedy routines I have worked out in many clubs around the Valley."

"Your comedy of last night was unusually well received by the young man you were entertaining in your cabin. His, uh, 'laughter' could be heard from one end of the Strip to the other."

"Well, he was a quick study like they say. I was just teaching him a few routines, and it was breaking him up."

"Let me repeat, Mr. Breckinridge. Rule one: You must not try to alter anything here. If you do, you derange or damage the future, and perhaps destroy us all."

"Mr. Williams, I will alter everything, including blowing up the back lot and keeping the world from ever seeing *Siren of Babylon* to get out of this place and home again."

"Oh, dear." Mr. Williams was suspiciously mild. He acts as if my threats mean nothing. *As if there is nothing that I can do to alter anything* which is a pretty horrible thought. Has he met me before like this? "Perhaps you need a—well, a hobby, a distraction, other than the amusing *impressions en travestie* that you delight us with from time to time."

"Such as?"

"Literature, Mr. Breckinridge." A black fist indicated the shelves of Heritage Club masterpieces in rich gilt-edged genuine plastileather. "I am devoting my time here—the two weeks I have in this quiet part of the world—to reading all of the world's great literature. All of it that I can read in two weeks of course.

Yes." He laughed as if he had said or was going to say something funny. "For me, even as we speak, the golden bowel has begun ever so slightly to most beautifully crack." Whatever that meant. It sounds like that complaint of Gertrude's in recent years which is spelled "diverticulitis."

"I've got nothing against reading books when there's time which is not much considering my busy schedule and how tired I am at night when we turn on the TV, Mary-Ann and I."

"Alas, we have no proper TV here. Even the sinister Milton Berle has not yet begun his mission. But there are films to contemplate."

"I hate movies. I'm not . . ." I was going to say "Myra" but I stopped myself. "Anyway, we can't even get in to see *Call Northside 777* down the road while *The Three Musketeers* won't open, even if we could get in, until after . . . after we're all gone from here. Isn't that right?"

"Yes." I did not like this stillness that Mr. Williams let surround the one word.

"Except we're *not* going away from here because we start the picture all over again."

"Yes." More stillness; black as ink, his face.

"Mr. Williams, you've been through the shooting of this film twenty-three times. Once for each year since you checked in."

"Yes."

"Each year you go from the last day of shooting July 31, 1948, to the first day of shooting June 1, 1948."

"Yes."

"You started doing all this in 1950."

"Yes."

"So for twenty-three years you've been going from June 1 to July 31, and back again."

"Yes.

"Well, explain me this little thing. Time is passing outside. There are new arrivals most every day which is how you've been able to keep up with what's happening back there like your very radical remarks about our President to me just now suggested.

Well, if this is the same eight-week period which it has to be for everybody who's really in 1948, then how can it change with each passing year for us since nearly every day someone is arriving from the future and on the day he arrives somebody else has probably arrived that same day, too, but the year before or the year before that and so on back to 1950?" I am going mad, I think, as I try to think things through and write them down in this account book.

"Well, are we all coming here at once?" I asked. "And if everybody is, then the last arrival, but I mean the very *last* person ever to catch *Siren of Babylon* on the Late Late Show and get caught in it, is already here, and the game is up. But who is it? Who is the last one, and what happens to everybody when he gets here?"

"Is the universe infinite or finite? If it is infinite, there is no last."

"This is a con game, Mr. Williams, and you are the number-one con around here."

"Mr. Breckinridge, I promise that in time, yes, within our eight-week *pousee-café* of days, you will adapt as we all have, as we all must." But as he said this I saw that same strange look in his eye that I had noticed in Rooster's eye when he looked past me at Mrs. C. Y. Bowles with a questioning look but also with a troubled look and with—well, with this *frightened* look. I think they think that if I start rocking the boat I might in some way wreck their little game whatever it is. I hope they are right but I don't know how in hell to really start rocking. The possibility I am the last person to arrive here went through my head, but how could I be when J. D. Claypoole has more news of the Watergate than anybody?

"Feel free," said Mr. Williams, "to call on me at any time. Just check with Rooster . . ."

"Who must be pushing seventy now that it's 1973."

"But it's only 1948, as you can plainly see. And that, I fear, is all that it will ever be for us. Or for Rooster—this summer anyway. Good day, Mr. Breckinridge."

I had a lot more to say but I saw it was no good. As I started toward the door, the phone rang and Mr. Williams answered it. "Hello, L. B.," he said. "Yes, I've read the script. *The Miniver Story* has *everything*!"

I shut the door behind me wondering if the L.B. he was talking to was really L. B. Mayer and if so is Mr. Williams in the pay of the studio, to help them read books maybe? It is very clear to me that he is not your average nigger by a long shot.

I went out to the Thalberg pool where I found Iris in her one-piece Jantzen with the small tit built up to match the big one which I suppose is easier to do than to squeeze the big one down to the size of the small one.

She was chatting with Mr. Telemachus who was fully clothed, drinking a beer and holding a copy of weekly *Variety*, the bible of show business.

"Word's got around," he said, not in a very nice way I thought. "You've been up to see Mr. Williams."

"What's he like?" Iris was sitting cross-legged beside the pool, careful to hold in her stomach. She is a good-looking girl and though I never thought I'd cheat on Mary-Ann, I feel that these are highly extenuating circumstances and I need Iris to keep me a hundred-percent normal guy in a hundred-percent abnormal situation.

"Black," I said, meaning to be nasty too.

"So I've heard," said Mr. Telemachus.

"I saw him once a few years back," said Iris, "at least I *thought* it was him and he looked more, you know, South American or Mexican."

"How could you have seen him several years ago when he only checked in the first of June?" I was going to get to the bottom of all this or burst.

"Easy, fella," said Mr. Telemachus, doing John Carradine.

"There you two go!" Iris was ecstatic. "Talking that funny talk of yours."

"What did what I just said sound like?"

"Careful!" From Mr. Telemachus.

"Don't ask *me* when *you* know! I mean you're the one talking crazy talk."

Well, we were getting nowhere and what with one thing and another and my being nervous I went up to Iris's room and had, all in all, a good time though I was kind of shocked even shook up when just before we got started she said, "Why, look at your poor weenie! How red and raw it is! What've you been doing, you bad boy?"

"I could never explain in a million years," I said, wanting to murder, yes, murder Myra who without so much as a by-your-leave went and used Dr. Mengers' remarkable invention to fuck Steve Dude's obviously very tight and plainly Brillo-y butt and then left *me* to have to live not only with a raw and fairly sensitive cock (at least on the underside where the skin from my wrist is) but with the possibility that Steve himself might come back at any time to get even.

Somewhat relaxed by my meeting with Iris, I went on the back lot to look for the exit. Just past the Andy Hardy street I ran into Maude who was escorting this dazed-looking new arrival, a woman of perhaps thirty in a negligee and holding a glass half full of whiskey, the way she had been holding it while watching the Late Late Show.

I should say here that I am one of the few people ever to arrive fully clothed since most people who are caught by *Siren of Babylon* are either in their pajamas or underwear or stark naked as it is late at night or early in the A.M. for them when they hit the Strip. There is a special wardrobe and makeup room in one of the Chinese pagodas left over from *The Good Earth* where the naked ones are given bathrobes and slippers so that they can cross the boulevard without getting arrested.

Maude was delighted with the newcomer, Helen Bird of Jackson, Michigan. "Helen is a beautician with the latest news of *Vogue* and she tells me Mr. Kenneth is absolutely nowhere as of today—May 16, 1973," said Maude, remembering his manners and introducing Helen Bird.

"April 17, 1973," I answered—and realize as I write this down while waiting for the scene where the exit is to come up that it has been one month now that I have been separated from Mary-Ann though only about two weeks here.

"Oh, God. God!" Helen Bird started to sob as she finished off her drink.

"This girl didn't spill a single drop even while going through the *CREDITS*." Maude was very admiring.

"What am I doing here?" Helen Bird was not only confused but she was drunk as altogether too many out-of-towners who watch late-night television tend to be upon arrival.

Luckily, along came Mrs. Connolly Yarborough Bowles dressed for badminton. "Thank you, Maude. For a job well done. I will take the lady in charge. To register her. To see to her special wants."

Helen Bird and Mrs. C. Y. Bowles then fell into one another's arms and had a good cry as Mrs. C. Y. Bowles led the very upset and plastered lady to be registered at the Thalberg Hotel.

"Maude," I said, "what happens when you come back to the day you first arrived?"

There it was again. That tricky *knowing* look. This time from behind Maude's giant dark glasses.

"I don't understand, sweetie."

"Maude." I held Maude's fat round neck in between my pretty large strong hands. "I suggest you play ball, Maude." I was quiet but menacing. "Answer my question. What happened when *you* came back again to that first day when you arrived?"

"That's it! I *arrived*, sweetie. That's all." Maude squealed and tried to get away.

"I mean, Maude, what happened on the first anniversary of your arrival?"

"Eight weeks is hardly a year, sweetie."

"Maude, I am going to start squeezing your fat neck right here on the Strip and if you don't want a pair of ugly bruises which not even Max Factor can cover up on your neck, you better tell me what happened."

355

"You come through again." Maude sounded frightened, and not so much of me as of the second floor of the Thalberg Hotel where the telescope was trained on the two of us. "You're not supposed to know. Nobody's supposed to know until it happens. It's a rule. You come through like the first time."

A moment of hope. "Does that mean you go *back?* So that you can come through again?"

"No. You just go back to where you first came in. For you that's the Grand Staircase. Now, sweetie, do stop crushing my blouse."

I let my hands fall. "Then what happens?"

"Why, nothing. You just keep on."

"Just like before?" I was getting scared, let me tell you. The vibrations are getting worse around here by the minute. I could feel Mr. Williams' telescope practically burning a hole in the back of my neck.

"Well, of course like before." That was what I call evasive.

"Maude, is *every*thing repeated?" This was the question that I was too scared to ask before because I was too scared even to face the possibility that *we just go round and round doing the same thing over and over again.*

"No, silly!" Straightening his clothes, Maude backed away with a last sneaky look at the telescope. "It's always different."

"Except for coming back once every eight weeks . . ."

"Well, yes. And some other things repeat. Little things. Oh, you'd hardly notice. After all, there's always somebody *new* arriving. Like Helen Bird who has given beauty treatments to all the Ford girls when she was working at Grosse Pointe near the country club where—what a hoot!—they wouldn't let Christina Ford in because they didn't know it was her! Oh, Helen Bird has a fund of fun stories!"

Then Maude was gone and I went on into the movie where I am now waiting for the Grand Staircase scene to come around in another forty minutes.

Sudden light goes on in my head. How did Maude have time to hear so many stories from Helen Bird about the Fords in

Grosse Pointe when the Helen Bird I just met is absolutely drunk and makes no sense?

Maude has brought Helen Bird in before. That is the plain awful truth and that means I'll have to start meeting everybody for the "first" time again as soon as I make my first re-entry. But I'll get out of here first.

21

No, you won't! Ever. Long before the Grand Staircase scene I was myself again.

The insufferable Myron has an uncanny ability to reappear when he's least wanted (as if he is ever wanted by anyone save the mongoloid Mary-Ann). I had hardly got past the prelude to the fugue that was to transform Steve Dude into Stefanie Dude when Myron re-entered the atmosphere, as we say at Cape Canaveral, and stayed my hand, thus depriving the world, temporarily, of Stephanie and 1974's world famine.

Worse, it is going to take me hours to rebuild my *maquillage*, which now includes false eyelashes exactly like those worn by Miliza Korjus in *The Great Waltz* (a favorite film of the late Marshal Stalin) as well as an Ilona Massey beauty mark on my chin. Need I say that the total effect is now ravishing, even without my once and future bosoms?

I have made up my mind that if the plastic surgeon in Culver City has not come back from Lake Arrowhead in time, I shall make a date with another surgeon farther afield—in Brentwood, say, and go under the knife June 1 which will give me eight weeks in which to become whole again. I assume of course that the local beauty-butchers and blowers of silicone make house calls. If not, then I assume that I shall be able to *persuade* one of them to do what I want him to do, since it is not possible for me to fail. In this I resemble God at the moment he created the universe with a single fart. Yes, I am happy to give my imprimatur to the big-band theory that is generally accepted as being the first movement of the music of this and all the other spheres.

But I have now begun to outdo the prime mover himself as I weave this cage of old time, salvaged from the cloacal confusions of that mindless universe the first mover has so wisely surrendered to me. Slowly, carefully I now draw to myself the very stuff and essence of all time, pulling from heaven's farthest limit those strands of aging light whose golden surfaces reflect the entire history of a billion stars which like so many fireflies have been extinguished, drowned, sucked into the last *FADE OUT* which is *FADE IN* to the other, to the negative universe beyond the quasars and the pulsars of our knowing, beyond that unbelievable weight of total darkness where, until the opening of my eyes, our race's imagination always came full stop and there was nothing until I saw fit to reshape past, present and future in my own image as there can be no other if we are to survive as the regnant species.

Right off, I must change the décor of *Siren of Babylon*. Then I shall present to various interested parties the notes I have been making all afternoon on how to save Metro from Kerkorian and Aubrey by re-establishing the studio as of this date (1948) to its rightful place as principal purveyor of the world's dreams. This means that I—and I alone—shall determine *what* is dreamed by the human race within this cage of time through whose radiant bars only I can view eternity just as I am now—at this very instant—creating the cage itself.

On the back of one of Myron's dumb Chinese fortunes I wrote "Wednesday night. Same time, place. Bring director. M."

During the long commercial and station break in the middle

of the Execution of the Guilty Priestess Scene during which Steve looks his very best as one of the guards standing at attention behind Louis Calhern's throne, I got down to business. Yes, I have interfered and changed the future.

As I hurried onto the set, I was conscious of a sudden overwhelming blast of what I can only think was purest ozone—so the earth's air must have been when human life first stirred in the loins of some mute mutancy.

I crossed to Steve, who was frozen into attitude, mouth slightly—and I fear a bit stupidly—open. I pulled up his Babylonian skirt; yanked the ancient jockstrap to one side and saw with delight *proof* of my intervention, my power to restructure the universe and re-create *Siren of Babylon* as well as the human race: the pubic hairs were gone and I knew what I needed to know—that this scene was shot *after* our meeting at the Mannix Motel. From the length of the rough stubble in his rosy crotch (the prickly heat was going away), I guessed that three days had passed since our first meeting.

Briskly I slipped back the foreskin I had come to know so well (to the creatrix of new worlds *not* to indulge in such detail is to commit the only indecency, gaseous critics notwithstanding); inserted my *billet-doux*; re-covered the delicate violet-colored head, which in a state of erection becomes a stormy dark purple like the volcano in *The Hurricane* (Jon Hall, Dorothy Lamour; 1937) and thus provides a vivid color-contrast to those feather-induced white jets that on Saturday night arced into the air as high as his chin during an early phase of that initiation for which he had been prepared from the top, regarding me, quite correctly, as someone supernatural because—this was said while we were still in the bar and his ordeal not yet begun, "Golly, I just don't know how you was able to get that Chinese fortune cookie to—well, to where you did." I witnessed the first of many blushes. "I mean, Jesus H. Christ, you must've given me a knockout drop or something on the set or in the dressing room during makeup to be able to put that thing where you did."

I gave him a mysterious smile. "Myra has her little ways, not to mention her plans, her *big* plans for you, Steve Dude, star-to-be."

Chuckling to myself as I recalled the scene, I took from my handbag a bit of pink ribbon and tied it in a bow around the tip of his rather longer than average foreskin. Then I let his skirt fall back in place.

I looked at my watch: three minutes to go before the station break ended. Time enough to alter time.

I went over the priestess who is about to be executed and unsnapped her gilded breastplate to reveal a pair of teats as fine as any ever fondled by L. B. Mayer during the lunch hour at—or under—his desk in the Thalberg Building.

I then undid the girl's hair in such a way that each nipple was hidden by the horsehair wig someone in makeup had created for her, obviously working on the cheap in order to keep for himself the human hair assigned for the job. Presently I shall put a stop to this petty pilferage.

I was nearly caught in the scene. But the tugging sensation began just in time for me to duck out of what was, luckily, only a Med Close Shot. Had it been a Long Shot I would never have made it and so would have been forever visible as a mike shadow on the wall.

I waited until the Guilty Priestess Scene was played again. Oh, joy! My handiwork was visible: the girl was plainly half-nude. Triumph! I have now altered *Siren of Babylon* as well as world history by inserting near-nudity of the topless variety *in a 1948 film.* Done tastefully, as I do everything, I am certain that the scene will be accepted by the Breen Office and the domestic gross of the picture will of course be substantially increased.

I must confess that there is a specific and personal reason for this particular intervention. If the film should become a hit (and I can make it one with a few more alterations), then it will *not* be sold to television in 1950 and if it is not sold to television in 1950 my enemy Mr. Williams will not enter it that year or in any other year, and we shall suddenly find his suite at the Thalberg Hotel empty.

So, baby, the jig is up! You're on your way back to Albany.

Wednesday! In three days I have changed the world.

I have made further alterations in the costumes and makeup of *Siren of Babylon*. With extraordinary cunning, I have suggested male and female nudity but in a way that not even the eye of the keenest editor or the most devoted censor could object to: a battle scene in which, for an instant, male buttocks are bared for the first time in glorious color. So quickly does the shot come and go that it is hard to believe one's eyes. Breasts hover in the middle distance while in the farthest reaches of the harem bathing scene there is even beaver. But, as always, Good Taste is my keynote, and of course swiftness. Swiftness is my be-all and end-all.

Each day when I return tired but happy from my labors of creation, I am aware of new tension on the Strip. The telescope in Mr. Williams' window is always turned on me as I come and go from the back lot. Mrs. Connally Yarborough Bowles looks at me with true terror whenever our paths cross and averts her eyes, hurries on.

Maude of course is a comfort. Unfortunately the arrival of Helen Bird has entirely distracted him from our usual diversions. "You don't mind, do you, sweetie? Helen's still a little upset about being here and . . ."

"And you want to know all the latest gossip from Grosse Point."

"Not just Grosse Point, sugar! Do you know that Helen Bird has given beauty treatments to Rosemary Kanzler in Saint Moritz?"

"And who the fuck," I said with some amusement at Maude's impressionability, "is Rosemary Kanzler?"

"Sweetie, really! Your values are so Hollywood and so high-brow."

We had a good laugh over that in the bar of the Mannix. Maude cannot believe that I am not as interested as he is in the doings of the jet set. But despite his silliness, Maude is an invaluable ally and, thanks to Maude's clever fingers and a few beauty hints picked up from Helen Bird, I am now looking like a million dollars, like an absolute dream walking!

Even Telemachus is responding to my seductiveness. He came over to my table after Maude left. "Well, Myron, that's quite a get-up." This oafish effort at sweet-talk misfired.

"Get lost," I jeeped but then had a swift change of mind though not of heart, since I find him physically and morally repulsive. "I was joking." I gave him my Irene Dunne warm little chuckle. Even gave him a touch of *The White Cliffs of Dover*. "Sit down, Telemachus."

Telemachus sat down at the table, eyes staring at me with that awe I am used to no matter how much I may want to be simple, to be warm and immediate, able to forget for a happy hour or two my sovereign responsibility to re-create the human race. "Well, Myron, you've been causing quite a stir on the Strip."

"You don't say?" I parried.

"Your ears should be burnt to cinders."

"Oh, dear! My poor rep. That's all a girl has, you know." I was Ann Sothern as the early *Maisie*.

"Yeah. There's a rumor going around that you've been doing things to the flick on the back lot."

I showed him my set of Ann Sothern Disapproving Pursed Lips immediately belied by the Saucy Twinkle in my eyes. "How could teeny-weeny Myra do a thing like that to that great big ole turkey?" Baby talk, courtesy Ginger Rogers.

"By pulling the bras off the chicks and the jocks off the studs." That was brutal.

"You got proof?" Barbara Stanwyck struck.

"I'm just telling you that's the word going around."

"Well, kiddo, I suggest you don't go running off at the mouth if you want to keep that full set of ivories in your fat head."

Telemachus looked alarmed when he saw me reach for my handbag. "Just thought a word to the wise . . ."

"Of course, darling," I husked, having previously shrilled: I like to alternate the two swiftly, for effect. "You don't happen to recall offhand what the domestic gross of *Siren of Babylon* was?"

"One mill two." Telemachus prides himself on knowing every gross by heart.

"Are you sure?"

"Of course I'm sure. Anyway, it's inked right here." He held up the worn copy of domestic and worldwide grosses of all Hollywood products 1930–1968.

I took the book and leafed rapidly to 1948. Eureka! Excelsior! Oh, world! Oh, time! I practically shouted, "It says here one million three."

"I don't believe it. You're looking at the wrong line." He grabbed the book; stared at it; gasped. "But it's not possible."

"*You* must've been looking at the wrong line all along, silly goose!"

I wanted to howl my triumph from the rooftops! But I did not dare, for Mr. Williams may yet try to stop me. After all, once the picture is in the black (and I can put it there in a few more days), no more Mr. Williams on the Strip!

22

When I came to this morning in the cabin of the Mannix, I found out that I have been missing for several days and from the way people act Myra has been busier than a bird dog. Among other things she has destroyed all my clothes so I was forced to dress up in a pair of women's slacks and a blouse but without her goddamn padded bra which I went and shredded the way the big companies and the Federal Government shred their highly secret papers when the Comsymps in the Senate are after them. But more of that anon.

I really believe we are now at the crunch, as in a short while it will be August 1 and we will all be back to square one which is the first day of shooting but I will either be dead by then or out and that's a promise, Myra, you bitch.

Realizing what a funny sight I must look with my short hair and frilly blouse and slacks and wedgies and the awful tweezered eyebrows, I still forced myself to go to the Thalberg Hotel in order to see Mr. Williams and warn him what Myra is up to.

Except for one table of canasta-playing ladies, the lobby was empty, as it was the beginning of lunch in the restaurant. I could hear the out-of-towners in there yakking away as happy as can be. Only Chicken was at the desk. He looked shook up when he saw me and I can only pray that Myra has not tried anything funny with what is after all a great little guy.

"What can I do you for . . . sir?" That is a little joke that is popular with boys that age in California even now when the moral rot has just begun to set in of which more anon.

"Is your father here?"

"No, sir. He's gone to Encino to buy meat."

"Well, I want to see Mr. Williams."

"Oh, he's not to be disturbed today."

"Well, you tell him . . ."

Something very strange happened at that moment. There was like a shadow in the room the way you suddenly get one in Burbank when a plane flies over where you are waiting in the parking lot for someone to land and you're not ready for the shadow to come because there are no clouds and the smog looks even.

Chicken kept staring at me; his eyes looking really scared and peculiar and his rosy cheeks didn't look so rosy but he never took his eyes off mine.

"No, he's not here," he repeated in a hoarse voice.

"But Mr. Williams is always here."

". . . like three months ago." I didn't catch the first part of what Chicken was saying, as I was talking, and I didn't know what was three months ago nor did I care, as I was eager to get to Mr. Williams.

"Well," I said, "tell him that there is a plot against his life." I thought this would certainly get Mr. Williams interested in talking to me but Chicken went right on talking right through me but never taking his eyes off mine and never losing this really scared look.

". . . going to be torn down" was all I got out of what he said after I finished saying what I'd been saying which he plainly wasn't listening to.

"You sure look good," he said, and then he smiled and I

swear it made me feel real warm all over and wish that Mary-Ann and I could have had a little shaver like Chicken with a Hawaiian shirt and Keds around the house even though we belong to Zero Population Growth and swear by Dr. Paul Ehrlich whose reports on what is happening to the world through overpopulation by the coloreds is just frightening.

"Telephone's ringing," said Chicken, even though I couldn't hear it ringing. "So long now. Have a good day now."

Chicken ran into the office back of the desk and shut the door. The shadow in the room went away, too, and I turned around frustrated as per usual to find Mrs. C. Y. Bowles looking very serious and sad.

At first she was not too friendly until she saw I was Myron. Query: Has everybody here got it worked out that I am sometimes taken over by an enemy or do only Maude and a few others of that ilk understand?

"We have received bad news . . . Myron?"

"Yes, yes, Mrs. Bowles. I'm sorry about this get-up but my clothes are all at the cleaners and I had to borrow these duds from a waitress at the Mannix."

"Say no more." Mrs. C. Y. Bowles showed me a *Los Angeles Times* dated July 19, 1973, which means I have been gone from home for almost four months back there though only a matter of weeks here. "This was brought by a recent arrival. A lady of refinement. From Sherman Oaks. She was studying the listings. For a maid. White. Then she joined our little family."

Well, that paper was full of the most awful things about what is happening to our President and country that you could imagine. Some time ago our President bugged his own office so that everything anybody said in it would be all a part of the record and I believe him when he says that he did this so that future generations as yet unborn will have this important historical record of all the important historical things that he and his visitors talked about but naturally the television senators are acting like he did this to get something on the people he talked to who did not know that what they were saying was being recorded for posterity, but as Mrs. C. Y. Bowles said, "Now at last our President will be able to confront his accusers. With tapes of what he *really* said to that terrible Dean Rusk. He will show the world he is innocent."

But I showed her where the paper said that the White House would not let the TV senators hear the tapes.

"Of course they will. In time. First those parts that deal with delicate. And recent negotiations. Between sovereign powers. Intended to ensure peace. With honor. In our time. Will be cut out. In the interest of national security. Then. After that. And only after that. *Altered* tapes will be given to those awful TV senators."

"I hope you're right."

"One ray of light," said Mrs. C. Y. Bowles, "in all this darkness. The Supreme Court. They have outlawed smut. Each community can now decide what it wants to ban."

Well, I was pretty thrilled to learn that the Court says that whatever is obscene is what your average John Q. Citizen thinks is obscene and no Commie talk about freedom of speech and the First Amendment allowed.

23

I lie on the bed of my cabin at the Mannix overwhelmed with grief. During Myron's brief period at the controls this afternoon he learned that in a matter of three weeks we have lost Betty Grable, George Macready, Veronica Lake, Joe E. Brown, Robert Ryan, Lon Chaney Jr. (the recovery from beriberi was obviously not complete: shall I ring him up to say how sorry I am?) and, most terrible of all, the inimitable, the sublime Ernest Truex so arresting in *The Adventures of Marco Polo* (1938) where his resemblance to the late Harry S. Truman gave added resonance to a part that in anyone else's hands might have been secondary. Finally, in this terrible season of falling stars, there died one whom I need not—cannot apostrophize, so close am I to her in every way: Fay Holden—Mom Hardy. If there is a 1974, 1973 will surely be known as Götterdämmerung.

Late at night.

The despair of this afternoon has been replaced by elation. 1973 may yet be a marvelous year. I cannot guarantee the stars who have twinkled their last twink this (1973) summer will still be alive in the post-Myra 1973 but I do guarantee that they will be working to the end and that the Metro Contract Players system will not be jettisoned and the studio will be in the blackest black. Yes, I have begun my takeover of Metro.

I arrived in the bar of the Mannix at sundown, beautifully gowned and coiffed (Myron got off with my padded bra but Maude had an even sexier one in his closet and my bosom now resembles Bonita Granville's in *Now Voyager*). A few out-of-towners greeted me respectfully. Several locals stared with awe and wonder. I radiated charm and quiet authority.

Right on schedule Steve Dude (soon to be Stephanie) entered with a short bald man who wore a large diamond on a finger which he referred to as his "pinkie."

"I see you got my message, Steve." I batted my Miliza Korjus eyelashes at Steve, who blushed.

"I sure did, Myra, and I sure would like to know just how you get these messages to me—I sincerely would, honestly."

I turned to the bald man, who was staring at me with ill-disguised excitement. "You are Mark Dyson." (Steve had promised to bring me the right-hand man of top-flight producer Pandro S. Berman).

"No, honey!" How I hated the intimacy in the bald man's voice, the smug male superiority. "I'm Sydney Spaceman. I'm in Casting, and Steve here told me there was this most unusual-type girl holed up at the old Mannix and I told him I'd drop in and take a gander."

"A goose is more like what you'll get."

"Isn't she something, Mr. Spaceman?" Steve is my slave.

"You can say that again."

I was all business. "Do you realize how much money Schary's *Intruder in the Dust* currently being lensed will lose at the box office?"

"A packet, I should guess." Sydney smoked a cigar. Eddie Mannix himself brought us Sazeracs.

"Or the sequel to *Mrs. Miniver* that Sydney Franklin will meg as *The Miniver Story*. Do you know how much that turkey will lose?"

"Lose? It isn't even made."

I had my documents ready. I gave him a sheet of paper with the various pictures currently in production or in pre-production; and the losses (to be fair, I also listed the occasional accident—the flicks that were profitable).

Sydney Spaceman was stunned. "But how do you know all this? How do you know what we're planning to make?"

"Myra's like one of those clear buoyants." Darling Steve is eager to be helpful.

"It doesn't matter how. I know."

Sydney was staring at the sheet, puffing his cigar. I sipped my Sazerac daintily and winked at Steve. Again he blushed.

"How," said Sydney finally, "do you know we're talking about using that cunt Garland in a picture which hasn't even got a title yet but you call *Summer Stock*, a lousy title, with Chuck Walters directing?"

"I know, Sydney. I know. And take a look at the red ink. The losses."

To my astonishment and relief, Sydney was able to read the figures I had so neatly printed in red. This is a breakthrough. I had assumed that the ground rules are immutable but obviously they are not. The locals on the Strip cannot read Mr. Telemachus' book of worldwide grosses, yet this very evening top-flight sub-casting director Sydney Spaceman had no difficulty in understanding the report I had prepared on the future of Metro's current product. Obviously the strands of control emanating from Mr. Williams' suite are weakening . . . or there is a way *around* the rules as Mr. Williams was the first to discover some weeks—years—ago when he made his killing on the stock market with future information.

"Now, honey, all this is crazy of course. I mean there's no way of knowing how much a flick will lose *before* you make it otherwise there'd be like no erasers on your pencil." Oh, the smugness! I will break him when I take charge of production.

But for now I am playing it warm and womanly, purest Kay Francis.

"Some of us, Sydney, can see the future as it is," I jilled. "Some of us . . . well, one of us—myself—would like to see the future as it *ought* to be. That's why I've prepared these figures."

"Yeah, yeah, yeah." *He did not listen to Myra Breckinridge.* Before I set down my burden, Sydney Spaceman will be in the mailroom at the William Morris Agency and that is a solemn vow.

Nevertheless I continued graciously to jill in my jeep. "I have my crystal ball, Sydney!" Under the table I pinched Steve's soon-to-be-detached-from-him bean-bag. Steve yelped.

Sydney ignored the cry. He was still staring at my report. "What impresses me, Myra," he said at last, "is your info. How do you know what's being discussed by Mr. Schary and Mr. Mayer? I'm on the inside and *I* know. But like take this item for Gable—*Any Number Can Play.* That's still being scripted."

"Sydney, I know. That's all. Now what I want is a meeting with Dore or L. B. For reasons that are too complicated to go into, I'd like either one—or both—to meet me here any day this week. They're invited to drop in at the end of the day for one of Eddie Mannix' special Sazeracs and a chat about upcoming product."

Sydney gave Steve a look. "You weren't joking."

"No, sir," said Steve. "I wasn't. I sincerely wasn't."

I indicated the various memoranda I have been working on for the last ten days. "I have a number of projects that will save the studio."

"Metro is sound as a dollar, honey, and don't need saving."

I gave him the previous year's losses, this year's losses and next year's losses but he gave me a superior smile, an unfair exchange. "O.K. So what're some of your big ideas? You want us to make you a star?"

"You've done worse." I was cold. "In fact, you've done no better since Lana was put into orbit. But that is of peripheral interest. Take a look at Steve."

Sydney looked at Steve, who sat up straight as any vain young stud will do when he thinks stardom may descend upon him.

"Good-looking kid. He's got a chance on the lot."

"Has it occurred to you, Sydney, that Steve would make a ravishing girl?"

Steve inhaled his Sazerac and started gasping and gagging. Sydney nearly put his cigar in his mouth wrong way round. "But he's *not* a girl."

"I reckon Myra knows that pretty well." Steve recovered his manly poise.

"Sydney, listen to me closely. This is a biggie. I see this film in which *Steve is turned into a girl before our very eyes.* We'll even show the operation. After all, you can't cheat the audience. Naturally the surgery will be in Good Taste and should occur no later than the second reel. From then on we tell a happy story, the life not of Steve but of Stephanie—a joyous fun-loving sterile Amazon, living a perfect life *without* children, and so an example to the youth of the world, a model for every young male, and our salvation, humanity's as well as Metro's."

For half an hour I acted out the film for their benefit. I confess that I brought tears to my own eyes. When I was finished, there was absolute silence. Steve looked pale and troubled, and Sydney simply looked stupid. "I don't get you, honey. I mean so maybe there's some box office in something so gruesome, like Frankenstein. But what is the lesson for the youth of the world?"

"To reduce world population before it is out-of-hand." I gave them statistics; tried to warn. But as I suspected, the thought is too new in the pre-Myra 1948: the approaching end of the human race is as yet unsuspected.

So I changed my tactic. Tried to show what fun the picture would be. How much money it would make in comparison with, say, *The Miniver Story.* "Here is a treatment I've written—and registered with the Library of Congress, so no fucking around, Sydney. Not that I don't trust you, boychick."

Sydney took the treatment as though he was afraid it might burn his fingers. "Frankly I can't see L. B. or Dore going for this kind of material. L. B. wants to show wholesome young pig people who love their moms and the flag while doing dumb goyisher things in the suburbs, and Dore likes social uplift."

"L. B. is on the skids with the front office in New York. Dore's on the rise. His success with *Battleground* now in preparation for 1950 release will make it possible for him to do what he wants—for a while, anyway. That's why I'm sure that once Dore knows how important this flick is for all mankind he'll give it the green signal in the name of social uplift."

"How do you know L. B. is on the skids? How do you know *Battleground* is being discussed at the top level?" At that moment I made Sydney Spaceman my slave.

"Darling Sydney, never again ask me *how* I know anything. Just take for granted that I know it. L. B. will ankle the studio in June 1951."

"What? I didn't hear that?"

For the first time double-talk. I repeated the date. Sydney could not understand me. I wrote the date on a paper napkin. To him it looked like a hieroglyph. Then I led him to the desk of the Mannix Motel and I took down the Utter-McKinley Mortuaries calendar and I flipped to the month of June. Then I pointed to number 1 to 9 to 5 to 1. Sydney understood! Triumph! I have broken the most important ground rule.

"L. B. is leaving June 1951?"

I nodded. I did not add that if my intervention in the affairs of the studio is a success, Schary with his dull uplift pictures will be the one to go and L. B. (shorn of those race horses that ruined his pre-Myra career) will be back at the tiller, making more great product. But I must proceed a step at a time.

"Wow," said Sydney Spaceman.

"Wasn't I right about her." Steve was proud of his creatrix.

"Well, I'm not about to say she really knows future grosses. How could she? But I will say this, Myra, you know everything that's being said out loud in the executive dining room and whispered in the executive sauna."

"So shall we consider my scenario?" I jilled amusingly.

"Making *me* into a girl?" Steve was shocked at the idea.

"Well, Steve, you got to admit it's *different* . . ."

"And," I said, "what will ensure worldwide boffo grosses will be that Steve really does become a girl between the first and second reel, and on camera."

"Oh, Jesus H. Christ, Myra! I mean—like shit! I don't go for that. That's crazy." Steve was deeply disturbed.

Sydney laughed. "Well, I don't think we have to go all that far realism-wise. But now you mention it, Steve would be a luscious number with that red hair . . ."

"Oh, come on, Mr. Spaceman, I ain't no fag."

"Nor am I, Steve. But I am like you—a cog in a great industry. You want to be a star, don't you?"

"Well, yeah, but I don't want to lose my nuts."

"A small price to pay, darling." I patted his cheek (he shaves, alas, and will need electrolysis).

"We'll fake the operation, if Myra doesn't mind." Sydney seems genuinely intrigued by the overall subject matter.

"You're the boss," I jilled, jeeping to myself. "Until I am."

After a new round of Sazeracs, Steve and Sydney departed. Steve was apologetic. "I got to see my girl tonight. She thinks I been tomcatting too much."

"Don't you want to stay here and let me de-kink you some more, darling?" I was all jill.

"No, thank you, ma'am. I'm straightened out for a long time after last time and I mean that sincerely." I did not press the point because I now realize what a coup it will be to transform Steve *during* the picture. Everyone on earth will want to see him before and after. Also, my message to the world will be all the more effective. Close Shot—scalpel. Cut To: bean-bag.

24

I don't know what Myra has been doing but she has been making contact with the locals in a big way.

I got up this morning myself again but shaky and found on the doorstep of the cabin a huge basket of fruit covered with cellophane and silk bows as well as two bottles of champagne and a telegram from someone called Sydney, saying "Welcome aboard," and a lot of other stuff. I suppose she has gone and got herself into the movies which was always her wish. I still have not been able to break her code but it makes no difference now as I have made up my mind that today is pretty near my last day here.

Myra has not found where I keep my clothes and I cannot get at hers without breaking down the closet, so we are even, I suppose. Anyway, I was at least presentable when I met Whittaker Kaiser in the luncheonette of the Mannix for breakfast and there he was with Iris, happy as can be.

"Long time no see," giggled Iris.

"Yeah. Long time." The waitress slapped some coffee down in front of me.

"Oh, he's in one of his moods!" Iris was radiant. "Tell him the good news, Whittaker."

Well, Whittaker was all smiles which is a lot worse, let me tell you, then his usual loony sheriff from Selma, Alabama, number. "We're getting hitched, Myron, I got to have a woman all the time."

"Isn't he cute?" Iris asked me and I couldn't say anything, but knowing what Whittaker feels about the fair sex I couldn't help but imagine her a few weeks from now hanging upside down on a meat hook in the larder after some big quarrel. Of course she is stronger than he is so maybe she can take care of herself. But if I were her I would never turn my back on Whittaker Kaiser.

"Actually she's knocked up, that's why I'm marrying her." There was a lot of cheerful laughter at this and then they talked about all the children they were going to have because Whittaker does not believe in contraception.

"How," I said to Whittaker, "can any of us have children back here when we're not allowed to interfere with the locals? And having a child by one of *them* back here is bound to change the future?"

Iris yelled like a wild Indian. "I'm going to find out what that crazy language is if it's the last thing I ever do!"

Whittaker paid no attention to her. "Mr. Williams has given a good ruling. He says that since the baby is never going to get born during our eight-week shooting schedule, there is no serious chance of changing things."

"Yes, but she'll still be pregnant when she goes on into August and we come back to June!"

"Mr. Williams doesn't think so and he ought to know. What really matters is that he's asked Rooster Van Upp to ask me to take over the kitchen of the Thalberg and I've agreed. How could I say no? That's the only game in town food-wise." Then Whittaker went and told us as per usual what a great chef he is and how he would be even better if there was any competition on the Strip or anywhere else for that matter for him to measure himself against, and I left. There is obviously going to be no more talk from him of getting out of here or of kidnapping Mr. Williams. He's settled in. That means I am on my own. The only one who wants out.

I am now back in the movie. That is, I'm at the point where you watch it being made. I am sitting on the ground, my back to that blue-gray barrier I have got to get through *today*. I know the exact spot where our President was shoved through it but for the life of me I can't tell how it's different from any other part of the TV screen.

Technicians walk around me and don't see me. I still find this creepy. From time to time everybody freezes while there is a commercial. Fact, I just now heard this used-car dealer selling his GM lemons on the TV. Also, in the past half hour I have heard several times from behind the barrier someone who I guess is Benjamin R. Laskie the director say, "O.K., action" and "This is a take" and "Print that one."

It is frustrating to know that just behind that glassy whatever-it-is there is a whole real world you can move around in, even if it is 1948.

But there has also got to be another world out there that is home for me because I swear to God that I just now heard Mary-Ann's voice, sounding a million miles away, calling, "Myron, you come up to bed now."

Did I imagine this?

No. She *has* to be there, too, and our TV and rumpus room has to be there with the TV on. Also Pat and Tricia and Julie must also have been there at the White House when our President left them for a much-needed vacation back here unless he was already on vacation with his friend Bebe Rebozo in which case he probably wanted to check out *Siren of Babylon* as a possible emergency White House in case of enemy attack.

Anyway, right after I heard Mary-Ann, I got so depressed and lonesome that I picked up this Babylonian sword that was lying about and started pounding with the hilt on the barrier, but nothing's happened so far and, worse, though I hit it real hard there is no noise either. It is like pounding solid air but I am going to keep at it. Someone will hear. They have to.

25

I have heard, Myron.

We are now at the crunch. The nitty-gritty. Something is about to give. We cannot continue like this: a body divided against itself must decompose, as Raymond Massey might well have said.

I was appalled to find myself hammering at the barrier with the hilt of a Babylonian sword. What if I . . . if Myron had actually broken through to the other side? I shudder at the thought. Even more chilling—he had nearly stepped, by accident, *through the exit*!

Needless to say, I stopped pounding and stuck the sword (which is very sharp) into my . . . Myron's belt. As always, I am excited to be back in the picture. I never tire of Maria and Bruce and Louis—not to mention Steve Dude strutting about in the background, face dark with Max Factor Octoroon.

Myra Breckinridge is still in the picture.
I have been here for two whole showings.
I sit cross-legged now at the edge of the Before the Walls of

Babylon Scene, happy to record in this ledger my encounter with J. D. Claypoole, the FBI's principal contribution to Watergate.

During one of the commercial breaks, I walked onto the set of the Banquet Scene and started to rearrange the Disneyland letters of Jehovah's disagreeable message in order to spell out *my* name on the wall.

I am aware that such a dramatic change in the big sky god's well-known text might smack of self-advertisement, but then, as I am the first to confess, my genius (though universal in its application) is also profoundly American in its nature. Like my countrymen, I am always thrilled when someone entirely without talent is able to become through strenuous and even pathological publicizing of himself a part of the nation's consciousness and for a season famous because that is our American way.

I stress the absence of talent as a *sine qua non* because in a real or even would-be democracy actual excellence is resented and disallowed: witness the constant sniping of the movie reviewers at the truly great films, particularly those starring Lana Turner and William Eythe. What these "critics" do not understand is that the *mythical* aspect of the authentic star made it mandatory for him *not* to act (after all, any idiot can act—look at Laurence Olivier, look at Joseph Wiseman) *but to be*—and need I spell out the simple law that nothing gets in the way of pure being so much as talent (world-making genius of my sort is something else again)?

Take, for example, Ardis Ankerson (known as Brenda Marshall and later of course as Mrs. William Holden) in her first role (*Espionage Agent*, 1939). Ardis demonstrated this mythic quality in spades. With her high cheekbones, sharp chin and bright hazel eyes, brunette Brenda-Ardis radiated godhood— another Pallas Athena in the line of Frances Farmer. *But Ardis did not receive the support that she deserved from either the press or the Industry.* Also, she was too shy to draw attention to herself —and why should she? Is the Virgin Mary expected to hang out a sign in front of her bungalow? or buy space in the trade papers when Oscar-time comes around? So Brenda-Ardis and Bill Holden were married and she retired from the silver screen and I only hope, *pray*, that she has found some happiness in her private life—a long shot, I fear, since Holden as star is no more than pale carbon to a true mythic figure like James Craig.

"What the fuck are you doing, Breckinridge?" was Claypoole's greeting to me as I tried to substitute the second letter of Jehovah's message with a "Y" (the first letter, significantly, is "M").

"Out of the sight line, you FBI fruit!" I shouted as I hurled the letter "Y" at his head and it connected. Unfortunately it was made of plastic (the letter "Y"—not the head, which is of solid bone) and hardly creased his crewcut.

At that moment we were pulled out of the set and the action began again. I was thrilled to see that Jehovah's message on the wall lacked an "e." I hope there was consternation in the Valley at this lacuna but I doubt it, since reading skills are agreeably low in Southern California.

"You know the rules, Breckinridge. Jesus! Look what you've done to the writing on the wall! Typical Commie trick. Don't think I don't know what you're doing: sending your messages to your Chinese friends, the way you do in those fortune cookies. Don't think I haven't got your number, Mac, because I have." This confused harangue was heard by me with a small patient Eve Arden smile.

"Are you on duty here?" My voice was plangent with only a hint of jeep.

"*Special* duty, Mac, assigned by Mr. Williams himself. Mayday. Mayday." Claypoole was sweating and for all his bravado I detected terror in his dull eyes. But then, who does not fear his creatrix?

"I must be about my work, shit-head." I smiled at him as I started to turn away.

"No more interfering. That's an order."

I responded to this "order" with three or four peals of Deanna Durbin girlish laughter.

Claypoole then pulled a revolver from the holster under his jacket. Luckily for me, in the grand old lavender-and-lace tradition of the FBI, the revolver was backwards in its holster. For an instant Claypoole held the weapon by its muzzle. As he started to switch it around, I let him have the Archangel-Three-Wing-Twist and Chop.

The gun flew in one direction. Claypoole flew in another. With a grunt he reeled backward *into the action of the picture*, and what I have from the beginning suspected was an axiom of this not only parallel but uniquely vertical universe proved to be true: Claypoole's momentum was so great that the delicate rejecting force that keeps us out of the action was not able to expel him; instead, he entered the scene and fell into the open arms of one of the officers standing just behind Nebuchadnezzar's throne in the Council Scene. The extra seemed not to notice what had happened, since we are no more than mike shadows to players who are to us divine images on celluloid.

The scene continued without a hitch, but my original theory about this special universe (whose laws I make and so must joyously obey) was perfectly demonstrated, for like two bits of mercury pushed too close together, the actor absorbed Claypoole. For an instant I saw two men, one clinging to the other. Then there was only one: the extra. If I were interested in Claypoole's fate, I would take the time to work out *where* he has gone (if anywhere) but I have other tasks to perform prior to tomorrow's meeting with Dore Schary. In fact, time is of the essence if I am to halt nature's planned death for the human race in the late (pre-Myra) seventies.

I removed from my pocket the dental floss that Myron always carries about with him. I tested the Babylonian sword on the floss. The sword is sharp as a razor. Obviously some extra has been playing around with the props.

At the start of the Battle Beneath the Walls of Babylon Scene, the longest of the commercial breaks begins. The soldiers freeze.

From behind the blue-gray barrier I could hear the far-off voice of a used-car salesman.

I ran to the nearest soldier, a burly young man who stood with legs wide-spread, spear in hand, looking up at the painted canvas walls of Babylon.

I pulled up the military skirt and tucked it under his belt. He wore no underwear. A nondescript American rosebud stared at me with its blind eye looking somewhat startled, if such lethal objects (capable of filling up the universe with hungry replicas) can be said to have expression. The balls hung loose in a crinkly scrotum.

Deftly I took the sharp point of the sword and made an incision in the man's right groin. I know by heart where all the tubes and arteries are hidden. With hindsight, as they say in Washington, I confess now that I was fearful that there might be bleeding which could not be stanched since I had no clamps, but to my relief, the blood was as frozen in the young man's veins as everything else. He could not bleed any more than he could move or breathe during the commercial break when all the players are in a state of suspended animation like so many live frogs congealed for the winter in a pond.

With the dental floss I quickly tied off the seminal tubes. Then I repeated the same operation in his left groin. A perfect vasectomy! And far better than surgery in a doctor's office because not a drop of blood appeared on the pink skin.

When the tugging began, I had just time enough to pull down the soldier's skirt.

I hurried across the sight line as the commercial ended and the action began.

I was on tenterhooks! Would he notice what had happened?

Bruce Cabot's magnificent voice resounded across the desert. "Charge, oh, men of Babylon!"

My soldier (my creation!) had been frozen with his spear aimed at the walls of Babylon. As the action started, he suddenly dropped the spear and grabbed at his crotch as though someone had kicked him. For an instant the soldier clutched at himself.

Then, very stiffly, he started to walk out of frame. The battle continued, as always.

I was waiting for him—not that he could see or hear me. I stood next to a technical director who spends most of his time going back and forth through the barrier with instructions from the director.

"What's wrong, Sam?" The technical director actually knows all the extras by name, but then, Metro is one wonderful family under the benign fathership of Dream Merchant L. B. Mayer, whose bacon I mean to save.

"I think I got hit with a rock or something." I looked at the man's heavy-set bare legs, fearing to see blood trickling down. But my sutures held.

"Go see the doc."

"Yeah." The extra walked shakily into the blue-gray barrier. I was relieved. He will now get proper medical attention, and best of all, he will never be able to add another human being to this pullulating planet.

An hour after my successful vasectomy of a member in good standing of the Screen Extras Guild, Mr. Williams himself appeared on the set. He wore a panama hat, a white suit, carried a cane—very natty all in all, and very frightened.

"You must leave the film immediately, Mr. Breckinridge. That is an order."

"How can what *I* have invented order me to do what I have no intention of doing?" I felt the power rise in me. At last we were face to face. Myra the creatrix and the uppity dinge from Albany, New York.

"The question of *a priori* invention has no single and certainly no satisfactory answer."

"You see the answer all about you. You see it in my eyes, don't you, Mr. Williams? You see the end of the game I allowed you to play for twenty-three years. Now it's over. I am about to put this picture *in the black*."

"That is not possible. The past is past. What was is."

"What is *was*, Mr. Williams." Like a gladiator in the divine *Quo Vadis*, I swung the enmeshing net of my dialectic over Mr. Williams; then hurled at him the trident of my logic.

"I am here as the savior not only of Metro-Goldwyn-Mayer but of the human race."

"No, you are simply here to meddle. To be absurd. To change for your own amusement the balance of history."

"You prefer that I let the studio make *The Miniver Story*, and lose a packet? Do you prefer that a quarter century from now the nearly doubled population of the earth will suffer from famine, from lack of energy, from the collapse of Western civilization as represented by the as yet unmade films of Bertolucci and of the dread Peckinpah? Do you prefer that I allow one billion too many people to be born when I—and I alone—can stop their conception right here at the source? Finally, do you in your heart of hearts really want to see Kerkorian and Aubrey at the helm of MGM?"

Mr. Williams was staggered by the Greek fire of my argument. But he did his best to rally. "You cannot change anything that is essential. Even if you could, you must not because this atrocious studio—this dispenser of slick kitsch—must die. The cinema, the most depressing and demoralizing of all pseudo-art forms must be destroyed."

At last the horrible, the unsuspected, plot was revealed. I was, I confess, staggered and sickened.

Like the total villain, the world-destroying monster he is, Mr. Williams did not spare me the full horror of what he has done. "Yes, Breckinridge, I am destroying the cinema, bit by bit, step by step. Why do you think *The Miniver Story* is being made? And all those other turkeys? Because *I* have got through to the front office! It is *my* advice they are taking, not yours!" Oh, the enemy is more cunning that I suspected. I am still shaken by this exchange:

"The Word must regain its primacy—which is what is happening now. As of 1973 worldwide box-office grosses have plummeted—thanks to what I am doing here—and the crack in the golden bowl is once again visible to the young people of the seventies who laugh at Lana Turner as they read Holkien and Tesse and Vonchon and Pynegutt."

I could not let him rave on. As I have suspected for some time, Hollywood has been controlled for twenty-three years by a demented educated Negro: an erratic black comet loose in the Gutenberg galaxy just as that galaxy spirals into extinction to be replaced by the electronic picture which flashes classic films from television set to television set, from eye to eye, all 'round the world, joyously bouncing off satellites as it unifies in beautiful simultaneity a world for centuries kept in solipsistic disarray and separation by the written and the (invariably) wrong word.

"I see your grand design, Mr. Williams, and I am happy to be able to shatter it. You are my creation."

"No! No, Breckinridge. You are my aberration."

"This is my universe."

"It is mine. Look! Darkness. My darkness." Mr. Williams pointed at the dark sky opposite, to the inside of the TV set where we were lodged.

I laughed at him like Bette Davis in *The Little Foxes*. "Shall I give you proof of my power? Shall I send you back to Albany in 1950? There to die in due course, long before 1973?"

"You cannot." But I saw the terror in his black face.

"I can and I will. I shall put *Siren of Babylon* in the black."

"You don't dare!"

I raised high my Babylonian sword. "In the first reel, with a single gesture, I shall change the history of the cinema, and send *you* back to Albany."

With a horrendous cry, Mr. Williams *fled*. There is no other word; if there was I would not use it.

I sit now writing in this book, waiting for the picture to begin.

My plan is simple. Just before Maria Montez enters the set for her first scene, I shall unsnap her breastplates.

From Encino to Van Nuys the audience will be ravished. More

to the point, I am certain that that scene will be accepted by the Breen Office in (pre-Myra) 1948 because . . .

The *CREDITS* are starting. The MGM lion just roared.

Here comes Maria Montez. She has just left her trailer on the other side of the barrier. The makeup man is with her. How beautiful she is!

26

I am Maria Montez.

27

For eight glorious days I have been—and am—Maria Montez, the star of stars at Universal Pictures currently on loan-out to MGM for *Siren of Babylon*, in a deal pacted by top-flight ten-percenter Louis Schurr.

It is Sunday. I sit at my beautiful writing desk in my palatial home at the corner of Tower Road and San Ysidro. Through the windows I can see my Japanese gardener pruning my roses. A tourist bus has just gone by, and I could hear the guide saying, "That's the house where Maria Montez lives with her husband Jean-Pierre Aumont, the French film star."

Jean Pierre. *My* husband. My magnificent eyes brim with happy tears as I think of him, of our happiness together. Of our darling daughter Tina, aged two years old (she was born on St. Valentine's day 1946)—and taking a nap as I write these lines.

At times I find it hard to remember that I am still Myra Breckinridge, on temporary duty, as it were, within this gorgeous body so soon to die.

I look at myself in the mirror on the wall opposite. I am . . . *she* is so beautiful! I *must* find some way of preserving her—of preserving us. I have already told my darling Jean-Pierre that if ever I say that I am going to Arden's to lose weight in the hot paraffin baths, he is to stop me. But Jean-Pierre just laughs. Apparently Maria Montez is just like me: a willful spitfire—yet fun-loving, gracious, womanly, a star!

I have Mr. Williams to thank for this exquisite experience. In a desperate attempt to save himself, he vaulted me from dull earth to radiant paradise.

As Maria Montez stood, waiting for the cue to begin the first scene of the picture (though not the first scene to be shot), I started toward her, ready to tastefully adjust her costume.

When I was a few feet from Maria Montez, Luke suddenly appeared: a mountain of a man, who is—was—from foothills to peak devoted to Mr. Williams.

"Get lost, buster!" I jeeped.

Luke lowered his head and, like a maddened buffalo, charged me.

I immediately struck the Early September Gourd position, but for once I fear that I was too slow: the mountain was moving faster than Mohammed realized.

Luke knocked the wind from me—something no man has ever done before or ever will again. That is a vow.

Clutching this ledger in one hand, I fell backwards against Maria Montez (needless to say, none of the people on the set were aware of Luke and me).

It is a most peculiar and disagreeable sensation to collide with a body that simply does not respond. Maria Montez did not feel me hit her. I, on the other hand, felt most painfully the sharpness of her jeweled breastplate as it jammed into my *poitrine*, not to mention the barbaric spikiness of her right earring as my face grazed her cheek.

Then darkness: a sense of being sucked into a vacuum. For an instant—an eternity?—I did not exist. There was nothing. Time stopped. The universe vanished as its creatrix ceased to exert control over her gorgeous finitude of starry spirals.

Finally my eyes opened of their own accord and I saw a different world from any that I have ever seen before.

The sky was an intense cobalt-blue; brighter than any sky could ever be this side of Natalie Kalmus and the Technicolor process. Yet it was no more than an authentic 1948 California sky seen with 1948 Santo Domingan eyes.

From far away I heard the makeup man say, "A little powder, Miss Montez. We're getting a shine."

I looked about me to see where I was and discovered that I was where I had been before. Only everything was now different. That was my first reaction and, as always, it was precise, despite obvious disorientation.

Right off, I knew that I was not myself—or rather, that I was myself but someone else as well. Myself *augmented* by someone marvelous rather than *diminished* by something cretinous like Myron.

Next I realized that all my senses are now different from what they were. The sky to my new eyes is more vivid than any I have ever seen before outside a movie. My sense of smell is more acute—no, not more acute, different: I am conscious that I move in a cloud of gardenia scent that protects me from the slightly sweet sweaty smell of the makeup man who is applying powder to my forehead. I shrink from the odor, not liking it (because I do not like him?). I also hear in a new way. The sound of grips laughing and joking in the distance annoys me; makes it hard for me to concentrate, and concentrate I *must* in order to achieve absolute mental clarity, for I am the star of the picture and, presently, will be obliged to climb a steep wooden staircase at the back of the "marble" staircase down which I shall soon, superbly, descend.

Looking back, I still turn to ice with a terror that is remembered not in tranquillity but in glory.

I am standing there. I am nervous. I am breathing hard. I am perspiring beneath the golden breastplate.

The makeup man knows that I am jittery. He murmurs soothingly, "That's fine, Miss Montez. And those new eyelashes are real beautiful. You look like a million."

"Thanks," I say. *My voice is different!* No longer do I possess the fabulous range of Myra Breckinridge, who could, at will, re-create a dozen stars with no more than a sigh or a gurgle of laughter. No, the voice now is bronze. The voice is a trumpet. The voice is that of Maria Montez.

I am she, I say to myself, and she is . . . me? I start to shudder convulsively. A sudden panic. Will I be able to give a performance? Can I, very simply, cut the mustard?

"What's the matter, Miss Montez?" It is the assistant director.

"Nothing." The voice—the marvelous voice—is coming from me! "I think I'm a little faint. The heat."

In an instant a folding chair with *Maria Montez* painted on the back is brought me. Then the director hurries over to me. Benjamin R. Laskie himself (one of the metaphysical arguments on the Strip is now answered: there *is* a Mr. Laskie, and a camera crew, and a camera, and a studio beyond that). The blue-gray barrier no longer exists for me: I have made the journey to the other side traveling, need I add, first class.

Laskie is short, fat, with a nose like the bowl of the pipe he always holds clenched between his yellow teeth. "Hey, baby doll, you under the weather?"

"On top of it, Mr. Laskie." I flash a smile at him and would have given a fortune to be able myself to see and enjoy the smile that clearly rocks him, as it does all normal men.

"*Mr.* Laskie! How about that! Well, baby doll, you're the boss. When you want to roll, we roll."

As much as I enjoy the badinage between superstar and staff director, I *am* nervous. Although I have seen *Siren of Babylon* perhaps a thousand times and know all the dialogue, I am fearful that I might not (oh, shame to confess even to this ledger such weakness, such uncharacteristic timidity!) that I might not be able to play what, after all, is one of the most difficult roles ever essayed by any star of the silver age.

I also realize the terrible responsibility that has suddenly been thrust upon me. History requires me to give a performance which will not be topped (at least pre-Myra) until Lana's luminous work in *The Prodigal*, almost a decade later.

"I'm ready." I pull myself together, conscious of my beauty, of my total command.

"You got all the words, baby doll? You want I should get you your coach?"

Coach! What could he mean? Dialogue director, I assume. Or perhaps Maria is studying English, since her accent is quite pronounced. Curious. Although I am a master of the English language and think entirely in English, whenever I speak, Maria's accent takes control. A lucky thing for our career, but puzzling.

Slowly I climb the steep staircase in back of the set. I am conscious of the sharp smell of raw pine and I am careful not to let my skirt sweep against the occasional viscous splotches of oozing resin. If there is one thing a star hates more than a tropism, it's a viscosity.

At the top of the staircase I stop and wait for my cue.

Ecstasy. No other word. I, Maria Montez, the most beautiful woman on earth superbly if barbarically gowned and exquisitely coiffed, am standing at the top of a flight of shallow simulated marble stairs.

Lights on huge cranes are focused on *me*. A mike boom is above my head. Beneath me stands Louis Calhern, as Nebuchadnezzar, waiting for me to descend, fearful of my oracle.

Beyond the set I can see past the back lot to the gleaming white sound stages of Metro—until now hidden from me by the blue-gray barrier.

I look in the opposite direction, toward the Strip, where I can see the crummy Thalberg Hotel, not to mention the unspeakably sordid Mannix Motel; and I wonder how I had ever settled for such a sleazy life. I, who was born to be a superstar in my native Santo Domingo, I mean Red Bank, New Jersey.

Does Mr. Williams suspect what has happened? Are the out-of-towners watching me? But of course they are. Myron has just arrived. He and Maude are standing at the bottom of the stairs. I narrow my eyes: yes, there are two unaccountable shadows just below me. Then the lights are readjusted and the shadows of Maude and Myron vanish.

Laskie waves to me. "O.K., baby doll. We're rolling."

I hear the bronze trumpet of my voice say the dialogue I have heard a thousand times but never dreamed that I myself would one day say not only for the camera but for all time, "Greetings, oh, King of Babylon. From the goddess whose servant I am!"

I cannot believe it is I. The grips as well as the extras are transfixed with delight and awe as I begin my descent, every inch of me a goddess. Even Louis Calhern, a supercilious New York stage star, cannot keep out of his face an expression that can only be described as worshipful.

"I come with gifts, oh, Priestess, for the Sun." Mr. Calhern comes in late on his cue, as usual, and I (always a good sport) have to return to my place when Laskie yells, "Cut!"

Mr. Calhern says, "Oh, damn. Sorry, Miss Montez. I was off my mark."

"It could happen to anyone," I say graciously, always the star and yet warm and human with everyone, even featured players from the New York stage who look down on Hollywood and only come out here to make money. Well, *we* know camera, and camera is the only thing worth knowing.

The day of triumph ends when I throw my arms up to heaven and pray to the Goddess of the Sun to defeat the enemies of Babylon. So powerful is my reading of this very beautiful speech written especially for me at Dore Schary's insistence by Leonard Spigelgass that the grips burst into spontaneous applause when I finish and Laskie shouts, "Print it!"

On a cloud called Nine (an expression one often hears in 1948 though what its origin is I know not), I am borne to my trailer (exquisitely frilly and pink), where makeup is removed with the help of a maid and I put on my usual clothes, a glamorous star-style Travis Banton creation with open-toed shoes.

I allow the maid to arrange my hair, since I have not a clue as to how Maria Montez looked off-duty circa 1948. Now I know: *on duty*. To be a star is to be constant, immutable, shining.

A chauffeur-driven limousine whisks me through Culver City—how empty the streets are compared to now (1973 pre-Myra) with half as many cars, I should think.

I stare through the car window like a Martianess, delighting in the quaint costumes, in the crewcut boys—until I realize that my glances might be misinterpreted and I must not, in any way, compromise Maria Montez, a Universal superstar and sex symbol who is, nevertheless, a *perfect* wife and loyal in every way to Gallic heartthrob Jean-Pierre Aumont.

My darling Jean-Pierre. What happiness I have known this last week! Except for one thing. I cannot understand one goddamned word he says because he insists on speaking French to me, the son of a bitch, and when I say, "No, no, my dearest. Let us practice on our English like my coach says we must," he just laughs and jabbers away like a deranged wine steward.

It is a great strain, which I am beginning to show. Not only does he keep talking French to me but the only people we ever see in this town are *not* Lana, Judy, Bette and Dolores Moran, who are at their zenith, but all the goddamned French actors like Charles Boyer, who is, I must confess, a treat to look at even without his hairpiece but *what* the hell is he talking about all the time, what are *any* of them talking about?

"Caramba!" I exploded last night after dinner here at home with a dozen French-talking Europeans mostly under contract to Warner's. I do intersperse my conversation with Spanish words and phrases picked up from the PRs who used to hang around Columbia when I was Myron the First and a fixture in a local bar frequented by youths of the lowest class.

"We must practice our English, *muchachos*."

But it did no good. Everyone laughed and this French or German writer whose name I still don't know (and obviously I don't dare ask him his name since Maria Montez is an old friend of his and a lapse of memory of that sort might have serious repercussions), this writer with the face of a lion and the brain of a burnt-out orangutan did his party number which consists of gulping down the contents of a huge glass of brandy and then chewing up the glass (in our house Baccarat crystal) and swallowing it. Everyone is thrilled when he does this except me. I hope he hemorrhages internally.

Last night when he finished munching on the crystal, I shouted,

"*Ole!*" Then I threw open the door to the cabinet where our beautiful crystal goblets are kept, and said, "Start eating, *zapata!*"

The roar of laughter from the guests was reassuring. I am obviously convincing in the role of a fun-loving superstar but I have been, I must confess, deflected these last few days from my true goal, which is the salvation of MGM in particular, and of the world in general. The two are interrelated, as I mean to prove.

My position now as Maria Montez is not the bowl of cherries it might seem to the casual observer. Although I am in a place of power, I am far too conspicuous to be able to operate freely. I must watch not only the usual p's but the troubling q's. I am also seriously handicapped by being unable to use Maria Montez's memory. There it all is, in her head, completely available to me except for the fact that all her memories are in Spanish, and since I have not the time to take a crash course at Berlitz in order to rob the memory bank, I am obliged every minute of the day to "wing" it, as we stars say.

28

Back on the set of *Siren of Babylon*.

I am giving the performance of the decade. Everyone says so. The daily rushes are studied by L. B. and Dore, and Laskie says, "Baby doll, the studio's yours! Nobody but *nobody* dreamed you could give a performance like this in what is—let's face it —a corn you cope ee ah."

"*Caramba*," I said, smiling brilliantly. "Each flick we make during this period can be only one thing, immortal—you dumb bastard," I added, throwing in a half dozen Puerto Rican gay chuckles.

"You break me up!" Laskie gasped, breaking up.

I firmly believe that I am now able, *through performance alone,* to put *Siren of Babylon* in the black, eliminating Mr. Williams, whose diabolic advice to the front office here has until now been creating turkeys galore.

Once Mr. Williams is safely back in Albany, I shall have a free hand to create a new product. To introduce a cycle of Beat films. To revive the Andy Hardy series (I saw Mickey, the adorable little shaver, in the commissary yesterday and he *whistled* when he saw me!). Finally, I must put a stop to *The Miniver Story*. I also expect to get—no, I must be fair—I expect Maria Montez to get the Academy Award for the performance I have been giving on the back lot during these last ten days of shooting which include all the key character scenes.

An amusing encounter in the commissary at lunch today. I entered the noisy room with top-flight ten-percenter agent Bert Allenberg—a tall, ugly, amusing man who wants to get me away from Louis Schurr, but I am totally loyal. Nevertheless, I enjoy Bert and we are the best of friends.

Just inside the commissary door, before you get to the writers' table on the left where Leonard Spigelgass reigns supreme, I ran into Sydney Spaceman and Steve Dude. Steve gasped, the way extras do whenever they come face to face with a total star.

"Steve!" I flashed my full smile.

"Gee, Miss Montez. You remember my name!"

"I make it a point to know the names of all my fellow workers in this great Industry."

"I'll go get us a table," said Bert, who only handles top-flight six-figures talent and plainly did not want to be bothered with an extra like Steve or a sub-casting director like Sydney Spaceman, who said, eagerly, nose-browning, "The rushes are just great, Miss Montez!"

"Thank you." I was mischievous. "I hope you are making plans for that big picture, starring Mr. Dude?"

"What was that again, Miss Montez?" S. Spaceman could not believe his ears.

"The world is waiting to see—*Stefanie*! The first fun-loving Amazon, to be created especially for the screen."

"Jesus H. Christ!" Steve Dude was stunned.

"How did you know about that—uh, project, Miss Montez?" S. Spaceman was bewildered.

"Because I do not make a movie without consulting Myra Breckinridge. All us stars do. She is, frankly, infallible. I must confess to you that, believe it or not, I was dubious about the script of *Cobra Woman*. Quality-wise I feared that it lacked class.

Well, Myra convinced me that I could overcome the dialogue and I did, as the world knows! *Caramba!*"

Bert came back. "Table's ready, Maria."

"Where is Miss Breckinridge?" asked S. Spaceman. "I made an appointment for her with Eddie Mannix here a few days ago but they said she wasn't living at the motel any more."

"*Quién sabe?* Myra travels far and she travels fast. But do exactly what she tells you to do, Mr. Spaceman, and you will triumph." I blinked my dreamy dark eyes at Steve. "Stefanie," I whispered. "You will be a star. you will change the world. Obey Myra." Their minds were blown.

I enjoy lunching in the commissary and always refuse to take a star's table, preferring potluck. I also enjoy passing between tables crowded with extras and featured players wearing color- ful costumes. On all sides I feel their worship, and draw strength from the ecstasy they feel in the presence of a superstar on loan-out from Universal.

I am always stopped at least half a dozen times by people who know Maria Montez or pretend to know her. I am gra- cious—and at least they all speak English, unlike that floating crap game of French-talking lounge lizards at home. I must have it out with Jean-Pierre. It'll do his career no harm to practice his English with me.

Bert was most interesting at lunch. "You're wrong, you know, about wanting to change your image."

"But I don't want to change. What gave you that idea?"

"You did. Couple weeks ago. When I saw you at Joe Paster- nak's house. You said you wanted to give up the sex-symbol business. Underplay the tits. Be like Paulette Goddard, who you said gets away with murder and doesn't have to throw her cunt around on the screen."

I smiled. "I am a big tease, dear Bert." I really laid on the PR accent. "I love Paulette and respect this girl's taste in jewels but I am happy like this. The way the good God made me." I threw out my *poitrine* and cried, "*Ole!*" to the merriment of those nearby.

Then after we had our laugh Bert got down to business and told me top-flight producer Sam Zimbalist of *Boom Town* fame is considering me for a project and would like to meet me. I graciously agreed to an appointment.

I also learned to my amazement that I am—that Maria Montez is—on the skids at Universal and that she has been inked to topline a little stinker in France next month with Jean-Pierre and Lilli Palmer. I must nip this project in the bud. For one thing, Maria Montez must make a major Hollywood film next. For another, how the fuck am I supposed to make a flick in French when the only sentence I have picked up so far is *Je m'en foute*?

29

I seem to be gaining a little weight and must watch the old calories. Fortunately, I know a great deal about dieting, a subject no one understands back here. They think that if you want to lose weight you must sweat, which is idiotic and dangerous, as poor Maria Montez will soon demonstrate unless I find a way of saving her.

I am tempted to become a beauty counselor. With what I know about the emetic properties of grapefruit, I could make a fortune.

Tomorrow is the last day of shooting. There will be a party on the back lot. Will the shadows of Mr. Williams *et çie* be on hand? But I forget. Tomorrow is August the first, which means that they will all be heading back to June the first, thank God.

After today's shooting I went straight to Mr. Zimbalist's office and we had a most interesting and fruitful conversation. I truly believe that I have now begun the salvation of Metro.

As I swept imperiously into the inner office, Mr. Zimbalist came from behind his desk to greet me. He is tall, with a loud deep voice. Although he has the blue lips of a carp, his eyes have a warm twinkle and he is a genuinely good person as well as a top-flight producer with a track record that is the envy of all Hollywood despite the shellacking he is going to take on the upcoming *Beau Brummell* unless I intervene.

"Miss Montez! I'm glad you could take the time to come see me."

"Call me Maria . . . Sam!" I husked in a PR way, and then sat down on the legendary director Sydney Franklin, whose presence in the room I had not noticed since he is very small and gray and had not risen to his feet at my entrance; he had remained seated as "I am not feeling so good, Miss Montez. Please forgive me."

I forgave him. He forgave me for sitting on him. I noticed with surprise that he was wearing gloves. Later Sam told me that Sydney was afraid of germs!

I took the bull by the horns, as is my wont. "Sydney, do not—I repeat—do not make *The Miniver Story*. You will lose a packet for the studio and seriously affect your own track record as a bankable staff-megger."

Sydney and Sam were stunned that I knew so much about a project still under wraps. "Nice meeting you, Miss Montez," said Sydney, creeping to the door. "I'll bear that in mind what you said about *The Miniver Story*. I really will."

"Let's hope he does, Sam." I flashed my teeth at Sam Zimbalist. Pushed out my *poitrine*. Tossed my head so that the earrings jingled (holes have been pierced in my ear lobes—I confess that it took me an hour to get up sufficient nerve to put on my earrings for the first time).

"Maria, I've got a couple of properties that might interest you. We're all pretty impressed by the work you're doing for Ben Laskie. The dailies all last week were sensational and everybody's talking about them in the executive dining room. I give away no secrets when I tell you that L. B.'s kicking himself that Universal got you instead of Metro."

I accepted this flattery as my due. It is true that Maria Montez's performance in *Siren of Babylon* was marvelous (pre-Myra) but she lacked the *total* authority I have brought to the role. After all, Maria Montez never saw herself play the part a thousand times. I have. I also know how to gild your average lily.

Laskie is stunned that I now do every scene in a single take. "Baby doll, you got perfect concentration. I don't know what's come over you the last few days."

Sam chuckled suddenly. "Laskie's being a naughty boy. Some of the stuff he's trying to get away with! L. B. was fit to be tied when he saw that scene where the girl has no top to her costume."

"Did L. B. *cut* the scene?"

"Of course. You can't release a picture with a scene like that. Funny thing is, Laskie swears it was an accident. Some joker, that boy! But if the picture is profitable that's all that counts."

Not until I see the final edited version of the picture will I be able to determine to what extent my changes have remained in the film. It is a fact that the last time I looked at Mr. Telemachus' domestic grosses I had added a hundred thousand dollars to the total. Was this increment a result of the performance I am now giving or of earlier changes? It is all very puzzling. Obviously I must put time in its place. If I don't, that tragic pre-Myra world of Nixon, Peckinpah and Paul Morrissey will so derange the world's monetary system that the making of multinational picture productions will be a financial no-no.

I enjoy Sam. He worships me. I can tell. But we are decorous. Each happily married. Fulfilled. He has a wen on the back of his neck.

I warned him about *Beau Brummell*.

"How did you know we were thinking along those lines?"

"Because I do and because I care and because I love this Industry. Sam, I'll tell you what I want to play. *Ben-Hur*. As a silent, Metro made a packet on that flick first time around. Now *you* make it again as a talky, as a *super* spectacular!"

Sam narrowed then popped his eyes at me: a trick many people back here do in imitation of top-flight megger Vic Fleming, a he-man who is everyone's idol except mine. "Funny you should mention *Ben-Hur*. Dore and I were talking about the property at lunch today."

"Don't just *talk*, Sam. Make the picture! Make it *now* for release in the early fifties—not the late fifties." I was tactful. Did not tell him that he would indeed produce *Ben-Hur* in 1958, and during the production die in Rome of a heart attack brought on by the harassment from a panicky post-Dore Schary front office complicated by a lifelong habit of each day drinking several quarts of milk and cream. Sam's *Ben-Hur* is his monument, of course, and it did save Metro briefly. But my plan is more basic. If the picture were to be made in 1948 instead of 1958, Metro will be able to weather the fifties and L. B. will be at the helm until his pre-Myra death in 1957.

"That's not much of a part for you, the girl friend of Ben-Hur," said Sam.

"*Caramba, Samba!* I mean Sam." We both broke up at my funny error. "I want to play the part of Ben-Hur."

"How?" Sam looked stunned.

"The way I am playing the *Siren of Babylon*, the way I play everything—like Maria Montez, superstar."

"Well, this is an unusual approach, Maria, and I'd better sleep on it. Off the top of my head, I can't see L. B. going along but . . ."

"Good taste will win the day, as it always does with me. I won't play Ben as a man and I won't play him as a woman. I will play Ben-Hur like Montez, larger than life!"

"I see what you mean," he said, seeing.

I think I have half convinced him. But he did not react as well to my idea of transforming Steve Dude into a fun-loving sterile Amazon. Sam did think, however, that if there was sufficient uplift in the presentation, Dore might be willing to try it on for size with the leadership of B'nai B'rith and Planned Parenthood.

All in all a successful meeting.

As I was coming out of the Thalberg Building, where my car was waiting beneath a magnolia tree, I saw Judy Garland talking to top-flight musical-comedy producer Arthur Freed. They were talking very earnestly to each other and she was clutching at his arm, and frowning. It was strange, suddenly, seeing Judy, who has been dead for four years now (1973), still alive and pretty if a bit plump, and troubled.

I came up behind them, not knowing if she was a friend of Maria Montez or not. "Judy!" I said, projecting superbly.

Judy Garland jumped like a frightened gazelle. "Maria *Montez!* Oh, God!" Judy started to giggle uncontrollably.

"Ole," I said firmly, pushing Arthur Freed to one side. "I want to say a few words to you, Judy. In private. Because no one else has the courage to tell you."

Still giggling mysteriously, hysterically, Judy accompanied me to the foot of the magnolia tree. I saw in the distance a half dozen fans approaching down the street, coming from the funeral parlor which shares the site of the executive building. We would only have a minute together.

"Judy, you are destroying yourself with drugs and booze."

That stopped the giggles. "What do you mean drugs?" There is—was—an Irish spitfire in Judy. Unfortunately, she had no neck; otherwise, she was every inch a star.

"Nembutals are barbiturates and barbiturates are drugs like heroin. You're about to miss the chance of your career with *Annie Get Your Gun.*"

"I'm making it. And what the fuck business is it of yours . . ."

"You're going to be replaced by Betty Hutton."

"You've got to be kidding! Betty Hutton makes Deanna Durbin with that penguin arm look talented." Here Judy, I fear, did a cruel imitation of her rival girl singer and fellow immortal Deanna Durbin, now happily retired to France.

The fans started to shout our names.

"Cut the clowning, Judy. Put yourself away. Dry out. Get off the pills. If you don't you'll be dead in twenty-one years."

"That's a hell of a long time off and besides . . ."

The fans were upon us. Regally signing autographs, I made my way to the car. I shall save Judy yet.

I told my chauffeur to go home by way of the Strip. Morbidly, I wanted a last glimpse of the out-of-towners before they go back to the first day of shooting tomorrow.

"Stop here," I said as we approached the Mannix Motel.

If memory serves, I am on schedule, I thought as I got out of the car. It was dusk and though several locals saw me as they entered the bar, I was not recognized.

Just inside the bar Maude was sitting with Helen Bird, drinking daiquiris. Maude gasped when he saw me. I held my finger to my lips and flashed an intimate glance at him. I was so placed beside the jukebox that the other inmates of the bar could not see me clearly.

Maude hurried over. "Miss Montez, this is an honor! I'm Nemo Trojan but call me . . ."

"Maude. I know."

"You do!" Maude was delirious with joy. "May I have the honor—the *privilege*—of planning a totally new coiffure for you?"

"It's too late, I'm afraid."

"Too late?"

"Because you go back to the first day of shooting tomorrow and I shall go on into August." I must say it was wicked of me to stun poor Maude like that but I could not resist a little mischief.

Maude's round damp face was a study in putty. "You *know*?" he hissed.

"Everything."

"How?"

"Myra told me."

"Where is she?" There was now real terror in Maude's face.

"Off the Strip."

"I know. I heard. But *where*?"

"Safe and around. She is my constant adviser. Tell Mr. Williams that, thanks to Myra, I am certain to get the Academy Award for my performance in *our* movie!"

"Oh, no! Please, Miss Montez! Stop her! Stop Myra! This picture has got to bomb or we're all done for."

"Only the early arrivals like Mr. Williams will be done for. Don't worry, sweetie. The picture will have been sold to television by the time you hit the Strip."

"But it won't be the same!"

"Nothing will ever be the same, thanks to Myra Breckinridge."

"Maria Montez!" I heard a familiar voice behind me. I turned and there was Whittaker Kaiser in cook's apron and chef's hat. He was now impersonating a serious earnest breathy criminal of the Nixon variety. "I've always had this existential idea of you, Miss Montez. I've always felt that what you needed was someone like me, not only a real man in a feminized world but a cook who understands not just the black beans and rice you were brought up on but the castrator goddess you represent, despite your vulnerability."

"Why don't you"—and margarine would not have uncongealed its vegetable fats in my beautiful mouth—"go fuck yourself? You dumb . . ." I sought a Maria Montez word. Found it. "¡Cucaracha!" I even remembered to pronounce the exclamation mark upside down in the Spanish manner as I swept out of the bar and into my limousine, confident that I had now totally demoralized Mr. Williams and sent him back to Albany.

30

It is late at night in my beautiful mansion on Tower Road. Jean-Pierre is sleeping. Crickets can be heard in the garden. A lovely silvery moon casts shadows through my window. The air is scented with jasmine. I am perfectly happy but deeply troubled.

We must not make that film in France. But Maria Montez has signed the contract and Louis Schurr says we must go through with it. I don't know what to do.

Sam Zimbalist is eating out of my hand. He is activating the *Ben-Hur* property. At Warner's, Irving Rapper is willing, he tells me, to show on the screen the transformation of Steve Dude *if* I agree to play the part of the plastic surgeon. Although I am too big a star for what is only a supporting role, I told Mr. Rapper that in the interest of curbing world population I would even consent to do a cameo, so strongly do I feel on the subject. Finally, Sydney Franklin has decided not to go ahead with *The Miniver Story.*

All these marvelous things are beginning to happen, thanks to my being so well located in time and space. But now we must go to France where that asshole writer is waiting for us to buy him some more brandy glasses to munch on. I am in despair.

Yet I must count my blessings, too. It is wonderful being Maria Montez, even if I don't understand a word my darling Jean-Pierre says to me.

Where, I sometimes wonder, is Maria Montez now that I am where I am? Is she deep down inside? If so, will she ever forgive me for having put two pounds on her magnificent body in the last few weeks? I have, by the way, gone to the doctor. Maria's heart is sound—so it is simply bad luck what is going to happen three years from now when she takes that hot paraffin bath at Arden's. A terrifying thought: if she dies, will I die? Is this possible? Although death is simply Mother Nature's way of saying slow down, am I pushing too hard? I must try not to brood. *Che sarà sarà.* And I have my work to do.

Busy days now. Making plans. Packing. Studying French in secret. Soon I'll be *acting* in French. *Zut alors!*

Tomorrow I make a personal appearance at the opening of a branch of Penney's in downtown Los Angeles. Curious the sense of *déjà vu* I have—as though I have done all this before. Yet of course I have not. This is the first time. It has to be.

My darling Jean-Pierre. I have just kissed him on the forehead. He is smiling in his sleep. Does he dream of me? How happy we are.

31

I don't guess I'll ever be able to make any sense out of this ledger which has gone with me through thick and thin. So much of it is written in a funny kind of code which I have so far not been able to crack and so I will probably never figure out what Myra was up to but I can guess—*no good!*

I was able to read the part where she is or thinks she is Maria Montez and it is funny now that I think of it that this part must be true because I now remember everything about that morning when my mother Gertrude the practical nurse happened to read in the paper that Maria Montez would make a personal appearance at the opening of a branch of Penney's in downtown L.A. where we had been visiting my uncle Buck Loner, the Singin' Shootin' Cowboy Star of Radio and so on.

I can still hear Gertrude saying, "I got to see that swell-elegant Maria Montez in the flesh and I'm taking Myron with me even if the doctor does say he should be kept in a strait jacket all the time."

That part—the out-of-my-head part—I don't remember at all as I was off my rocker for about three weeks. But I sort of remember hearing in my head Gertrude discussing going to see Maria Montez.

Then next thing I know there is this crowd in front of Penney's with newsreel cameras, and all of us fans lined up on the sidewalk, waiting until this limousine drives up and out steps Maria Montez, looking very tall and beautiful though, frankly, after my experiences inside *Siren of Babylon*, I am not very eager to see her ever again or any other movie star for that matter on the TV or anywhere else.

Well, as the flash bulbs go off and the newsreel camera buzzes away, Maria Montez makes her way through the crowd. When she gets to us, my mother Gertrude the practical nurse says, "Oh, what a thrill it is, Maria, meeting you who I have always thought the absolute tops!" Or something like that.

As Gertrude says this, I can still remember after what is now one fourth of a century the way Maria Montez's eyes suddenly open wide and her mouth just falls open. She starts to back away from us but Gertrude has grabbed her arm.

"I want you to meet my little boy Myron who loves all your movies, though he has not been himself lately, jabbering away in this language nobody can understand though of course he can talk as plain as you when he wants to but he won't talk at all now. He just sulks all day."

While Gertrude the practical nurse is saying all this, Maria Montez just stares at me, her face white as a sheet. Then she gives a funny little cry, "Oh, no. No!" There is pleading in her voice.

So that was it. The crunch. The next thing I know I am sitting here in the TV and rumpus room in front of the TV, watching the last credits of *Siren of Babylon*.

I think I have got a pretty good idea now of what happened. As Myra wrote, she became Maria Montez and Miss Montez became me—but me as I was back in 1948 aged ten years old. I can imagine what a shock it must've been for your average world-famed movie star like Maria Montez to have to spend three weeks of her valuable time inside yours truly aged ten years old. What she was talking all this time through me that nobody could understand, thank God, was her native Spanish. Then I guess once she figured out that she was stuck and that complaining would do no good, she just clammed up and hoped for the best which finally happened in front of Penney's that morning with me.

Of course, Maria Montez then went right on the way she was meant to go on and in due course she took that hot paraffin bath at Arden's and conked out, I'm sorry to say. But the moving finger, once it has writ, moves on and there are no erasers, Myra to the contrary—thinking she could change the world, given enough time back in 1948 and an expensive wardrobe.

Much relieved to be home again, I went straight upstairs and crawled into bed beside Mary-Ann who was sound asleep.

32

We are having a barbecue in half an hour and I am filling up the last pages of this ledger while the coals are burning in the barbecue pit out here in the back yard.

I have been deeply troubled as are we all by the Constitutional crisis of today, Sunday, July 29, 1973. The TV senators are demanding the tapes that the President has made of his many historical conversations in his various offices around the land. Worse, however, is the request of his own son-in-law Cox for copies of those tapes, even though Cox works for the President, too.

Fortunately, Mr. Nixon is going to hang tough and in this frame of time he's going to hack it, I am sure, although many of his admirers in the Valley are upset as who is not?

A funny thing happened this morning. I drove over to Culver City to a butcher I know who sells dandy sirloin for a barbecue and after I bought the steak at a price so ruinously high that you can well believe that the Communists are deliberately wrecking our economy by buying up all the grain so that the cows and baby chicks have to be killed because the cost of feeding them is too high for a profit thus making shortages galore in the richest and best country on earth, I decided it might be fun to see if the Thalberg Hotel is still standing so I drove along the Strip where I spent so many awful days and nights.

Well, you wouldn't recognize anything. The back lot of Metro is built up. The movie house where *Call Northside 777* was is gone as is the Mannix Motel and everything else except for, believe it or not, the Thalberg Hotel which is still there, very run-down as it is about to be torn down.

I parked in front and went inside the lobby which is very different than it used to be, modernized with lots of neon but dusty and likewise run-down.

There was no one in the lobby but behind the desk was this fat baldheaded man who was just staring into space, talking to himself.

Fat and bald though he was, I recognized Chicken Van Upp. "Hi, Chicken," I said, "remember me?"

Well, he looked scared to death and started mumbling how the hotel was no longer in business and being torn down.

"Where's Rooster?" I asked. "In the office?"

"No, he's not here."

"You've put on a little weight, Chicken."

"Fact, he died like three months ago."

"Sorry to hear that, Chicken," I said. "What're you going to do with the hotel?"

"It's sold. Going to be torn down."

"Sorry about that."

"You sure look good," he said. Well, there wasn't really much more we could say to each other after that. Then the telephone rang. "Telephone's ringing," said Chicken. "So long now. Have a good day now."

As I turned around to go out, I thought I saw a card table with four ladies sitting at it playing canasta. But that was twenty-five years ago and when I blinked my eyes this sort of double-exposure effect went away.

I felt kind of sorry to see how Chicken has aged and also sorry that there isn't much point for us to go fishing together or skinny-dipping as he is now older than I am and because he's fat looks even older than he is which must be forty-one or two.

Well, I am nearly at the end of this ledger. Everything has turned out all right for yours truly and after the latest series of hormone injections I don't think we'll ever be hearing from Myra again.

I am also happy and relieved that nothing serious was dislocated by all the crazy things she was allegedly up to back in 1948 on the Strip. It's the same old country that it was when I got into the picture with a lot of problems, true, but also with the know-how how to solve those problems in the good old American way like John Wayne tells us on the new disk he has just cut.

One peculiar thing just cropped up that did make me a little uneasy. Last night when I was calling up different people to invite them to today's barbecue, I called Sam Westcott who is a very able attorney in Van Nuys and active in Republican politics. "Sam," I said, "you old galoot, why don't you and Becky come on over for some barbecue like around sundown tomorrow?"

"Sure would feature it, Myron." We talk Western together, our joke, you might say.

"And bring the young genius."

"The young what?"

"Bring Sam Junior if he's around so as we can congratulate him on getting that Nobel Prize."

There was this silence on the other end of the line. Then Sam said, "Myron, are you plumb loco? There ain't no Sam Junior. You know I been a stud mule since before I married Becky and used to hang around all them starlets when I was doing extra work in the movies and had one of the first spontaneous vasectomies ever recorded by medical science."

"Hell, Sam, I was just joshing you," I said and quickly told him the latest joke about these two Mexicans. Sam likes Mexican jokes.

But it is real strange that Sam Junior doesn't exist now when

I know for a fact that he was the fair-haired boy of the whole country before I got into *Siren of Babylon* with his population-control efforts which were all the rage with whole countries asking him to come on down and help them out.

Well, maybe I imagined all that about Sam having had a son, just like I allowed the out-of-towners to convince me that *Siren of Babylon* had been a flop in its day when of course it was a smash hit and Maria Montez was awarded the Academy Award for her performance.

Thank God, Myra was not able to change anything at all except maybe keeping Sam Junior from being born, and despite her meddling, this country is just like it was which is just about perfect no matter what the Com-symp senator from Massachusetts John F. Kennedy says as he starts his race for the President by unfairly and maliciously taking advantage of Mr. Nixon's current misfortunes.

Luckily, there's not a chance on earth of John Q. Citizen buying Mr. Kennedy's radical line since his only claim to fame is being the brother-in-law of Marilyn Monroe which is hardly sufficient qualification for being the President of these United States, as our good governor and next Republican President Stefanie Dude, the fun-loving Amazon, said last night on the television during an interview from the governor's mansion at Sacramento.

Since there are only a few blank lines left to this page, I will sign off by saying that the highly articulately silent majority to which I am darned proud to belong are happy with things as they are and that we are not going to let anybody, repeat *anybody*, change things from what they are.

33

!sevil aryM

FOR THE BEST IN PAPERBACKS, LOOK FOR THE

In every corner of the world, on every subject under the sun, Penguin represents quality and variety—the very best in publishing today.

For complete information about books available from Penguin—including Puffins, Penguin Classics, and Arkana—and how to order them, write to us at the appropriate address below. Please note that for copyright reasons the selection of books varies from country to country.

In the United Kingdom: Please write to *Dept. JC, Penguin Books Ltd, FREEPOST, West Drayton, Middlesex UB7 0BR.*

If you have any difficulty in obtaining a title, please send your order with the correct money, plus ten percent for postage and packaging, to *P.O. Box No. 11, West Drayton, Middlesex UB7 0BR*

In the United States: Please write to *Consumer Sales, Penguin USA, P.O. Box 999, Dept. 17109, Bergenfield, New Jersey 07621-0120.* VISA and MasterCard holders call 1-800-253-6476 to order all Penguin titles

In Canada: Please write to *Penguin Books Canada Ltd, 10 Alcorn Avenue, Suite 300, Toronto, Ontario M4V 3B2*

In Australia: Please write to *Penguin Books Australia Ltd, P.O. Box 257, Ringwood, Victoria 3134*

In New Zealand: Please write to *Penguin Books (NZ) Ltd, Private Bag 102902, North Shore Mail Centre, Auckland 10*

In India: Please write to *Penguin Books India Pvt Ltd, 706 Eros Apartments, 56 Nehru Place, New Delhi 110 019*

In the Netherlands: Please write to *Penguin Books Netherlands bv, Postbus 3507, NL-1001 AH Amsterdam*

In Germany: Please write to *Penguin Books Deutschland GmbH, Metzlerstrasse 26, 60594 Frankfurt am Main*

In Spain: Please write to *Penguin Books S. A., Bravo Murillo 19, 1° B, 28015 Madrid*

In Italy: Please write to *Penguin Italia s.r.l., Via Felice Casati 20, I-20124 Milano*

In France: Please write to *Penguin France S. A., 17 rue Lejeune, F–31000 Toulouse*

In Japan: Please write to *Penguin Books Japan, Ishikiribashi Building, 2–5–4, Suido, Bunkyo-ku, Tokyo 112*

In Greece: Please write to *Penguin Hellas Ltd, Dimocritou 3, GR–106 71 Athens*

In South Africa: Please write to *Longman Penguin Southern Africa (Pty) Ltd, Private Bag X08, Bertsham 2013*